LORD RUSHLAKE
MAKES
A
MISTAKE

by

Catherine Bowness

1

ACKNOWLEDGMENTS

With love and gratitude to

Sophy King for the design of the book cover

Sophy and Ben for invaluable technical and emotional support
as always

and to

Janis and Lyn for their endless patience, helpful advice and continuing
encouragement

Contents

Chapter 1...6
Chapter 2...14
Chapter 3...23
Chapter 4...30
Chapter 5...37
Chapter 6...45
Chapter 7...54
Chapter 8...61
Chapter 9...70
Chapter 10...75
Chapter 11...83
Chapter 12...92
Chapter 13...103
Chapter 14...112
Chapter 15...119
Chapter 16...126
Chapter 17...134
Chapter 18...143
Chapter 19...153
Chapter 20...162
Chapter 21...169
Chapter 22...177
Chapter 23...186
Chapter 24...194
Chapter 25...201
Chapter 26...209
Chapter 27...217
Chapter 28...225
Chapter 29...233
Chapter 30...240
Chapter 31...248
Chapter 32...256
Chapter 33...264
Chapter 34...272
Chapter 35...280

Chapter 1

It was more than a year since Lord Rushlake and his friends had been involved in investigating unpleasant goings-on in Society and, although much had healed, there remained a degree of internal discomfort – perhaps wariness - which, being persons who prided themselves upon their self-restraint, none of them liked to mention.

Lady Amberstone had returned to Yorkshire along with her young friend, Helena Patchett.

"Much as I've enjoyed staying with you, Horace," her ladyship had said one morning at breakfast a few weeks after the investigation had been wound up, "I believe I must go home. I cannot give up my life in my own house entirely."

He smiled. "Of course not. You have been a most delightful – and useful – guest and, although I wish you would stay here for ever, I perfectly understand your need to go home."

"Thank you," she said, concentrating upon achieving a perfectly even coating of butter upon her toast in order to conceal an unexpected moistening of the eyes.

"Of course, I do understand that, lacking both parents and wife, you may not object to having an old fogey such as I hanging around quite as much as the next person might, but there is really no need to flatter me. Please don't hesitate to invite me again if you think there is anything with which I could assist – or which you think I might find stimulating - enjoy would surely be the wrong word," she finished on a self-deprecatory note.

Thus did the old lady reassure her nephew that she had not been too upset by the recent events and would relish being involved with any other cases that might come his way, but stopped short of demonstrating too ghoulish an interest in such things.

"I will indeed, and am glad to hear you say it. As for being an old fogey, I can only suppose you want *me* to flatter *you*."

"Reassure, I think. As to the other, it is of no use to refine upon things over which one has no control," she finished, dabbing at her lips with her napkin and managing at last to meet his eyes.

"No. But," he added after a moment or two, "I suppose we did have some control. If we hadn't interfered, do you think Bodley would have succeeded in solving the case?"

"I'm certain of it - eventually. I'm afraid that his mind was not always exclusively fixed upon the job – and for that I believe one member of our team was responsible."

Lady Amberstone was referring to the *tendresse* the detective had developed for her friend, Helena Patchett.

However, in spite of this – and Miss Patchett's probable reciprocal sentiments – the two women set off back to Yorkshire a couple of days later, parting from the Earl and his remaining guest, Aunt Saffy, with grateful thanks, numerous protestations of affection and heartfelt expressions of hope that they might meet again soon.

It was not until they sat down together for luncheon that Aunt Saffy broached her own presence.

"I believe I should be leaving too," she said somewhat tremulously.

"Where were you thinking of going?"

This was not an idle question for Aunt Saffy, an indigent and distant relative – *not* an aunt – had originally been engaged as a chaperone for Horace's unmarried sister, but this young woman had been staying with another sister almost since the moment she had arrived in London and thus had no need for Aunt Saffy, rendering that lady's presence in the Earl's house unusual, for surely he had no need of a chaperone. A lone female continuing to live with him would look odd even if she was at least fifteen years his senior.

"Well, that's something that we should perhaps discuss," she said. "I am, as I'm sure you must know, very ready and willing to continue to act as Titania's chaperone, but it's quite clear that she doesn't need me. Do you think I should wait around – somewhere – in case she does decide to leave Jenny's household, or should I look for another position?"

"Do you want another position?" he asked bluntly.

Saffy, as with the Marchioness earlier when her departure had been discussed at the breakfast table, concentrated upon buttering a piece of bread. She did not, therefore, see his expression as she said, a little thickly, "No; I own I don't, but what I want and what I should do are not necessarily the same."

"I don't want you to leave," he said quietly. "I enjoy your company and, although it is perhaps a trifle odd for you to remain without Titania, I think we can square Society by pointing out – at frequent intervals – that you are, if not precisely my aunt, at least a cousin of some sort. Perhaps we should spend an hour or two trying to work out whether we're fifth or sixth cousins – or even something more distant - and how many times removed."

This speech caused Aunt Saffy to have to blow her nose before she could speak again. When she did, her voice quavered.

"You are so exceedingly kind, Horace, that I hardly know how to respond. Of course, I would love beyond anything to remain here, where I am so very comfortable, so excessively well looked-after – my every want catered for and – and so on. But, just because you are kind, I should not take advantage and force you to put up with an old, superfluous woman hanging around when you, perhaps, might wish to – to lead a different sort of life."

"Don't be silly," he returned. "Whatever sort of life are you imagining I might want to lead? Are you thinking that, if you weren't here, I could bring all sorts of unsuitable females home and indulge in drunken parties – *orgies*, even? You exert no constraint upon me; if I want to indulge myself in too much liquor or the company of improper females, I could perfectly well do so, as you very well know. This is a huge house, you go to bed early – I don't suppose you'd even know who'd been here of an evening after you'd retired. And, even if you did, I have no doubt that you would keep your own counsel. You're very welcome to stay, become *my* companion – I have no other, after all."

He stopped, realising suddenly that his last remark had not been as courteous as it could have been, and blushed fierily.

She, who had been concentrating upon a piece of cheese which seemed unusually difficult to cut, looked up and saw the colour in his handsome cheeks.

"We neither of us have at the moment," she said gently, "but you will, one day, and do you not think she will consider my presence peculiar at the very least?"

"If she does, she will not be the right woman for me," he declared stoutly. "I believe you should stay, Saffy, if only to make sure I don't marry the wrong sort of person. If she is wedded to convention and a stickler for the proprieties, I don't think she and I would get along very well once the initial romance had faded.

"I daresay," he added, "that, in any event, Jenny will soon get tired of Titania, or Titania of Jenny, and then she will come back here – or run home to Rushlake. *Then* you will be needed again by her and will be obliged to forsake me."

"Don't you think she will be married before the end of the year?"

"I don't know. I haven't asked Jenny for a report on how she's getting along and whether there's a queue of suitors lining up. I suppose that, although she's well past her majority, if one did decide to put in an offer, he would feel bound to speak to me first. No one has as yet."

It was later, when the pair met again over a cup of tea in the drawing room that the Earl said, "Please don't feel obliged to remain here if you would rather find a new position. I offered because I would like you to stay and I assumed – but should not have done – that you would prefer that than be obliged to look for another post."

"I would infinitely prefer to stay here," she said softly, "particularly if it is more a case of your wishing to retain my services in case Titania should need them again than if you are simply being kind. That is really not necessary; you have already fulfilled all possible obligations concerning kindness towards me."

"That was part of my reasoning," he acknowledged. "I thought that, if she does scuttle back to the country, she would surely prefer to have you accompany her than be obliged to find someone new."

In point of fact, he did not think this since he knew that his sister found Saffy extraordinarily irritating, but he hoped that this particular situation would not come to pass.

"On the other hand," he went on with a smile which caused poor Saffy's heart to melt in her bosom, "I'm afraid I might be lonely here without you."

She returned the smile, but hers was sad. "It's my belief you were being kind. Why, you haven't even managed to lay off any of your servants and, far from dispensing with Marshall's services at Rushlake, you've provided him with an assistant to do all the work! You know – I'm sure you must – that Titania has little patience with me – indeed forcing her to put up with me again would probably be the worst thing she could envisage!"

He grinned at this, realising that the flashes of insight which Saffy had shown during the recent case had been by no means transient. She was, he was convinced, far sharper of intellect than she generally demonstrated, her habit of humility concealing a lively intelligence.

"Wouldn't it be depressing for you too?" he asked curiously.

She did not speak at once so that Lord Rushlake knew that the answer was in the affirmative.

"I am very fond of Titania," she said at last, "but we are such different people that there are times when we do not altogether understand one another. All the same," she added hastily, "I would be perfectly willing

– if she was – to take up my position at Rushlake again. It is a most comfortable house and the country round there is lovely."

"I believe we must hope she will marry," he concluded.

The next day he called upon his sister, Jenny, and, as luck would have it, found that Titania had gone out for a walk with a new friend.

"A male friend?" he asked.

"No; a female one."

"Do you think," he asked, "that any of her admirers are likely to come up to scratch?"

"I would have expected at least one to do so had I not seen her dismissing him impatiently only a couple of days ago. She is very exacting, you know."

"Who is he?"

"Lord Martindale. He's a Viscount at present but stands to become Earl when his father dies. It's an old title but unfortunately doesn't seem to come with much else. I mean, they're not at all well off – I rather think his grandfather sold a lot of land."

"Gambling, I suppose? Does this one take after his grandfather?"

"In that respect? I don't think so; he's quite dull."

"Is he? Is he after her money, do you think?"

"Probably," Jenny admitted in a despairing tone. "The thing is, you see, that she's quite sharp in manner sometimes – a result of being a bit older than the usual *débutante*, I suspect, as well as having effectively run Rushlake for years. She's frightened most of them off, but he's still hanging around."

"Oh dear. Are there any others?"

"Well, there's Cranver, but I suspect he'd lead *her* a merry dance while she'd lead Martindale by the nose. I wouldn't, if I had unlimited choice, choose either."

"I suppose Martindale would do," her brother said, "although if he is so easily routed I should think he'd allow her to bully him unmercifully. Did – do – you think she likes him above half?"

"Probably a little above half but I'm not sure that's enough. In any event, I imagine he's got cold feet now. I don't think Cranver has, but then I'm not convinced he's serious."

"No," the Earl agreed.

"Why do you ask?"

"Because we're getting to the end of the Season and we will, I suppose, have to decide what to do next. Has she mentioned anything to you about going back to Rushlake – or alternatively moving back in with me in London?"

"Not in so many words, no, but I get the impression that she's becoming a little desperate as the Season winds down. Of course, she never expected to find a husband, but all the same I think she's disappointed."

"No doubt – and do you think she may be dreading going back to Rushlake with Aunt Saffy?"

Jenny frowned.

"Are you wondering what to do with her?"

"Yes. I've suggested she might like to stay in London with me, but I get the impression that she thinks she'll be a nuisance. She's mentioned looking for another position."

"But you thought it might be useful to keep her in reserve for Titania again?"

"Yes."

"I don't think Titania would want that. She really doesn't care for poor Aunt Saffy."

"No – and I'm not sure Saffy cares much for Titania. But how long can you bear to keep her - Titania?"

"I don't mind her as a matter of fact. She gets along well with the children and is quite independent. So long as I don't try to organise her, we manage quite well."

"So I take it you're saying that, even if Titania does go back to Rushlake, she would rather not have Saffy there?"

"Yes."

There was a short silence while they both pondered the dilemma. It was Jenny who broke it.

"So will you tell Saffy to look for another position?"

"No, I don't think so. I might keep her myself."

"*What?* Whatever for? Won't she drive you mad in the same way she did Titania?"

"No, I don't think so, because, you see, I'm a man and we live in London so that I can always go out if I need to get away from her. I'm wondering if I can put her to use as a sort of housekeeper? She seems very assiduous in attending to the linen, and Mrs Robinson, who is supposed to be the housekeeper, hasn't been much use during the years the house has been empty. I think I might set Saffy above her and either sack the woman eventually or hope she leaves of her own accord."

"*Well!*" Jenny said. "How long will you keep her – Saffy? Will you allow your wife – when you take one – to turn her out in five to ten years' time? Wouldn't it be better to send her on her way now?"

"I've already invited her to stay."

"Oh dear! You really are too quixotic for your own good! But do you think she could manage the servants? That's one of the things a housekeeper is expected to do and Saffy – well, she's always struck me as a bit *limp*. I can't imagine her sacking anyone – although you don't seem to be able to either!"

"I could put her into a sort of *châtelaine's* position, above Mrs Robinson, so that Mrs Robinson would still be in charge of the maids and so on but would have to answer to Aunt Saffy."

"Lord! I should think Aunt Saffy would be more terrified of having to deal with Mrs Robinson than of having to find another position."

He smiled. "Perhaps. I'll put it to her. The thing is that I've grown quite attached to Saffy and don't want her to feel she has to leave. If I put her in charge of Mrs Robinson, nominally, she might not feel so much that she was receiving charity."

Jenny laughed. "And it'll stop you having to deal with Mrs Robinson – or, rather, you'll have to deal with her at one remove."

"Just so. And, it will effectively be a demotion for Mrs R so that she may feel her pride has been hurt and leave of her own accord. Then I can appoint another, under-housekeeper, to do as Aunt Saffy bids."

"I think you must grasp the nettle, little brother, and dismiss Mrs Robinson. Tell her Aunt Saffy is taking her place, and *then* appoint a more biddable under-housekeeper."

He did not wait for Titania to return from her walk but went home, sent for Mrs Robinson and told her, without speaking to Aunt Saffy again, that his cousin, Miss Hemsted, would be taking over the running of the house so that Mrs Robinson's services were no longer required.

Mrs Robinson was a stout, brusque woman, who had no trouble controlling the maids but, during the time when the house had been empty, had not done her job with quite the degree of assiduity that Jenny, knowing much more about housekeeping than her brother, would have demanded.

It was clear that she had not expected to be given notice at this juncture, for the Earl had been in residence for several months. She flushed an uneven red, her eyes began to bulge and, for an awful moment, he was afraid that she was going to quibble. He had never given anyone notice before and suspected that his manner had been too apologetic. Her next words convinced him of this.

"Have you found fault with my work, my lord?" she asked sharply.

"As a matter of fact, yes. The house was in a very shabby, not to say dirty, condition when I first saw it with my sister. There was a great deal of dust, a musty smell and a vast amount of mending which hadn't been done. I appreciate that we arrived without much warning, but your job was to keep it ticking over until I did move in."

"Huh!" she exclaimed, glaring at him. "It's not my place to criticise your decision, my lord, but, from what I've seen, I don't think Miss Hemsted will find it easy to manage the staff."

The Earl did not think so either and neither did his sister, but, as he was not prepared to discuss this with the outgoing tyrant, he said mildly, but a trifle frigidly, "Thank you for the warning. I'll provide you with a reference and am willing to give you a month's wages while you look for another position. If you wish to leave before that, I shall not try to prevent you."

Mrs Robinson glared at him.

"I don't know what your mother would have said!" she tried.

"I don't think you do either," he returned, rising. "She died long before you were engaged."

For a moment they stood facing each other, she glaring and breathing hard, he wondering if he would have to summon Ford to eject her.

"Thank you, Mrs Robinson," he said curtly, sitting down again and drawing a piece of paper towards him as though to continue with the rest of his work.

There was nothing she could do but leave and he, when she had gone, heaved a sigh and ran his hand through his hair. Mrs Robinson was the first person he had dismissed in his life and he had not found it a pleasant experience.

Chapter 2

Mrs Robinson left at the end of the week, much to the Earl's relief, for her malevolent presence seemed to permeate the whole house. On his sister Jenny's advice, he explained the situation to his butler, Ford.

"Is there," he asked, "one of the maids who would be able to take over the management of the female staff under Miss Hemsted's direction?"

Ford, who was glad to see the back of the tyrannical but lazy housekeeper, admitted that he thought it might be difficult to promote one of the junior staff to what was a fairly senior position and one, moreover, where she would be obliged to seek the advice of an even more inexperienced supervisor.

"For," he explained as tactfully as he could, "Miss Hemsted is not accustomed to managing household staff."

"No," Rushlake agreed. "That is why we need somebody to carry out her wishes – she does, after all, know how a house should be run. Whoever becomes what you might call her second-in-command will answer directly to Miss Hemsted, who will have her own ideas about what she wishes to achieve."

"Yes, my lord, I understand that, but I don't think any of the present female staff are at the stage where such a promotion would be easy for them to assume – or where they would be able to do what Miss Hemsted might ask of them."

"I see. Is it your opinion then that I should engage another housekeeper to act under Miss Hemsted's direction?"

"Yes, my lord, that would be my advice. Would you like me to place a suitable advertisement?"

"Not just yet. I believe I'll discuss it with my sister first. She's bound to know of someone suitable."

"Indeed. An excellent idea, my lord."

Ford bowed and withdrew.

Later that evening, when his lordship joined Aunt Saffy in the drawing room, he told her that the position was vacant and that he would like her to take it up – not, he hastened to add when he saw her face, without some appropriate person being engaged to deal directly with the servants.

"Oh!" she exclaimed, beginning to flutter like an uneasy moth. "Did you dismiss her or did she leave of her own accord?"

"I dismissed her – told her you were going to take over."

"Oh, no! I wish you had warned me. I don't think I can. At least, if that is what you want me to do, of course I'll try, but I'm afraid I don't think I'd be much good."

"Why not?"

"Why …? Well, I don't think I have the *authority* somehow – I mean, I'm not really in the habit of telling others what to do – I've been more accustomed to doing what I'm told."

"I know that – and I thought it was time you turned things around. I know – or I thought I did – that you have found doing others' bidding a burden and I wanted you to be free while at the same time doing something for me."

"Oh, yes, I *do* want to do something for you, dear Horace. Indeed, I would do *anything* for you, but I'm rather afraid that what you've asked will be beyond my capabilities."

"Nonsense! Do you know, I wasn't sure I could dismiss the wretched woman – it was the most frightful effort and there was a moment, after I'd told her to go, when she just stood there and glared at me. For an awful moment I wondered if she was going to hit me – or spit at me! But it passed off and now I feel so confident I believe I could dismiss them all. Should I do that, do you think?"

"Oh no, not Ford! You couldn't get rid of him – why, he's been here since your father's day, hasn't he?"

"Yes, but I feel I should bring in a new broom."

"Not to Ford!" she repeated. "But I think you were quite right to get rid of the housekeeper. The more I see of this house, the more I think she neglected her duties quite *dreadfully* before you moved in."

"There," he said with some satisfaction, "you see, you know just what needs doing."

"I believe I do, but I don't think I know how to do it."

"Neither did I!"

"No, but it's different for you. You pay their wages and you're a man. I'm just an oldish woman and you want me to deputise for you, really, and I think that would be awfully difficult."

"Why? Because of me breathing down your neck?"

She flushed, but said gamely, "Yes. You see, when you're doing something for yourself, it's not so difficult to gather one's courage and do it, but when you're doing it for someone else, it's so much more difficult. I would be so afraid of letting you down."

"I don't think you could. The thing is that I don't know anything about housekeeping – you've already pointed out a lot of Mrs Robinson's deficiencies so that, in truth, you know much more about it than I do."

"I'll try," she promised but her voice was despairing and she could not look at him.

"I'm sorry!" he exclaimed. "I'll get Jenny to find some candidates and you and I will interview them together – perhaps with Jenny there too. She'll know what's needed."

"Yes, she's bound to, but – the thing is, she'll probably choose a first-rate person but I won't be able to manage her because I – I'm just – I don't know how I'd go about telling anyone what was required."

"Don't be silly, Saffy. You've been telling me what's required; why in the world couldn't you tell a servant?"

"Because I'm too feeble. It's easy to tell you because you're so sympathetic and you're not going to refuse to do it, but the housekeeper wouldn't be – she'd be bound to want to get the better of me – and she would."

"If she tried, she'd be out on her ear!" he said, laughing, "and I could practise my dismissal technique again."

"Oh, pray!" she begged. "It's no laughing matter."

"It is – or it ought to be. I need a housekeeper and, lacking any knowledge of the sort of person I want – except that I would infinitely prefer her to be entirely different from Mrs Robinson – I'm asking you, who do know what's required, to help."

"When you put it like that," she said, "I don't feel quite so intimidated, but the thing is, Horace, that I've never been in a position to command servants and lack authority."

"You have the authority I've vested in you," he pointed out.

"Don't you think," she murmured some time later when they had drunk their tea, "that it might be better if I looked for another position as a companion? I know how to do that, you see."

"If that's what you want, I won't prevent you, but I don't believe it is."

He studied her face for a few moments while she tried not to flinch and look away. Eventually he said, "Will you indulge me so far as to interview these wretched women with me? Then, if you still want to go somewhere else as a companion, you shall."

"You are so very kind, Horace, but I cannot conceive it possible that you really wish to share your house with me, even for a short time."

"Why should I not? You're not much trouble, you don't try to order me about or get me to do things I don't want to do. I suppose I should be ashamed of myself for taking advantage of your good nature – and your gratitude, which I promise is quite unnecessary. I'm grateful to you because I can sit in my own drawing room of an evening, drink tea, chat about what's going on in the world and receive sympathy and understanding. If you weren't here," he went on, warming to his theme, "I don't think I'd sit here of an evening; I'd go out, probably drink too much, possibly play cards too often and lose money, or find some unsuitable female to pursue who would be bound to make excessive demands upon me."

"But that's what you should be doing – and I won't try to stop you because that would be mean. You're a young man, you're supposed to do all those things you've listed – and as for the young women, well, isn't it about time you found one whose wishes you want to indulge?"

"No, I don't think so – not – not to settle down with."

"Well," she said, "finding the right young woman isn't quite like buying a new coat – or even a new hunter, is it? You have to get to know a person, find out whether you like her, whether you're compatible – that sort of thing. Is there," she asked a little tentatively, "anyone you do find just a little bit appealing?"

"No."

"Perhaps," she suggested slyly, "there is someone but she seems to be already suited."

"Good lord! Are you implying I've got my eye on a married woman?"

"Have you?"

"No – not, I'm afraid, even a betrothed one. Why do you all want to marry me off?"

"I think," she said at last, having given the matter some thought, "because we love you and we want you to be happy."

"Thank you, but I'm perfectly happy."

"Good. You don't have to tell me about anyone on whom your eye has alighted," she went on earnestly.

He grinned at her and said, "Since we're talking about people's happiness, what do you think about Helena and the detective?"

"Oh dear," she said, "they're wasting an awful lot of time, aren't they, when they don't have such a great deal of it? I mean, she's well into her thirties and he must be nearly forty."

"Yes. What do you think we should do?"

"I don't see what we can do. She's gone back to Yorkshire and he's still in London and really has no reason to go up there unless it's to see her. I don't think he dares because I'm not sure he thinks he's good enough – or, which is much more to the point, whether she thinks so."

"No; the man's an idiot. *We* all noticed so why hasn't he?"

"I don't think he can believe his luck," she said, carefully matching another length of silk before threading her needle. "I did try to tell her," she went on, "but she wouldn't listen – kept changing the subject. Have you tried to tell him?"

"No. He's not that sort of friend."

"Oh. Do you still see him from time to time?"

"Occasionally, but it's always I who seeks him out, never the other way round. I'm afraid he's uncomfortable with the difference in our stations and doesn't like to bother me with what he believes to be his inferior presence."

"No doubt."

It was not difficult for Saffy to understand the detective's point of view since she suffered from the same feeling of inferiority *vis-à-vis* the Earl.

"There's a difference between him and Helena too, although it's not so large."

"Do you think," he asked, "that they would be happy together? I mean, if they were to marry, I suppose she would have to come to London because his job's here."

"Yes, although if he were married to her he could afford to give up his job and move to Yorkshire."

"I don't think he'd feel comfortable with that. Whatever they were to do, there would be a huge disparity in their means. She could afford to buy a large house in London, which would be ideal for them both, but that would probably make him feel beholden to her."

"Yes, I know."

Aunt Saffy took a few careful stitches, bending her head over her work and thus allowing a short pause before she spoke again.

"It seems a shame though because they're two people who have somehow failed to find a spouse at the usual time but have, through your agency, met and taken quite a shine to each other, if their blushes are anything by which one can judge the matter."

"It was sheer luck that they met each other – nothing to do with me."

"In the first instance perhaps not, but you took a certain amount of trouble to bring them together again and now they've wandered off to opposite ends of the country and need to be brought together again."

He laughed. "Should I book a church for them and then bring her back by some ruse – not, I hope, another murder?"

She looked up, met his eyes and smiled. "I don't think you should go quite so far as to book the church, but I do think you'd better bring them together again."

"What do you suggest?"

"Well, what about inviting them both to Rushlake? It'll be Christmas soon which would provide the perfect excuse to gather them together again."

"What a splendid idea! I could invite Jenny and her family too, as well as Aunt Mildred, although I daresay she'll be spending the festival with one or another – or perhaps several – of her children and grandchildren. But what do you suppose Helena does usually?"

"I've no idea; I only met her here," Aunt Saffy said. "I suppose she must have some cousins or something, but she hasn't even any nephews or nieces since she was an only daughter, wasn't she? I shouldn't think she goes anywhere with your aunt because whatever *she* does, it'll be organised by her children."

"I'll write to her. What do you think about Bodley? Do you suppose he has some nephews and nieces – or even parents with whom he'll spend Christmas?"

"I should think he has *someone* – most people do – but that doesn't mean he wouldn't jump at an offer from you."

"Oh, I think it does! We're up against the inferiority dilemma again! He'll be thoroughly unnerved at the prospect of spending Christmas in a large house in the country with a whole family of aristocrats – and I won't dare mention Helena Patchett as mitigation in case he takes even worse fright at the thought of meeting her again."

In the end he decided to invite Helena Patchett first because he thought that, even if the detective found some excuse not to come, he would rather be left with her without him than him without her.

He mentioned his idea to Jenny, who was delighted at the prospect of spending Christmas at Rushlake.

"I haven't been there since Papa's funeral," she said, "and that was *not* a happy occasion. It'll be lovely to see the old place again. Is it just as it was when Papa was alive?"

He smiled. "Do you mean have I done as little to update it as I have in London? Yes, undoubtedly, but the housekeeper has kept it in much better order."

"I suppose," he went on, "that it will provide the perfect opportunity for you to leave Titania there?"

"Yes, it would, but, as I told you, I don't actually mind her staying – and if we let her go back to Rushlake now she'll never find a husband! She's fitted in very well. I assume she doesn't have any admirers in the country, does she? In fact does she have any friends there?"

"She denies both, but I don't think that's necessarily true. I'm sure there must be a few neighbours with whom she's on speaking terms at least, and possibly some admirers too."

"Whom else will you invite?"

"Well, Adrian Bodley of course."

"Yes, but I think you should muster a few more guests as otherwise he'll realise the whole thing is a set-up to bring him and Helena together again."

"Whom do you suggest?"

Jenny frowned. "A lawyer or someone of that sort; he'd bridge the divide between the aristocracy and the police."

"I doubt he'd see it that way. Do you know any lawyers?"

"I'm sure James does – or perhaps a stockbroker."

"Or a clergyman. I'm sure we could muster one or two of them – indeed there's a new curate at Rushlake – Marcus Stapleton."

"One of the Stapletons of Hinchcombe?"

"Yes; that's why I appointed him. Old Merrick'll be retiring soon and I thought one of them could do with the living. There may even be a lawyer amongst them."

"They'd be better advised to encourage at least one of them to go into stockbroking – might improve the whole family's finances," she said, laughing.

"I suspect they're far too snobbish to think of that," he returned. "I might suggest it to Marcus though."

In the end, after consultation with Sir James Wendell, they found a suitably well-connected lawyer, who was single and, having been brought to the house for dinner one evening to meet both his putative host, Lord Rushlake, and Titania, seemed eager to spend Christmas in Shropshire. His name was Thomas Benton.

"I think he was quite taken with Titania," Jenny confided to her brother.

"Good. He seemed agreeable. What did she think of him?"

"Well, as a matter of fact, she clearly preferred him to either Martindale or Cranver. He's quite a good friend of James's – was at Cambridge with him. We told him something about Helena and Bodley before you arrived, although afterwards I thought he might be just the ticket for Titania. I mean, she doesn't have to marry a nobleman, does she? What about the curate? Will she have already met him?"

"I shouldn't think so – he hasn't been there long and I don't think she did much around the parish."

"No – she's not much given to being charitable," Jenny agreed. "Too selfish and taken up with her own concerns."

"Don't you think she'd make a good clergy wife?"

"No, but I suppose she might change if she fell in love with a clergyman; in fact, there are any number of Stapletons to choose between."

"Really? How many?"

"There are at least six sons."

"Lord! Are there a lot of girls too?"

"I don't know. I haven't enquired into that – not much I can do for them."

"You could marry one I suppose."

"That," her brother said, more amused than annoyed, "is a low blow."

"Well, but she might be delightful. Perhaps we should invite the whole family."

"They'd think that rather odd, wouldn't they? We've never, to my knowledge, met even one of them."

"Didn't you meet the curate before you appointed him?"

"No. I left it to the Vicar to interview him. He's the one who has to work with him after all."

"How are they related to us?" she asked.

"Lord knows! They're a distant connexion – cousins of some sort, I suppose – a bit like Aunt Saffy."

"Is she related to them?"

"Possibly; I'll ask her later."

"Do you think the one ensconced at Rushlake will be successful? Turn out to be a leading light in the church?"

"I've no idea. Become a bishop, do you mean? Would that reconcile you to Tania marrying him?"

"Yes, I suppose it would."

"Whom do you favour at the moment for her – one of the two here in London, Martindale or Cranver, or my new curate?"

"Or James's lawyer friend. He's quite clever; I'm not convinced either Cranver or Martindale is – and I think they're both after her money."

21

"I don't think we want them then," the Earl said. "From what I hear, Cranver's a bit of a rake which would make him a bad husband. Martindale is rather a dull fellow but perhaps that's what one wants in a spouse."

"Male or female?"

"Either; the trouble is that, if a person's dull, it's difficult to work up enough enthusiasm to pursue them in the first place."

Chapter 3

He left her to persuade her husband that a Christmas spent at Rushlake would be enjoyable, and invited Adrian Bodley to meet him in a coffee house on Bond Street.

"I was wondering," he began, when the pair had sat down, "whether you might like to spend Christmas at Rushlake with my family."

"Oh!" the detective exclaimed, clearly taken by surprise. "What – that's very kind of you, my lord."

"Not at all. We would like you to join us, but perhaps you're accustomed to spend the festival with members of your own family."

Mr Bodley nodded. "I don't have a large family," he said, "but I do usually visit my parents over the festive season."

"Would they be very disappointed if you were to go somewhere else?" his lordship asked.

Mr Bodley thought they would, but he was also convinced that they would be even more keen for him to spend time staying with an Earl in a grand country house. If he were to go up in the world, they would think, he would most likely do so through his connexion with the Earl.

"I doubt it," he said in a rather dismal tone. "I mean, I've always spent Christmas with them, ever since I was a child, but I don't think they find my company particularly stimulating. I'm sure they'd perfectly understand if I were to accept your kind invitation, my lord."

In spite of judging this to be a distinctly unenthusiastic response to what he had perhaps considered kindly condescension on his part, Lord Rushlake managed to restrain himself from the sort of sharp retort which hovered on his lips by thinking of how amused his aunt would be when he retailed this put-down to her. So, instead of getting his own back, he evinced what he hoped was the right degree of pleasure at having his invitation accepted, remembered an appointment he must on no account fail to keep and left, having first paid the bill for the coffee and cakes they had consumed.

On returning home, he remembered that he had still to write to Miss Patchett to invite her to Rushlake and did so, although, after the disappointment of Mr Bodley's response, he was no longer so certain that he wished to encourage a union between the young woman and the detective.

After dinner that evening when he and Saffy were drinking their tea in the drawing room, she asked if there was something on his mind.

He smiled. "Yes, but I don't doubt I'm refining too much upon it. I feel somewhat spurned by Bodley."

"Really? Did he not jump at the invitation to spend Christmas at Rushlake?" she asked, surprised, for she too had expected the detective to fairly leap at such a grand invitation.

"No, he didn't, although he accepted. Indeed, I rather wish he had not if he is going to view it as an obligation."

"I should think it's not so much an obligation as a worry," she said gently. "Here, he can visit you from time to time – and you can visit him – but travelling all the way to Rushlake and spending several days in the sort of *milieu* about which he is certain to know little and which he will find intimidating, must be the sort of thing he wants but is uncertain he can deal with."

"Do you think that's what it is?"

"Yes, I'm certain of it. You see, up until now, he has – not to put too fine a point upon it – made use of you and your contacts to assist him in his job. Indeed, I doubt he would have been able to make the arrests he has without your assistance. And now, here you are inviting him to something for which he will feel wholly unable to repay you. It must be quite a burden for him."

The Earl nodded, watching his companion's face, which was bent over her embroidery.

He said, "Is it a burden for you to remain living here?"

She looked up then, met his eyes, blushed and nodded.

"Yes, but it is such an enormous pleasure – I'm so happy here – that I'm sure I shall soon grow accustomed to feeling beholden and – and find some way of repaying you."

"Your happiness is payment enough," he said gently.

"Thank you," she replied a little tremulously, but went on in a firmer voice, "The thing is, you see, Horace, that you seem willing to extend help and kindness to us all – but we, those of us who have grown fond of you, would like to do something for you. The difficulty arises because you don't need – or seem to want – anything. I've been wracking my brains, for instance, to think of what in the world I can give you for Christmas."

"Oh, Lord!" he exclaimed, relieved that the high flights of obligation and *noblesse oblige* seemed to have descended a little towards the trivialities of the Christmas season. "Shall I write a little list?"

"Yes, provided it doesn't begin and end with managing a new housekeeper or sacking one of the maids. Of course, I will do that if that is what you want, but I would like – oh so much – to wrap up a little present for you and give it to you on the Day."

"And I would love to receive such a thing but would infinitely prefer it to be a surprise, which I know will add to your burden but, really, I cannot think of anything I either need or want just at present so that, whatever you find, I'm certain it'll be just what I want!"

"Very well. Have you finalised your list of guests with Jenny yet?"

"Not quite. I've written to Helena, but of course, as Aunt Mildred won't be coming, she may not want to either. I didn't like to say I'd twisted Bodley's arm to get him to attend so that she won't know that there will be any particular reason for her to make such a long journey on her own."

"Shall I write too and casually mention that I think he may be coming?"

"Don't you think that might frighten her away?"

"I don't think Helena is easily frightened; I think the detective is – by social situations with which he is unfamiliar. And he's undoubtedly positively terrified of his own sentiments towards Helena. I assume that's why he was unable to mention them when she was here. He was, in my opinion, afraid to put it to the test for, if he had made her an offer and she had refused, I don't think he would have found it easy to recover from what he would have seen as the humiliation."

"Do you think him proud?"

"Yes, in an odd sort of way. He feels himself to be inferior – certainly to you, but possibly to her too, for she is excessively rich and he has, I suspect, only his salary upon which to rely. It would be a huge step up for him to marry her."

"Yes, I know, but, if he wants her, he'll have to face up to it."

"Indeed. Shall I write to her then?"

"If you think it will assist, yes, please do. I was wondering if I should ask Aunt Mildred to come after Christmas – for New Year perhaps when she will not be under the same obligation to stay with her close family. You could mention that to Helena, although I do want Helena to come for Christmas. If she doesn't, if she were to decide to wait and come with Aunt Mildred, I daresay Bodley would already have left, for I must suppose he won't get an indefinite amount of leave from his job."

And so both wrote more letters later that evening and waited with bated breath to receive replies. His lordship's were not only to his putative guests but also to his servants in the country to prepare them for the ordeal ahead. He informed them of the event, although, as he pointed out, he was not yet certain of the number of people that was expected, a fact which he would communicate as soon as he had received replies to all his invitations. Otherwise, he promised that he would leave it to them to decide upon the assignment of bedrooms and the menus, thinking, probably correctly, that they knew much more than he about the proper things to serve to a large party over Christmas.

"I hope," he confided to Aunt Saffy the following day at luncheon, "that the servants won't be too thrown by what will no doubt seem to them to be a sudden decision to fill the house with guests."

"I should think they'll be pleased," she said encouragingly. "After all, they're lucky enough to work in a beautiful place and must, when your parents were alive, have catered for large parties from time to time."

"Not recently though. My mother died a long time ago, as you know, and my father never remarried. I don't think he entertained much at all; certainly I don't remember it. Perkins, in any event, never knew my mother."

"No," Aunt Saffy, who had spent much more time at Rushlake recently than the Earl himself, said, "but Mrs Baines, the housekeeper, is quite old. I should think she did."

"Possibly," the ignorant landowner replied lightly. "I don't remember Mrs Baines – I mean, I have of course met her now, but I don't remember her from when I was a child – and I recall very little about Mama. Did you know her?"

"Your mama? No, although I think I may have met her as a child. So far as I can recall, she was a little like your – and her - Aunt Mildred, although not of course so very decided in her manner."

He laughed. "Was Aunt Mildred's husband unusually easy-going?"

"I didn't know him, but I should think he must have been, although I don't mean that he was under her thumb precisely. I believe he doted upon her – gave her almost everything she wanted – so that she has become accustomed to getting her own way."

Replies to the missives arrived the following day. The servants professed themselves eager to provide whatever was required for his lordship's guests and had already begun to air the rooms, check the linen, polish the silver and glass and so forth. Orders had been issued for festive food, including poultry, assorted vegetables – although most of those would come from the estate itself – fruit, coffee, tea etcetera. The Earl, reading this enthusiastic list of things which must be purchased, was glad that he had not to find them himself for he had no idea where the best coffee could be purchased or the most fashionable blend of tea.

Lady Amberstone, his Aunt Mildred, said she was looking forward to coming and was only sorry that her own family obligations meant she could not come for the actual Day. She would, however, she promised, do her best to arrive on the twenty-seventh of December at the earliest. She would certainly hope to be well ensconced by the beginning of 1845.

He had, fearing that they might otherwise take umbrage, invited his two eldest sisters and their families but was not surprised when they declined. They had, of course, come for their father's obsequies, but did not otherwise pay much attention to their natal families, being much more taken up with their spousal ones.

Amongst the eagerly awaited replies, there was one from Helena Patchett, who declared that she was honoured by the invitation and, remembering how much she had enjoyed (for the most part) her sojourn in London with him and his family, was delighted to accept.

It had been decided that Aunt Saffy would travel, as she had when she had first come to London, in a carriage with Titania, while Jenny, who had a husband and three children, would make the journey separately with her own family.

After much thought, his lordship, prompted by Jenny, decided to go down a few days before the others in order to make sure everything had been properly arranged, for, she pointed out, it would be quite awful if he were to arrive after any of his guests and even more frightful were he to discover that the appropriate arrangements were not in place. In the end, unnerved by the number of people coming, he asked if she would accompany him in order to oversee any last-minute preparations.

"Goodness! Are you admitting that you need me?" she asked teasingly.

"I believe I am – and you will be quite within your rights to remind me of it for years – although I hope you will not."

"Very well," she rather surprisingly said. "James can bring the children later and I will travel with you. I suppose you'll be taking a carriage, not riding?"

"I think so."

"What about Aunt Saffy and Titania? Will you make them come later too? I suppose I'd better send Tania back to your house when I leave."

He thought about Titania's likely reception of the news that she was to be put back under Aunt Saffy's aegis and Aunt Saffy's uncomplaining acceptance of the situation, and said, no, he rather thought they should come too. They could, he suggested unguardedly, all travel together.

The journey, when they set out on it a few days later, was an agreeable one, for everyone was looking forward to the projected party. Jenny was pleased to have been designated an expert in the matter of organising the household, Titania was glad – although she did not say so – to get away from London and her rather tepid admirers for a little while and Aunt Saffy was delighted to have been included in the family party.

His lordship, sitting beside the younger of his two sisters in the backward facing seats, was treated by them all as the person on whom they could rely – even Jenny deferred to his decisions about where they should stop and what time they should eat – so that he began to feel more like the head of the household with every passing mile.

When they arrived at Rushlake, they were welcomed by the servants, who lined up in the hall to be introduced to Jenny, who was to act as mistress of the house.

She was given her mother's room. The Earl, a little anxious about this, asked her, as the housekeeper was about to lead her upstairs, if she objected to this.

"Not in the least," she returned. "I take it as a compliment. Thank you, Horace."

The other two went to their old rooms and the Earl allowed himself to be shown to his father's chamber for the first time. It had, while he was in London, been cleared of his father's effects and furnished with such of his own as had been in his boyhood room.

When he had washed his hands, he knocked upon the door next to his and, upon being bidden to enter, went in to find his sister standing by the window, looking out upon the garden.

"There are plenty of bedrooms if you would rather not take this one," he said quietly from the door.

She turned and he saw that there were tears on her cheeks.

"No, I must pull myself together," she said. "It's years since she died. It's just that this room brings it all back."

"I know – so does Papa's. There's no point in being upset; I can easily ask them to move your effects."

She shook her head. "No, I want to stay here and remember her. I was nineteen when she died and so full of myself and my own happiness that, to tell you the truth, I've hardly thought about it since. Do you remember her at all, Horace?"

"Not much. What was she like?"

"Unselfish – to a fault, I think now. She never complained about being ill, although I now realise she must have been when I came out. She took me around London, we went to party after party, she listened to me going on about James for ever and, all the time, she must have known that she hadn't got long."

"And Papa? Did he know, do you think?"

"I don't think he wanted to. If she was unselfish, he was abominably selfish, as you know. I wonder if she'd always been so, so compliant or whether Papa's irascibility had forced her to fit in with him. She was beautiful and none of her daughters are – only her son. I realise now that you're like her in more than looks; you have that magical ability to think of other people and their feelings. Lord, I find myself envying whoever gets to marry you."

"Goodness, what an encomium! You're getting sentimental, Jenny."

"It must be the room, but, you see, I never noticed how like you are to her before. I might have done if you'd been a girl. Somehow, one doesn't expect a man to be so agreeable."

"Oh, well," he said lightly, "sleeping in my father's room will probably put an end to that."

Chapter 4

Lady Wendell took over the management of the house with enthusiasm, beginning by complaining to the housekeeper that the drawing room sofa was almost threadbare in places. The next morning, wandering in to inspect it on his way to breakfast, the Earl found a young girl industriously darning it.

She jumped up, curtsied and explained that her ladyship had wanted someone to mend it as soon as possible and, there not being sufficient time to buy new material to cover it properly, it had been decided that she would do her best with her darning needle.

"I'm sure you'll make an excellent job of it," his lordship said, not admitting that he had failed to notice the problem when he had been here last.

When he went downstairs, he found Jenny and Aunt Saffy already at the breakfast table. There was no sign of Titania.

"Saffy tells me," Jenny said, "that Tania rarely rose in time for breakfast when they were living here before. It seems she's reverted to her old ways."

"It's still early," he said. "Did you make her get up for breakfast in London?"

"Not exactly, but I think she must have picked up on my disapproval. I suppose there was more to do there. Saffy thinks she stays in bed in order to pass the time when she's down here."

"Very likely," he agreed. "Perhaps you'd better find her a task."

"She could have mended the sofa if she was any good at sewing," Jenny returned.

Titania appeared as the other three were on the point of leaving.

"Is there anything you would like me to do?" she asked innocently, helping herself to eggs from the dish on the sideboard.

"You could take over mending the sofa," Jenny suggested.

"I don't suppose I'd do a very good job. Shall I have a look at the stables, make sure there are enough horses for anyone who comes without one, and enough space for people who bring their own?"

"Yes," Horace said. "That would be very helpful."

"I could do the sofa," Aunt Saffy murmured.

"There's a girl doing it at the moment, but I daresay there are plenty of other things she could be doing if you think you could bear it," his lordship said.

"Of course I could bear it. I've done a great deal of sewing during my life," Aunt Saffy explained, "and, although I know you both think my choice of pattern for cushion covers exceedingly dull, I won't have to make a choice for the sofa. All I can do is try to match the colours as best I can."

"If you would like to do that," his lordship said gently, "you can send the girl back downstairs. I suppose someone must have provided her with something approximating the right colour, so you can simply carry on from where she's got to."

"Unless of course she's made an awful mess of it," Jenny said, "when you'll have to undo it all and start again. It should keep you occupied for ages."

The three women having found themselves jobs which suited them, the Earl went off to speak to his bailiff.

The next few days saw both master and servants scurrying about preparing for the influx of guests and, by the time the first ones arrived, the house was sparkling, there was a vast decorated tree in the hall, a smaller one in the drawing room and the hosts were apparently relaxed and ready to welcome their friends and relations.

The first to arrive was Jenny's family. Her husband, Sir James, rolled up soon after breakfast on the day before Christmas Eve, with their three children positively bursting with excitement but trying to appear too sophisticated to show it. There were two girls, aged fourteen and twelve and a boy of ten.

"Will our cousins be coming?" the boy asked.

"No, but there'll be lots of other people," his mother explained, much to his disappointment.

"But I thought it was a family Christmas," he said.

"Yes, it is, but unfortunately neither your Aunt Sarah nor your Aunt Anne will be coming so that your cousins won't either."

"So who is coming?" the elder girl asked, to which question her mother was obliged to admit that all the guests were grown-ups.

"Will there be no other children?" the younger girl asked.

"There are bound to be some in the neighbourhood," Jenny told her.

"I suppose there'll be some Thetfords. They're all girls and I think one or two are still in the schoolroom. I'm sure the Vicar will know of some more," their Uncle Horace put in.

"They'll be poor," the elder girl said with disdain. "We won't have anything in common with them."

31

"That is a shockingly disagreeable remark!" Jenny exclaimed, flushing with anger. "In any event, the Thetfords, if they are the same sort of ages as you, aren't poor; their father's a Viscount."

"That doesn't mean he's rich though, does it?" the child, Aspasia, returned. "And they'll be country children, used to running about in the mud. What will we talk to them about?"

"I don't know – whatever you usually talk about amongst yourselves, I should think," Jenny snapped. "Probably how utterly horrible your parents are."

"Oh, that'll be easy then!" the child retorted.

She was about to be sent to bed without any lunch when her Aunt Titania emerged from the small dining room and, not having heard the discussion, invited the children to come and look at the stables and see if there were any horses they might like to ride.

"For riding in the country," she explained, "is so much more fun than in London."

Jenny, probably for the first time in her life grateful to her younger sister, muttered, when they had gone out, that it was much more dangerous too.

"I'm sure Tania will look after them," Sir James said soothingly.

"Yes, she taught me to ride," the Earl said.

"Hmn," Jenny said, "and just see what a bruising rider you've turned out to be."

"Yes, but I'm still alive and that's because she taught me well. You'll see, they'll learn a lot from Tania. You may have had to teach her to dance, but she can teach them to ride. Come inside, James, and let me pour you a drink."

The grown-ups followed their host into one of the sitting rooms, where, furnished with glasses of sherry, they soon fell into discussion about how merry the house looked and what fun it would be to spend Christmas together. Sir James explained that Mr Benton, invited to be Titania's new *beau*, had at the last moment cried off, citing his parents' inevitable disappointment at his planning to abandon them to a dull Christmas without him.

Jenny, still ashamed of her elder daughter's behaviour and anxious about the dangers of the country, continued to look piqued until Aunt Saffy came and sat down beside her, saying gently that she was sure everything would turn out all right.

32

"How can you be sure?" Lady Wendell asked sharply. "Tania'll take them on a long ride and they'll probably fall off into the mud and miss their lunch."

"I don't think they're going out just at the moment," Saffy murmured. "They just went to look at the horses; after all, they're not dressed for riding, are they?"

"No, but knowing my sister, she wouldn't let that deter her. If they say they want to go off immediately, I daresay she'll let them."

Aunt Saffy, however, was proved right and the three children and their aunt soon returned, the children now talking nineteen to the dozen about the various horses and which ones they wanted to ride.

"Are any of them the right size?" the Earl asked.

"Oh, yes, I think so," Titania replied. "Aspasia can ride Nyssa, Clara will be all right on the bigger of the two ponies and there's still Horace's old Jason, the one he used to ride as a boy. Of course, he's quite old now but I'm sure he'll be just the thing for William, who's not a very experienced rider yet."

"He liked me!" William told his mother. "I gave him a carrot and he looked *very* pleased."

"I expect he was. Thank you, Tania, for saving the situation."

"Not at all; dearest Jenny, you've looked after me wonderfully in London, the least I can do is help the children get used to the country."

On this positive note, the family settled themselves into the house and waited for the rest of the guests to arrive.

The first to do so was Mr Bodley, who had been invited for luncheon and arrived at precisely the right moment, so much so indeed that Jenny wondered if he had been waiting round the corner before presenting himself.

The Earl greeted his friend and took him upstairs to his chamber himself. The detective, on entering the hall, which was several sizes larger than that in the London house, had looked anxious and as though he wished he had found an excuse to turn down the invitation.

"I'll show you to your room and then we'll sit down to luncheon. You're the first guest," his lordship said, leading the way up the stairs, along what seemed to Mr Bodley an almost endless corridor and into a comfortably appointed bedchamber.

"Am I too early?" the detective asked.

"No; you've arrived at exactly the right time. Someone will bring up some hot water in a minute if you want to wash. Shall I wait to take you down again – don't want you getting lost?"

The other man smiled nervously and assented, although he said, "I suppose, if I can find my way around London, I should be able to find my way downstairs."

"I should imagine so, but the thing is that you know London, you don't know Rushlake, and it's exceedingly easy to go the wrong way and then get into a bit of a panic and keep going round in circles. The thing to remember is to turn right out of your room and keep walking until you get to some stairs. When you reach the hall there should be a footman hanging about who can show you the way to the dining room. We do have a bathroom or two now – my father had them put in shortly before he died. Shall I show you where the nearest one is?"

"Oh, yes, please. But you said someone would bring up some hot water? Will this person bring it in here or to the bathroom?"

"The bathrooms have hot water piped in and waste pipes to take it away again when you've finished with it, but I thought you might prefer to have some water of your own in the first instance."

Mr Bodley, unfamiliar with such modern – and expensive – equipment as bathrooms with running water, expressed his gratitude for this consideration, but, the matter not having been mentioned by his host, was obliged to enquire about the location of a water closet.

"Lord! Sorry – of course you want to know that, especially when you've travelled such a long way. Come with me."

Mr Bodley, rather wishing that his lordship had delegated the job of showing him to his room and left a tour of the water closets and bathrooms to a servant, of whom he would not have found it so difficult to ask a question, meekly followed his host out of the room and down the corridor.

It was some twenty minutes later that the two men descended the stairs and joined the rest of the party in a pretty sitting room, from whence they made their way into the dining room for luncheon.

Aunt Saffy greeted him with pleasure and enquired about his journey.

Relieved to be speaking to someone as insignificant as Lady Titania's former companion, Mr Bodley was able to talk about his journey freely and indeed to ask her a few important questions, not only about the house and its various conveniences and inconveniences – the fact that it was so large that one would get a good deal of exercise simply walking to and from one's chamber being one of its less endearing qualities – but also to ask her about the other guests.

Aunt Saffy, perfectly aware that the whole set-up had been prepared with the one thought in mind of getting Mr Bodley and Miss Patchett together again, listed the various guests, inserting Miss Patchett's name somewhere in the middle so that he should not guess the purpose of the party.

"Oh!" he said, the telltale colour rising in his cheeks. "Is Lady Amberstone coming then?"

"No – at least not immediately. I believe she generally spends Christmas with her eldest son and his family, who live in the main house in Yorkshire. She's intending to come later – I hope you'll still be here then."

"Oh, doesn't she live in the main house?" he asked, recalling the vast residence in which he had first met the redoubtable lady and the number of policemen he had had to gather to surround it in order to be certain that the criminal he was about to arrest would not be able to run away.

"Oh, no! She lives in the Dower House, which is close by, so that it will not be difficult for her to join her family over the festival."

She smiled, perfectly understanding his awe and sense of alienation from a way of life which clearly struck him as so different from his own that he could barely contemplate it.

"They're all such elevated persons," she murmured sympathetically, "that if one were to allow oneself to dwell upon their position in Society, one might feel quite intimidated. It's as well, I always find, to concentrate upon them as individuals. They're perfectly ordinary in that way – no different to anyone else really."

"Oh, there I must disagree with you, Miss Hemsted. They are very much more courteous than the general run of people."

"*This* family may be," she agreed, "but it is by no means the case that the aristocracy in general is any more inclined to courtesy than anyone else. Indeed, sometimes, I've found them to be positively rude. The thing is, you see, that they look down on one if one is not from the same stratum of Society."

"But I understand that you are," he said.

"Not really. I'm very distantly related to Rushlake's family, but my branch has never had either a title or much money. Consequently, we've hung around on the fringes – or I have - taking employment from them when it's offered, but always well aware of the difference in our stations."

"Don't you find that uncomfortable?"

"Yes, of course I do, but I don't see what else I can do but clutch their coat tails. His lordship has been very kind."

"Yes," Mr Bodley said with a somewhat depressed air. He had also found his lordship kind but was acutely aware of the differences between them.

"The thing is," she said gently, "that sometimes one does feel a little *condescended* towards, but he doesn't mean it. I believe he genuinely doesn't see any *appreciable* difference between us; it is we, you and I, who feel it and refine upon it."

"I don't think Miss Patchett feels it," he said.

"No – and she should be our example. She always behaves naturally."

"Yes, but then she isn't quite like me either, is she? She has a great deal of money and therefore influence."

"She does have money and that gives her confidence. I don't think she has any more influence than you, Mr Bodley. You're an important person – your job is to uphold the peace, catch criminals, make sure everyone else is safe. Now *that* is what I consider influential."

"You're very kind," he said, "but, of course, I'm not here in that capacity at the moment, am I? I believe, in the execution of my duty, I can feel a little more confident but here, now, well I admit I'm nervous."

"Of course you are, but I'm sure you'll soon get used to it."

After luncheon, everyone returned to the sitting room where they were served coffee. Lady Wendell, in her capacity as hostess, came and sat beside Mr Bodley and engaged him in conversation about his knowledge of the area – which was non-existent, he never having had occasion to visit Shropshire before – and generally sought to put him at his ease.

Later, when the party went out for a walk shortly before darkness fell, he found himself walking beside Sir James Wendell, who, being a mere Baronet, seemed a little less intimidating. By the time they returned to the house for tea and prepared to greet some new arrivals, Mr Bodley was feeling a little more relaxed.

Chapter 5

The rest of the guests arrived later that afternoon. Mr Bodley was relieved to find that they were not all members of the aristocracy, although he could not pretend that any of them came from quite such a lowly position as he.

Miss Helena Patchett arrived by herself and was greeted with great pleasure by the members of Lord Rushlake's Team, who were now all assembled, apart from Lady Amberstone.

Mr Bodley, hanging back, saw her, could not take his eyes off her and found, to his amazement, that her eyes sought his and that, meeting them, she seemed unable to disengage hers.

"You've come a long way," he said with a startling lack of originality when the crowds parted and the two were within speaking distance of each other.

"Not I think quite as far as if I'd gone to London," she returned with a matching absence of imagination.

"No, I suppose not. It's not only north to south but also north to west," he persisted, sticking doggedly to English geography in the hope of calming his rapidly beating heart.

"Yes; I've never been to Shropshire before. It seems very pretty."

"Indeed. You will no doubt not be at all surprised to hear that, until I visited Yorkshire, I had hardly left London. Now I've branched out as far as Shropshire."

"I haven't travelled a great deal either," she admitted. "I came to London when I was eighteen and scuttled back to Yorkshire as soon as the Season was ended. I haven't left since, except to accompany Lady Amberstone to London, and now to come here. It was quite an adventure."

"Does his lordship possess any properties in other countries?" he asked, relaxing sufficiently in her agreeable presence to extend the geographical scope and, in doing so, essay a touch of humour.

"I don't think so, but he may have relatives on the Continent. A lot of people do."

"Yes, of course."

"Have you taken a holiday from your employment?" she asked, the subject of Lord Rushlake's properties failing to offer much in the way of engagement to either party.

"Yes. I hope there won't be anything that will need investigating. In any event, were there to be an unpleasant incident of some kind, it would not of course be my business to intervene. I mean, there must be policemen in Shropshire."

"I suppose so, but I shouldn't think they'd have your expertise in matters relating to violent death."

"No; indeed, one has to hope not. I'm certainly not expecting to have to do anything more arduous than try to ride a horse or – or shoot something, I suppose."

"Shoot something?" she repeated, raising her eyebrows. The last time she had seen Mr Bodley there had been a great deal of discussion about shooting, although his had not been the hand upon the trigger.

"Yes, I gather we're to go out with guns tomorrow," he said.

"Partridge?"

"I believe so. The thing is," he confided, "I've never shot anything in my life."

"No, nor I."

"I don't suppose you'll be expected to."

"Probably not; I shall just have to follow you with the other women."

"I'm sure you can stay here if you don't want to come. I shouldn't think Aunt Saffy follows the guns, does she?"

"I've no idea. No, probably not. Would you rather not go either?"

"Infinitely, but I don't see what excuse I can find to stay at home; on the other hand, I've never handled a rifle and rather suspect that my eyesight isn't up to shooting a flying bird with any degree of accuracy."

"I shouldn't think that matters. There'll be plenty of other people who'll do it well – his lordship, I should imagine in any event. It seems to me that the important thing is not to shoot a person."

"Oh, lord! Just think what the Commissioner would have to say if I killed a person over Christmas!"

She laughed. "I'm sure you can avoid that without the least difficulty. All you have to do is shoot up into the sky – there won't be any men – or following women – up there."

"It's all very well for you to laugh; you'll be sitting here quite comfortably with Aunt Saffy and won't be in the least danger of doing anything so utterly shocking as shooting the wrong thing."

Helena did not think that sitting at home with Aunt Saffy while everyone else went out for the day would be at all amusing. She might be safe, but she would be bored. Aunt Saffy was a dear, kind woman, who had nursed her with immense patience and gentleness when she had been injured the year before, but she was not the sort of person with whom one could engage in an interesting conversation. She did not appear to have any opinions and, if she had, was clearly averse to voicing them.

"Do you wish you hadn't come?" Helena asked after a pause.

"I do rather, but pray don't tell his lordship; he's convinced he's doing me a great favour by inviting me."

Helena did not think that was why Mr Bodley had been invited, or why she had been. It was her opinion that Lord Rushlake – egged on no doubt by his female relatives – had got up the entire party with the aim of getting her and the detective together.

"If you don't want to go shooting, why don't you tell Horace? He's bound to let you off – he's the most understanding man I ever met," she said.

This turned out not to be the most tactful thing to say since Mr Bodley immediately took umbrage, drawing the conclusion that he was not.

"I think I'll have to go," he said, rather tight-lipped, and moved away, leaving Helena to wonder – and eventually light upon – the reason for his sudden pique.

"Why's he gone off in a miff?" the Earl asked, joining her where she had been abandoned upon a sofa in front of the window.

"I *think* it was because I said you were 'understanding' and he assumed, by that, that I did not find him so."

"Well, I don't think he is, particularly. If you want an understanding man, I believe you could do better than Adrian."

"Oh!" she said, flushing and hoping he was not putting himself forward in the detective's stead.

The Earl, seeing the blush and connecting it, correctly, with what he had just said, laughed.

"He is too anxious to fit in to be able, just at present, to understand anyone else's point of view unless it coincides exactly with his own," he said. "I daresay you can teach him to be understanding. Why were you talking of such a thing?"

"Oh, because he's got cold feet about going shooting tomorrow."

"Yes, of course. Why doesn't he cry off? Then he could spend the day with you."

"And Aunt Saffy."

"She's much too tactful not to keep out of your way if he's in the house," he assured her.

"I'm afraid he's gone off me," she said, pouting a little.

"He'll get over it. Shall I suggest he stay home with you tomorrow? I can say that you don't want to have to talk to Aunt Saffy all day."

"No!" she exclaimed, horrified. "Really, Horace, you cannot move us about like puppets just because you think we've developed some sort of *tendre* for each other! You know, both Lady Amberstone and I hung around for ages in London last year to give him a chance – which I was eager for him to take – but he muffed it and – well, I can't hang around for ever."

"No, but I suppose you'll hang around until after Christmas when Aunt Mildred'll turn up."

"Yes, but I might try talking to one or two other gentlemen. Whom do you recommend?"

"Ah, well, some of them were invited for Tania's sake so I think I'd prefer it if you didn't make a move on any of them – unless you think *he* might prefer her."

"I'm sure I don't care whom he prefers!" she exclaimed, going red with anger.

"Let me introduce you to an old friend of mine; his name's Vincent Lovatt and he's a younger son, so unlikely to inherit much to speak of. Indeed, his older brother, who's presently Viscount Surdis, isn't expected to inherit much either."

"If he's an old friend of yours, I shouldn't think he's very old though, is he? Too young for me, I should imagine."

"He's thirty. They're near neighbours and it was his sister, who is more my age, with whom I was used to be friends. She's married now and isn't here. Come, let me introduce you."

"Isn't he one of the ones you've earmarked for your sister?"

"No, they've known each other since they were children so they've had plenty of opportunities; whether she'd accept if he came up to scratch, I've no idea."

"Why don't these wretched men come up to scratch?" she asked rhetorically.

"No idea!"

"Yes, you have – and so have I. They're not entirely smitten. I don't know what's the matter with me," she added. "I've always considered marriage to be wholly unnecessary and have enjoyed my single life."

"You can still enjoy it. You're just feeling hurt and therefore determined to punish poor old Adrian. I suppose I should have realised that bringing you both here would make matters worse as he's so unnerved by the whole thing – you know, the grand house, the other guests, the interminable meals sitting between a couple of intimidating females – that all he wants to do is run home."

"He's revealed himself as pathetically lily-livered!" she snapped. "I hope you're not expecting me to sit next to him at dinner tonight."

"Oh yes, I am, but you can have Vincent Lovatt on the other side."

He took her arm firmly and led her across the room, weaving gracefully between a number of people until they came upon a young man who was talking to Titania.

"Vincent," he said. "I've brought a very good friend of mine to meet you. She usually hides herself miles away in Yorkshire, but I've managed to persuade her to leave her fastness for a few days. Helena Patchett."

"She's a friend of my Aunt Mildred," Titania said to Lord Vincent, not at all put out. "I've known Vincent all my life," she explained to Helena, "we were used to play together as children."

Both she and Horace smiled conspiratorially as the other two shook hands. Rushlake, reassured by her manner that he was not upsetting his sister, wandered off in search of the detective.

He found him talking to the curate.

"Ah, I suppose you've already introduced yourselves," he said smoothly. "Marcus Stapleton is the curate here, but he is also a cousin of mine."

"Of course," Mr Bodley said rather sullenly.

Lord Rushlake grinned. "Marcus has been here a few months and is, I hope, content with his job."

"Oh, yes, indeed, my lord. I hope the Vicar is pleased with me."

"He hasn't complained," Rushlake returned, "and I hope you won't find us too overpowering."

"I'm trying not to feel too intimidated," the young man answered with his charming smile. "But your presence – and that of your sisters - does make me feel a little anxious about delivering one of my first sermons."

"We were just comparing the advantages and disadvantages of our careers," Mr Bodley said stiffly.

The curate looked a little embarrassed as the detective continued, "I chose the Police Force because it seemed like an attractive occupation. I believed I'd be doing something useful."

"Just so," the curate agreed smoothly. "But I suppose it can sometimes be dangerous."

"Yes, and then one is frequently dealing with the dregs of society," Mr Bodley pointed out, although in this house he felt this description probably applied to himself.

"Curates do that sort of thing too," Marcus said gently.

"I shouldn't think there are many such persons here in the country though, are there?"

"I'm afraid there are a good many everywhere."

"Yes, of course," the detective muttered, beginning to wonder whether this conversation was going in the right direction.

"The thing is," Marcus continued, "that in the Church we focus on redemption - try to persuade people to become 'good', whereas I suppose in the police force you must simply be trying to stop them doing something bad."

"Yes," Mr Bodley agreed heavily, "although people sometimes commit crimes because they have no other obvious means of providing for themselves and their families. There have been occasions where I have felt quite sorry for a criminal."

"Perhaps you should consider a change in career – to the Church. We try to show our Saviour's compassion towards everyone, but it can be difficult."

"I don't think," Mr Bodley murmured, flushing uncomfortably. "I mean, I'm not certain I'm a believer, you see."

"Oh, I don't think that matters," the curate replied blithely. "We quote the scriptures, we talk about God's compassion, we try to lead the way to a more righteous way of life, but ultimately it's more about helping them as best we can on Earth than about leading them to God – God as a metaphor," he finished on a low note.

"Oh!" Mr Bodley said, not having spent much time thinking about metaphors and having assumed until this moment that men of the Church were necessarily convinced of the truth of the gospels.

Mr Stapleton laughed lightly. "Going into the Church is the sort of thing that one is expected to do if one is a younger son," he explained, "and certainly it sort of 'mops' one up, if you see what I mean, but – well, it's a perfectly agreeable life, although I own I sometimes hanker after the wicked pleasures of the metropolis."

"Would you prefer to be a policeman?" Mr Bodley asked.

"I must admit it sounds rather fun," the curate confided. "Do you spend a lot of time chasing criminals?"

"Eventually, yes, but I'm a detective so that most of what I do is investigate what appears to be criminal activity; when I find out who the miscreant is, it is more often the job of a less experienced policeman – or more likely several of them – to chase after him."

"I see. And then, when you've caught him, you lock him up?"

"Yes. Then of course he has to be tried in a court of law."

"Of course. Do you ever worry that you've got the wrong fellow? I mean, if you did, and the poor chap were hanged, I assume that would be distressing."

Mr Bodley nodded. What the curate said was true, but he tried, not always successfully, not to dwell upon that aspect of his job.

"A man isn't hanged without a fair trial," he said.

"No, of course not. You deliver him up to the law, as it were?"

"Yes. And ultimately," he said, feeling a strong desire to pass some of the responsibility to his interlocutor, "he will come before God."

"Indeed – and if he has been found guilty and hanged that will be sooner rather than later," the curate agreed, still with what Mr Bodley considered an unbecoming degree of levity.

"Yes, but I suppose if he wasn't guilty, God would forgive him and let him enter the gates of Heaven."

"One hopes so," the curate said with a slightly mocking smile, "but He might, in those circumstances, chalk up a black mark against the lawyers – and the jury – who had got it wrong."

"And the policemen," Adrian concluded.

"Just so."

Having discussed the relative degrees of responsibility of catching, convicting and punishing the wrong man, the curate enquired how Mr Bodley had become acquainted with the Earl.

"We met in the course of a case – a missing person with whom he was acquainted and for whom I was asked to search," Mr Bodley replied.

"Oh, I see! I take it the person was found and restored to his family."

"Oh yes – her family."

"Ah. And you have remained friends since?"

"Yes," Mr Bodley said firmly.

By the time he moved on to speak to another of the Earl's guests, Mr Bodley was feeling a little less disgruntled and had to some extent got over his disappointment at what he could not deny had been a poor showing towards Miss Patchett. He had been looking forward to seeing her again but seemed unable to make a definitive move towards her. Later, in the privacy of his chamber, he realised that he had once again failed to take the bull by the horns and, by thus missing his opportunity, most likely given her over to one of the other gentlemen, of whom there seemed to be a great many.

Helena Patchett, upon being introduced to Lord Vincent Lovatt, at first judged him to be the sort of aristocrat whom she found most irritating, a gentleman who had little in his head apart from hunting, playing cards and pursuing young women in an insensitive manner. Seeing how easily he got along with Titania, and hearing that they had known each other almost all their lives, she considered that, if only he were a little more intelligent, he and the Earl's sister would surely have been able to make a perfectly respectable match of it. He was not, she was convinced, the sort of man for whom she had much time.

Chapter 6

The following day was Christmas Eve.

The women busied themselves around the house, tucking sprigs of holly behind any of the pictures whose frames they could reach and threading glass baubles and pieces of fruit with silk which, following the new fashion introduced by Prince Albert, they hung from branches of the Christmas tree. The younger ones stood on chairs to increase their reach and eventually resorted to making use of a tall young footman so that no picture in the main rooms remained undecorated by the end of the day.

The men, meanwhile, took rifles and set out into the further reaches of the estate to shoot partridge. Most of the gentlemen were perfectly accustomed to doing this and, it being a surprisingly warm and mercifully dry day, were happy to be outside, walking and exchanging anecdotes upon any subject other than Christmas, a topic upon which most of them had heard quite enough for that year.

Birds were put up by the beaters, shot and picked up by the dogs. Quite a generous bag was collected and most of the sportsmen were delighted with their achievement by the time they made their way back to the house. They were looking forward to changing out of their by now scratchy outdoor clothes into softer indoor ones before joining the women in the drawing room for tea. They had been supplied with a rather grand picnic in the middle of the day by the servants, who had set up tables, chairs and rugs in advance.

Adrian Bodley, unfamiliar with this sort of pastime, felt more relaxed by the time the party began, under a darkening sky, to make its way back towards the welcoming lights of the house. He had managed to shoot a couple of birds, although he did not think that was cause for much celebration since the poor things seemed to find it so difficult to get into the air that they were really very easy to hit.

As he walked, he found the Earl beside him.

"Did you enjoy yourself?" his host enquired.

"Yes, indeed," Adrian replied with somewhat forced enthusiasm.

The Earl laughed.

"It wasn't perhaps as bad as you expected?"

"No, although I think I was inclined to aim a little high, mostly I think, on account of being afraid I might hit someone by mistake."

"It should be fairly difficult to hit anyone because there are, as I'm sure Stapleton explained when we set out, all sorts of rules about where one should stand in order to avoid being hit."

"Yes, yes, he did, but somehow once one's got out here, there are so many people milling about and I was so anxious not to do the wrong thing that I fear I was sometimes in the wrong place. He had to pull me back a couple of times, for which I'm very grateful."

"We won't go out tomorrow," the Earl reassured him, amused, "but we'll probably join the Hunt on Boxing Day. Don't feel obliged to come if you would rather not."

"No," Mr Bodley murmured. "No, thank you. I think I'd better though, don't you? I mean the women won't want me hanging around inside when all the other men have gone out."

"Miss Patchett might," the Earl said after a pause while he wondered whether he should make such a bold remark.

"Oh! I fear you're behind the times," the detective murmured. "She seems to have taken against me – I rather think I said the wrong thing."

"Possibly, but I don't suppose she'll hold it against you. She's a sensible woman, won't take umbrage, I shouldn't think."

"I think she did – and then she went off and starting talking to Lord Vincent Lovatt, which – well, she seemed to be getting along awfully well with him."

"Everyone gets along with him; I shouldn't suppose it means they'll be getting married."

"No; well, I'm sure I wish her very happy."

The Earl, fearing that his attempt to bring his two friends together was in danger of failing, said, "Not my business to advise you, Adrian, and I'm a lot younger than you, so probably don't know anything about the matter, but it seems to me that – or it seemed to me when she was last in London – that you and she were well matched, but that you bottled it at the last minute."

"Yes, I did – and now I've put my foot in it."

"Hmn, I know you think you have, but I'm sure it's not as bad as that. I would advise – although I don't know why you would think I'd know anything about it – advise you to take the bull by the horns and make a definite approach. The thing is that, if you don't, she may find someone else or just go home to continue her life in Yorkshire by herself. If you're not successful the first time, I don't think you should despair but – well, nothing ventured, nothing gained!"

"I know," Mr Bodley admitted.

He returned to the fence later that evening, after dinner, making a determined effort to command his lady love's attention by sitting down next to her as soon as the gentlemen joined the ladies in the drawing room.

She smiled at him, although he interpreted this friendly gesture as being a trifle frosty.

"Did you enjoy the shoot?" she asked.

He nodded but, turning down the corners of his mouth at the same time, gave the impression that his enjoyment had not been unalloyed.

"I own I was relieved to see there were no gaps at the dinner table this evening," he said.

She smiled again, this time with much more warmth and humour.

"Did you truly think you might have shot someone?"

"In truth I had little idea what or whom I'd shot," he said, "although Rushlake told me I'd got two partridge. I found the whole thing horridly confusing."

"I'm sure it must have been," she agreed. "I've been reminding myself all afternoon how fortunate I am to be female."

Lord Vincent Lovatt appeared in front of them bearing two cups of tea, which he proffered.

"I understand you two have met before," he began, drawing up a low chair and sitting down beside them.

"Yes, we met in London nearly a year ago," Miss Patchett said. "I'm beginning to feel like a much-travelled person. I've spent years in Yorkshire, going nowhere, and have now visited both London and Shropshire. It's been very exciting."

"Really? Have you never left these shores?"

"No. I'm afraid I'm a very dull person."

Lord Vincent laughed at that and asked what he was expected to reply.

"Why, that I'm perfectly fascinating in spite of never having done anything in the smallest degree exciting!"

Mr Bodley, perceiving this skittish response as flirting, began to look sour again.

"Well, of course you are," Lord Vincent said lightly. "Do you suppose I would have brought you a cup of tea if I had considered you dull?"

"I imagine you found me so odd when you spoke to me before that you wanted to investigate a little further. I daresay I'm not his lordship's usual sort of friend. The thing is, you see, that I live quite near his Aunt Mildred; indeed, she and I, despite the difference in our ages and rank, are by way of being friends."

"Oh, that I can readily believe," he replied. "I hear she is a most unusual and lively person – and so are you."

"Unusual to you," she corrected, "but I suspect I am an only too common type to be found in Yorkshire."

Mr Bodley sipped his tea and managed to remain in his seat only by reminding himself sternly of his host's advice. He must not give up and cede his place to the irritating lord.

Lord Vincent did not stay long, for his self-imposed duty at this point of the day was to furnish the other guests with cups of tea and exchange a few words with each, behaving, Mr Bodley considered, quite as though he were the lord of the house.

When the other man had moved on, Mr Bodley, finishing his tea, asked whether Miss Patchett would like her cup refilled.

"Oh, no, thank you. Have you," she asked, apparently determined to engage with the detective, "been busy recently?"

He frowned.

"Professionally," she explained.

"Ah, well, there've been the usual crimes, but nothing involving the aristocracy, I'm glad to say."

"I'm sure your work has been making the streets of London safer," she hazarded, at a loss as to how to initiate a conversation which he would find sufficiently interesting to abandon his ill temper.

"I doubt it," he said glumly. "I mean, one removes one rat but that doesn't have much of an effect upon the rodent population in general."

"I disagree," she said. "By removing one, whether male or female, you will prevent that particular rat from reproducing again."

"Are we talking about rats or humans?" he asked, a lurking smile briefly illumining his face.

"Either, but really, I suppose, humans."

"I don't investigate many female murderers," he admitted, "although there are a number of them."

"Does someone else usually look into those – or do they remain uninvestigated?"

"Females," he said slowly, "are more inclined to kill their domestic partners – not always husbands – whereas many of the men I pursue in the course of my job are what you might call professional killers. Sometimes they've been paid to kill someone – or occasionally several people – but often they've killed another man in the course of a fight."

"But," she persisted, "don't the police pursue women who've killed their domestic partners, as you so tactfully put it?"

"Yes, but I'm a detective. My job is to *find* a murderer in cases where the perpetrator is not obvious; it usually is in the case of a woman killing her man."

"Of course – silly of me – I didn't think of that."

"Not silly at all," he said more gently than he had spoken so far. "You only have experience of that peculiar case in which we were both involved recently. Are you quite recovered from your injuries?" he added, frowning at her and perhaps recalling his extreme anxiety about her at the time.

"I believe so, but sometimes I wonder if my brain has been addled permanently. I mean, just now, I didn't show a great deal of intelligence, did I?"

"On the contrary, Ma'am, you drew a conclusion based on your experience. The fact that it was inaccurate was on account of the information you possessed rather than upon any inability to reason."

"Thank you."

She fell silent and, after a minute, he said, "Are you disappointed in what you now realise forms the large part of my job? Did you think it involved more romance than it does?"

She shook her head. "Now you're jumping to an erroneous conclusion about me. I cannot, have not and hope will never consider investigating the killing of one human being by another as in any degree romantic."

"I didn't mean that!" he exclaimed. "I suppose I thought you would be unlikely to understand the unpleasantness of the society in which my job obliges me to work."

"You were right. I don't understand that and shudder to think of it. Coming here must seem very strange to you – everything so beautiful, clean and comfortable – and the guests so polite and agreeable."

"That," he said slowly, "is the superficial appearance of it, while the appearance of my *milieu* is ugly, dirty and cruel. But both involve human beings in all their greed, competitiveness and sometimes spite. I don't mean," he added quickly, "to cast aspersions upon his lordship's friends and relations, but, beneath their fine clothes and shining hair, they have, I don't doubt, the same difficulty in maintaining pleasant relations with each other and the same envy towards another who seems to have more than they."

"Yes," she said. "I believe that, at bottom, we're all the same, but I don't think I find it easy to understand that people who appear to have so much should so deeply resent someone they perceive as having more. I suppose," she finished with a little downturn of her mouth, "that I am spoilt and have always been protected from the more miserable aspects of human behaviour."

He smiled. "Yes, I think you have, but, in spite of that, you show a vast amount of human understanding."

"Don't you?"

"Not so much, but then my job is to find the sort of people who have committed the most serious crime there is – taking the life of another human being. I can't afford to be understanding – or forgiving. That," he added with some bitterness, "is the sort of thing upon which Mr Stapleton is presumably an expert."

"Not necessarily," she returned rather tartly. "Of course clergymen are expected to dole out forgiveness and understanding, but they're generally doing so on behalf of God."

"You mean you don't think he feels that himself?"

"I've no idea; I've only spent five minutes speaking to him – and he seems a perfectly agreeable person – but one must know a person much more intimately to embark upon such a subject, especially perhaps when it is their job."

Mr Bodley blinked at her and blushed because it seemed to him that she had just said, more or less overtly, that she and he were intimately acquainted. He wondered if that meant what he hoped it did, but, in spite of Lord Rushlake's advice to take the bull by the horns, he was unable to do so and simply stared at her, probably with his mouth open.

She, beginning to feel a little more confident that he was interested in her, observed, "You and I have known each other much longer and it seems to me that our common experience recently has almost forced us to speak of such things – certainly to think of them."

"Yes," he agreed, "but I'm afraid it's only served to make our differences more obvious."

"I didn't say we were identical," she corrected, amused.

"If we were, we'd have nothing to discuss," he agreed. "Tell me how you've occupied yourself in the North since I last saw you."

"Oh, in an excessively boring manner. I've reverted to my usual lone walks, charitable visits and so forth."

"I understand there will be hunting on Boxing Day," he said, "if there isn't shooting. Will you do that?"

"Hunting, yes, shooting, no. I enjoy hunting. Will you?"

"I don't think so. It's one thing to be given a gun and told to shoot a large, low-flying bird, but quite another to get upon a horse and hurtle around the country."

Dinner on Christmas Eve was richer, more prolonged and accompanied by an even more astonishing variety of wines than the one the night before. As course succeeded course, Mr Bodley, seated beside Miss Patchett, grew not only fatigued but also a trifle inebriated. He was not accustomed to dine so late in the evening and, having only one or two servants, had developed a simple palate. He had, introduced to the custom by the Earl, begun to take a small glass of port after his dinner, although he, living alone, drank it in his sitting room rather than at the table.

The quantity and variety of wines caused him considerable anxiety. He noticed that Miss Patchett, probably more accustomed to grand dinners when she visited her friend the Marchioness, took only a small sip of each and thus remained as clear of mind at the end as at the beginning, whereas Mr Bodley, not wanting to waste what he was given and observing how much the other male guests managed to swallow, tried to keep up with them and soon found himself feeling distinctly fuzzy in the head.

This was all very well when he was speaking to Miss Patchett, for he was certain she understood perfectly and would neither comment upon the matter nor judge him, but the lady on his other side was Miss Thetford, the eldest daughter of Viscount Thetford.

She was, he judged, considerably younger than Miss Patchett and probably younger than Titania, but, having already informed him that she was the eldest of her family, gave the impression of considering herself to be a person of great importance.

She had grilled him on the subject of his job, which it was clear she considered an occupation for the lower classes; indeed, he almost had the impression that she expected him to smell of the gutter and, in order to avoid this contamination as much as possible, kept her nose elevated whenever he was speaking to her.

"Whereabouts in the country is your house?" she asked now.

"In London; I'm a member of the Metropolitan Police."

"Yes, I know. You've already told me that, but I was wondering whence in the *country* you hail."

"Oh, only London, ma'am. If you mean, do I have a country house, the answer's no."

"La!" she exclaimed, apparently stunned. "Do you spend *all* your time in London?"

"Yes, every day and night – unless of course I'm obliged to follow a criminal out to the country – and then I go wherever he goes!"

"I see. Is this the first time you've visited Rushlake?"

"Oh, yes. It was very kind of his lordship to invite me."

"Indeed." She paused while she allowed this conclusion to sink in, while he, for his part, wished that Miss Patchett would cease to speak to Lord Vincent and allow him to turn away from Miss Thetford. This young lady now had her nose so high that he wondered how she contrived to find her dinner upon her plate.

"I imagine you must feel a touch uncomfortable – the company is not that to which you're accustomed and ..."

"No," he agreed readily enough. "And I'm not at all accustomed to shooting. In fact, I've never shot anything in my life until this afternoon."

"Good lord! Weren't you afraid you might kill the wrong thing?" Miss Thetford seemed suddenly to come to life, lowered her nose and directed a hard blue stare at him.

He laughed. The large amount he had drunk and his consequent confusion had removed most of his inhibitions and the *naïveté* of his questioner suddenly seemed wholly delightful. She meant to be disagreeable but, no longer wanting either to please her or to care whether he fitted in with the company or not, he found he did not mind.

"Yes, terrified, but I gather I didn't do anything of which I should be ashamed."

"I suppose," she said, the nose going up again, "that you have a different idea of what's shaming than I."

"No doubt. Tell me what you find shameful, ma'am, and we can discuss our different attitudes."

She stared at him for a moment consideringly, and he realised, even in his befuddled state, that she was dredging her mind for the most shocking thing she could think of.

"Well, it's my belief," she said at last, "that killing your wife so that you can marry someone else is excessively shameful."

Mr Bodley blinked.

"More than shameful," he murmured, smiling rather wildly because he thought she was making fun of him and his profession, "wicked, illegal and altogether to be deplored."

"Yes. I thought you would say that!"

"I'm sorry to be so banal," he retorted, now rather irritated.

"It's a banal thing to do," she returned, and suddenly her face changed as a dark shadow crossed it, made her mouth tighten and her eyes begin to stare.

"It's what that man over there did," she said, nodding towards her father on the other side of the table.

Chapter 7

The evening, when the gentlemen joined the ladies, took the usual form of one of the ladies performing on the *pianoforte* while another sang. Since this was usually forced upon unmarried women, the only two who were available were Titania and Miss Thetford, Miss Patchett being – at least at first – considered too old.

Titania dashed off a sonata with competence but no feeling. It was dull and, to anyone with a musical ear, probably excruciating. Miss Thetford opted to sing a song, chose a Christmas carol and then looked around for someone to accompany her, Titania having shot her bolt with her own indifferent rendition of Chopin. It was Aunt Saffy who, no one else coming forward, offered tentatively to accompany the performer. She was not, she insisted, a good pianist but she had some familiarity with Christmas carols and very much liked them.

"Perhaps you should sing one then," Miss Thetford retorted.

"Oh, I don't think anyone would want to hear me sing," Saffy murmured, smiling weakly.

"I'm sure I don't know why not," Miss Patchett suddenly said. "When I was ill, you sang to me most beautifully. I found it both soothing and stimulating. You have a lovely voice."

Aunt Saffy blushed fierily at this praise and attempted to deny the possession of any such thing.

"Well, I should like to hear you sing again," Miss Patchett persisted. "Will you – when you've accompanied Miss Thetford?"

"If – well, I should imagine people will have had enough of being sung to," she demurred.

Miss Thetford, who had probably thought at first that being accompanied by such a dull, ageing creature would diminish her own performance, suddenly changed her mind, hoping perhaps that the contrast between her own youthful countenance and Miss Hemsted's faded one would serve her well.

"Thank you," she said with an assumption of sweetness. "It is very kind of you."

Saffy, rising to her feet and approaching the *pianoforte*, enquired which carol the other had in mind and, upon being informed that she rather liked 'Hark the herald angels sing', applauded such a choice and seated herself at the instrument.

Miss Thetford, positioning herself carefully, enquired, as her pianist waited, hands poised above the keys and head turned enquiringly towards the singer, whether she had the music to hand.

"Oh, yes," Saffy replied gently, "it's in my head."

"Oh. Very well, let's begin then."

Saffy, bending her head respectfully towards the keyboard, began the introduction and surprised everyone by both the accuracy and charm of her playing. Considering herself to be very much the junior partner in the endeavour, she did not look at Miss Thetford until the latter had missed the moment when she should have come in, but simply repeated the last couple of phrases before glancing interrogatively at the other.

Miss Thetford, this time aware of her cue, took it and launched into a rather painful rendition of the well-known carol. Her voice was not unmelodious, but she embellished the piece to an unnecessary degree, trying, it would seem, to turn it into an operatic aria.

When it came to an end, she was applauded politely and, enquiring of Aunt Saffy if she could play 'O Little Town of Bethlehem', flung herself into this too.

Two pieces being the usual to be performed after dinner, she bowed politely to the applause that followed and returned to her seat, well pleased with her performance.

Saffy rose from the *pianoforte*, received something of an ovation herself, bowed and blushed and attempted to return to her seat. But Miss Patchett was having none of this and rose with an offer to accompany the older lady if she would favour the audience with a rendition of another carol.

"Oh, no, dear, I'm sure people have had quite enough," Saffy murmured with becoming modesty.

"Well, I have not," Miss Patchett stated uncompromisingly, "and I have the greatest wish to hear you sing again. I remember your rendering of 'Once in Royal David's City'. Indeed, it was that which brought me round after I'd spent some time in a state of senselessness. Pray repeat it for me now."

"Perhaps I could sing it later when no one else will have to hear," Saffy said.

"If they don't want to hear, they can talk," Helena said.

No one had been able to talk during Miss Thetford's performance for they were all too much on tenterhooks as the next high note heaved into view to be able to think of anything else except the importance of the lady reaching it and moving on to the calmer waters of a lower register.

Helena had by this time seated herself at the *pianoforte* and, apologising in advance if she played the occasional wrong note, began on the introduction. Saffy, now forced to take part, returned to stand beside the younger woman and, when her cue arrived, began to sing in the same simple, pure manner in which she had sung to the invalid several months before.

Nobody spoke and the hush which fell upon the party was quite different to the nervous anxiety which had attended Miss Thetford's performance. Perhaps it was unfortunate that both women had chosen – or been obliged – to sing carols, for Saffy's rendering of the well-known words and tune was magical.

It occurred to Lord Rushlake, listening with amazement to Saffy's performance, that Helena had very likely intended to make the contrast obvious. She had grown attached to the modest, retiring Saffy during the time they had spent in London and wanted to 'draw her out' in a way that the older woman had probably never experienced before.

Begged to sing another by the admiring audience, Saffy nevertheless declined in a firmer manner than any of her acquaintance had heard before and made her way back to her seat while Miss Patchett was begged to play something else.

Helena complied and the evening ended with several sets of card games and a good deal of laughter. Everyone was flattered to have been invited, pleased to see old friends and distant relatives, well fed and sufficiently well oiled with alcohol to be expansive but not drunk.

Helena, making her way upstairs later with Aunt Saffy, was thus separated from Mr Bodley, who had wanted to praise her performance.

He felt frustrated in his endeavour and found, at first, that the myriad strange and unsettling experiences of the day prevented him from falling asleep, but - giving way at last to his great desire to think – and dream – of the lady for whom he had conceived such a deep admiration, he found on closer iterance of what they had said to each other that they had seen eye-to-eye far more than they had not, and that, in short, he had little about which to worry – at least on that score. He was, however, deeply troubled by what Miss Thetford had said shortly before the ladies had been swept from the table by Jenny Wendell.

Mr Bodley, left on tenterhooks concerning the matter, did not know whether the dead wife was Miss Thetford's mama, although he guessed it was on account of the barely suppressed rage with which the young lady had uttered the accusation.

He wondered if this murder was supposed to have happened recently and whether the woman to whom he had been introduced as Lady Thetford was the one for whom his lordship had removed his wife. How long, he wondered, had Lord and Lady Thetford been married? Presumably the present Viscountess was not Miss Thetford's mama; indeed, she did not look old enough to be – unless she had been little more than a child when she had given birth to the angry young woman.

Trying to resolve this conundrum, Mr Bodley eventually fell asleep, determining to ask Lord Rushlake at the first available opportunity whether there had been any gossip in the neighbourhood concerning the Thetfords.

The next day was Christmas Day and the party met in the dining room for breakfast with many expressions of hope that the day would be, variously, merry, happy, joyous and so on. It was of course only the party who had spent the night in the house that sat down to breakfast together, so that neither the Thetfords, Lord Vincent nor indeed Mr Stapleton were there.

Most of the party had already seen Marcus Stapleton earlier in the chapel where he had been officiating in a minor capacity at Holy Communion and had, after the Sacrament, been able to exchange greetings with him. He was, he was happy to tell them, expected to join them for luncheon – and indeed dinner.

The Thetfords were also in church and Miss Thetford greeted Mr Bodley with every appearance of pleasure. It seemed that, common as he was, she was pleased to be gracious enough to overlook their differences – or perhaps it was that she recalled her accusation of the evening before with some embarrassment and wished to be certain he had not taken her seriously.

Mr Bodley, recalling not only what she had said, but how she had said it and his own disturbed sleep, could not help his eyes dwelling upon the family with embarrassing frequency.

Lord Thetford was a man of about fifty, his wife at most half his age. She was a good-looking young woman, not precisely pretty, but well-dressed and with a noticeably fine figure. They sat one on either side of Miss Thetford, who, Mr Bodley judged, was probably not much younger than her stepmother. Also present were what were evidently the younger Thetfords, two girls of, he guessed, about sixteen and twelve.

Aunt Saffy, who was possibly one of the few people present to whom the Sacrament meant more than the usual thing to do on Christmas morning, looked happy and relaxed. She had, like everyone else, dressed smartly – or as smartly as she could – in a dark dress which fitted her rather better than most of her garments. Its clearly delineated waist and wide skirt revealed a figure considerably better than anyone would have guessed from her usual ill-fitting outfits, and the effort she had made with her hair made her face appear, if not precisely pretty, at least less faded and raddled than usual.

After the service, while they were all standing around shivering outside, Miss Thetford told her that she looked so well this morning that she would not have recognised her.

Aunt Saffy, amused by this bid for her approval, and knowing exactly what the younger woman meant, smiled gently and said, "I always find Christmas such a happy time – and this year, with everyone gathered together, is particularly pleasing."

"Where do you usually spend it?" Miss Thetford asked curiously, knowing, as a neighbour of the Earl, that he and the youngest of his sisters always spent the festival at the Hall, and that she had never seen Saffy there at that time of year.

"Oh, I generally stay with one of my brothers," she admitted. "I don't like to impose on the Rushlakes all the time, you see."

"Goodness! But this year you're here!"

"Yes; his lordship invited me. I was very touched," she added, blushing.

"From all I hear, he's an excessively kind man," Miss Thetford said.

Aunt Saffy, always charitable, did not allow this undermining comment to distress her and agreed wholeheartedly, but managed to reply in a tone of ineffable sweetness that, now that she was no longer a companion to dear Titania, she took the invitation as a great compliment.

"Oh, are you not? So have you another position lined up for the New Year?"

"No; his lordship has asked me to stay on at his house in London."

"What? Are you to be *his* companion now?" Miss Thetford asked, unable any longer to conceal her contempt.

"In a manner of speaking, yes," Saffy returned complacently although her heart was hammering uncomfortably in her bosom and she found herself for the first time in her life wanting quite dreadfully to slap the arrogant young woman's cheek.

"Good God!" Miss Thetford exclaimed, beginning to grasp something of the character of the woman she despised and finding herself infuriated. She was a similar age to the handsome Earl and, there not apparently being any other rivals on the scene, had been hoping that she might be the first person he sought if he wanted female company.

Aunt Saffy greeted this exclamation with another gentle smile and turned the tables upon the younger woman by enquiring how long she had been acquainted with the Earl.

"Oh, forever!" Miss Thetford replied confidently.

Saffy's nod reminded Miss Thetford that, having known the Earl for most of his three-and-twenty years, he was unlikely suddenly to find her irresistible.

"I hope you won't be too shocked by the way young bachelors behave in London," Miss Thetford said, clearly determined to cause the older woman annoyance.

"Oh, I'm too old to be shocked by much," Saffy assured her, "and in any event, as we both know, his lordship is far too well-mannered to put me to the blush."

"Yes, of course. I suppose, when he marries, you'll have to look for another situation," Miss Thetford concluded with what she hoped would pass for a sympathetic expression.

"Of course," Saffy agreed readily.

Miss Thetford, having failed to find a place into which she could insert her dagger, nodded brightly and allowed herself to be gathered up by her stepmama, who was bearing down upon them.

"Do you know," she said, "Miss Hemsted is going to continue to keep Rushlake company in London."

"Indeed? Just fancy!" the other replied. Whatever she thought of the Earl of Rushlake, and whatever her relations with her stepdaughter were, she was not competing for she had already managed to attach a Viscount of her own.

Saffy smiled vaguely and, spying Miss Patchett and Mr Bodley speaking together a few yards away, made a determined effort to leave the Thetford ladies, both of whom, she was well aware, wished to discountenance her as well as each other.

She wondered, as she reached the pair whom she considered her friends, why some people took such pleasure in trying to make others feel uncomfortable and unwanted. She had been at the receiving end of such behaviour almost all her life and had long ago decided not to allow it to upset her. It was, she told herself firmly, only a little scratch, soon forgotten and not worth refining upon.

"Shall we go inside?" Helena asked. "It's very chilly out here."

"Yes, do let us. Isn't it a pretty chapel?"

"It is – and I thought Mr Stapleton acquitted himself well," Helena said.

The three friends walked the small distance between the chapel and the house together. The chapel could be reached from inside the house, but, unless it was raining, it was customary for the church-goers to go out into the fresh air, walk a few yards across a terrace and enter as though it had been an independent church. This route was followed after the service too, thus enabling the congregation to stand around outside chatting to each other.

Chapter 8

On getting back from the service, the Earl's guests made their way to the drawing room where coffee was served and small presents were exchanged. Hanging these on the Christmas tree had been one of the tasks the ladies had undertaken while the gentlemen were out shooting the day before. They consisted largely of little parcels containing sweets or nuts, or perhaps some dried flowers or herbs.

Those who were related gave each other additional small gifts, which were still, on the whole, uncontroversial and fairly impersonal, such as embroidered handkerchiefs from the ladies, or perhaps, for a closer relative, embroidered slippers. The gentlemen gave the ladies such things as gloves, scarves and, most frequently, small books.

Those who were unfamiliar with the customs of the household had agonised over what to present to the guests with whom they were acquainted. The person to whom this task had seemed monumental was of course Mr Bodley. He had, when he voiced this concern to his host, been assured that he was not expected to provide any gifts for anyone, although he could, if he particularly wished to do so, give something to his closest friends, by which the detective understood that he should purchase – or somehow acquire – something for the people whom he had got to know during the last case on which he had been assisted by the Earl.

Much relieved by this, he was still anxious about what he could choose for the Earl himself, Aunt Saffy and, of course, Miss Patchett. He was determined on something a little more personal, a trifle more aligned with the character and taste of the recipient than the list of possible objects implied, although how he could fit this requirement into the rigid lines of propriety, which he was so terrified of overstepping, he was uncertain.

In the end, after toying with the idea of purchasing a silk scarf or a rather charming little vase for Miss Patchett, he was so afraid of getting it wrong that he decided instead on a book. Choosing a book for his beloved was fraught with difficulty because he was well aware that his choice would with certainty reveal his own character and abysmal level of education as well as his position in Society. However, he eventually resolved that, if he was ever to have the courage to make her an offer, he was under an obligation to inform her accurately of the sort of person he was and there seemed little more revealing than his choice of book. If he got it wrong, she would know they had no future together and he, watching her as she opened it, would know that too. It would, he told himself, save a deal of discussion as well as fruitless agonising.

He spent hours in several different bookshops and eventually chose a slim, leather-bound volume of poems by Elizabeth Barrett Browning. He knew this poet to be popular with the ladies and hoped that Miss Patchett, who was a remarkably independent-minded female, would appreciate this nod in the direction of feminine ability. He did not suppose that she would not already have read most of the poems, but hoped that she would be taken with the beauty of the volume he chose with its soft leather cover on which the title and author's name was inscribed in gold lettering.

While he was poring over books, he found an elegantly bound copy of some of Edgar Allan Poe's works, which he hoped would amuse the Earl. That left only Aunt Saffy and, far less intimidated by her imagined reception of a gift from him, he chose a copy of Charles Dickens's new Christmas novella, *The Chimes*. Thus, in one shop, he found all the presents he required. He would not, he was relieved, have to search for something to suit Lady Amberstone because she would not be with them for Christmas.

He had wrapped his three gifts and tied them with ribbon – blue for the Earl, green for Miss Patchett and yellow for Aunt Saffy - and thus knew, without having had to write upon them, for whom each parcel was intended.

He gave the Earl his when he had finished distributing the presents from the Christmas tree and was pleased when his lordship, upon opening it, exclaimed with what seemed to Mr Bodley to be genuine delight at the choice of book.

"Just the sort of thing that fascinates me!" he said.

"Oh," said Mr Bodley, feeling the tell-tale colour rise in his cheeks. "I daresay you've read them before, but I thought it an appropriate gift from one person interested in mysteries to another."

"It is not only appropriate but delightful – and most excellently chosen! Thank you."

Aunt Saffy received her gift with surprise – she was not accustomed to personal presents of any sort at any time – and opened it with a heightened colour. When she saw what it was, she jumped up from her chair and approached the detective with what for an awful moment he feared was an intention to kiss him. But she stopped short a few feet away and expressed her pleasure and gratitude in such a heart-warming way that he found himself moved almost to tears.

As for Miss Patchett, well, he would have been delighted if she had flung herself into his arms in the joy of the moment, but she did not. She smiled shyly, expressed her appreciation and apologised for having got him a terribly dull object in return. She handed him a small, rather flat parcel which turned out to hold a leather bookmark with his name carefully cut into the leather above a pair of handcuffs. He was overjoyed by this evidence of her having thought of him some time before Christmas and laboured to produce something that was at once personal and impersonal.

"I don't suppose you get much time for reading," she said, "but, if you do, I should think it would be useful to be able to mark the place you have reached. I always find it so difficult to remember where I am in a book and, while that doesn't matter at all with poetry," she glanced tenderly at the book he had given her, "I consider it rather important with other books."

The rest of the day passed pleasantly enough. After luncheon, which was attended only by those who were staying at the house, most people went for a walk and returned as the sky was darkening to embark upon a game of charades.

This was enjoyable, although Mr Bodley found himself the butt of a good many jokes about his profession and speculation about why he did not immediately know the answer. He was forced to explain that this was a very different 'game' to tracking down criminals. In truth, he found it extraordinarily difficult because he did not have a particularly large vocabulary and was ignorant of the sort of things such a group of persons might be trying to depict. The acting veered between the inadequate and the exaggerated, but, while this did not help him to contribute much to his team, it did elucidate the characters and degree of self-belief or otherwise of the rest of the party.

Miss Patchett, on whose team he was fortunate to find himself, proved to be extraordinarily good at it. In her quiet way, she soon had the measure of the other side's bombast and cut her way through it with gentle determination, bringing triumph in the end.

The winners were rewarded with little parcels of sweets and everyone went off to change for dinner in high spirits.

Miss Patchett came down for dinner in a, to Mr Bodley, quite ravishing green velvet gown, which fitted her to perfection and showed off her fine skin and glowing eyes.

Aunt Saffy, making an unusual effort to fit in with everyone else in their finery, wore wine red. She had draped a dark shawl, patterned with red flowers and a red fringe, over her shoulders, and had made what must have been a positively superhuman effort to dress her hair so that it was all confined in a bun rather than having a number of uncontrolled wisps hanging about her face. Behind the shawl, Mr Bodley caught a glimpse of what looked like a rather fine pearl necklace, a piece of jewellery which was no doubt something she had inherited but rarely found the opportunity to wear.

Titania, looking handsome in blue, noticed the necklace too. She was wearing the one her brother had given her nearly a year ago when they had been looking for an earring amongst their mother's jewels.

"That's a very fine pearl necklace, Aunt Saffy," she said, tweaking the shawl aside to peer at it.

"Yes, isn't it? It was my dear Mama's – and she left it to me in her will. My sister-in-law, who of course got most of Mama's stuff, was quite annoyed, but it was clearly stated in the will that it was to be mine. I treasure it," she finished, tears filling her eyes as she remembered her mother and her mother's care of and love for her.

"Lord! My Mama didn't leave me anything!" Titania returned. "Papa left me a fortune to give to my husband – if I ever get one – but Mama didn't mention me when she died – so Horace has everything. But," she added, brightening, "he gave me this necklace. He allowed me to choose anything from Mama's jewels and this was what I chose."

"It is lovely," Aunt Saffy said apppreciatively. She had already seen it and heard Titania express her gratitude for her brother's gift before.

"I don't think he's ever given Jenny anything to make up for the one earring he gave her, to which he was never able to give her the pair."

"No," Saffy said. She knew, as did both Titania and her older sister, Jenny, why Jenny no longer had either earring.

"I expect he's forgotten all about it," Titania said generously.

Saffy nodded non-committally; she thought it odd that Jenny had not mentioned it; she was not usually a person who failed to make her wishes known.

But when Jenny, Lady Wendell, came into the room, both women noticed that she was wearing a very fine pearl and sapphire necklace which neither had seen before. She, also in blue, no doubt chosen to match the jewels, joined them.

"I see you're admiring my necklace," she said, although how she could have told from the doorway remained anyone's guess. "Horace gave it to me for Christmas," she explained. "He said it was to replace the earring."

"It's much prettier," Titania said. "Was it from Mama's hoard?"

"I assume so; I mean, he surely wouldn't have bought me a new one, would he?"

"I didn't think she'd care for a new one so much as an old one," the Earl said, joining them. "It's also a mark of gratitude for her acting as my hostess this Christmas."

"Oh, I'm enjoying that – so far," she said, smiling at him.

The same neighbours joined the house party for dinner.

Titania found that she was sitting between Lord Vincent Lovatt and Mr Stapleton. The latter exerted himself to charm her and, with his handsome face and flattering manner, more or less succeeded.

Like the rest of her family, she had never met him before – and was rather sorry that she had not for he was certainly far more stimulating than any other man she knew.

He had, he told her, only recently come down from Oxford, where he had been a year or two behind Lord Rushlake. In spite of them being connected in some distant way, they had never met there either. This piece of information caused her heart to sink a little for Horace was her younger brother and, if this delightful young man was his junior, he must be more than a few years younger than she.

"And you've decided to enter the Church?" she prompted for want of anything else to say and to give herself a chance to recover from her fear that her extra years would be bound to make her seem positively old to him.

"I don't think it was precisely a decision. The thing is, you see, that I have an awfully large number of brothers and my family is not precisely full of juice, so that the eldest being set to inherit what little there is, the next one having been despatched to the army and number three to the navy, my place was clearly the Church."

"Oh, I see. Would you rather have done something else?"

"Not particularly, although I own one of the services would have been my first choice, but, really, I'm quite content, particularly now that your brother's found me such an agreeable position – and indeed, even more so now that I've met his sister."

She smiled. She was old enough to know that what he said – as well as the warm look in his eyes – was probably assumed for the occasion - and helped by the large sherry of which he had already disposed – but she could not help responding with pleasure. He was so very handsome and she knew that, if she wanted him, she could most likely have him – in spite of the inconvenient age difference - if only on account of his admitted poverty and her wealth.

She had remained largely indifferent to the many admirers – more likely of her fortune than her person - that she had met in London and was perhaps primed to find the attentions of such an accomplished flirt stimulating. The look in his eyes when they rested upon her face and the fascinating twitch of his lips as he teased her went to her head as quickly as the sherry, especially since she had lived at Rushlake for most of her life without finding any *beaux*. Lord Vincent, who was slightly older than she, was a good friend but neither his presence nor his expression set her blood racing as Mr Stapleton's did.

The fact that – to those disinclined to eat or drink more than they wanted – dinner seemed almost interminable, its innumerable courses following one upon another, suited her well as it enabled her to flirt without being interrupted very often by Miss Thetford, who sat resentfully upon his other side. He did not seem interested in her, only turning to her occasionally when Titania remembered to speak to her other neighbour, the reliable and familiar Lord Vincent.

So delighted was Titania by the curate that she could have sat there all night and was almost disappointed when, nearly three hours after they had sat down, Jenny rose from the table and led the women out of the room.

"Lord, my dress is too tight!" Titania exclaimed, casting herself almost supine upon a sofa.

"I thought it an unwise choice in view of the dinner you must have known you'd have to eat," Jenny said, amused. "Whom were you trying to impress?"

"What in the world do you mean? No one!" the younger woman cried, but the change in her colour belied the denial, although in truth she had not known when she dressed that she would find herself desperately eager to impress the curate.

"Do you know, Tania, I think you've spent all those months in London acquiring new admirers and treating them with contempt only to come home and take a positive shine to Vincent after all these years!"

"Nonsense! It was agreeable to see him again after a gap. I'm very fond of him – in a perfectly prosaic way – as he is of me. If we'd wanted a romance, I don't doubt we would have tried one before. In any event, he's a pretty down-to-earth sort of person."

"What's wrong with that?" Jenny asked. "Just the sort of thing one wants in a husband. Why, one would grow excessively tired of a man who was constantly spouting poetry or going into eulogies about one's eyes."

"Oh, I think that would be rather pleasant – for a little while!" Saffy said with a yearning look.

The other two stared at her.

"Is that what you've hankered after all these years?" Titania asked tactlessly.

"Yes, of course. Haven't you?"

"Well, I'm too young to have been hankering after anything for very long," Titania replied impatiently.

"Oh," Helena said quickly, seeing Saffy's dejected expression, "I don't think it's only related to age, you know. When one is very young, when one first becomes a little more interested in the opposite sex, one dreams of such things almost twenty-four hours a day, but, when one gets a little older, one's dreams become a touch shorter and a touch less frequent, but one still dreams."

"Do you dream of Adrian Bodley?" Titania asked, still too eager to protect her own new feelings to worry about anyone else's – and wanting perhaps to check that she was not the first to feel this way.

"I think of him sometimes," Helena Patchett admitted. "But I don't expect him to go into rhapsodies about my eyes. Indeed, if he did, I think I might fear he'd taken leave of his senses for, although there's nothing precisely wrong with my eyes, they're not the most beautiful in the world."

"So what do you think about him – or wish he would say or do?" Titania asked. She had drunk more wine than she was accustomed to and seemed to have lost not only any iota of tact she might once have possessed but also all sense of propriety.

Helena blushed, but said, "Oh, when there's something I find amusing – or particularly interesting – I imagine telling him and seeing his reaction. I *like* him, you see. At my age, it's not all about my appearance. At least, if it was, I can't conceive why he would take any interest in me."

These four were not the only women in the party. There were several others, including Lady and Miss Thetford, who were all agog during this discussion. Lady Thetford, only recently married, looked smug that she had managed to attach the man she wanted, and Miss Thetford looked disgruntled because, in spite of being younger than Titania, she had failed to attract the attention of either the Earl or Mr Stapleton.

Miss Thetford, who had of course noticed that the curate, in spite of sitting beside her at dinner, had spent most of the time talking to Titania, murmured that she rather thought Lord Vincent had been gazing at Titania with what seemed to her to be a more than friendly expression. Did they, she enquired, have an 'understanding'?

Titania laughed. "Lord, no! I daresay he's inebriated!"

This put-down did not please Miss Thetford, who looked furious.

"I suppose you prefer one of those London gentlemen whom you've met recently but seem to have left behind," she snapped.

"Oh, dear, no, I don't! I can tell you it's a great relief to have escaped from them."

"Just fancy you having so many admirers!" Miss Thetford observed, fanning herself.

"I don't. So far as I can see, I haven't any. In any event, most of them admire my fortune more than me!" Titania returned confusingly.

This airy remark seemed to infuriate Miss Thetford even more, no doubt, Saffy deduced, because *she* had neither a fortune nor a great deal else to recommend her – and certainly seemed in want of admirers.

Saffy should have been sympathetic for she had never had any herself and had suffered similarly from an absence of either fortune or looks, but she found Miss Thetford such a disagreeable character that it was hard to feel much sympathy for her.

"I must say I rather like Mr Stapleton," she said provocatively for she had noticed Titania's excitement as well as Miss Thetford's disappointment.

"Isn't he too young for you?" Miss Thetford snapped.

"Me? Good lord, yes. No, dear, I was thinking of you."

"*Me?* A curate?"

"He may be a bishop one day, even an archbishop, I suppose. He seems very knowledgeable as well as being of excellent character, but of course he *is* very young."

Thus did Saffy, so gentle and kind, manage to insult Miss Thetford in a place that was particularly painful for, although she was the youngest female present, she was in point of fact slightly beyond the usual age for acquiring *beaux*.

Miss Patchett, who had been listening to this repartee with considerable amusement, did not trouble to hide her laughter at this remark and so drew Miss Thetford's ire upon herself.

"And who are you?" Miss Thetford asked.

"Helena Patchett from Yorkshire. My father was a mill owner."

"A *mill owner?*"

The contempt in the lady's voice was ill-directed at Helena, who replied gently, "Yes. It wasn't of course such a respected occupation as a clergyman, but vastly more lucrative."

Miss Thetford, realising that she was heavily outnumbered by the Rushlake ladies, flushed with temper and took herself off to join her stepmother, a woman she would normally have avoided.

"I own I don't much care for that young lady," Helena said in a low voice.

"No, neither do I," Saffy agreed, "but, all the same, I'm a little ashamed of having been rude to her. It was uncalled-for."

"On the contrary," Helena said, "*she* called for it by trying to insult you. Pray don't refine upon it. I daresay she is used to being the most sought-after female in the neighbourhood."

"Only because there aren't any others," Saffy replied with something approaching spite.

Chapter 9

While the ladies were making friends – or re-establishing enmity - the gentlemen were settling down to their port and, relieved of being obliged to find agreeable things to say to ladies when they were feeling a little the worse for wear, fell to discussing the earlier shoot.

In this, Mr Bodley was at a disadvantage since a good deal of the discussion took the form of comparing this one with previous outings.

"Did you enjoy your first experience of shooting?" Mr Stapleton asked. He had been the gentleman who had taken the novice under his wing.

Mr Bodley, supposing that his mentor knew perfectly well whether he had enjoyed the outing or not, decided that he probably would not cause an outcry if he told the truth.

"Well, I own I was a little confused – and afraid I might shoot someone in the party by mistake."

"I know," the curate said, smiling in a friendly fashion. "I was too the first time I went out. I'm hoping to come on the hunt tomorrow."

"I'm not sure I'll join it," the detective said, "as I'm not an experienced rider. I've spent all my life in London, you see, so that any riding I have done has not been of the kind that I believe will be necessary."

"There'll be plenty of people," the curate explained, "including villagers – and indeed some ladies. The thing is, the keen fellows will be up there in the front, leaping hedges and ditches and so forth, but there'll be a sizeable number trailing along at the back, I promise, so that as long as you can keep your seat across fields – no need to jump as it's usually possible to open gates if one's not in a particular hurry – you'll probably find you enjoy it."

"I'm not sure," Mr Bodley murmured, remembering that Miss Patchett had said she enjoyed hunting and wondering if she would be one of the ladies in the front.

"It's quite a jolly thing to do on Boxing Day," the curate continued, "because one's generally eaten and drunk a good deal more than is good for one and sitting on a horse is less onerous than walking for miles carrying a gun."

"Yes, I suppose so. I own I was thinking of remaining in the house."

"Ah! I can understand that's tempting, but I'm fairly sure you won't regret it if you come out. However, it's your choice! Don't take any notice of me."

"You were extremely helpful with the shooting expedition, sir, so that I very much value your judgment."

One of the other men also urged him to join the hunt.

"I own I'm not a frequent joiner of hunts, but it really is the most splendid fun," he said. "I'll wager you'll like it."

"I don't suppose I shall if I fall off," Mr Bodley countered, striving for humour.

"You won't – and as Stapleton says - you don't have to be in the front. There's no shame in bringing up the rear."

"Well, I'll think about it," Mr Bodley promised, intending to ask Miss Patchett whether she intended to go.

"And we'll see how many of the women we can persuade to come out with us," the young man continued. "It's more fun without them, really, but, if you don't want to be going hell for leather, you can always decide to keep an eye on them."

Very soon the whole table was discussing hunting and planning the route to be taken on the morrow. The more they went on about it, the less Adrian wanted to be part of it.

An older gentleman sitting opposite declared himself to be the Master, as well as the local magistrate, and joined with the others in encouraging him to join the party.

"Thank you, sir, for your encouragement," Adrian said, wishing he could think of some way of changing the subject.

"I say, aren't you the London detective?" this man, Sir Wilfrid Pace, asked.

Adrian admitted that he was and explained that he had not spent much time in the country. London, he pointed out, was very different.

"Oh, yes, certainly. Might be different countries, different planets, what! But you're a detective, sir, you must be accustomed to chasing after criminals. Tomorrow you'll be chasing a fox – that's the only difference! Ha! Ha!"

"Well, not really, sir. It's the terrain that's different, you see. I'm not used to fields and ditches and so forth. And, as a matter of fact, pursuing criminals is more often than not done on foot."

"Lord, yes, I suppose it must be. Oh, well, I still hope you'll join us."

"I hope you will too," Lord Rushlake said later, as the gentlemen processed out of the dining room to join the ladies.

"I thought I might keep Miss Patchett company," Adrian confided.

"Don't let me interfere with that," his lordship said, "but she might like to come out with us."

"She did say yesterday that she enjoyed hunting so I suppose that she will," Mr Bodley said dejectedly.

"In that case, I'd advise you to come too. It's really not too arduous, you know – people don't often fall into ditches!"

"Oh!"

Mr Bodley was disappointed; he had assumed, until Miss Patchett had confessed to enjoying hunting, that, because she was not a noblewoman, she would not be keen to do something which, to him, seemed the very essence of an aristocratic pursuit. He was beginning to think that the difference between him and all these other people was not so much a question of class as one of habitat. The majority of them lived in the country, at least some of the time, whereas he never had, having been born and brought up in London.

It was the first thing he asked Miss Patchett when he sat down beside her.

"Do you intend to join the hunt tomorrow?"

"I was thinking of doing so," she admitted, alerted by his anxious tone to his doubts.

"Do you – you said yesterday you liked it?"

"Yes. One has to do something," she explained, "and the opportunities for entertainment in the country are really quite limited. Are you thinking of crying off?"

"I've never ridden to hounds," he said, "and am, I own, terrified of falling off and breaking my neck."

"You might, I suppose," she said in her usual pragmatic way. "It has certainly been known to happen, but not generally to a person who's never hunted before. I'm sure Horace – or his groom - will find you a reliable horse and all you have to do then is to give it its head and let it take you the best way round. There's no need to compete with anyone."

"Very well," he said morosely. He knew now that his dream of remaining in the house with his beloved – and perhaps screwing up his courage to ask her the question to which he so desperately wanted an answer – was not to take place upon the morrow. In consequence, he thought he must pull himself together and join the hunt for, if he did not, what in the world would she think of him? Probably that he was too feeble for words and certainly wholly unsuitable to be the man with whom she might consider spending her life.

The rest of the evening passed pleasantly enough, Titania and Miss Thetford were prevailed upon to play and sing again – as was Aunt Saffy, who had gained such approval the previous evening that everyone was positively longing for a repeat performance.

This time, though, Miss Patchett was noted as a reasonably young and unmarried woman who might prove to be another enjoyable entertainer.

Unlike any of the others, she did not squirm or blush or plead incompetence or a lack of musicality, but rose serenely from her seat beside Mr Bodley and made her way to the *pianoforte*. After a low-voiced discussion with Titania, a sheet of music was unearthed and Miss Patchett sat down to perform it, Titania offering to turn the pages. Mr Bodley wished he could but, not being able to read music in any but the most rudimentary fashion, was afraid that he would get it wrong and either fail to turn a page or turn it before the pianist had reached the right moment.

The piece was a Beethoven sonata, which Miss Patchett, to the amazement of the entire room, performed not only with competence but with what might be described as uncommon musicality. It turned out that she was a remarkably able pianist in spite of hitting one or two wrong notes.

"My!" Jenny exclaimed in admiration when Helena resumed her seat. "Will you not play something else?"

"No, I don't think so. I believe I've shot my bolt with that – rather an ambitious choice, I'm afraid."

"It was simply tremendous!" Saffy said.

"Thank you."

"I don't know much about music," Mr Bodley murmured, "but that sounded terrific. I didn't know you could play."

"Most women can," Miss Patchett said lightly, "at least they can if their parents had ambitions for them. It was one of the things one was obliged to labour over as a child."

"But it sounded – well, if you did labour over it, you've been very successful," he said.

"I did labour as a small child," she said, "but, after my parents took me to a concert when I was eleven years old, I realised that it could – if one could only concentrate enough upon it – become something important in one's life. I suppose that, if I'd been a boy, I would have worked hard at my academic studies but, since I knew that I would never be able to pursue them to any very great degree, I concentrated upon being able to play instead – and I own it has given me huge satisfaction."

"It gives others satisfaction too," he said softly. "I've never heard anything so wonderful in my life!"

"Oh, that's due to Beethoven," she returned. "I've grown very keen on his music recently but, when I was a girl and expected to perform after dinner I wasn't used to play anything half so exacting – or pleasing. I'm glad you liked it. When I was asked to play, I was so unnerved I couldn't remember a single piece – that was why I asked Titania to find me a sheet of music. When I saw that one, which I *have* been practising, I couldn't resist – although I'm not sure it's the sort of thing one ought to play after dinner, especially on Christmas Day."

After that the card tables were put out and everyone played something or other – whist on some tables, hearts on one or two and a riotous game of Old Maid on one.

By the time some of the older guests began to leave or retire for the night, everyone had enjoyed the day and some, at least, were looking forward to the more outdoor pursuits likely to take place on Boxing Day.

Mr Bodley, laying his head upon his pillow after having bid an affectionate good-night to Miss Patchett, began, as was his custom, to go over the day in his head. He was not altogether pleased with his performance – he never was – but believed he had acquitted himself satisfactorily at the dinner table as well as during the games afterwards. He had been one of the whist players as it was a game he did at least know how to play; indeed, it turned out he was better than many, managing to recall most of the cards others had played so that he was able to assess what remained in people's hands. In this he was probably assisted by the fact that, afraid of misbehaving and aware that he had imbibed too much the night before, he had limited his consumption of strong liquor as much as he was able.

Having run over what he might have got wrong, he began to agonise about the morrow for he had, on bidding her good-night, promised Miss Patchett that he would join the hunt in the morning. It seemed to him that there was a great deal he could misjudge here but he tried to comfort himself with the thought that at least he was unlikely to kill anyone inadvertently, his main worry with the shooting.

Finally, he went over the delight of hearing Miss Patchett play Beethoven so skilfully. It had been enormously pleasing but, at the same time, it only reinforced his anxiety that she was so far above him in every respect that it was almost ludicrous to aspire to her hand.

He did not spare a single thought for Miss Thetford's curious revelation of the previous evening. If he had thought about it, no doubt he would have dismissed it as fanciful.

Chapter 10

After the hunting party had set out the following morning, Aunt Saffy found herself alone in the house for the first time for many months. She did not sit idly toying with a book, or indeed admiring the pretty pearl brooch the Earl had given her for Christmas. She set about not so much tidying the rooms, for there were maids to do that, but making sure that the servants were doing what was necessary, including preparing and transporting the luncheon that was to be served to the huntsmen and women after an hour or two in the fields.

The majority of the Christmas Day guests had returned to their own houses from whence they would probably join the hunt. The Thetfords, Lord Vincent Lovatt and Mr Stapleton were amongst those who had climbed into their carriages and been taken home very late the evening before. The curate, not having his own carriage, had accepted a lift from Lord Vincent with gratitude.

Those that remained in the house – or who would at any rate sleep in it again tonight – included all those members of Lord Rushlake's team who had assembled again, and certain other friends and relatives. They had all donned riding clothes and set off, including a nervous Mr Bodley to whom Saffy had whispered some words of encouragement as he went out with the surge of eager riders.

Saffy, having dealt with the servants, went up to the nursery apartments where she found the family nanny engaged in a long, unidentifiable piece of knitting. She lived in the Hall in this apartment, provided with everything she could possibly want except an infant of whom she could take care. She was waiting, not particularly patiently, for his lordship to marry and produce an heir. Of this she somewhat despaired for she had come to the family when the eldest daughter was born and was already middle-aged by the time Horace made his appearance.

"I shall be long dead by the time he produces an heir," she muttered morosely to Aunt Saffy, having furnished this other superfluous female with a cup of coffee and a small biscuit.

"No, you won't," Saffy responded cheerfully. "I'll wager he'll provide one within the next ten years."

"That's too long for me – and just look at the guests. Not one of them is a young woman, apart from that Miss Thetford – and there's more than a whiff of scandal hanging about that family."

"I own I didn't like her much," Saffy admitted.

Nanny sniffed. "*She* doesn't like her stepmother – tries to make everyone believe she poisoned her mama!"

"Really?" Saffy asked, interested.

"Yes. The thing is, you see, that *this* Lady Thetford was the governess – there are several younger sisters as well as Julia – Miss Thetford."

"I see. When did the first Lady Thetford die?"

"Oh, not long ago – probably not much above a year. They're only just out of mourning – and he's married the governess in considerable haste. I understand she's already expecting!"

"Oh, dear! Of what did the first one die?" Saffy, having recently been involved, albeit distantly, with a murder case, was more interested than she might have been before she went to London.

"I don't think that's very clear. She sickened, took to her bed – it was just after the youngest of her children was born – she's about two now. She didn't improve, indeed she got worse over quite a long period and then died."

"Oh dear! It sounds as though the poor woman's death was more closely related to the recent birth than anything else."

"Yes," Nanny agreed darkly. "Miss Thetford maintains that it only happened because the baby was another girl."

"I see. Are they all girls?"

"Yes – four of them. It was a terrible birth apparently; Lady Thetford was despaired of, but she did recover, although I *gather*," Nanny's eyes darkened and she leaned closer to Saffy to whisper – although there was no one else present, "the doctor said she'd never be able to have any more!"

"I see. So does Miss Thetford think it was her papa who killed her mama or the governess? I mean, was it more a question of wanting a son – and therefore needing a different mother – or regularising a *liaison* which had already begun?"

Nanny pursed her lips. "Does it matter? A bit of both, I should say."

"Yes, I think it does matter. If it was a question of wanting an heir, I would imagine Lord Thetford more likely to be responsible, whereas, if it was a question of the governess wanting to be a Viscountess, more likely she was the culprit."

"Serve her right if she has a girl too!" Nanny said vindictively.

"Did you know the first Lady Thetford?"

"Not to say 'know', no, but she was popular in the village. She did a lot of charitable work. I've never heard any scandal attach to her."

"Until her death."

This interesting thread having petered out, the two women moved on to speculating upon Titania's possible husband, Nanny insisting that Lord Vincent Lovatt had always been her choice and she believed her late ladyship would have agreed with her.

"He was quite put out when she went to London," Nanny explained. "Thought he'd lost his chance. I hope he takes it now she's back."

Saffy did not doubt that Nanny, although she appeared to spend her whole time in her own wing, knew what was going on in the village and, allowing the old lady to bring her up to date, she generously reciprocated with any snippets of information she had managed to garner concerning Titania's suitors in London. She did not though, on account of loyalty to her former charge, mention the young lady's flirtation with the curate, which she had observed taking place the night before.

This conversation went on for some time, indeed it took them up to luncheon, which they took together in Nanny's quarters. After luncheon, as Saffy knew, Nanny was inclined to retire to bed for a recuperative rest. Saffy therefore took herself off to some imagined task as soon as they had finished, promising to return the following day.

Meanwhile the hunting party set off in a good deal of jostle and excitement. The guests who had spent the night at the Hall were provided with mounts, Mr Bodley managing to secure one which he was assured would carry him steadily all day and not be in the slightest degree over-stimulated either by the other riders or the hounds.

Miss Patchett, taken aside by Titania and grilled upon her previous experience in following the hounds, was provided with a rather more lively mount which Titania assured her was the best in the stables, apart, of course, from her own favourite and his lordship's, which was, in any event, far too large for the average-sized Helena.

Having been assisted to mount, Helena made her way back towards where Mr Bodley had, with some difficulty and much relief, managed to take his place upon his saddle.

Lord Rushlake, mounted upon a handsome black horse, joined them, reassuring Mr Bodley that he would be bound to enjoy the outing.

"Do you think so?" Mr Bodley enquired sceptically.

"Yes; I'm convinced of it."

"Will there be any other inexperienced riders with whom I can potter along at the back?" the detective asked.

"Oh, I should think some will join us when we get to the White Hart. That's where we meet the rest of the village and anyone else from outlying ones who wants to accompany us. You must not be so despondent."

"I don't want to hold Helena up," Mr Bodley confided in a low voice, his gaze straying to the young woman, who was talking to Titania, with whom on this occasion she had more in common than usual.

"I'm sure you won't; in any event, unless she's already promised to act as your nursemaid, I should think she'll most likely tear off with Titania, who's a very keen rider and must have been looking forward to today ever since she left Rushlake to come to London."

"Oh, I hope she will," Mr Bodley said fervently. He already felt so deeply inferior to his beloved that he really did not want her to see his poor riding skills and judge him accordingly.

Miss Patchett, however, had other ideas. Once everyone was mounted, she made her way to his side and, as the party set off, the hounds barking excitedly and the riders jostling for position, proceeded side-by-side with the anxious detective.

"Don't you want to be in the front?" he asked.

"Not in the least. I enjoy the riding but I'm not at all keen on being in at the kill."

"That won't be for ages, will it?" he asked. "You can drop back when it looks likely."

She smiled. "Do you want to get rid of me?"

"No; I'm just concerned that riding beside me will spoil your enjoyment."

She smiled again, this time somewhat cryptically, and they continued together.

Mr Bodley soon found that the horse that had been chosen for him was one after his own heart. It proceeded steadily and determinedly, taking no notice of the hysterical hounds or the other horses.

"Do you think it's quite old?" he asked Helena *naïvely*.

"Middle-aged, I should guess. It's not going to let anything ruffle its calm but, equally, it's not so old it's likely to stumble. Horace has done well by you, as usual."

"It was the groom who chose it," Mr Bodley said.

"Yes, of course, but the thing is that Horace has made sure his stable's equipped with all sorts of different horses to suit a variety of riders."

"Do you think he bought some of them just for this party?"

"I've no idea; he may have done – or perhaps he borrowed or hired them. I mean, most of the time nobody lives here except Titania and Saffy. Saffy doesn't seem to ride at all and Titania, although I know she's very keen, can't need more than two or three to choose between. In any event, that one's too big for her."

"She's a tall woman," Adrian Bodley murmured.

"Yes, but not heavy – and not as tall as you in any event. I shouldn't think he'd generally keep such a large stable in the circumstances."

"He's a very generous host," Adrian said.

"He can afford to be, but yes, he is."

They proceeded contentedly side by side at the back of the party until they reached the inn where the local guests from the night before and several villagers joined them. Amongst them were four Thetfords, for Miss Thetford's younger sister, Veronica, was there together with the curate and Lord Vincent Lovatt.

The whole group proceeded for some time without there being any sign of a fox. Mr Bodley and Miss Patchett still brought up the rear and were occasionally obliged to jump a hedge or a ditch, an action which, the first time it occurred, almost caused Mr Bodley to give up altogether.

"It's nothing to be concerned about," his companion told him with what seemed to him to be an unnecessarily breezy attitude. "That horse'll take you over perfectly safely. He must have been this way any number of times before and probably views it as no more taxing than going upstairs two steps at a time."

"But how do you make him jump?" he asked, hanging back. On his sober circuits of the Park, he had never been required to jump anything. Rushing along at a canter was quite worrying enough without having to sail over a hedge.

"He'll do it all by himself," she said. "Just make sure you hold on firmly with your legs, relax the reins and he'll sail over."

Mr Bodley frowned at her, wondering, but not quite liking to ask, how she managed to 'hold on with her legs' when she was sitting sideways.

"He's done it any number of times," she repeated, moving in front of him. "Follow me."

He did, praying fervently that he would neither break his neck nor fall humiliatingly to the ground, and in next to no time he and his horse were on the other side.

Miss Patchett waited for him to catch up with her before saying, "There, that wasn't so bad, was it?"

"No."

There were a couple of villagers lingering awkwardly at the back too and the four of them followed the rest as best they could.

It was some time later that they came upon a sizeable bunch of riders, all paused, some dismounted, others still in their saddles, in front of what appeared to be a thick belt of trees.

"What are they waiting for?" he asked.

"I think there's been an accident," she said. "Someone's fallen."

They advanced towards the group but, being at the back, could not see what had happened. Not wanting to interfere and believing that he had nothing to add to the situation, Mr Bodley hung back but Miss Patchett, a rider who was not afraid of making her way through a number of horses and riders closely bunched together, advanced, telling him she would try to find out what had occurred.

"What is it?" she asked various people as she approached and urged her horse gently forwards.

"Someone's fallen – badly," a man told her. "It's a steep bank here – and you have to push through the greenery to reach the edge – and then you have to jump. Are you new to the neighbourhood?"

When she nodded, he went on, "Once you get used to it, it's not particularly difficult – you just need to know which is the best way through. Most of the horses know it – and most of the riders."

"Who was it who fell?" she asked.

"I'm not sure, but, judging by the panic which seems to be growing, it was a bad fall. Do you want to go through?"

She nodded. "Is there anything I can do, do you think?"

"I shouldn't think so; several people have already reached the lower field so they must have seen – or will have by now – what happened and no doubt they're doing all they can."

"Thank you," she said, but she did not turn round and go back; she continued forwards, the crowd giving way to her, until she reached the bank of trees and shrubs. Peering through, she saw that several people were indeed in the lower field and were clustered around a ditch which lay at the bottom of the bank. Someone had fallen into it. A riderless horse was standing, bewildered, at the edge of the crowd. It was equipped with a side saddle so that she drew the conclusion that the person in the ditch must be a woman. Anxiously, she searched for – and found – Titania, although there was no sign of Jenny.

"What happened?" she asked a man beside her.

"It looks like one of the Thetford girls," he said. "She took a tumble down the bank."

"Did the horse fall?" Helena asked.

The man frowned.

"I think it slipped and she tumbled off – fell heavily into the ditch. She hasn't got up," he finished gloomily.

Miss Patchett nodded and, turning, went back to where Mr Bodley was sitting upon his mount.

"I suppose someone's gone for help," he said.

"I should think so. I saw Horace down there with Titania."

"Where are Sir James and Lady Wendell?" he asked.

"I didn't see them – either they're still up here or they've gone for help. What do you want to do? Nobody seems to be going down now – at least not via the bank. We could turn round and go back the way we've come."

"I don't think I'd be able to find it," he said helplessly. "Isn't there another way down?"

"Probably, but I'm no more familiar with this area than you are. Shall we try to find someone who is?"

They were still standing uncertainly at the back of the crowd when Jenny reached them. She seemed to have been even further behind than they.

"What's happened?" she asked.

When she had been told, she looked horrified.

"Oh dear," she said, "I always knew hunting was dangerous. I'm glad I didn't let any of my children come. Aspasia was furious but I told her she wasn't a good enough rider yet to go gallivanting all over the country."

"No," Miss Patchett agreed. "Where's Sir James?"

"I don't know. He was with me."

"I didn't see him down there in the lower field," Helena said. "Do you think he could have gone for help?"

"No; he wouldn't know where to find it. He's hardly ever been to Rushlake; he must be here somewhere, probably nearer the front." She began to edge forward.

"Could we get down a bit further along, do you think?" Mr Bodley asked.

"Yes, probably, but I don't know the way. Some of these other people must, surely. I'll try to find someone to lead. Where's Lord Vincent? He'd know."

"I think he's down there already with Titania."

"Oh, damnation!" Jenny exclaimed. "All those eager horsemen and women have already got down, leaving us stranded up here."

She began to push her way forward and, unlike Miss Patchett, whom nobody knew, was soon recognised. In no time a concerted movement formed, led by one of the local villagers, who took most of the party back the way they had come for a short distance before descending a gentle hill, crossing a couple of fields and turning up close to where those who had already gone down the bank were congregated.

"It would have been much easier to have come this way in the first place," Mr Bodley murmured to Miss Patchett. "But I suppose the fox went the other way."

"I don't think anyone's seen a fox yet," she returned. "I imagine they go down that bank because they enjoy the challenge."

Chapter 11

"It's one of the Misses Thetford," somebody said. "Her horse must have lost its footing and she tumbled off. She's in a bad way."

Mr Bodley thought she looked as though she was. "Is there anything I can do?" he asked.

The man shook his head. "I don't think there's anything anyone can do," he said in a low voice.

"Should I go for a doctor or something?" Mr Bodley asked, longing to help but hoping his suggestion would not be taken up as he had no idea which of these seemingly endless fields might lead to the village.

"Don't think there's much even he could do," the other replied. "She'll have to be carried back. They'll probably put her on a horse as we've come too far to take her on foot."

The rescuers, one of whom was Lord Rushlake, were struggling to lift their burden out of the ditch and on to the field on which the now horror-struck hunt stood. The ditch was full of water, a quantity of which dripped off the body they carried. It could now be seen that it was a very young female, probably no more than sixteen or seventeen years old.

Some of the riders, all now on the ground with their horses beside them, had already got over the hazard before the accident occurred. Amongst them were Lord Thetford and his wife.

He, no doubt recognising the riding habit of the injured person, pushed his way through the crowd of onlookers who gave way with horror upon their faces.

"What's happened?" he demanded, although there did not seem to be much doubt.

"Her horse missed its footing as it came down the bank," someone said, "and she fell."

"Veronica!" he cried in despair. He stumbled forward and cast himself upon the body of his daughter.

"What …? We must take her home – fetch a doctor!" The Viscount's voice was hoarse.

Lady Thetford followed him but did not speak. Her face looked pale and anxious. She reached for his hand but he pushed her away, his interest centred upon his daughter.

"Papa!" This was Miss Thetford, the eldest daughter who had come to the Rushlake dinner the night before.

"Papa! Is she …?"

"She's lost her senses!" he cried, distraught. "Give her to me!"

Rushlake, in whose arms the inanimate body of the girl lay as limp as a doll, murmured something unintelligible and handed his burden to Thetford.

"Veronica! Dearest girl – pray open your eyes!" the father besought, cradling his child in his arms. One of her arms was against his chest, the other dangled uselessly towards the ground.

"Come, Papa," Miss Thetford, standing very close to the pair, was peering at her younger sister's white face and the distressing way in which her head lolled against their father's chest. "We must take her home."

She seemed to have taken charge, the father now too distressed to do anything more than clasp his daughter to his chest.

"Go away! Haven't you done enough harm?" the young woman hissed at Lady Thetford, who had approached her husband.

"She shouldn't have come!" Lady Thetford said. "She was too young! I tried to stop her. She didn't understand the danger!"

"No, she didn't," Miss Thetford snapped, a deeper meaning apparent in the emphasis she placed upon the words.

"She's a first-rate rider!" the father cried, beginning to stumble towards where his eldest daughter now stood, holding her horse.

"Oh, she could ride as well as anyone," the other returned sharply, "but she wasn't prepared for someone prodding the horse just as it was coming down the bank."

"What?" Lord Thetford shouted, turning briefly to look at Miss Thetford, a sudden wash of red suffusing his face.

"It was meant to be me," Miss Thetford said, now also red in the face. "She's wearing my old habit. That – that harpy wanted to kill me, not her! She got the wrong sister."

"Be quiet!" the father ordered in a voice of thunder.

"I will, for now," the young woman replied, "but I'll speak later. In fact, I'll tell that detective – he'll deal with it! It was murder, pure and simple."

"She's not dead!" the father cried and nobody dared to argue, although all those close by could see that there was no other explanation for the ghastly appearance of the girl.

Mr Bodley, hearing this, pricked up his ears as it were, but lowered his gaze. He did not believe Miss Thetford any more than he had the night before. He thought she was jealous of her new stepmother and bitter about her mother's only too recent death. Now she had another grievance which she wished to lay at the hated stepmother's door.

There was a painful silence which greeted this declaration, followed by people milling about, holding the horse, attempting to assist the father in arranging his younger daughter's body in as respectful a manner as possible.

The party, almost all of which was now in the lower field along with the girl and her family, found themselves stymied by the fact that they were the wrong side of the ditch and the bank to go home the way they had come. Leading a horse up and forcing a way through the shrubs would not only be difficult but seemed disrespectful, the danger being that the horse would stumble or blunder into the greenery and its burden would be knocked to the ground again – and perhaps roll back into the ditch.

"There is another way round," Lord Rushlake said. "It's a bit longer but will be easier. Do you know it?" he asked Lord Thetford, who was standing uncertainly at the head of the horse which bore his daughter's inanimate form.

"No; it's your land, Rushlake."

"Yes, of course. I'll lead the way, shall I?"

Lord Thetford nodded and, as Lord Rushlake walked past, leading his own horse, fell in behind him.

Nobody liked to remount and all followed respectfully on foot, their boots sinking into the mud as they walked.

"Shall I go back up and lead the rest of the party home?" Titania asked, noticing that some people still clustered at the top of the bank.

Jenny, to whom she confided her intentions, nodded.

"Yes, take them back. Can you get back up yourself?"

"Nefertiti can," Titania returned confidently. "Can someone please give me a hand up?"

Mr Stapleton, who had been standing close to her with a horrified expression upon his face, came forward at once and threw her up into the saddle.

"Would you like me to come with you?" he asked.

She shook her head. "I think your spiritual guidance is more urgently required this side," she replied, turning her horse and making for the ditch and the bank.

Several of the onlookers watched as she urged her horse across the ditch and up the steep, awkward bank.

"She can certainly ride," Miss Patchett confided to Mr Bodley as they peered, still on their feet, through the trees to the intrepid girl on horseback.

"Yes."

The detective looked almost stunned. He had been afraid of joining the hunt, had feared that his would be the broken neck and had joked, rather weakly, about the possibility; the awful event had sobered him so much that he found himself almost wishing it had been he who had tumbled down and landed in such an awkward manner. He had not seen the accident happen for he had been at the back with the other stragglers, but he had by now grasped something of what had happened.

Miss Patchett, perceiving the state he was in, led her horse to a fallen tree trunk and remounted without asking for help, Mr Bodley following suit and heaving himself up into the saddle once more.

Now being part of the group in the lower field, he and Miss Patchett followed the Earl and Lord Thetford, together with Sir James and Lady Wendell, until the Master, who knew the area well, suggested they make their way back to the village by the most direct route. Lord Thetford, he explained, was going towards his own house, but for everyone else it would surely be more sensible, now that the hunt had been aborted, to make their own way back. All had now remounted and the dogs, following their master, came with them as they rode, soberly, across a number of fields until they reached the road.

Titania and Lord Vincent, who had followed her up the bank, rode side by side at the front of the party which had not come down. He glanced at her from time to time, but neither spoke for several minutes.

"What a horrible thing to happen," he said after they had been riding for about ten minutes.

"Yes – and she was so young."

"I didn't know her well, although of course I know the family."

"I too. Presumably, she, Miss Thetford, is one of the people you see at the Assembly Rooms from time to time, although I suppose Veronica was too young to go there."

"Yes."

"Were you – are you - close to her?" she asked at last, acknowledging the tense in which they had been speaking of the girl.

"Not particularly. I have never found the family easy to get along with."

"No, but I think that one, Veronica, was probably easier than Miss Thetford. How many exactly are there?"

"I'm not sure; most of them are still in the schoolroom, although I believe the youngest is very young. Their mother died soon after that child's birth. I think there are four girls altogether."

"And now I understand the governess has become their mother. Is there then a new governess?" Titania enquired.

"I suppose so. She did not come out today, so far as I know."

"No. Well, if she had, what would they have done with the younger children?"

"And the former governess, the new Lady Thetford, was riding with some *élan* in spite of being – so I hear - in an interesting condition. They've not been married long – nor he widowed long."

"Did you," Titania asked, "hear what Miss Thetford said?"

"You mean accusing her new mama of killing her old one?"

"Yes. Is that something the village has been bandying about?"

"Yes; I don't know whether she's retailing what she's heard or whether she started the rumour. I should think it more likely that the first Lady Thetford died of complications after the birth, but he's married again in unseemly haste."

"Oh dear!" she said inadequately.

"Perhaps," her companion suggested, "we should involve your brother's new detective friend. Do you think he'd be able to get to the bottom of it?"

"Perhaps." Titania thought that it had not been solely Mr Bodley who had got to the bottom of the last case in which her brother had been involved, although perhaps he had contributed to the *dénouement*.

"I suppose he's on leave," Lord Vincent said. "Might not care to be involved."

"I'm not sure he'd be permitted to be," Titania said. "I mean, he's a detective with Scotland Yard, so he's officially a policeman, but dealing with a pernicious rumour surely wouldn't be quite proper, would it? And it's not on his patch, so to speak, up here."

"Perhaps not."

"Do you think she might have done it?"

"Quite possible, I should think – or perhaps he did."

"Yes. Wanted a boy, I suppose, and his poor wife had failed to provide one. She must have been quite old by the time she had the most recent one, too, because Miss Thetford's over twenty, isn't she?"

"I daresay he did want a boy – and he might have killed his wife in order to take another one – but I think it odd he should have chosen the governess," Lord Vincent said.

"Why? She's much younger than the first Lady Thetford."

"Yes, but the Thetfords are very high in the instep and the new one isn't the same rank – or even particularly pretty."

"Don't you think so?"

"Not to my way of thinking, in any event."

"Oh! What sort of female do you admire?" Titania asked this question purely in the interest of wondering why he did not care for the, in her eyes, extremely pretty governess.

He cast her an amused glance.

"Poor little dab of a thing," he said.

"Are you trying to flatter me?" she asked suspiciously. Titania was tall, a trifle masculine in appearance, being much like her younger brother, the Earl, and longed to be a tiny, pale girl. Both seemed to have forgotten why they were returning exactly the way they had come without having found or chased a single fox.

"I didn't think of it," he returned with a straight face. "Didn't think you'd care for that sort of approach."

"It never occurred to me that you might want to 'approach' at all," she said tartly.

"We've known each other since we were small children," he said lightly. "Is that why you've never seen me as a person of interest?"

"Possibly, but you've never shown any interest in me either. I mean, we've been friends – playmates, I suppose – for ever."

"Is the curate pursuing you?" he asked abruptly.

She flushed but managed to say, "I've only just met him – and he's by way of being a cousin."

He grinned.

"You're not an easy female to pursue, are you? You say you've known me for ever, which is why you've never thought of me as a suitor, and you've only just met him. How long would a more fortunate man have known you for, do you suppose?"

"I don't know," she mumbled, not wanting to be quizzed on the subject of Mr Stapleton when she felt so very unsure of his interest.

"And is he likely to be successful – when you know him a little better?"

"I've no idea. I've barely exchanged ten words with him. He's quite handsome though, isn't he?" she added, thinking that she should perhaps make an effort to reciprocate in the curious game which her old playmate seemed to have instigated. In any event, she felt sure she should try not to show how nettled she was.

He smiled. "I don't think I'm likely to be the best judge of that. Had you never met him before?"

"No; I told you, he's a very distant cousin. What," she tried by way of research into the curate's character, "does the neighbourhood think of him?"

"I believe he's quite popular, especially with the old ladies. After all, as you say, he's handsome and charming. He also appears to be articulate and well-read."

"And what's your opinion?"

"I think – and perhaps I'm biased because he's clearly a rival – that he's a little too full of himself. I find him over-confident and a trifle inclined to preen."

"I see. You say the old ladies like him, what do the young ones think?"

"Oh, I can see they like him too. Miss Thetford, for example, is clearly your rival; she blushes whenever he addresses her."

"Does she? What do you think of her?"

"I've known her almost as long as I've known you," he began evasively.

"But not so long," she interrupted, "on account of my being several years older."

"Are you?"

"Don't be absurd! You know I am!"

"Yes. And, as I said earlier, yours are the sort of looks I prefer."

"I didn't ask you about her looks."

"No, but I'm sure you were interested in my opinion of them. She is a very pretty young lady, but … well, perhaps it's her character which I find puts me off a little. She strikes me as a resentful person. She never misses an opportunity to criticise her stepmother, for example, and rarely fails to take one to criticise her papa."

"Why do you think she's resentful? I am too. I've always felt nobody wanted me when I was born – fourth girl, no boy in sight, terrible disappointment."

"Yes, of course; I understand that. I suppose she was a disappointment too in that sense because, with families like ours, boys are so ridiculously important. However, she was the first girl so can't have been such a crushing disappointment as that poor little thing who's lost her mother so recently."

"She won't remember her mother at all. How old are the others?"

"Veronica was sixteen, the next one's about twelve I think and then there's the baby. There were some others in between but they've all died for one reason or another."

"And Miss Thetford?"

"She's twenty-two, so not much younger than you."

"No. Why isn't she married?"

"Well, I didn't want her and the curate hasn't been here long, although I must say I haven't noticed him showing any interest. To my mind, she's always had her eye on your brother. Is she the sort he admires, do you think?"

"I've no idea what sort he admires, but I don't think he's ready to settle down yet."

"No; I don't think Stapleton is either, although he might if he thinks the price is right. I gather that, as a family, they're poor as church mice – or he falls heavily in love."

"Yes, I believe so. There are too many of them, that's part of the problem. There are at least ten children, several of them boys who will have to be found some suitable *niche* from which they can earn a living."

"Or collar a rich wife," Lord Vincent reminded her with heavy meaning.

While Titania and Lord Vincent led the party back towards the house on the home side of the brook, Lord Rushlake and the bereaved father led the way on the other side.

They did not speak except occasionally to discuss which side of a field would lead most directly to a gate. They proceeded at a walking pace, although, after they had gone a few yards, Lord Thetford mounted his own horse and Rushlake carefully lifted the dead girl from the one on which she had been so carefully placed and passed her to her father. The Viscount cradled her in one arm while directing his horse with the other hand.

They were followed closely by Lady Thetford and Miss Thetford, neither of whom spoke a single word.

After they had gone some way, the party split up with Lord Rushlake continuing with the Thetfords and Mr Stapleton, who had been one of the first to rush to the injured girl's aid, leading the remainder of the group which had already reached the lower field when she fell. The curate, who was a keen rider, declared that, since Titania had gone back up to lead the stragglers who had not descended, he would lead this party since he knew a way to reach the village without having to climb back up the fatal bank.

The Master and the rest of the hunt which had joined Lord Rushlake's party at the inn followed at an even greater distance, the hounds clustering around their horses' legs. It was when they reached the inn once more that the party broke up, everybody making their own way home from this point.

Chapter 12

Mr Bodley, riding side by side with Miss Patchett in the party led by Titania and Lord Vincent, was no longer worried about managing his horse, the hedges or anything else concerning the aborted hunt.

He was, however, turning over in his mind what Miss Thetford had said on Christmas Eve as well as what she had said just now. In spite of having been some way away when she had made her accusation, it had been delivered in a loud voice which most of the party must have heard. Miss Patchett certainly had, for she had glanced at him as the young woman spoke.

"What a terrible end to what was meant to be entertainment," he said at last.

"Yes. I daresay it reinforces your opinion of the inherent danger," she replied.

"I suppose it does. You said it didn't often happen. Were you simply trying to reassure me?"

"Yes, I was; it doesn't happen frequently, but often enough to give the sport a reputation as something dangerous. What is so particularly awful, I think," she went on, "is that she was so very young."

"Yes. That family seems to have been subject to a good deal of misfortune recently."

"Indeed. What did you think about Miss Thetford's accusation?"

"I was horrified," he admitted.

"Horrified by her saying it or by *what* she was saying?"

"Both, I suppose, but particularly the content. She accused her stepmother of killing her mother."

"Or her father of doing so. Have you had much conversation with her?"

"I was sitting next to her at dinner on Christmas Eve. She accused one or both of them of killing her mother then. I thought – hoped – that she was simply trying to shock me and chose that subject because I'd told her I was a detective."

She looked at him.

"Do you now think she may have meant it?"

"I'm much afraid she may have done. In truth, I don't know what I should do about it."

"Perhaps," she suggested tentatively, "you should tell Horace and see what he thinks."

When they reached the inn where the villagers had joined them on the outward journey, there was a parting of the ways, Lord Vincent and the villagers dispersing to their own homes and Mr Bodley and Miss Patchett continuing with Titania towards Rushlake Hall. They arrived before his lordship, who had accompanied Lord Thetford to his house. It was thus they who broke the news to the stable staff, who expressed a suitable degree of distress and sympathy.

Having dismounted and left their horses at the stables, they made their way back into the house and, Titania going straight upstairs, Mr Bodley and Miss Patchett stood indecisively in the hall for a few moments while they debated whether they should leave and return to their own homes.

"I don't know," Miss Patchett said, when Mr Bodley confided this dilemma. "We can't leave until Horace gets back in any event – and, in view of what Miss Thetford said, I don't think we can go until we've discussed *that* with him."

The house seemed very quiet and there was no sign of Aunt Saffy, with whom Helena longed to consult on the tricky situation in which she found herself.

She changed out of her riding habit and went to one of the sitting rooms. The usual time for luncheon had passed and no one had eaten the picnic. She wondered if it would be brought back to the house and whether it would now be served in the dining room, afterwards castigating herself for her selfishness in thinking about luncheon when a young girl was dead.

Mr Bodley joined her.

"Do you think the servants know we're here?" he asked.

"Probably not. Are you hungry?"

"I own I am. Where do you suppose Aunt Saffy is? Perhaps we could join her."

"We could if we knew where she was. And where's Titania? Why has she shot off upstairs without a word and not come down? I believe I'll ring the bell."

There was an appreciable delay before the bell was answered, but eventually Perkins appeared.

"Madam? Sir?"

Helena said, "There was an accident and the hunt was called off. His lordship has gone with Lord Thetford to his house and will probably be some time. I wondered if it would be possible to provide us with a small luncheon of some sort since we never reached the spot where the picnic was to be eaten."

"Certainly, Madam. I'll order something to be sent to the small dining room in, say, half an hour?"

"Yes, thank you. I suppose Miss Hemsted must be somewhere?"

"I believe her to be with Nanny Brown in her quarters," the butler explained. "Would you like me to send her a message?"

"Oh, I wouldn't want to trouble her," Helena murmured.

"Very well, Madam."

The butler bowed himself out again and the two fugitives were left alone once more.

Mr Bodley, who had longed to find himself alone with Miss Patchett, did not think this an appropriate moment to explain his sentiments so remained silent.

Helena said, "It's an awkward situation, isn't it? I mean, we feel uncomfortable being here alone and unable to speak in a natural manner on account of what has just taken place. But we were not acquainted with the unfortunate young woman, or indeed the family, and, while one is shocked and saddened at such a thing, we – or at least I – cannot claim to be personally affected by it."

"No," he agreed heavily.

"I wonder if Lady Amberstone will still come tomorrow, or do you think his lordship will write to suggest she does not?"

"I don't know," he said hopelessly.

They were still waiting for the half hour to pass and Titania had not returned when the door opened and Aunt Saffy came in.

"Goodness!" she exclaimed. "Didn't you go in the end?"

Helena explained what had happened. Aunt Saffy's expression grew increasingly grave as the recital continued until, when Helena recounted Miss Thetford's accusation, it assumed an expression that could only be described as horrified.

"Do you think there could be anything in it?" Helena asked.

"I've no notion, but it does indicate that the poor young woman is excessively unhappy!" Saffy said.

"Angry, I should say," Helena suggested.

"Yes; but so often anger is a person's way of dealing with unhappiness," Saffy explained. "She's very young, isn't she, and probably thinks she's entitled to an agreeable life – one does when one is young – and then losing her mother and acquiring a stepmother she dislikes won't have helped. I mean, she must be about at the point of having a Season, isn't she? Indeed, I daresay she may have missed it because of her mother's death."

"The stepmother was apparently the governess," Helena said.

"Yes – and I don't doubt that makes it worse because she probably thinks – oh I hate to contemplate what she thinks! What is Horace's opinion?"

"We haven't spoken to him since the accident," Mr Bodley said. "He's gone with Lord Thetford and the poor girl. I should think he might be some time."

"Yes, indeed."

She paused, looking from one anxious face to the other, and then said, "Something is troubling you, Mr Bodley. I mean, of course it's very distressing, but you look as though you're wrestling with some exceptionally tricky dilemma."

"Yes, I am. It's terrible – awful accident – such a young girl and so sudden and unexpected! I'm wondering – I'm sorry to be so ignorant, Aunt Saffy – but should we, I, leave, do you think? I mean, not before his lordship gets back, of course, but perhaps I should leave later this afternoon."

"Oh, I didn't mean that," she exclaimed. "I meant about the mother's death. It's your sort of dilemma, isn't it?"

Seeing his surprise, she added hastily, "Leave? I don't know. Perhaps you should ask Horace. The thing is that most of the people staying are actually his relatives so that I don't think he'll necessarily expect them to leave at once. I appreciate you aren't, but then you're rather a special sort of friend in a way, aren't you? And, in this case, where it looks as though some sort of foul play may have taken place, I should think your presence would be extremely helpful."

Mr Bodley looked even more horrified by this.

He said, "Do you mean you think I should try to investigate the first Lady Thetford's death?"

"Well, there wouldn't be any harm in doing so, would there? I mean you're not on duty, so to speak, just at present, are you? You're on holiday, but your expertise in looking at the facts and drawing conclusions might be invaluable."

Mr Bodley looked even more alarmed by this and was clearly relieved when Perkins came in to announce that a light luncheon had been laid out for them in the small dining room.

"Oh, thank you," Helena said. "Will you join us, Saffy?"

"No, no, thank you. I already had luncheon with Nanny; she's taking a little rest now. But won't everyone need something when they get back? I mean," Saffy became quite confused as she realised that she seemed to be taking control of the household, "they won't have been able to eat the picnic, will they? Have you told Perkins what's happened?"

"No," Helena admitted. "We didn't really know what to do, and you didn't seem to be here, so we – well, we – I'm afraid we felt rather hungry so I asked Perkins if we could have something."

"Oh, no, I was probably with Nanny when you got back. I think – do you think – we should tell Perkins so that he can get the kitchen to prepare something for everyone when they arrive – or perhaps send someone to bring the picnic back?"

It was agreed that this should be done and Saffy, who came down to sit with the others while they ate, informed Perkins of the situation when he came in with the soup.

"Oh, thank you, Madam; I'm sorry to hear there was an accident. I'll put something in train at once to provide refreshments as soon as the party gets back."

The two women talked, although inevitably they focussed upon what had just happened and the likely ramifications. Mr Bodley did not say much.

He was thinking about Miss Thetford's accusation, her furious tone and her father's reception of it. He had not been close enough to have seen the expressions of the people concerned since the interchange had taken place in the lower field while he had remained in the upper one, separated by the small copse and the ditch. All he had heard were the angry words and, putting these together with what she had said the previous evening, he began to wonder if he should mention the matter to his lordship.

They had just finished their luncheon when the rest of the party, minus the Earl, came in.

"Oh, I'm glad you've had something to eat," Jenny said when Helena had put her in possession of the most recent events in the house. She rang the bell to summon Perkins once more.

It was not long before a fresh bowl of soup was borne in and the new arrivals began to eat.

"Where's Titania?" Jenny asked, laying down her spoon.

"I don't know; she went off upstairs as soon as we got back and we haven't seen her since," Helena said.

"How very odd! Have you seen my children?"

"Yes, I did see them," Saffy said. "They came in just as I was leaving Nanny – I had luncheon with her, but I don't think they did – at least they did not join us. She sent them away on the pretext of having to have her usual rest. I don't know where they went after that because, by the time I'd made my *adieux* to Nanny, they'd disappeared."

"Oh!" Jenny said, beginning to frown.

"What were the arrangements for their luncheon?" Aunt Saffy asked.

"I asked for it to be served in the old nursery. But, if Nanny isn't with them, I wonder who is. I think I'd better go and find out."

She pushed her chair back and rose from the table.

"Would you like me to look?" Sir James asked.

"No; you don't know this house very well and you don't know the servants at all. I'd better go."

"No," Saffy said with more than her usual decisiveness, "you finish your luncheon. I've had mine, I know the house and the servants and am certain I can soon find them. Would you like me to send them down or simply report back?"

"You don't know the children though," Jenny murmured, oddly indecisive.

"It doesn't matter – they're the only children here so far as I know."

"Report back," Jenny said as Aunt Saffy left the room.

She found them immediately. They were sitting in the day nursery, talking in an animated fashion with their Aunt Titania.

"Oh, there you are!" Saffy said, going into the room. "Your mama was wondering where you'd got to!"

"Is she home already?" the eldest girl asked, surprised.

"Yes; she's just got back. Titania, have you had any luncheon?"

"Oh, yes, thank you. I sent for a bowl of soup some time ago. Would you like to join us? We were about to play a game."

Saffy looked at the faces round the table and thought that Titania was a different person with the children. She was no longer angry or resentful and seemed perfectly at home. She could understand now how easily and happily she had fitted into her elder sister's household.

"Not at the moment, thank you. I believe I'll go and set your mama's mind at rest."

"Was she worried about us?" Aspasia, the eldest, asked. "What did she think we'd be doing?"

"That was what she was wondering," Aunt Saffy replied, not wanting to be the person who told the children about the accident and their mother's naturally increased concern.

It was not until nearly teatime that Lord Rushlake returned.

He had continued to Thetford House with the bereaved family, nobody speaking. When they arrived at the stables, he surrendered his horse to the groom who came out to meet them and take the family's horses.

The shock and horror with which the sight of their master carrying one of his daughters' lifeless bodies was extremely distressing and reduced many of the stable staff to tears, for Veronica had been particularly keen on riding and had spent a great deal of time at the stables. Lord Thetford himself remained stony-faced.

"Would you like me to come in with you or would you prefer it if I made myself scarce?" Lord Rushlake asked.

The Viscount, glancing surreptitiously at his womenfolk, said, "I believe I would appreciate your company if you feel able to leave your guests for a little longer."

"Oh, they'll be perfectly all right – they're almost all my relatives in any event and will get along perfectly well without me."

"There's that detective fellow and the woman from the north," Lord Thetford reminded him.

"Oh, yes, but I know them well. They won't miss me for an hour or two."

Reassured that his neighbour was not in danger of committing a social solecism, the Viscount led the way into his house where, once again, there was a distressing reaction from the first person whom they encountered – the butler.

"You'd better send for the doctor," Thetford said, "although there's nothing he can do."

"Yes, my lord. My sympathies, my lord."

"Thank you. I'll take her upstairs to her chamber."

"Would you like me to carry Miss Veronica, my lord?" the butler asked.

"No, thank you. I can manage. She – she's not heavy," his lordship replied, his voice breaking.

"Come with me," he added to Lord Rushlake and the two men went up the stairs together.

Laid upon the bed, with her head supported by a pillow and still in her – or rather her elder sister's – habit, Veronica Thetford was a tragic figure.

"She was sixteen," the Viscount informed his companion.

"She is very beautiful," Rushlake said quietly.

"They are at that age," the father returned with some bitterness, "even if, later, they turn out to be nothing out of the ordinary."

The Earl stood respectfully some distance from the bed and gazed upon the porcelain countenance and long sweep of eyelashes of the dead girl, but there was something about the body which struck him.

"Are you sure that life has been totally extinguished?" he asked. He had never been a soldier and the only dead body he had ever seen was that of his father, who had been both old and ill when he had died, but there had been no doubt in his mind that he was dead. There was something altogether unmistakeable about the remains of a person from whom life and spirit has fled. This dread sense of vacancy did not hang about Veronica Thetford's corpse. The porcelain complexion was pale but not, somehow not, dead. It reminded the Earl of the story of Snow White – or even, perhaps, Juliet.

"What?" the Viscount exclaimed. "Her neck was broken."

"It seemed that it had been; perhaps it was not."

The older man drew up a blanket over his daughter's body and sat down beside her, clasping one of her inert hands in his. The Earl, unsure what to do, enquired whether he should leave.

"No, no, please don't! I – you're talking wildly but the women ... I can't face either of them."

"What about Nanny? Some of your children are quite young, aren't they? Do you still have a nurse to attend to them?"

"Lord, yes, but she's an old woman – in every sense of the word! She'll go to pieces when she finds out. Veronica was always her darling – such a gentle, loving girl – the best of the bunch."

"Yes," the Earl murmured. He did not believe what the distraught father was saying; he thought, simply, that whichever of his daughters had been cut down in this way he would have felt that he had lost the best.

"Did you see what happened?" he asked.

"Her horse – she was coming through the bushes at the top of that damnable hill and suddenly it went mad – as though possessed – reared up and hurled itself down the hill – failed to see the ditch, over which it should have jumped, until the last moment when it lost its footing and she fell, catapulted off its back."

"Straight into it?" Rushlake asked. "Or did she bang against the bank as she fell?"

"I don't know! What does it matter?"

"Probably it doesn't; it's just that, if she fell straight into the ditch, she might not have been so badly injured, but if she crashed into the bank on the way it may – that may have been what broke her neck."

"Oh, now you think she has broken her neck? Now you concede that she's no more?"

"I don't know," Rushlake admitted, trying to hold on to his sanity as the bereaved father began to work himself up into a temper and clearly saw a likely recipient of his rage standing before him.

"Look at her!" the father shouted, dropping his daughter's hand and jumping to his feet to approach his guest in a menacing manner.

"Would you like me to leave, sir? I'm sorry if I've added to your distress!"

The rage seemed to leave the Viscount as swiftly as it had arrived; his shoulders slumped, his head dropped and he said, "You cannot – nobody can add to my distress! It's as deep and horrible as it can be!"

"Yes, of course."

Lord Rushlake was beginning to wish that he had not, driven by pity, accompanied the man back to his house, let alone up to his daughter's chamber, there to witness the man's misery.

"You might have married her," Thetford said, perhaps to prevent his companion from leaving. "Would you have thought of doing so?"

Lord Rushlake, who was growing accustomed to people speculating about his marriage – either telling him to 'get on with it' if they were old or even, in at least one case, suggesting herself as a suitable bride, took little notice of this, reasoning that the likelihood of such an event was hardly worth a thought.

"I haven't thought of marrying anyone," he said apologetically. "I'm not much above twenty."

"No – and she was less than that – but, together, what a handsome pair you would have made."

Lord Rushlake, reflecting that this was not perhaps the best reason to choose a particular woman, found himself thinking that the Thetfords, with their already fraught relations amongst themselves, was not the family to whom he would choose to ally himself.

"She was a gentle girl." The father continued his reminiscence. "I have – had – four daughters."

"I have four sisters," Rushlake offered.

"Huh!" Thetford exclaimed. "And you were the youngest!"

"Yes."

"I wonder if my next child would have been a boy," Thetford said wistfully.

"Are you expecting one?" Rushlake asked, disconcerted by the tense and unsure what the Viscount meant.

"What? I haven't been married to this wife for long – my previous one died."

"Yes. My condolences on your loss," the Earl said formally.

"Aren't you going to offer me congratulations on my second marriage?"

"I – yes, of course. I had not thought this a moment to offer congratulations."

"No, it's not, but … dammit, everyone's talking about my new wife."

"I suppose they're bound to do so – being new and all that."

"I married her too quickly after poor Margaret died. I shouldn't have done that; it made everyone gossip, say Vera was already expecting – even that I'd killed Margaret. How could I have done that?"

"I've no idea," the Earl responded. "How did she die?"

"It was nearly two years after the last baby was born, but she'd been ill almost ever since. The doctor thought it was some internal problem – she never really picked up after the birth and then she kept being sick – couldn't keep anything down at the end."

"It must have been horrible," the Earl murmured, wondering if the first Lady Thetford had indeed been poisoned and now fairly well convinced that, if she had been, it had not been her husband who had administered it.

"Vera was the governess," the Viscount went on. "I daresay that added to the scandal – made people suspect I'd wanted to – that we'd …"

"People will always talk," Rushlake said gently when the Viscount fell silent.

The other man looked up at him consideringly.

"They were right though," he said heavily. "Margaret was so ill, spent all her time in bed and Vera – we used to talk about the children – the girls – and, somehow it just happened."

Lord Rushlake, although he was young and relatively inexperienced in the ways of the world and indeed even relations between men and women, did not think that the sort of thing to which Lord Thetford was referring 'just happened'. Such an act was voluntary and could not, in the strictest sense, have occurred without at least one of the pair making some kind of approach to the other and it being received in a positive manner.

He also wondered how 'talking about the children' could have progressed into what he assumed was thinking and acting in a manner which related not at all to the children – unless of course, even at that stage, his lordship had been focussing on 'the girls' and perhaps dreaming of a boy. Such a boy would not of course have been of much use to the Viscount and his family tree unless he had been married to the child's mother. That might have led one or both of the participants in 'what happened' to taking steps to ensure that the new union could progress to a legal one.

Thinking of this and reminding himself that they stood beside a bed on which one of the Viscount's daughters lay dead, Rushlake said nothing.

"You disapprove," the Viscount said in a depressed tone, "and I own I do myself. I wish I had not 'jumped the gun'. My eldest daughter, as you must have gathered, is furious and unlikely to forgive me."

Chapter 13

Lord Rushlake made a gesture indicative of there being nothing to be done except perhaps wait for Miss Thetford's anger to diminish, as all such reactions do eventually.

"Would you like to marry her?" the Viscount asked, scenting a solution to at least one of his problems and perhaps wishing to divert his own attention from the reason the two men were sitting in Veronica's chamber.

There being no sign of humour in Thetford's demeanour, Rushlake assumed this to be a real offer. He shook his head, trying to look regretful.

"You'd have got on better with this one," the Viscount continued in an acknowledgment that his eldest was not perhaps the most amenable of his children.

"How old are your other daughters?" Rushlake asked.

"The third one is twelve – you'd have to wait a little while but she's not much more than ten years your junior; the youngest is nearly three."

"There are large gaps between them," Rushlake observed for want of any other answer.

"There were others in between who died, either before birth or immediately thereafter. None was a boy."

"I'm sorry. You must be hoping for a boy next time."

"I own I am, but he will not take the place in my heart that Veronica held."

"No, of course not."

Lord Rushlake, having no wish to engage in a discussion of the misfortunes of possessing so many daughters or the necessity of acquiring a son, rose and made a determined effort to move towards the door.

"Please don't go!" Lord Thetford begged, rising too and making a gesture as though he would detain the Earl, before dropping his hand and saying, "I'd like you to be here when the doctor arrives."

Such a request at such a time was impossible to refuse and Lord Rushlake abandoned his attempt to escape and sat down again.

"She …" Thetford said, "do you truly think she may not be quite gone?"

"I'm sure I couldn't say," Rushlake began, wishing he had not said what he had for there was no more sign of life than there had been when he had spoken – only, still, the girl lacked that emptiness that he had noticed in his father. He wondered if perhaps it was because this corpse was young – and the girl was beautiful, still.

At that moment the door flew open and an old woman dressed in black stumbled in, keening like a Greek chorus.

"Oh, my darling," she cried, running to the bed and, ignoring the two men, flung herself upon the corpse.

"Nanny!" Lord Thetford remonstrated feebly. "Please don't disturb her!"

"Disturb her! Lord, what have you done, Mr Vernon?"

"I?"

"Yes, you, my lord!" Nanny returned, claiming the privilege of an old woman who had ministered to her lord when he was a baby and had therefore no scruples about telling him off.

"Wake up, child! Your papa's distraught – and no wonder! His behaviour's been appalling - shameful – but that's no excuse to deprive him of his reason! Who knows what he'll do next if you upset him too much?"

With which the old woman, who could not have been much above four and a half feet tall and was almost as round as she was high, took hold of the corpse's shoulders and shook the girl with such vigour that the two watching men gasped, first at the violence the wizened creature seemed able to exert and then, when her efforts did seem to wake the dead, at the result, for the corpse upon the bed choked – as Snow White did when the piece of apple in her throat was dislodged – and, sufficient air having by this means made its way into her lungs, began to moan piteously.

"There!" Nanny exclaimed with satisfaction, laying the girl back upon the bed. Her manner changing to one of rough tenderness, she gathered the girl into her arms, pressed the dishevelled head against her bosom and began to croon to her.

"There! There! You'll be right as rain in no time, my darling! You've given these men a nasty shock – and they well deserved it – useless creatures" – this last uttered almost *sotto voce* – "but now it's time to pull yourself together."

"What have you done?" the Viscount cried, echoing the old woman's earlier cry.

"Well, I hope I've stopped you burying another female in your family," Nanny responded brusquely.

The father tried to push the old woman out of the way but she would not be moved, holding fast to the girl, while the girl, now curiously animated, clung to her and began to sob.

"Nanny, Nanny, help me! It hurts!"

"I'm sure it does, my love," Nanny returned, still in that warm comforting tone. "Where does it hurt? Is it your leg or your back or what? What happened to her?" She shot at the Viscount.

Lord Rushlake had taken a step back but he found he had lost all desire to leave the room. He did not think the others were aware of his presence but it seemed to him that, if there was an old crime to be investigated, Nanny was about to do it.

"My arm, my head – oh, it hurts so much!" the girl whimpered.

"Have you sent for the doctor?" Nanny demanded, casting an accusing glance at the Viscount. "Or was it the undertaker?"

"The doctor, of course!" the man replied, outraged.

"Good! Where is he?" She looked round the room and her eye lit upon the Earl.

"Are you he? I don't recognise you! You're very young!"

"No, I'm not the doctor," his lordship replied, "I'm Rushlake – your neighbour. I came back with his lordship."

"Did you? Why?"

"We were on a hunt – organised by me, on my land," Rushlake explained. "I thought – we thought – she was dead and I – I hoped my presence would be of some comfort to his lordship!"

"A person your age? What do you know?"

"Very little, ma'am," he admitted, affording her the ghost of his heartstopping smile.

Nanny was not immune to it, or perhaps she would have shown a preference for any man other than the 'Mr Vernon' with whom she was clearly extremely annoyed.

"Did you think she was dead?" she asked.

"I wasn't sure."

She nodded.

When the doctor arrived, which was shortly after this, Nanny drove both the men out of the room.

Downstairs, Lord Rushlake expressed his relief that the girl seemed likely to recover and, making a determined effort, at last managed to leave. He found his horse being walked up and down outside, mounted it and rode away.

105

Coming into his own drawing room where his guests were drinking tea and commiserating with each other over the awful events of the day, he flung himself down, accepted a cup of cold tea from Aunt Saffy and said, "She's not dead after all!"

"*What?*" everybody exclaimed at once and barely listened, interrupting both him and each other to ask further questions, while he explained.

"Did you see Miss Thetford after you knew Miss Veronica wasn't dead?" Mr Bodley asked when there was a pause in the questions.

"No. I thought I'd already been there far too long. I suppose I should have done and could then have told you what her reaction was, but she was not downstairs when I was leaving and I didn't think it behoved me to ask to see her."

"Lord, no!" Jenny exclaimed. "They would be bound to have thought you were courting her if you'd done that."

"Thetford, when he thought Veronica was dead, suggested she'd make me an excellent wife," he murmured provocatively.

Jenny threw up her hands. "She did seem to be quite an agreeable girl – more so than her sister in any event - but I wouldn't advise allying yourself to that family – not after what Miss Thetford said."

"No."

"Said in the field?" Mr Bodley asked. "Would you like to know what she told me at the dinner table on Christmas Eve?"

"Yes!" everybody cried at once.

When he had retailed Miss Thetford's remark about her mother and stepmother, Jenny was even more certain that it would be more than unwise to wed into that family.

"For clearly they're at daggers drawn with each other," she explained.

"Nanny, our nanny, Nanny Brown, was talking about them when I had luncheon with her," Aunt Saffy said, and retailed the gist of the conversation the two women had had.

"Do you think something sinister did occur in that household?" Lord Rushlake asked Mr Bodley.

"I really don't know. What did you think, my lord? You've just spent some time there."

"Not with either the accuser or the accused though. I was with a distraught father, an unconscious daughter and, later, an agitated nurse."

"When Miss Thetford made the original remark at dinner on Christmas Eve, I thought she said it to provoke me – because I'd told her I was a detective. But then, barely two days later, there's an almost fatal accident in the same family. It does make one think!"

"Aunt Mildred will be here tomorrow," the Earl said. "Shall we ask her opinion?"

Everyone was perfectly willing to wait for the decisive old lady to give her view before taking any further action, but, in the event, something transpired before she arrived.

It was early the next morning, not long after breakfast, that Perkins announced that Miss Thetford wished to speak to Mr Bodley.

"To me?" the detective asked, startled.

"Yes, sir. I've placed her in the blue sitting room."

Mr Bodley looked at the Earl with his eyebrows raised.

"Not precisely the waiting room for callers whom Perkins judges should be sent away with a flea in their ear. You'd better go and speak to her – if you can bear to do so."

"Isn't it rather odd to ask to see me when it's your house?"

"Yes – quite rude, in truth – but, especially in view of what we were saying last night, I believe you should see her."

"Very well."

He rose and Perkins conducted him to the right room.

When he had gone, the rest of the family looked at each other in stunned silence.

"Unpleasantness seems to follow you," Jenny observed to her brother drily.

"If she's about to repeat the accusation she made on Christmas Eve, it took place long before I got here."

"I suppose," Titania observed with a small smile, "that, if you want to avoid people trying to make use of your new hobby – and your new friend – it would be as well to scrutinise their families for any unexpected or untoward deaths in the last few years before you invite them to your house."

"Did you know anything about it?" he asked.

"No, although of course I did know that the first Lady Thetford had died. But I didn't know he'd married the governess because *that* took place while I was in London."

"Had you met her before she came here for dinner?"

"No; why should I have done? I've been too old for a governess for years. I don't even know Miss Thetford because she's years younger than I."

107

While the Rushlake family were speculating upon Miss Thetford's visit, Mr Bodley was shaking hands with her.

"Shall I bring some refreshment, sir?" Perkins asked, having shown the detective into the small blue sitting room in which his visitor was impatiently striding up and down.

"Yes, thank you."

The butler withdrew and the two sat down opposite each other.

In the light of day, and not having imbibed any strong liquor, Mr Bodley saw that she was a young woman whose impatient air made her look many years older than she was. She appeared to be carrying a good deal of care and anxiety for her brows seemed to be drawn permanently into a frown and her eyes were suspicious. She was not a beauty although she was not unattractive except in her manner, which was both angry and entitled. It was clear that she saw Mr Bodley as little better than a tradesman and found it as odd to be sitting opposite him in Lord Rushlake's sitting room as she had found it to be seated next to him at a dinner table.

"May I enquire how your sister is doing?" he asked, unnerved by her haughty stare.

"My sister? You mean Veronica? Well, amazingly, she seems to be still alive, although she's not well and can't, apparently, remember anything of what went on immediately before the accident."

"I don't think that's unusual."

"No. The doctor thinks she may remember eventually. He said we must not *demand* that she remember, that she either will or she will not. She doesn't need to remember in any event because I saw what happened."

"That is very helpful," Mr Bodley said warily.

"She was pushed – or rather her horse was tripped – a stick was held in front of its legs as it was coming down the bank. I saw it! It stumbled and she fell."

"Did you see someone holding a stick?"

"Not precisely, but Veronica was wearing my old habit which I'd outgrown. I'm certain I was meant to be the victim because …"

The young woman stopped speaking abruptly as Perkins, preceded by a tactful knock upon the door, brought in a tray bearing coffee and a plate of macaroons. He bowed himself out and Mr Bodley, being the host, was forced to pour coffee for his guest. She watched him with such scorn, almost willing him to do something wrong, that he did indeed spill some of the coffee, but was able to take that cup for himself and furnish her with one in which there was no puddle in the saucer.

"Pray continue," he said, passing her the plate of macaroons.

She took one.

"My stepmama wants to kill me because I know she killed my mama."

He nodded.

"You said that when I last met you. What makes you so certain?"

"Mama was perfectly well; she'd recovered well after Letty's birth – she's my youngest sister – and then, suddenly, she began to fade. She lost weight, she was frequently sick and it wasn't long before she couldn't get out of bed."

"Are you certain she didn't contract an illness – a disease – of some sort?"

"It was only after Miss Morris – that was the governess's name before she married Papa – took to visiting her that she became so very ill. Of course Mama had seen Miss Morris often to talk about my sisters' progress in the schoolroom, but, when she began to be ill, she was there at least once a day. That was when she administered the poison."

"So she began to be unwell before you thought she was being poisoned? What form did the illness take?"

"Oh, it was perfectly usual. She was a little bit sick – indeed I thought – being older than my sisters – that perhaps she was expecting again. Letty was more than a year old when it started. But then she grew so much worse."

Mr Bodley nodded. "It must have been very distressing. How did your papa take it? I assume he called the doctor?"

"Yes. He seemed – I don't know – at first I didn't think he was very interested. I mean, I think he thought she was expecting again. She was always sick at first and often spent the first few months in bed. But then," her eyes became hard and angry, "Papa spent more and more time with Miss Morris and – poor Mama – I'm certain she knew what was going on because people – servants – always talk, don't they?"

Mr Bodley had only one servant so that this helpful and hard-working person had no one, at least not within his own household, to whom she could have talked, but he nodded for it seemed to him very likely that the servants would talk amongst themselves.

"Do you know which one told her?" he asked.

"No, of course I don't, but it was most likely her dresser. She was the one who was closest to her. But everyone knew Papa was carrying on with Miss Morris. I thought Mama was being poisoned all along but, when Papa married the harpy barely six months after poor Mama's death, I knew for certain."

"How long have they been married?" he asked.

"Four months – you see, it's not even a year since Mama died – and the witch is already expecting. I think she was before Mama died and that was why they got married so quickly – and why Mama had to die."

"Do you think your father knew about it?" he asked.

"What do you mean? Knew she was expecting or knew Mama was being poisoned?"

"Both."

"Of course he knew she was expecting – I'm sure she must have told him even before she was quite certain herself because it made Papa very impatient to get the ring on her finger – just in case the baby should be a boy, you see."

She paused and Mr Bodley waited for her to answer the second part of the question. She did, eventually.

"Yes, I think he did know – and perhaps he even helped her, because, you see, he wants a son and Mama didn't seem to be able to give him one."

"That's a very serious accusation," Mr Bodley said gravely.

"I know it is! Do you think I want my father to turn out to be a murderer? But I don't think it's fair that poor Mama was killed just because he wanted a son. And why did he have to marry that horrid governess? If he had to marry again, why couldn't he have married a person of the same rank? It's horrid, horrid, to have that person lording it over us!"

Her voice reached such a high note on the second 'horrid' that it hurt Mr Bodley's ears.

"Have you," he asked, deciding to move slightly sideways in his interrogation, "spoken to the doctor about your suspicions?"

"I asked him what Mama died from. He said it was something inside which had made her so very ill and that there wasn't anything to be done about it. I asked him when she was first ill and he said that she must have eaten something which disagreed with her. But later, when she didn't get better, when she got worse, that was when he said he thought there was something amiss inside."

He nodded and, thinking that her grief had made her search for someone to blame for her mother's untimely death – and that the too-swift remarriage of her father to the governess had added fuel to her suspicions – said gently that he would look into the matter.

110

"Will you? What will you do?" she asked eagerly, her face suddenly brightening.

"You must leave that to me," he said firmly, wondering how he was to get rid of her.

For a few moments they sat staring at each other until she jumped up from her chair.

"Thank you!" she cried.

"I'll ring for Perkins to show you out," he said awkwardly, unsure whether, as a guest in this grand house, he was allowed to do such a thing.

"Thank you so much!" she said again when Perkins arrived in answer to the bell.

Chapter 14

Lady Amberstone arrived later that afternoon and was greeted with joy by the entire household.

More tea was ordered and served in the drawing room where the conversation was, at least at first, taken up with the Marchioness recounting the various obstacles which had presented themselves during her journey and been, eventually, overcome. Indeed, it was not until after dinner that the abrupt end to the Boxing Day hunt was mentioned.

"Oh dear!" the old lady said. "And is the girl expected to recover entirely?"

"I believe so," her nephew responded.

"Well, that's good," she said cheerfully.

"Her sister cast a further blight upon the situation by claiming, in an exceedingly loud voice, that her stepmother had killed her mother – and had meant to kill *her*, not Veronica," Titania informed her.

"Oh! Is there any truth in that, do you think? Have we lit upon a suspicious death again?" Lady Amberstone spoke in a half-humorous tone, clearly not taking the matter very seriously.

It was Mr Bodley who answered this time.

"She came to see me earlier today," he explained, "and reiterated her accusation. She insisted that it was the stepmother who had caused the accident to her sister, mistaking her for herself, Miss Thetford, because she was wearing her old riding habit."

"Oh dear!" the Marchioness repeated, a little less lightly. "Did you think there was any likelihood of her being right?"

"I don't know," he admitted. "I was – am – inclined to think she is simply refining upon her sense of loss of her mother and, having decided to blame the stepmother, is seeking something else with which to blame her."

"Perfectly possible, I suppose, but it seems rather a drastic line to take. What do you think, Tania? I suppose you know the Thetfords."

"Not very well; Julia, Miss Thetford, is some years younger than I – and, as she is the eldest, I have not had a lot to do with any of them."

"No. Have they no sons of your age?"

"No," Titania retorted, blushing. "I wish you would all stop trying to marry me off."

"Well, my dear, I think we're bound to, you know. No sons: is that why the stepmother wanted to take her mother's place – or I suppose I should say why the father was prepared to countenance it? What is the stepmother like?"

"She was the governess," Jenny said as though this explained everything anyone could possibly want to know.

"Well, of course that's interesting and no doubt forms some part of Miss Thetford's wish to hold her responsible, but what sort of a person is she?" Lady Amberstone persisted.

"I haven't spoken to her much," Jenny returned. "She seemed quite dull, to tell you the truth. I remember the first Lady Thetford though from when I was growing up. She was a gentle woman and not, so far as I recall, ever very strong. She had four daughters, but they're fairly well spread out because she had a number of false starts or losses as well. Miss Thetford is something over twenty but the youngest is not yet three."

"Oh, is that what she died from – the birth?"

"I suppose it might have been, but, if so, it was somewhat delayed. The child was two when she faded away."

"But she was not very interesting either?" Lady Amberstone pursued.

"I suppose not. What are you getting at?"

"If the old one was dull and the new one is dull too, one can only suppose that Thetford prefers them dull – and that, to my mind, makes it less likely that he did away with the first one. I mean, why kill a dull woman only to marry another dull one?"

"Because she might have given him a son," her nephew reminded her.

"Oh, yes, of course. So who is his heir at present?"

"I've no idea."

"Hmn. Are there any old ladies in that household to whom I might be able to gossip?"

"Not so far as I know – or at least there's a terrifying old nanny, who revived the apparently dead girl by flinging herself upon her and shaking her vigorously. I was present when that happened," her nephew told her with a degree of pride.

"Good lord! Was Miss Thetford there too?"

"No."

"Very well." The old lady fell silent for a few minutes while Jenny refilled everyone's teacups.

"Anyone else new in the neighbourhood?"

"No – or rather, yes, there's a new curate – a distant connexion of ours, apparently," Jenny told her. "He's rather charming as a matter of fact."

"Married?"

"No."

"NO!" Titania exclaimed as her aunt's eye alighted upon her.

"How long's he been here?" the old lady asked, amused.

"A few months. He's a Stapleton," Rushlake told her. "They've got dozens of sons and no money so, hearing he was looking for a curacy, I offered him one."

"Very kind. So he – and his family – have a superfluity of sons and no money while the Thetfords have a number of daughters. Have they any money?"

"I should think so," Rushlake said. "Their estate looks well run, they're all expensively dressed and Miss Thetford looks down on almost everyone."

"Does she? Not, I presume, on you?"

"No."

"Hmn," the old lady said again and fell silent, leaving everyone to draw their own conclusions.

Since it was more or less time to change for dinner, the subject was allowed to lapse and the family soon dispersed to their own chambers.

After dinner, all three unmarried women were ordered to play or sing – or perform in some way to entertain everyone else. It did not occur to the old woman to ask Saffy to do so but Titania insisted she sing and offered to accompany her herself.

"Were you used to perform together when you lived here before – just the two of you?" the Marchioness asked curiously when everyone had done their duty.

"No. There wasn't anyone to make us do so, you see," Titania reminded her.

"So you practised on your own and Saffy – what did you do, Saffy?"

"I – well, I was Titania's companion so I did as I was bid," Saffy said, rather embarrassed.

"You have a delightful voice. I much enjoyed your performance."

"Thank you, my lady."

"What did you think of Miss Thetford's confidences?" Helena asked Mr Bodley.

"This time I didn't think she was simply retailing them for effect," he said slowly. "After all, she'd taken the trouble to come here and ask to speak to me. I'm convinced she believes them. But whether there is anything to be investigated I'm not sure."

"Isn't one of the younger daughters of a similar age to one of yours?" Lady Amberstone asked Jenny.

"Probably, yes," Jenny said warily.

"Perhaps we could invite them for tea?" Lady Amberstone suggested.

"If you're thinking of involving my children in a spot of surreptitious investigation, the answer's no," Jenny said at once.

"I understand your reluctance," Titania said, "but the children are fairly longing to find some friends. I think one of the Thetfords is exactly the same age as Clara and the one who was hurt, Veronica, isn't much older than Aspasia."

"No," Jenny repeated. "Last time you all interfered in a similar matter people got hurt."

"I'm not suggesting we get the children to ask questions," Titania said. "But, while they're chattering to each other, we can grill the grown-ups – and in any event the point would be to become a little better acquainted with the whole family. Do you think, Horace, that our distant cousin might be interested in Julia?"

"Isn't he interested in you?" her brother asked.

"He does seem to be, but I don't suppose it would be difficult to divert him to Julia, particularly if she has a reasonably-sized portion."

Titania, as she spoke, realised that she would not like it at all if Marcus Stapleton were to be 'diverted' to Julia Thetford with any degree of success; indeed, her suggestion was made more in the spirit of defence than intention. She was intelligent enough to know that her, or perhaps to a lesser degree Julia's, fortune must surely be the most attractive attribute either of them possessed. The curate was short of money and she did not doubt that he would make his looks and charm work for him to the best effect he could. To her shame, she knew that she would be perfectly prepared to take him on those terms. He must make the best use he could of his attributes, she of hers – and hers was her fortune.

"You're turning out just like your Aunt Mildred," her brother said teasingly, not knowing how engaged his sister's affections were already. "You seem determined to make matches."

"I'm trying to think of a way to sidle up to the Thetfords," she said lightly, sighed, and added, "I'll just have to call upon them, as a concerned neighbour, and enquire after Veronica, I suppose."

As luck would have it, Titania met Mr Stapleton on the road close to the Thetford residence the next morning. He was also upon a horse and greeted her with pleasure.

"I hope you're not going to be running back to London too soon. It would be delightful if you could stay in Shropshire for some time," he said.

"It's very pleasant here," she agreed. "I'm not sure how long we'll be staying – or indeed whether I'll go back with my sister in any event. I should think she must be quite tired of me by now."

"I find that hard to believe," he returned gallantly.

She shot him a rather scornful glance which made him smile all the more at her.

"How are you finding life in Rushlake?" she asked lightly.

"Oh, it is not so very different from Derbyshire," he replied. "But I own I miss Oxford."

"Perhaps the country doesn't suit you. There must have been a great deal more to do in Oxford."

"There was," he admitted. "It was very kind of your brother to offer me a place here – and I'm extremely grateful – but I do miss the bright lights of a city."

"Well, I daresay something will come up and you'll be able to move in a little while," she said brightly.

"Do you ever go to the Assembly Rooms?" he asked.

"I did occasionally when I lived here all the time, but I don't think I'd find them very amusing now, after having spent time in London."

"I suppose you used to meet Vincent Lovatt there," he said wistfully.

"Yes. I've known him all my life though, so it wasn't all that exciting to stand up with him."

"Would you stand up with me if we went one evening?" he asked.

"I expect so – if you asked me. I daresay," she added unwisely, "that if we stay here for some time, Horace will invite a few people over for a dance one evening. Would you come to that?"

"I would be delighted."

Having settled this to his apparent delight, she was filled with anxiety as she realised that she would be obliged to ask her brother to arrange an evening of dancing purely in order to fulfil her impetuous invitation. They rode on in silence for a little way.

"I suppose you're calling upon Miss Thetford," he said as the house came into view and they turned into the drive.

"No, I was intending merely to enquire how Veronica did. Have you any news on that front?"

"I believe she's recovering well. It's quite extraordinary when you think how – how everyone had despaired of her."

"Positively miraculous," she said. "God must have been listening to our prayers," she added rather facetiously.

"He always listens," he returned with a sort of *faux* unctuousness. "But He only does what we ask if He thinks it right."

"Yes, of course. Do you think He has plans for her future which He didn't want to change?"

"We cannot know what His plans are," he told her, still in a tone which struck her as a trifle artificial.

"Of course not!" she returned a little tartly, "but I should think He looked down, saw her innocent face and took pity upon her."

"The interesting thing about the dead is that they always look innocent, even when they're quite old," he told her. "That was one of the first things I noticed – in my job I see a good many dead people – and it was one which struck me."

"I suppose God has already wiped them clean of sin," she suggested, still teasing.

"Are you always so flippant on serious subjects?" he asked, amused.

"Probably. The thing is – with serious subjects – that they can pull one down a little if one takes them too much at face value. I suppose, in your job, you find such an attitude quite shocking."

"Not at all, but I wonder if you react in that way in order to avoid the natural distress you might otherwise feel."

"Very likely. I'm not close to any of the Thetfords, as you must know, but I own I *did* feel distressed when I thought that poor girl might be dead."

"Of course; it's natural that you should."

Arriving at the front door, it opened before they had dismounted and, upon seeing who it was, was pulled wider and someone inside was issued instructions, presumably to arrange for someone to take the horses.

Mr Stapleton dismounted and went to assist Titania so that they were welcomed into the house quite as though they had been a couple.

"I came to enquire after Miss Veronica," Titania said to the butler.

"She is on the mend, my lady," he replied. "Would you both like to come in and wait while I ascertain whether Miss Thetford is able to receive you."

"Thank you," Titania replied, allowing herself to be shown into a small sitting room, still alongside the curate.

"They seem convinced we came together," he said as the door was shut upon them.

"Yes. Whom are you hoping to see?" she asked.

117

"Like you, I came without an invitation to enquire after the family. I shall be happy to see Miss Thetford – or anyone else who can spare the time to speak to me."

"I'll leave you to do so," she said, "but, for myself, I believe I shall try to obtain permission to visit Veronica and ascertain for myself that she is recovering."

They did not have long to wait before Miss Thetford came into the room. She looked, Titania thought, so confident that she might have been the *châtelaine* herself. The greeting which she extended to the curate was charm itself, while her reception of Titania was a little more guarded.

"Paying calls together?" she enquired, arching her brows.

"We met on the road – by chance," Marcus Stapleton said. "We had both had a similar thought."

"Well, fancy that! Have you come to enquire about my sister?"

"Yes," Titania replied. "Is she well enough to receive visitors – for a very short time, you understand? I wouldn't want to tire her."

"Oh, I'm sure she'd be delighted," Miss Thetford replied at once, more, Titania suspected, in order to be rid of her while she entertained Mr Stapleton by herself than because she truly thought her sister would welcome a visit from a previously unfriendly neighbour.

"Will you wait while I take Lady Titania upstairs?" she asked the curate.

"Certainly. There is no hurry – pray take your time," he replied as what seemed to Titania to be a conspiratorial look passed between them.

Miss Thetford led the way out of the sitting room, up the stairs and along a corridor without speaking and Titania obediently followed her. At last they came to what she assumed must be the right door, amongst a line of identical ones. The older sister knocked upon it and, without waiting for an answer, led the uninvited guest inside.

Veronica Thetford was reclining upon a daybed in the window. She was alone and was holding a small leatherbound book in her hand. As the door opened, she looked up, directed a rather vague and not particularly warm smile at her sister before her glance moved on to the visitor behind.

"Lady Titania rode over to enquire after your health, Ronnie, and most particularly wished to see for her own eyes that you're recovering."

"Oh, how very kind," the younger girl said. "Pray come in, my lady."

Chapter 15

Titania, rather thrown to be addressed in such a formal manner, smiled and advanced upon the convalescent, whose slender form was draped in a rug and whose shoulders were wrapped in a soft shawl.

"I should have brought you some flowers or something," she said apologetically.

"No; why should you have done that? It's winter – there won't be any!"

"I'll leave you together," Miss Thetford said, whisking herself out of the room and presumably down the stairs to attend to her other, more desirable, visitor.

Titania approached the day bed and, at a gesture from her hostess, drew up a chair and sat down.

"I hope you're feeling better," she said.

"Oh, yes, thank you. The only difficulty is that I don't seem to be able to walk," the convalescent replied. "Dr Marvel tells me the sensation will return to my legs eventually, but I own I'm growing a little worried. Do you think he's just trying to comfort me?"

"I don't know; I'm sure he wouldn't say that if he didn't think it," Titania replied awkwardly.

"No. I don't like to complain, for I realise I'm very lucky to be alive, but it's excessively boring lying here all the time."

"Yes, it must be. Does your family come up and sit with you sometimes?"

It did not look to Titania as if they did. Veronica lay with a small table beside her on which was placed a candle, some matches, a carafe of water together with a glass and a small hand bell. She looked like a romantic painting, but Titania thought that looking like a painting all by oneself would not be a happy situation. She had laid the book she had been reading beside her, but on the pale face and in the luminous eyes lurked a shadow which, to Titania, not generally a person who thought much about how anyone entertained themselves without being able to walk and ride for a large portion of the day, spoke of a deep sadness – and indeed loneliness.

"Oh, yes, of course they do. They come when they can spare the time. Papa comes every evening and Nanny comes when she has got the children to bed."

"And Julia? I'm sure she must visit you frequently?"

"Yes, of course." But poor Veronica did not specify a time when her elder sister sat with her and Titania thought she looked unhappy.

"Is there anything I can do for you?" Titania asked.

"It's very kind of you to ask but, no, I don't think there is. I can, after all, always ring the bell and request whatever I need – as it were."

"Yes. Has Mr Stapleton visited you – or the Vicar?"

"The Vicar has but I've not seen Marcus. He's your kinsman, isn't he?"

"I believe so, but pray don't ask for the precise connexion for I don't know it! As a matter of fact, I met him as I was riding just now. I left him downstairs talking to Julia."

The girl nodded and, for a moment, her face brightened but she did not comment.

"Are you much acquainted with him – with Marcus?" Titania asked, noting that the patient had called the curate by his Christian name.

"Not really, no; that is to say, we have of course seen him around the village – and indeed Julia has met him at the Assembly Rooms – but he – he hasn't been here long and we haven't got to know him particularly well."

"No," Titania said and, searching in her mind for a subject on which she could engage the girl in a more meaningful manner, added, "He confided he missed the bright lights of Oxford so I daresay he does like to visit the Assembly Rooms."

Veronica smiled fleetingly. "I believe he's met Julia there on several occasions; I am – was – too young to go there, but, now, there wouldn't be much point, would there?"

"You mean because you can't dance at present?"

"Yes. I'll probably never be able to dance again. I don't think Dr Marvel thinks that I'll ever regain the use of my legs."

"I thought you said that he believed you would – eventually. What makes you think he doesn't in fact believe this?"

"I don't think he dared tell me. You know, what he said about sensation eventually returning, I think that was just him wishing to make me feel better. It doesn't, particularly as he apparently told Julia that he didn't think I'd ever walk again."

"Did she tell you that?"

"Yes – and, awful as it is, I'm grateful for her honesty."

Titania, who was by no means convinced that it was honesty rather than spite which had prompted Miss Thetford's remark, said, "Doctors aren't always right, you know. You mustn't despair. Can you stand?"

"No; I have no sensation in my legs. It's as though they belong to someone else. It's very odd to touch them, you know, to feel the flesh but not recognise it as my own."

Titania nodded. She was not accustomed to visiting the sick or to listening to anyone's woes. Being the youngest, apart from Horace, who was different because he was male, she had always laboured under a cloud of resentment that everyone else seemed to be not only more important than she was, but also to have the ability to make others feel better. *She* was always an irritant and powerless to influence anyone in a positive way.

Since she had been grown up and before she went to London, she had lived with Aunt Saffy who had always shown sympathy whenever Titania had claimed to have the headache or to be suffering from a cold in the head – or indeed bruises from falling off her horse – but she had never enquired how the older woman did – or indeed ever thought about how she might feel. Now, sitting beside this girl, younger than she and a gentle, sweet creature, cut down, damaged apparently beyond repair, she felt the first stirrings of pity as well as a powerful desire to help.

"How does it feel if someone else touches you?" she asked.

"I can't feel anything. I can only tell someone's touching me by watching what they're doing. Sometimes," she went on, suddenly becoming animated in a most distressing manner, "I feel like cutting them off. Do you think I'd feel that – if I sawed through the bone?"

"I don't know, but I don't think that would help. You certainly wouldn't be able to walk if you cut off your legs – and you might if you leave them alone. Has the doctor prescribed any exercises?"

"I can't do exercises when I can't move them!" the girl almost shouted at her.

"No, no of course not, but I wondered – forgive me, I'm very ignorant and stupid – if perhaps someone else – a maid – Nanny – could help by moving your legs for you - or something of that sort."

"I don't see how that would help. My arms still work," she added, trying to demonstrate a more positive attitude.

"Have you been outside? Would you like me to take you for a drive one day?"

The girl's face lit up so brightly at this suggestion that Titania had to blink to hold back her tears. It seemed that, for the first time in her life, she had had a positive effect upon another.

"Oh, I would love that! Would you – could you do that?"

"Of course I could. Shall I come tomorrow? It's quite cold outside but, if you were well wrapped up and perhaps provided with a hot brick, I think you'd be all right. We don't have to be out for long but it would give you something else to look at for a little while."

This suggestion seemed to break the ice between them and, looking round the room for some other entertainment, Titania suggested playing a game of cards.

"Oh, yes, I'd like that too – but there aren't any cards here."

"I can bring some next time I come. But, first, shall we go out tomorrow?"

"Yes, oh yes, I should like that so much."

The two young women concentrated upon arranging a suitable time for Titania to arrive in a small carriage to take the other for a ride.

"I'll bring a groom with me," she said, "just in case we need any help. In any event, he can carry you down if there isn't anyone suitable to do so here."

"We have enough servants," Veronica said, "although they don't seem to do much. Whom should I ask to bring me down?"

"I suppose," Titania said hesitatingly, "that you should probably seek permission to go out. I mean, you're not well and perhaps it wouldn't be as good for you as I think it would. In any event, you're not very old, are you, so I suppose you're not allowed to go out by yourself?"

"I'll ask Nanny. Shall we ask her now?"

Titania agreeing to this, Veronica rang the bell and asked the maid who answered to fetch Nanny.

The old woman bustled in and exclaimed with surprise when she saw Titania.

"My Lady Titania, isn't it?" she asked.

"Yes; how do you do, Nanny?"

"*I'm* very well, but poor Miss Veronica here isn't at all well. She can't use her legs at the moment, you see."

"No, she was telling me about it. I thought it might cheer her up a little if I took her for a drive tomorrow – I'll make sure I bring enough rugs as well as a hot brick – but do you think that would be all right?"

"Oh yes!" Nanny said at once. "She was used, Miss Veronica, to be so keen on riding and being out of doors, I should think it would do her a power of good."

"Oh, that's excellent."

When Titania went downstairs she found the curate still being entertained by Miss Thetford. The butler, meeting her in the hall whither Nanny had escorted her, informed her that the pair were drinking coffee in the small drawing room.

Titania, wondering whether the butler thought her arrival with the curate indicated that they had been on an outing together, allowed herself to be shown into the room where the pair were sitting deep in conversation over the coffee cups.

She did not think that Miss Thetford looked particularly pleased to see her; indeed, the face that had been rosy with pleasure when the door had first opened became red with annoyance.

"Oh, Titania!" she exclaimed.

"Julia! I've just been talking to your poor sister."

"Yes. Marcus explained that you'd come to visit her – and that you met outside."

"We did indeed. I wonder," she went on, putting her head thoughtfully on one side as she gazed upon the pair, "whether you might like to drop in on her, Marcus, while Julia and I have a little cose together?"

The curate, looking as guilty as if he had been caught with his hand in the collection box, jumped up at once.

"I would very much like to see her," he said, "but was not certain she was well enough to receive visitors."

"Well, I may of course have tired her with my visit," Titania said, "but I believe she would like to speak to you."

"Did she say so?" Julia Thetford asked sharply.

"No, not that I can recall. I just thought it would be an opportunity for you to enquire after her health, Marcus. We can ride home together – or at least down the drive – when you're ready to leave."

Having thus demonstrated an unnerving resemblance to her Aunt Mildred, Titania watched coolly as the curate turned to Miss Thetford and, taking her hand, bid her *adieu* before leaving the room.

"Would you like some coffee?" Miss Thetford asked ungraciously but correctly when he had gone.

"Oh, I would, but I don't suppose he'll be long, will he?"

"Long enough for you to drink some coffee, I suppose," Julia returned, ringing the bell.

"I didn't know you were close to my sister," she went on when the order had been given and Titania had seated herself in a chair opposite her reluctant hostess.

"I'm not, particularly; she's a great deal younger than I – as are you – but I've been thinking about her so much recently that I determined to pay her a visit. It's my belief, you see, that when one is incapacitated, one is always pleased to receive visitors, even those to whom one is not particularly close."

123

"Yes, of course; how thoughtful of you! Do you think she'll enjoy speaking to Marcus?"

"Oh, I'm sure she will; he's so very charming – and handsome – isn't he?" Titania asked with a guileless air which drew a deep blush from her hostess.

"Is he a cousin of yours?"

"I believe so – but, if you were to ask me to show you how we're related on a family tree, I'm afraid I'd fail dismally. Have you become quite good friends with him since he came here?"

"I don't know that I would quite describe us as 'friends'", Julia said, trying to imply that 'friendship' was not what either party sought. "I mean, he's usually awfully busy and – well, I don't think Papa would like me to claim friendship with him precisely."

"Why not? His pedigree is unexceptionable, so far as I know."

"Oh, not because of that; if he's related to you, I'm sure *that* aspect must be above suspicion, but Papa is very careful about his daughters spending any time with young men."

"Oh, I see. Yes, of course. And what about your stepmama? Does she try to prevent you conversing with a young man by yourself?"

"She's horrid!" Julia exclaimed, suddenly abandoning her hostess expression and flushing with anger.

"I'm sorry to hear that," Titania said. She was not the sort of young woman who had ever spent a great deal of time with others of her age and sex and was not therefore in the habit of discovering things by means of gossip. She had, however, since going to London and spending time in her older sister's company, learned a good deal about the way women ran their lives – and frequently other people's.

"I," she went on confidingly, "was lucky enough never to have a stepmama. Papa didn't marry again."

"It's not just that Papa's married again but that he did so with such improper haste!" Julia exclaimed. "And the governess!"

"Yes, that must have been distressing. Did she ever teach you?"

"No; she came after I'd left the schoolroom. She's taught Veronica and of course Mary as well. I'm sure," Julia leaned forward, "that she meant to unseat poor Ronnie, although it's my firm belief she thought she was tripping up my horse, not Ronnie's."

"Why do you think she did that?"

"Because she knows I know she killed Mama and she wants to kill me before I can tell anyone!"

Titania frowned and, trying to think of a way to frame her next question, allowed her mouth to fall open.

"That's awful!" she said at last. "Are you sure?"

"Of course I'm sure! I wouldn't say so otherwise."

"How did she do it? And do you think your father knew – knows?"

"Yes, I'm sure he was in on the plot to kill Mama, but I don't think he meant – thought – she'd try to kill me! I went to see that detective you've got staying with you earlier this morning. I told him."

Titania nodded.

"Is he going to investigate?"

"I don't know. I'm not sure he believed me. I mean I think he thought I was hysterical, although I wasn't, I was quite calm. But I don't see why she should get away with it."

"No, indeed. How do you think she did it?"

"She poisoned Mama – over several weeks. Mama was perfectly well after the baby was born – perfectly well. She got up, she was doing everything she'd always done – and then suddenly she got ill. She kept being sick and she got weaker and weaker. It was horrible to watch."

"It must have been. What did the doctor say?"

"He thought she must have been ill before – you know, with something horrid inside – and, after the baby was born, it got worse. He said that sometimes happens. It's my belief that sort of thing happens when a woman has had another girl – and there aren't any boys in the family."

Chapter 16

"Have you – did you mention your suspicions to your father?" Titania asked, aware that Miss Thetford had in fact accused him of assisting the governess's dastardly actions.

"Yes, I did! I – he was very angry. He said I was imagining it. I told him I knew he'd been – been passing the time with her – but that, although that was shocking, especially when poor Mama was so ill, he had much better send her away now because people would undoubtedly draw the most horrible conclusions. Didn't you know about the rumours?"

"No; I've been in London for some time."

"Not that long! Mama died before you left."

"Yes, I know that now but - I'm sorry – I went to London very suddenly. Horace came down – he hadn't been for a very long time – and suggested I go to London – and so I did. I believe your mother died just before I went and – well, I'm sorry, I would have called if I'd been here."

Caught on the back foot, Titania felt uncomfortable because, in truth, she had heard that Lady Thetford had died but, the two families never having been particularly close, she had not considered how important the Thetfords would rate the attendance at her funeral of at least one of the Rushlakes. Horace, if he had known, would most likely have insisted they delay their departure to London until after the obsequies; he was punctilious in such matters but, having travelled to Rushlake on a whim, he had not enquired closely into recent events in the village.

She also wondered whether, if they had been aware of the rumours at the time, it might not have been better to have remained in the country and investigated this case rather than dashing back to London to look into the mysterious death of a man none of them had known.

"Nobody thought there was anything in it at first," Julia admitted. "But then they didn't knew how Papa and Miss Morris had been behaving."

"No, of course not. Did Veronica know?"

"I didn't discuss it with her; I thought she was too young," Miss Thetford said. "But I'm sure she must have noticed. And then they got married almost at once! Everyone noticed that and they all assumed she was already expecting."

"But wouldn't it – I mean that was some time ago now – be showing by now if she had been?"

"I should have thought so, but I wouldn't be surprised if she hadn't lied – you know, told Papa she was expecting so that he would be desperately keen to marry her before the baby was born in case it was a boy. I don't know if she is now; I did think so, but it seems awfully unwise to have gone hunting in her condition – I wouldn't have thought Papa would have permitted it."

"Perhaps he tried and failed to stop her," Titania said. From what she had seen of the Viscount and his wife, she was convinced that the woman made the decisions and her husband was forced to go along with whatever she decided. Also, although he was no doubt keen to ensure the birth of a living boy, she had already achieved what she wanted – the title 'Viscountess'.

Miss Thetford clearly had the same opinion of the balance of power between her father and her stepmother, for she said, "I don't think she's much inclined to obey him now she's got the ring on her finger."

"No," Titania said weakly, wishing she were anywhere but facing Miss Thetford's bitter face.

"Of course he might have to kill her too if she doesn't provide him with a son!"

Titania, thinking that the identity of her mother's murderer seemed to fluctuate alarmingly in Miss Thetford's mind, asked, "Do you – was she an agreeable governess?"

"She didn't teach me!"

"No, I know, but do your sisters – did your sisters - like her when she wasn't their stepmama?"

"I don't think they *dis*liked her, but she was always trying to flirt with Papa – and I didn't like that – especially when Mama was still alive."

"No, of course not."

"Do you think Marcus is still upstairs with Ronnie?" Julia suddenly asked as another of her anxieties came to the surface.

"I don't know."

"But wasn't he going to accompany you home?"

"Oh, yes, I did suggest that – but I daresay he's forgotten." While talking to, and listening to, Miss Thetford, Titania's new *tendre* for her distant cousin had faded from her mind – or perhaps, unlike her hostess, she was not so ready to find cause for jealousy in every glance, pause or reference.

"Do you think he might have?" Julia asked, beginning to look hopeful that at least one of her potential rivals might not, in fact, prove to be one.

"Very likely. He said good-bye to you, didn't he, so I daresay he wasn't really intending to wait for me. I think I should go now, but would you like me to ask Horace what he thinks about – about what you've told me?"

Miss Thetford flushed, this time, Titania was convinced, with pleasure.

"Would you mind?"

"Not in the least."

Titania rose and said, "Thank you for the coffee."

Miss Thetford, rising too, said with something of a yearning tone, "Will you come again?"

"Of course, if you would like me to. I'm coming tomorrow in any event to take Veronica for a drive."

"May I come too?"

"Yes, of course," Titania said, rather taken aback and not particularly pleased. She did not find Julia's company altogether pleasing and she did like the wan Veronica. It seemed to her that the elder sister made a point of always looking on the bleakest side of any question while the younger strove to look upon the bright side.

A groom was waiting in front of the house with her horse and her kinsman was pacing up and down nearby.

Once she was mounted, he joined her and together they made their way down the drive.

"You've been a very long time," he said. "Did you find Miss Thetford's conversation riveting?"

She frowned at him. "I suppose it was," she said after a pause. "Did you find Veronica tired?"

"Yes. I felt sorry for her," he admitted in a gruff tone.

"Yes, I did too. I'm going to take her for a drive tomorrow. Foolishly, I mentioned it to Julia and she's coming too."

He laughed. "May I come as well?"

"Good lord! We'll need a bigger carriage if there are to be four of us."

"Would you prefer it if I did not?"

"No. You can drive if you like and we'll sit in the back and gossip."

"Won't Veronica have to lie down?"

"I don't see why; she was more or less sitting up on the day bed, but she'll have to be lifted in and out and provided with enough cushions and rugs and so forth to be comfortable."

"I can do that. You won't need to bring a groom if I come."

They had reached the place where their ways parted and, with a smile and a nod, they separated and Titania continued towards her ancestral home.

As she rode, she thought about what had just passed and the three people with whom she was intending to spend the following morning. She was not sure whether Marcus Stapleton was pursuing her or Julia Thetford. She had not missed Julia's look of annoyance when she heard that Marcus and she had ridden up together or her fear of them spending another large slice of time alone together as they rode back. She suspected the other young woman had fallen victim to the curate's undoubted charm, but then she did not doubt that she was also, presumably much more, interested in Horace. The Earl was slightly older than his kinsman and an infinitely better catch. Julia, she thought, might take a good deal of pleasure from being in the company of the curate, but she would surely prefer to receive an offer from the Earl.

As for her, Titania, she did find Marcus exceedingly attractive, particularly when she was in his company. She had forgotten about him while at the Thetfords, but had felt the same almost irresistible tug towards him during their ride back.

Her only other close male acquaintance in Shropshire was Lord Vincent Lovatt, but she did not think he was a suitor. She wondered if Julia was interested in him. The Thetfords were well enough off and it seemed likely that she would receive a reasonable marriage settlement but it would not be much in comparison to what Titania knew would be hers. She suddenly found herself wondering if Lord Vincent had noticed that Julia Thetford had blossomed, at least in appearance, in the last couple of years. There might not even be so much to deplore in her character if one knew her well, as no doubt he did. It was her manner, which struck most people as a little too abrasive, that put one off, but then this was a fault that she knew afflicted her as well. Did growing up in this out-of-the-way place lead to women developing sharp tongues? Would even the sweet Veronica acquire one as she grew older?

And what of Julia's disturbing accusations? Had the governess poisoned the first Lady Thetford, and had her father connived at the killing – or even suggested it – and had someone tried to kill Veronica or – surely far more likely as she herself had suggested – Julia herself?

Handing her horse to the groom at the stables, she ordered a carriage to be made ready for the following morning's drive and went inside.

She ran into her brother in the hall.

"Where've you been all day?" he enquired. "Well, in point of fact, I don't need to ask, do I?" he added, observing her riding habit.

"I went to visit Veronica Thetford," she said, according him a rather smug smile so that he might judge her outing as compassionate rather than selfish.

"Did you? How did you find her?"

"She is the sweetest girl," she said. "She is recovering in the sense that she seems to be in full possession of her wits, but she cannot walk. Oh,

Horace, she cannot feel her legs – it's as though they belong to someone else! Is that not terrible?"

"Terrible indeed," he agreed.

"I have arranged to take her for a drive tomorrow morning," she confessed.

"That's a very kind idea," he said approvingly.

"Yes, but unfortunately both her sister, Julia, and Marcus Stapleton are insisting on coming too!"

He laughed. "Well, it will make a nice little outing. Is Marcus coming on your account or Julia's, do you think?"

"Julia's, I assume. Would you be disappointed if she chose him?"

"Good lord, no! I own I don't particularly take to Julia Thetford – she has a sharp manner and a discontented expression. Would you like me to come too to see if she prefers me – and leave him for you?"

"Heavens, no! You'd spoil everything!"

"Why?"

"Well, to begin with there wouldn't be room in the carriage and then, of course she'll set her cap at you, which may make him look more closely at me, but I would infinitely prefer not to be chosen *faute de mieux.*"

"But is she simply comparing bank balances or has she fallen in love with him?"

"Perhaps she has, but it's my belief that if she'd fallen in love she'd be thinking about that and not refining upon whether the governess or her father or both of them killed her mother – and tried to kill her, unfortunately mistaking Veronica for her."

"Did she speak of that?"

"Oh yes. We began by my going up to sit with Veronica and she entertaining Marcus, whom I'd met as I rode towards the house; then we swapped and he went upstairs and I went down. Do you think there's anything in it?"

The Earl had by this time steered his sister into the library where they could speak without being overheard.

"It seems a little far-fetched, but it's true that Thetford has married again exceedingly quickly – and a bride whom most of Society would consider wholly unsuitable – so that there's bound to be gossip."

"What did Adrian Bodley think?"

"I think he rather wishes he hadn't come!"

She smiled.

"Isn't he getting anywhere with Helena?"

"I don't know, but if he feels obliged to look into an old murder and a new attempted murder he won't have time to concentrate upon her."

None of this was mentioned again until after dinner when everyone reached the drawing room, the three men joining the ladies after an unusually short interval.

Mr Bodley chose to sit next to Titania, a move which, until she understood the reason, made Helena look a trifle miffed.

"We were talking about Miss Thetford's accusations," he said, "and, before I interfere in any way, I rather wanted your opinion."

"Really?" she asked, surprised. No one had ever sought her opinion on any subject before except perhaps horses.

"Yes; you saw Miss Thetford earlier and his lordship tells me she confided her suspicions to you too."

"She did, although not in a manner which seemed particularly confidential," she returned.

"Did you think there was likely to be any truth in what she said?"

Titania frowned in an effort of concentration, and then she said, "I wonder if perhaps we should be looking more closely at poor Veronica's accident. What I mean is, if someone did cause it with the intention of killing her – and if that person had in fact mistaken her for Julia – one has to ask why someone wanted Julia dead. And the answer to that is presumably that Julia had been making apparently wild and hysterical accusations about her mother's death; but perhaps they weren't so wild after all."

Mr Bodley, who had listened carefully to this somewhat confused reasoning, said, "You mean, I take it, that we shouldn't concern ourselves in the first instance with who might – just possibly – have killed the first Lady Thetford, but start at the other end of the puzzle with who might have wanted to remove Julia Thetford?"

"Yes."

Nobody else was making any pretence of talking amongst themselves as all were listening with enormous interest to what Titania and the detective were saying.

"Is – was – Veronica Thetford a good rider?" Lady Amberstone, who had never met any of the family, asked.

"I think so," Titania replied. "She is certainly very keen on it – more so than Julia, I should say. The thing is, you see, that Veronica is nearly ten years younger than I and Julia about four. Consequently, I have not met either of them when I've been out, but my impression – really based

131

on very little except that one aborted hunt on Boxing Day – is that Julia is not a particularly eager rider and would have been relatively more easily unseated than Veronica. In truth, I find it surprising that Veronica did fall, although it's a steep bank and there's a great deal of greenery in the way."

"Was there anyone who looked less shocked, less upset, than everyone else when the accident took place?" Mr Bodley asked. "I wasn't in the field where she fell," he explained to Lady Amberstone.

"I don't think most people were looking at other people's expressions," Rushlake said. "We were all too fixed upon what had happened and trying to get Veronica out of the ditch."

Mr Bodley nodded. "Who was in the field where she fell?"

"I was," Rushlake said, "I was leading the party with the Master; Titania was there too and all the Thetfords, including Lady Thetford. Were you there, Jenny?"

"No; I haven't hunted for some time and have to admit that I was a trifle nervous of getting down that bank – and James was hanging around trying to give me confidence."

"Helena was doing the same for me," Mr Bodley said. "What about the villagers?"

"About half and half, I should say," Rushlake said. "The real villagers – I mean not the gentry – were probably hanging back because they didn't want to push in front of us. Not many of us were in the lower field. As well as the Thetfords, Marcus and Lord Vincent Lovatt were there."

"Yes, but were they waiting there when Veronica fell, or did they come down at much the same time as she did?" Bodley asked.

"Ah, I see what you're getting at. The Master and I led the way and Thetford came soon after. Where was his wife, Titania? Did you notice?"

"No, not then. Several of us burst through at much the same time. In fact, that might have been how she fell – I mean it might not have been anyone prodding or tripping the horse – it might just have been that we were all jostling about and the horse got knocked. Vincent was with me – he came through at much the same time as I did. The thing is that he and I have often ridden that way and know the bank so we weren't so nervous as some people."

"But did you come through before Veronica – or after – or at the same time?" her brother asked.

Titania frowned in concentration, trying to remember the exact sequence of events at that horrid bank. Certainly, she was in the lower field when Veronica's presence in the ditch was noticed, but when had she fallen – and who was coming down the bank at the same time? Shockingly, she rather thought she had been, along with Vincent Lovatt, who had been riding neck and neck with her most of the time.

"I'm not certain," she admitted. "The whole thing – the descent, the crowd, the excitement, the dogs – we all rushed down together. I don't see that there's any way of proving – or even suspecting – that someone caused her to fall on purpose."

Mr Bodley nodded.

"It was most likely an accident," he said, "but I believe there is sufficient doubt – as well as Miss Thetford's accusations – to warrant my investigating in a low key manner.

"Shall we start by everybody here trying to remember exactly where they were when she fell? Did anybody notice the horse losing its footing?"

Chapter 17

Jenny and her husband, along with Miss Patchett, who had all been in the rear of the party and hovering about at the top of the bank, did not have anything to contribute to this. The first thing they had noticed was not the shouting, which had been going on for some time and which was not unusual at that point in the route, but female screaming.

"Did you scream, Tania?" Horace asked.

"When I saw her in the ditch? I don't think so; I was shocked, which I think rendered me silent. I didn't notice her coming down the bank at the same time as I, but several people were so that – well, I know Vincent was there because we were very close – within touching distance as we had been almost from the moment he joined us."

"When did *you* notice what had happened, my lord?" Mr Bodley asked his host quietly when the women began to explain something of the characters involved to Lady Amberstone.

"When the screaming began, I think. I was halfway across the lower field by then, along with the Master and several others. I heard it and it didn't seem to me to be the usual sort of excited yelling that is sometimes a response to scrambling down that bank. It sounded more terrible."

"Where was Lord Thetford?"

"He was with us – the Master and me."

"So he came down before Veronica?"

"Must have done, yes."

"And where was Lady Thetford?"

"She was on the same side as we were. I know that because, when Veronica fell, she was one of the first to scream."

"But you didn't see her come down?"

"No. As I say, I was the first down, closely followed by the Master, and we set off across the lower field at once."

"Were the dogs with you?"

"Yes."

"So she couldn't have tripped over a dog?"

"I don't know. The dogs more or less keep together but there are a lot of them so that there's sometimes quite a long straggle of them. They're used to horses, and used to dodging their legs, so it doesn't seem very likely that her horse tripped over one. I suppose it's possible though. I think," he added, "that you're quite right and what we need to find out is if anyone did see the fall."

"Yes, but it's difficult to know quite what to do – or how I'm to ask people because this isn't my area and in any event there's no proof – at least at present – that it was anything other than an accident."

"No. I'm afraid we'll have to pursue our preliminary enquiries in a rather underhand fashion. We can, between us, speak to everyone and see what transpires from that."

"Yes, but Miss Thetford has asked me to look into her mother's death."

"Hmn. Did you tell her that she should report the matter to the local constabulary?"

"No. I didn't altogether believe her, you see. I thought she was exaggerating due to her dislike of her stepmother – and I suppose her grief at her mother's death. The thing is that if somebody did poison the first Lady Thetford, it can't really have been anybody but the second Lady Thetford or Lord Thetford, unless there's another bitter woman lurking in the background."

"No. And who would have wanted Veronica's death other than the same stepmother, presumably because she thought Veronica knew the truth, her father, which seems very unlikely, or Miss Thetford herself?"

"Don't forget," Mr Bodley said, "that Veronica was wearing Miss Thetford's old riding habit. They're not unalike to look at, especially from behind. It seems more likely, especially in view of her accusations, that whoever caused the horse to stumble – if anyone did – thought it was Miss Thetford's."

"Yes, but there's the same narrow list of possible murderers: the stepmother, the father, the other sister or some other disgruntled female."

"Or a disgruntled lover," Mr Bodley said.

"They haven't got any lovers, have they? Veronica is sixteen – she can't possibly have any!"

Mr Bodley gave his host a strange look. He was surprised by his lordship's certainty that a girl – a very pretty one too – would not have any lovers at the age of sixteen. Girls of her rank were expected to be married by eighteen; the fact that her older sister was not – and was already over twenty – had very likely concealed the younger girl's potential for attracting suitors – or lovers.

The Earl grinned.

"That opens up the possible list of suspects – and the one at the front is Miss Thetford herself. I'm fairly sure she doesn't have any lovers – she's constantly eyeing me and I've noticed her assessing Marcus."

Mr Bodley nodded.

"So, in order to make it look as though she was the target, not her sister, she dressed her in her own old habit? No, I don't believe it. And I'm as certain as I can be that she wasn't her mother's poisoner."

"No," the Earl agreed, getting quite carried away with the line they were taking, "but she may have made up that whole story to take suspicion away from herself about Veronica."

"Perhaps. But would she really have tried to kill her sister if she thought she was trying to take her suitor? And, in any event, she made the first accusation before Veronica's accident."

"True and, as I said, Miss Thetford doesn't appear to have any suitors anyway so that it would be more a case of not wanting her sister to steal a march on her than annoyance at actually losing a lover."

"I think we'll have to rely on assistance from Lady Titania, my lord," Mr Bodley said. "Would you have any objection to that?"

"I don't think she'd take much notice of me and I believe she's already begun to question the suspects."

"Yes, but she might be putting herself in danger by doing so," Mr Bodley reminded the Earl.

"Well, but whom else can we ask for assistance? I can ask around in the village, and perhaps call upon Thetford to enquire after Veronica, having been the person who accompanied him home that day. Neither Miss Patchett nor Aunt Mildred know any of these people, never having been here before."

"There's Aunt Saffy, I suppose," the detective suggested. "She was used to live here and, although she may not have spent much time with the young people, she would have heard any gossip, wouldn't she? And she could ask around the village too."

"She could," the Earl agreed. "She could start by repeating her visit to Nanny, who, although she rarely leaves her quarters, is bound to know what's going on."

"What about the men?"

"What men?"

"Lord Vincent Lovatt and Mr Stapleton. Has your sister got any other admirers so far as you know?"

"I don't think either of those two do admire her. Vincent Lovatt's been her friend since childhood and Marcus is probably a bit young, although I appreciate that marriage to my sister might solve a lot of his family's financial anxieties."

Mr Bodley nodded.

"Would you approve if she chose him?"

The Earl grinned.

"I think my sister Jenny would think him rather beneath Titania; on the other hand, I'm certain she wants her to find somebody. I don't know the young man well so cannot comment upon his character, but he seems perfectly pleasant and well-meaning. I would not suppose, however, that Titania would see much in him."

"And Lord Vincent?"

"She's known him for ever so that, if she were to have favoured him, I would imagine she would already have shown some sign of it. As for him, I don't think he precisely *admires* her, although clearly he likes her. In truth, I don't think either is quite what she wants – and I don't think either is thinking seriously about her."

"And do you think," Mr Bodley pursued, "that Miss Thetford has her eye on either of them?"

"I have no doubt at all that she has her eye on me," the Earl returned with a cynical lift of one eyebrow. "As for the other two, well, again, she lives here so must have known Vincent Lovatt all her life. Marcus is of course fairly new but he has no money, nor any pretence of being likely to inherit any. She will have a portion, but not, I wouldn't have thought, large enough to make up for his deficiencies in that regard. He couldn't afford her and she, if she did decide on him, would have to reconcile herself to life first as a curate's wife and then, eventually, with any luck, a dean's or even a bishop's. I wouldn't think either is quite what she has in mind. She doesn't strike me as the sort of female who would be happy to 'slum it', as it were. I think she's ambitious and is in any event still pretty young. So far as I know, she hasn't been presented yet."

"Will she be? By whom?"

"By the wicked stepmother, I suppose, so that, if that's what she wants, she had better start to butter her up a little and cease to accuse her of murder."

"We've come back to where we began," the detective said in rather a depressed tone. "Do you think I should try to investigate her accusation?"

"Lord! It's no use asking me!"

"I beg to differ, my lord. I'm staying in your house as your guest; I don't want to institute some sort of enquiry if it will embarrass you."

"If you think murder has been committed, it seems to me that it's your duty to look into it, whatever I think. For what it's worth, it's my opinion that Miss Thetford is refining upon a matter which has upset her considerably and for which she has received little more than the usual sympathy – and possibly none at all from her father, who has done his best to upset her further. As for the accident, I think that's what it was – an accident."

"So you don't think there's anything to investigate?"

"No. But you're the detective; if your experience and training tells you something different, pray don't hold back on my account."

Mr Bodley was not altogether satisfied with this result and took the matter to his beloved later.

"Do I think somebody killed the first Lady Thetford in order to replace her with another? And do I think that, further to this, somebody tried to kill at least one of the Misses Thetford, although it doesn't seem entirely clear which one was the target?" Helena asked.

Mr Bodley, although he was amused by this succinct summary of the dilemma, could see that his *inamorata* had no more idea of the guilt or otherwise of a person or persons unknown than his host.

"Shall we ask Lady Amberstone what she thinks?" she asked, realising from his still troubled expression that her answer had disappointed him.

"Yes. She's bound to have an opinion, isn't she?"

"She doesn't know any of the people," Helena said, "and is unlikely to have much interest in them, but let us by all means ask her opinion. We were, earlier, trying to give her a summary of the characters involved and speculate upon any reasons any of them might have had to do away with one or two of the others."

Lady Amberstone, when the matter was put to her, was, rather to the surprise of the others, extremely interested. As she pointed out, she did not know any of the people mentioned, not even Lord Vincent and Mr Stapleton, so that she had no axes to grind and no friends or relatives to defend.

"But why should either of the young men want to kill Lady Thetford?" Helena asked.

"I can't imagine," the old lady responded immediately, "but that's one of the things we would need to find out. But, I don't know why, or whether you want to save yourselves the trouble of investigating both a murder and an attempted murder separately, you are so convinced that the two matters are related. It seems to me quite likely – and remember I don't know any of these people – that someone did want to hasten the first Lady Thetford's passage to the next world for reasons which are fairly obvious.

"As for putting a period to Miss Thetford's existence: well, it could be related and be seen as a solution by the murderer to the young woman's suspicions, or it could be that whoever wanted to finish her off, had his or her own reasons related to his or her relations with her. What sort of young woman is she?"

"Not very appealing," Titania, who had been listening, said. "She is overbearing, high in the instep and ambitious. I can't imagine she would have any serious interest in either of the young men, although she's certainly affected by Marcus's charm – and what on earth has made you add either to the list of suspects? She has set her cap most determinedly at poor Horace, who will have none of her."

"Oh dear!" the old lady said with a sad look. "How very unfortunate! If she is so disagreeable, I'm afraid it's only too likely that she harbours vast quantities of resentment towards a whole host of people, including perhaps a more appealing younger sister."

"And vast numbers of people would be only too relieved if she disappeared," Titania agreed.

"So you think it likely that she was the target of the riding accident, not her sister?" Lady Amberstone asked.

"Veronica is still very young and can't really be considered a rival yet – although I'll wager she will be if Julia hasn't managed to escape the family before she grows up. I liked her: she's brave, uncomplaining and gentle."

"She won't be so much of a rival if she can't get out of bed," Lady Amberstone observed with brutal pragmatism.

"Oh, the poor child!" Aunt Saffy exclaimed. "Is it not thought that she will recover – in time?"

"I don't think anyone knows," his lordship told her. "Would you like to meet them all, Aunt?"

"Well, I suppose if I'm to put forward an opinion, I probably should, although I can't quite think how you'll achieve it."

"You could bring the two girls back here for tea after your drive," the Earl suggested.

"That's an excellent notion," his aunt responded, "but I really need to meet the father and his new wife as well."

"I think you may have to wait until Sunday for that. They generally come to this church where my cousin, Marcus Stapleton, will probably be officiating."

"Excellent. How many of the young men are going on the drive tomorrow?" she asked her niece.

"Only the curate – Marcus. Do you want to be introduced to Vincent Lovatt too?"

"Oh, lord, yes. Where can I run across him? Will he come to church too?"

"I'm not sure – he doesn't always."

"Can you invite him for a drink or something?"

"It'll look as if I'm setting my cap at him," Titania complained, blushing.

"Are you?"

"Certainly not! I've known him all my life."

"And liked him? Would he be such a bad husband?"

"Oh, pray, Aunt, don't try to matchmake! I'm sure he'd be a perfectly amiable husband, but he's my friend and I should think he'd be horrified if he knew you were trying to persuade him to admire me."

"I'm afraid I can't think of any tactful way to bring him here," the Earl said. "He's a younger son so that the fact that my land marches beside his father's is of no interest to him. Does he ever come here, Tania?"

"No. I often meet him when I'm out riding but we just ride together. He'd think it very peculiar if I invited him back to meet my aunt."

"Oh, dear!" Lady Amberstone sighed. "How fortunate that I packed my habit! I'll just have to come out with you the day after tomorrow. Tomorrow we'll concentrate on the two Thetford daughters and the curate, then we'll try to run across your playmate the next day and complete the picture on Sunday at church."

Everyone stared at her, their mouths open until the old lady, having given them a chance to make a comment – or at least shut their mouths - spoke into the silence with a distinct bite to her tone.

"Did you think I was too old to get in the saddle?"

"Of course not, Aunt!" It was Jenny who spoke, the woman who prided herself upon her ability to manage even the most taxing social situation. "It's simply that you've never mentioned riding."

The old lady raised her chin and directed a haughty stare at her relatives.

"I don't think anyone talks about what they do every day with any great frequency," she observed. "It would be quite dreadfully boring. Of course I ride – lord, I have to do something other than embroider or visit the poor. I didn't bring my habit to London because the riding there is fairly limited – involving nothing more stimulating than trailing round the Park and stopping to gossip – but I have brought it here because Shropshire is a little different to Yorkshire and I hoped there might be some pleasant places to visit."

"There are!" Titania assured her. "I shall enjoy going out with you, dearest Aunt."

"Good. Will you come too, Jenny?"

"No, I don't think so. You see, I live in London almost all the time and am consequently more accustomed to those dreary rides round the Park. I own I was quite unnerved by joining the hunt and have been seriously put off going out again by the accident. I'll leave wandering about the country on horseback hoping to meet Tania's suitors to you."

"Have you any more suitors, dear?" the Marchioness asked.

"I haven't any, which is why Horace took me to London – and I'm afraid I haven't been very successful there either."

"What do you like doing?" the old lady asked her.

"Riding."

"In that case, I should think you'd be better to look for one in the country. Those tiresome men in London have no interest in anything but lounging about drinking and wasting money."

"That's true," Titania agreed. "But there simply aren't any in the country – not for miles and miles around."

"If you don't find one in the next few weeks, you'd better come and visit me in Yorkshire," the Marchioness said. "I know plenty of perfectly respectable young men who like riding and haven't tried to murder any of their relatives."

Titania smiled.

"I'm going off the idea of getting married at all," she said.

"I can understand that, but the thing is, if you don't, what are you going to do? You can't live alone without setting the gossipmongers going and, in any event, that would be dull and lonely. You won't be young for ever. While you are, you will attract suitors – or friends as you insist on calling them – but when you get a bit older, you'll be judged either eccentric or disagreeable. I don't recommend it."

It took some considerable time to divert the Marchioness from her favourite line of discussion but, when her eye alighted on Miss Patchett, the Earl intervened and suggested it might be time she took a second husband herself. Clearly, he said teasingly, she could think of little else.

She blinked at him, too shocked by his temerity to say anything for a moment, then rallied and burst into laughter.

"Find me one then!" she challenged.

"I own I can't think of one offhand," he admitted, "but I'll give it some thought. In the meantime, I wish you would leave the rest of us alone."

Those who had not a spouse at present had been given food for thought and retired to bed with plenty to entertain them.

Chapter 18

The next morning, Titania came down to breakfast dressed for a drive and full of enthusiasm for the outing.

Informed by Perkins that the groom had brought the carriage to the front door, she finished her coffee, rose and, bidding the others *adieu,* went out to take the reins.

"Would you like me to accompany you, my lady?" Bloom enquired.

"I don't think you need – or indeed that there will be room for you," she replied. "I'm picking up Mr Stapleton, as well as Miss Thetford and Miss Veronica."

"Very well, my lady, but I suggest you take Jim here," he pointed to a boy of about sixteen standing in the background, "in case of need. If you find his presence irksome – or that he takes up too much room – you can turn him out and he can walk home."

Titania laughed.

"Very well. You can sit beside me, Jim, until we've picked up the gentleman, and then you can hang on at the back."

The boy, blushing, jumped up beside the young mistress and the carriage moved smartly down the drive, Bloom watching in some amusement. He did not doubt that her ladyship could handle the horses although he did doubt that the curate, who in his opinion was 'soft', would be much use in any circumstances which might require either brute strength or subtlety. He was sorry that Lord Vincent was not to be in the party, for he had heard that he was a fine horseman.

Titania made her way to the curate's modest abode, which was not far from the Hall. He was waiting outside in the January sunshine, looking, Titania could not help noticing, extremely handsome and agreeable.

She pulled up beside him and Jim jumped down and ceded his place to the young man, himself going to stand at the back.

"Good morning," the curate said cheerfully. "Would you like me to drive?"

"No, thank you. Does the vicar keep you busy?"

He laughed. "Are you wondering how I have the leisure to come for a drive? There's plenty to do and, when I go home later, I shall give my mind to writing a sermon for Sunday, but I consider this to be an act of charity – taking an injured young woman for a drive. Visiting the sick is undoubtedly one of my jobs."

"Of course. Had you met Veronica before the hunt?"

"Once or twice. Like you, she's a keen horsewoman."

"Was."

"Will be again, no doubt."

"I'm not so sure that she'll ever be able to ride again without a great deal of help. I suppose someone could get her into the saddle but – oh, it doesn't bear thinking about."

"Don't you think she'll recover the use of her legs?"

"I don't know. I hope so. What do you think of the rest of the family?"

"The Thetfords? I don't know them very well. They come to church every Sunday and I've been over there for drinks, and once for dinner, but I haven't seen a great deal of them. Oh, and there was one occasion where we met – quite by chance – in the Assembly Rooms."

"Really? Whom did you meet there? Not, I imagine, Veronica."

"No; Lady Thetford had brought Miss Thetford. *He*, his lordship, wasn't there."

"Ah! Did you dance with them both?"

"I did, although not both together. Are you wondering what I thought of her ladyship?"

"Yes."

"She seemed very agreeable. She enjoys dancing and didn't want for partners."

"No; and how did she seem to get along with her stepdaughter?"

"Ah! Well, they sat at a table together but, since both spent most of the time dancing, they weren't obliged to converse with each other much. Why do you ask?"

"Because Julia, Miss Thetford, complained to me about her new stepmama and – well, really, one can't help noticing that Thetford married her very quickly after he was widowed."

"Yes, he did. I suppose you're taking Miss Thetford's part – is she your friend?"

"By no means; she's younger than I, but I suppose I can put myself in her shoes for long enough to understand that she must have been upset by her father marrying so soon after her mother's death – and choosing the governess!"

"She was there," Mr Stapleton pointed out.

"Indeed. Are you taken with Miss Thetford?"

"No. She is not really the sort of female I admire."

"Oh. What sort would that be?"

He cast her a sideways glance by which she understood him to mean that he admired her. Whether he did or not, she was uncertain, mainly because she was not used to male admiration, but also because, in truth, she wished he did. Since meeting her kinsman, she had become aware that that organ which she had always believed was in some way deficient in her own bosom, was in fact perfectly adequate – indeed distressingly similar to every other young lady's upon meeting an attractive young man.

She also recognised that Miss Thetford, as a type, was not dissimilar to herself. They were both determined young women who were disinclined to put up with things for which they had no sympathy – and not very skilled at getting young men to take care of them.

She had wondered, indeed, in an introspective moment, if it was Julia's likeness to herself which made her dislike her. She could see her own faults reflected only too plainly and found, to her surprise, that this fact had opened her eyes to her own difficulty in gaining suitors, although it had not resulted in much kindness towards the other woman. Men, she suspected, did not like women who expressed strong opinions – or women who accused others of doing something reprehensible; they preferred the sort who hung admiringly upon their every word, looked upon the bright side and expressed gratitude and pleasure for the smallest things.

It seemed to her that, if Marcus did not take to Miss Thetford, he would be most unlikely to take to her, although no one – except perhaps her brother – knew so well how exceedingly useful her fortune might be to the indigent curate.

It did not occur to her that the sort of young woman whom she had suspected her distant cousin might admire was personified in the gentle Veronica and it was something of a revelation when she noticed it. She could not, indeed, mistake it when they arrived at Thetford House to pick up the injured woman and, recognising it immediately, she felt the most profound disappointment. He did not admire her; it was merely his usual charm of manner which had, for a short time, fooled her into thinking that he did and which had, treacherously, prompted her own heart to open.

They met Lord Vincent Lovatt outside. He, whose house was on the other side of the Thetfords, had, he explained, ridden over to enquire after Veronica and been invited – if there was room – to join the party. Miss Thetford, on the other hand, was unable to be with them, having taken up instead the offer of a trip to the shops issued by her stepmother.

Titania thought it odd that Lady Thetford's accuser should have chosen to go out for the day with the hated ex-governess in preference to spending it with two young men, her sister and Titania. It made her wonder if she was disliked even more than the stepmother and whether, tomorrow, it would be she who would be accused of poisoning the first Lady Thetford and tripping up Veronica's horse.

She was busy thinking about this, and striving to find a plausible explanation for the young woman's defection, when Lord Vincent, who had broken the news to her, asked if he could be of assistance in getting Veronica into the carriage.

"I daresay someone from the household may want to bring her down," Titania said, going towards the door to announce her presence.

The door was opened before she had applied her knuckles so that she realised someone must have been looking out for them. It was a footman who opened it, but, lurking behind him, was his lordship himself.

"Lady Titania," he said warmly, coming forward to greet her. "It is so kind of you to offer to take Veronica out. She's here in the hall waiting for you. She was so impatient that she could not bear to stay in her room."

"Oh, I'm so glad!" she exclaimed, favouring the Viscount with a beaming smile. "I've brought two stalwart friends to carry her out." She gestured to the two young men hovering behind her.

"Lord – it's to be quite an outing," Lord Thetford exclaimed, "but I believe I'll carry her out myself and get her settled."

"Of course."

Titania stepped back. She could see Veronica sitting, apparently normally, in a chair at the back of the hall, her legs securely wrapped in a woollen rug.

Lord Thetford lifted his daughter and carried her with enormous care out to the waiting carriage where he laid her upon the seat facing forwards. Nanny ran after him carrying extra rugs and a footman followed with several hot bricks wrapped in cloths. These were bestowed around her.

"No, I want to sit up, Papa," she said. "It would be no use going for a drive if I can see nothing but the sky – and in any event there wouldn't be room for all these kind people who are to accompany me."

She, apart from not walking out to the carriage on her own legs, looked extraordinarily well. Her eyes were bright, her cheeks pink – especially when those eyes rested upon the curate's handsome young face.

It was then that Titania noticed the curate's expression as Veronica was settled in the carriage and suffered the bitter pill of defeat. She had arranged this outing to please the unfortunate girl and she had invited her kinsman because she wanted to spend the day with him, using the ready excuse that a strong young man might be of great value in the circumstances.

She could not pretend that she did not see the way the curate's eyes were as though magnetically attracted to Veronica's enchanting face and, suspecting that Lord Vincent, who had come to enquire after the girl of his own accord, was experiencing the same excitement, felt betrayed. It seemed she had already taken up a position as the sort of female who *did* things but failed abysmally to raise a young man's pulse. Her failure to attract any offers in London seemed now not to be so much a misfortune as only to be expected.

She also thought she knew exactly why Miss Thetford had chosen to spend a day in her stepmother's company in preference to being passed over by the young men in favour of her younger sister. She would have suffered pain from being ignored by the young men, neither of whom seemed able to take their eyes off the injured girl; the advantage of going out with her stepmother might be that she would be able to persuade her to buy her a dress or at least something with which to adorn herself.

Whether Lord Thetford noticed the young men's expressions, Titania was unsure, but suspected he did not. From his point of view, Veronica was a child; it was Julia for whom he wished to find a suitor. In any event, talking all the time in a low voice – no doubt telling his daughter how to take care of herself – he rearranged her limbs so that she was sitting upright, with her feet upon the floor of the carriage. The rugs and hot bricks were moved accordingly and Titania, who had wanted to make Veronica happy, to compensate in some way for the disaster which had befallen her, felt a nasty creeping sensation which she realised with horror was jealousy.

When all was arranged satisfactorily, the Viscount kissed his daughter's cheek and wished her an enjoyable morning.

"Oh, I'm sure I shall enjoy it no end, Papa," she said brightly, casting him a loving glance. She did not look at either of the young men, both of whom were now standing beside the carriage, waiting to be told to take their seats.

"Who's driving?" the Viscount asked when he was satisfied that his daughter was safely bestowed.

"I am," Titania replied. "Lord Vincent can sit beside me and Marcus can sit with Veronica."

She found she could not bear to have the curate beside her when it was only too plain that he would infinitely prefer to be in the back, although she had, as she made her way towards Thetford House, intended to have him there.

They all took their designated places without argument, Titania gathered up the reins, the boy attached himself at the back and, with a final wave at the Viscount watching them, Titania turned the carriage and swept out of the drive, keeping to a prudent pace while they remained within sight of the anxious father.

"This is a treat!" Lord Vincent said to Titania.

"Really? Do you like to be driven?"

"By you, yes! And I'm delighted that you allowed me to accompany you."

"Oh," she said, "Pray don't take it as too much of a compliment! I daresay you will prove to be useful and, Miss Thetford having cried off, I would have felt like the coachman, sitting alone in the front."

"You could have had Veronica beside you and relegated your cousin to the back, but I'll try to do my best to assist in any way I can."

"Where would you like to go, Veronica?" Titania asked, turning her head to squint at the passenger in the back.

"Oh, I don't mind a bit. It's wonderful to be out."

"Very well; I'll see how scenic a route I can devise."

Emerging from the drive, she turned left and encouraged the horses to pick up speed. Soon they were bowling along at a sprightly pace.

"Is she enjoying it?" Titania asked Lord Vincent.

He glanced back before replying, "Oh, yes, I believe so; she's deep in conversation with Mr Stapleton."

"Hmn," she said. "Do you think there's something between them? Should I have made him sit beside me?"

"Possibly, but they both look happy. We can swap places if you think it your duty to separate them."

"Do you think I should?"

"She's a little young to be flirting with a *beau*," he replied soberly.

She nodded.

"I don't think they can get up to much that's harmful in the circumstances," he said reassuringly. "I'll keep an eye on them."

They drove for about an hour before Titania pulled in to the side of the road and turned to look at the passengers in the back.

"Are you enjoying yourselves?" she asked innocently.

"Oh, yes!" Veronica replied at once. Her cheeks were even pinker than when they had set off and her eyes brilliant. She was a remarkably pretty girl.

"I've brought some coffee and cake for us to have a little feast if you feel able to eat something."

"Oh, yes, indeed," the girl replied eagerly.

She was, Titania thought, still young enough to have an insatiable appetite and had not yet, perhaps, begun to think about the danger to her figure of indulging in cake.

"In that case, I believe I'll turn off here and find a suitable place to stop for a little while and then, after we've had our repast, you could have a turn at driving – that is, if you would like to."

"Oh, yes!" the girl breathed, joy illuminating her face even further until, Titania thought with some bitterness, its brightness rivalled that of the pale winter sun. She wondered, glancing at the sky, if it too would take umbrage at being outshone.

She turned off the road and went down a narrow track at a slow pace, making sure that the carriage bumped as little as possible. Eventually, she drew into another, narrower, track and brought the vehicle to a halt.

"This is all Rushlake land," she explained, "so that I know it quite well. We can disembark if you would like and sit upon the grass for a little while, but as it's winter and not very warm, I believe it might be better if we remained in the carriage."

Everyone agreeing to this, she ordered Lord Vincent to bring out the picnic basket, which had been stowed under the seat. Coffee was poured, cakes were passed round and everyone ate and drank with enthusiasm, all being young enough to find the pleasure of eating out of doors, without plates and with rather thick, indifferent cups, to be almost as exciting as all the rest. It felt, Titania could see reflected on Veronica's face, like some sort of childish feast.

When they had finished, Titania ordered the two men to help Veronica to change places with her.

"I think I'll leave Vincent sitting beside you, Veronica," she said, "because I'm sure he'll be more than able to help if you have any difficulty. I'll sit in the back with Marcus."

"I'll lift you out," the curate said at once, perhaps afraid that, if he did not stake his claim, Lord Vincent would perform this service.

Jim let down the steps, took the reins from Titania and waited while the curate lifted Veronica, carried her out of the carriage and back, this time

149

into the driving seat, watched by both Lord Vincent and Titania. She did not doubt that this intimate moment gave them both enormous pleasure – indeed she could see it reflected on their faces. She found herself wondering how they had managed to form a romantic connexion so quickly but guessed that it must be love at first sight. How galling to be obliged to watch it! He looked as though he was carrying something infinitely precious and she looked entranced at being in his arms.

The rugs and hot bricks were rearranged. There was nothing that Veronica was obliged to do with her feet so that, having placed her firmly upon the driver's seat, wrapped her up and handed her the reins, no one saw anything amiss.

Titania climbed back into the carriage, this time at the back beside the curate. Veronica set the carriage in motion.

She was a good driver, as Titania had expected knowing her love of riding, but she did not, at least at first, set the horses to a trot, but kept them soberly walking.

Titania, sitting beside her kinsman, fell to wondering what would come of what she was certain were romantic feelings on his part – and perhaps on hers too.

It was usual in families like the Thetfords for all the girls to receive a similar portion, although of course the boy – if there had been one – would have inherited everything apart from those portions. Veronica would not therefore be likely to come with any less than Julia, but, if she never regained the use of her legs, she would not be much use to a curate, who must make his way in the world and who would be expected to have a wife who would share that burden. She would need to be able-bodied to visit the poor and the sick, to organise charity events, to run a household that, unless he rose rapidly in the hierarchy of the church, would not be well off. There would not be a vast number of servants and the incumbent's wife would therefore have to do a good deal herself. She did not see how a woman who could not walk would be able to do anything much. No doubt she could be supplied with a bath chair, but someone would need to push it and, not only would that require a dedicated servant to do nothing much else, but it would also be difficult to manoeuvre round the sort of small abode which a curate could afford. Even were Marcus to be promoted to a parish of his own, most vicarages were supplied with a number of bedrooms, and indeed reception rooms, but none were large.

Veronica was not yet seventeen and had therefore several years ahead in which to acquire a wealthy suitor of the kind who could support her.

Titania did not think that they would be slow to come forward even if she never regained the use of her legs, for she was an exceptionally pretty young woman with a character which appeared to be both compliant and cheerful. Where her older sister drove suitors away by her forceful and angry manner, the younger attracted them by the very opposite. She wondered if Veronica knew this. She was certain that Julia did – and resented it.

She did not think that Lord Thetford would be keen on Marcus for either of the girls. He was not nearly as wealthy as Rushlake, had several daughters for whom he must provide, and had now acquired a new young wife who would be bound to add to his quiverful of children.

And what of Marcus? She had thought that he needed a rich wife – and that she herself would have provided him with the perfect opportunity to improve his fortunes. She was not much older than he and she had thought that he was interested – possibly as with all her previous suitors, more in her money than her person - but she did not think now that he had eyes for anyone but Veronica. Had he already given his heart when she, Titania, had arrived at Rushlake? Or was it the awful accident which had focussed his mind on Veronica? Did her helplessness appeal to him, make him look at her afresh?

Did Julia have her eye on him too? Did she prefer him to Horace? It was clear that she wanted to attract Horace but, at bottom, did she prefer the curate? It would not be peculiar if she did, for the Earl did not spend long in the country, had not indeed attended any social events until this Christmas. She suspected that she would take Rushlake, if he could be induced to make her an offer, even if she preferred Marcus. Would Marcus take her, Titania, if he could have her, rather than the one he clearly preferred?

"I've forgotten," she said at last, "how long you've been here. I'd already gone to London when you arrived, hadn't I?"

"Yes. I've been here just over three months. It's a pity you weren't here when I arrived for you could have shown me the ropes and introduced me to the neighbourhood."

Titania thought that he meant it was a pity he had not seen her first for he might have fallen in love with her, but that it was now too late.

"Oh, I've never done much in the neighbourhood, so I don't suppose I would have been much use. In any event, you seem to have made friends – particularly with the Thetfords. I suppose you first saw them at church?"

"Yes, but then I was invited to tea soon after I arrived. Lord Thetford had just got married and," he cast his companion an amused glance, "was having trouble with his daughters disliking his new wife. I believe he wanted to divert their attention to something new."

She laughed.

"And were his tactics successful?"

"Oh, yes; we've become firm friends."

"With both Julia and Veronica?"

"Of course, although I've only met Veronica a few times – when I've come to tea or when we've met by chance on a ride. As I told you, I've danced with Julia at the Assembly Rooms which, of course, Veronica is too young to attend."

"She wouldn't be able to dance now, in any event," Titania said bluntly.

"She'll get better, won't she?"

"I don't know."

They both fell silent and she, glancing surreptitiously at his profile, thought she detected both misery and confusion upon it.

Chapter 19

While his sister was taking Veronica for a drive, Lord Rushlake called upon Lord Thetford, ostensibly to enquire after his injured daughter.

Shown into a sunny morning room, the Earl was soon joined by Lady Thetford, who came in explaining that her lord had gone out to discuss farming matters with his bailiff. This was precisely what his lordship had hoped to hear; he had chosen a moment when he thought it likely that the Viscount would be from home.

"Oh, I'm sorry to disturb you," Rushlake replied smoothly. "I can call at another time. I came to ask how Veronica does."

"Surely you must know that she has been taken out by your sister," Lady Thetford said, a frown creasing her smooth brow.

"I did know that, but since I did not suppose that she would value a visit from me, decided it was a good moment to speak to her father – and of course you."

"Me? Don't you know that I'm the wicked stepmother?"

He smiled.

"You don't look very wicked to me," he said, not altogether truthfully, for he thought Lady Thetford had a hard look about her. She was good-looking in a peculiarly unappealing way; that is to say that her features were even and symmetrical, her nose was straight and small, her eyes brown, but not warm, and her lips a little on the thin side for true feminine beauty. She had a vast quantity of chestnut brown hair, or it was dressed in such a way as to make it look very thick.

"I have inherited a number of stepdaughters," she said, "and they were not pleased when their father married me. I've never been sure whether that was because I was their governess at one time – and therefore already despised – or whether they would have disliked anyone who took their mother's place."

At a loss as to how to react to this observation, his lordship smiled gently. It seemed this was the right response for she suddenly smiled back in quite a different manner – no longer either formal or hostile, but on the contrary friendly and a touch collusive.

"Will you sit down and join me in some refreshment?" she asked.

"I would be delighted, but don't want to take up your time if you're busy," he responded, matching her manner.

"I'm not often busy," she admitted, ringing the bell. "I haven't been married very long and was used to having every hour of every day taken up with managing my charges. Becoming a lady of leisure has left me with a great many hours to fill so that the arrival of a near neighbour, of whom I have heard but with whom I have barely exchanged two words, is an unexpected delight."

"Why, thank you, ma'am," he said, beginning to see a little of what must have attracted Lord Thetford.

It seemed that Lady Thetford's style was one of flattery, friendliness with a touch of self-deprecation – although he suspected this was feigned – and a sort of half-concealed flirtatiousness.

Coffee was ordered and they sat down together to drink it and to eat the little biscuits which accompanied it.

"Have you known my stepdaughters long?" she enquired.

"I've known of their existence ever since the first one was born – they being such near neighbours, but I am not acquainted with them. I left home for Oxford some years ago now and have hardly been back since, except when my father was dying, and that was not a time to socialise."

"No, of course not, but Julia isn't much younger than you. Had you ever thought of courting her?"

He laughed, amused although a little discomposed by her bluntness. "Almost everyone I know – at least all the women – are constantly enquiring about my future plans *vis-à-vis* setting up a family. My aunt goes on and on about it. Are you hoping you might be able to get rid of her?"

She laughed at that.

"Well, I own I wish I could find her a suitor, but I can see you're not interested. I suppose I shall have to take her to London and have her presented. She's bound to find a husband there, isn't she?"

"It's possible, but my sister hasn't," he warned.

"She's a little older, isn't she?"

"A little, but not appreciably. She is, however, a woman of strong opinions and outspoken manner – not unlike Julia. Did you ever teach Julia or was she too old for the schoolroom when you first arrived?"

"She was a little old but was lingering there, having nothing else to do. She missed being presented at the proper time, first because her mother was expecting and then subsequently because she was unwell. Then, of course, her mother died and a period of mourning had to be worked through. "

"I see. It's unfortunate, isn't it? Much the same happened to my sister, Titania – although the timescale was even more protracted. Our father died and, once the period of mourning was over, she was already a little old. She came to London this year and stayed with another of my sisters, Jenny."

"But she hasn't 'taken', has she?"

Rushlake laughed. "I don't think they do when they're a little more mature – and particularly if they have minds of their own. She's had plenty of admirers but their sentiments haven't been reciprocated. You could bring Julia to London next year – she is still young."

"Yes, but she has a smaller portion than your sister, and unfortunately next season will coincide with my adding to the family."

"Really?" Lord Rushlake, who had heard the rumours and observed the slight swelling of his hostess's figure, nevertheless affected astonishment.

"Yes! Haven't you heard the gossip?"

"I never listen to such things! Of what does it consist?"

"That I was already increasing when we married!"

She said this with a good deal of defiance and his lordship, believing her to like sparring with him, took the hint and queried, "And were you?"

"I *thought* so," she returned with an arch look, "but unfortunately it was not to be."

"I see. I'm sorry," he replied with as much sympathy as he could muster. He had heard rumours that she had pretended to be expecting in order to force the Viscount into marriage almost before his dead wife was cold in her grave.

"Yes; it was disappointing, but I think *this* time all should go well."

"Indeed; I hope so."

"And what of Veronica?" he asked after a delicate pause. "Does the doctor think she will recover the use of her legs?"

"He refuses to be drawn on that. I certainly hope so, for I cannot conceive how we are to find her a husband if she remains immobile."

"And what," he asked boldly as she poured him another cup of coffee, "do you feel about Julia's accusations? I hope you don't allow them to upset you."

"What? You mean that I poisoned her mother? It's absolute nonsense, of course. I assume you know that?"

"I know very little," he returned softly. "Pray enlighten me if it does not distress you too much to speak of it."

She stared at him, her brown eyes so wide open – to indicate surprise, he thought – that he almost feared they might pop out.

"I was the governess, as you know," she said, biting into a biscuit with such small teeth that he wondered if, by some extraordinary fluke, she had retained her infantile set. "It is true," she went on, affecting an air

155

of embarrassment which he did not think she felt, "that Lord Thetford and I became attached to each other while his wife was alive. It was very unfortunate – we tried to fight our sentiments – but – I'm sure you must know – one cannot, if one feels strongly, altogether eradicate those feelings no matter how hard one tries. The thing was, you see, that she was very ill – in truth she never quite recovered from the birth of the last child – and it is not surprising when you think that she had had a number of children already as well as several miscarriages and stillbirths – she was not young and was – and the doctor agrees with me – not well when she embarked upon the most recent. Unfortunately, expecting a baby can, I understand, hasten an illness already settled in the system. Because she was so ill, I dealt mostly with his lordship about anything concerning the girls. It was him whom I consulted when there was anything amiss with any of the children and – sharing our anxieties about them as well as about her ladyship – we grew close."

She paused and he nodded, not daring to make a comment in case it should cause her to clam up or lose patience with him. He could not help thinking that he was an odd confidant – a young man, younger than she, unmarried and inexperienced in such matters. Perhaps that was what drew her to speak; perhaps she would have been more reluctant to confide in his aunt, who would probably have thought that, in the circumstances which she had described, the proper course of action would have been to seek another position.

It did not occur to him that she might have begun her relations with Lord Thetford in a similar manner – confiding in a man about matters which women usually discussed with others of the same sex and thus laying the path for him to express – and perhaps eventually feel - sympathy.

The Viscount, Rushlake thought, had no doubt been flattered by her confidences, tried to help and perhaps, one day when she had appeared particularly distressed or anxious, put an arm around her to comfort her. Or perhaps it had been the other way round: he had become distressed as he contemplated the – probably fatal – illness of his wife and she had comforted him.

"We should not," she went on, "have given way to our feelings, but I'm afraid we did – once – and then, after that, it was difficult not to – to do so again."

He nodded, but did not speak, sensing that she had begun on a confession which he hoped would lead to a degree of enlightenment as to the recent events in her household.

"After the baby was born – and it would be idle to pretend that its sex was not a disappointment to his lordship – we – grew closer. We tried to hide it, but I suppose there is always somebody – most likely a servant – who becomes suspicious and then looks out for confirmation of their suspicions. I believe that was how Julia got to know of our mutual affection.

"It was understandable," she went on, nodding and trying to look sympathetic, "that she was upset. Her mother was very ill – and then of course she died. In those circumstances, I think she was looking for someone to blame and I was an easy target – a woman who was all alone, who belonged somewhere between the servants and his lordship, a young woman who was, in some sense, standing in for their mother – because of spending a great deal of time with the children – and she – well, she's the eldest, she was close to her mama and the other children looked up to her. I believe she thought she was offering something with which they could identify: a wicked person whom they could blame as opposed to their saintly mother simply succumbing to a common malady. It's extraordinary, isn't it," she went on, her tone hardening, "how people become saintly once they're dead? She wasn't – and she wasn't above complaining about her situation and her illness. Indeed, she was exceedingly captious; that was one of the reasons his lordship liked speaking to me."

Again, Lord Rushlake nodded, but he could not help feeling some sympathy for the Viscount who, it seemed to him, had married again – in haste – and saddled himself with another captious wife. He doubted her ladyship bothered to show him the same degree of understanding now the ring was upon her finger.

"Of course, Julia's attitude convinced the younger children of my wickedness and I became very unpopular; indeed, they began to behave exceedingly badly, being excessively rude and hostile. I told his lordship I believed it would be better if I left but he begged me to stay."

She stopped, rose and went to stand in front of the window.

He stood up too, not liking to remain seated when she was upon her feet. "It must have been terrible," he said without much conviction for he did not believe that a woman as ambitious as Lady Thetford would have allowed a little – temporary – unpleasantness to divert her from her design.

It was, in any event, a situation that was by no means unusual: a faded, dying wife, a young governess with more than passable good looks, an anxious and frustrated man, and an angry and miserable set of children.

It must, he supposed, have been horrid to be set up as the wicked seductress – and yet it seemed to him that that was precisely what she had been.

"You can have no idea!" she exclaimed, suddenly growing angry and turning round to glare at him, although he could not help thinking that, if that was the case, it was not for want of her telling him. He wondered if she was angry because, in spite of her effort to convince him of the disagreeable nature of her situation, he remained unconvinced. She had failed to sway him and his attempt to show sympathy had clearly been inadequate. She had seen straight through him.

In her anger, she looked magnificent and he thought that this sort of mood suited her much better than the one where she had been trying to engage his sympathy. She was not, he judged, a natural victim, being much more suited to the role of predator. It was like watching an eagle pretending to be a sparrow.

"No, I don't," he admitted. "I have no experience of such a thing, but I do understand that you must have felt very alone and unsupported, except by his lordship. I daresay that drew you closer and that you believed he was the only person in the world who understood."

"Yes, that was so," she snapped, "but it was not the whole. I – we hadn't been as careful as we should have been – and I found, as I mentioned just now, that I was expecting. I discovered this soon after Lady Thetford died and didn't know what to do about it. In the end, I told him. He was the only one I could tell because he at least knew how it had come about and – and I suppose I thought he was the most nearly involved."

"Indeed." Rushlake was at a loss as to how to reply to this confession. He felt uncomfortable and out of his depth.

She, clearly irritated by his bewilderment, retorted, as though it must be obvious to an idiot, "I lost it!" and burst into tears.

"Oh, I'm sorry," he murmured, not sure whether this was the right response.

In a sense it was because Lady Thetford, having at last elicited some conventional words, abandoned her position by the window and cast herself upon his chest, sobbing as though her heart would break.

Lord Rushlake, wholly unused to such behaviour, stood stock still but, feeling something was required of him and still hoping to extract more from her, placed his hands warily upon her back, being careful not to exert any pressure.

"Lady Thetford," he remonstrated, moving his hands to her arms and attempting to separate his body from hers. He was not successful, being insufficiently forceful. She continued to cling to him so that he began to feel almost asphyxiated by a combination of her substance, hair, tears and scent, all of which were overpowering.

"My lady," he said more firmly, now exerting his superior strength to prise her off his body. "You must not!"

"Why not?" she countered, allowing herself to be separated a small distance, just enough for her to be able to speak directly into his face, her own mere inches from his.

"You're a married lady," he explained, "and should not stand so close."

"You mean you don't want me to?" she exclaimed, once again infuriated and growing so red in the face that he could feel the heat burning his own cheeks.

"No, I don't," he agreed, "and you should not. What would your husband say?"

"I've no idea!" she replied, now so angry that she was almost spitting into his face.

She still stood alarmingly close and he held her off, but was beginning to wonder how in the world he was to escape and how he was to deal with the rage which he sensed was burning hotter at the rejection. Did she, he wondered, with a sort of creeping horror, frequently behave like this? Indeed, was this what she had done to Lord Thetford, who, being both older and, at the time, fairly desperate himself, had succumbed to her assault?

He was saved, vastly to his relief – and surprise – by the door opening and a feminine exclamation of horror, disgust and, oddly, relief.

"What are you doing?" this person exclaimed.

Lady Thetford, recognising the voice, allowed herself to be put away from her prey. He, the Earl, turned and saw the flaming face of Julia Thetford, who was standing in the doorway.

"I told you, didn't I?" she asked, no doubt reading his face correctly and relieved that she might no longer have to search in vain for proof of her accusation.

"You told me several things," he replied, "but not about this!"

She gave a derisive laugh.

"Mama!" she said with horrid sarcasm, "You've become agitated again. I believe you should retire to your chamber for a spell."

"I was telling his lordship my troubles," Lady Thetford said furiously. "He was comforting me."

"Really?"

"Yes – and in any event it's none of your business what I'm doing! How dare you come in here and accuse me?"

"I didn't," the younger lady replied. "I asked you what you were doing – not that I couldn't see for myself. You were trying to seduce our poor neighbour, who is far too polite to tell you the truth! I'm sure you can see," she went on, now addressing the Earl, "the sort of thing that's being going on in this house ever since this terrible woman was first employed."

"I can see that everyone is very distressed – and disturbed," his lordship said helplessly. "I believe I should leave."

"Why did you come?" Miss Thetford asked.

"To enquire after your sister's health."

"Ah! But she's gone out with your sister – and two men, I understand."

"Yes," Rushlake agreed, wishing he were anywhere but in this room being stared at by two women who detested each other and were clearly seeking to use him to punish each other.

"She is just the same," Miss Thetford said. "But she was very much looking forward to her outing today. It is kind of your sister to take her."

"Not at all. I believe she realised that they share a mutual interest in horses: riding, driving etc."

"Unfortunately that is the case," Miss Thetford said. "It is sad because now it looks unlikely that my sister will ever be able to ride again."

"I daresay something can be arranged so that she can," the Earl said, "and I'm certain she will be able to drive."

"Let us hope so. I see you've had coffee – but would you like another cup which you can drink with me?"

"That is excessively kind of you, but I believe it's time I was going home."

During this polite but distant exchange, Lady Thetford glowered in the background. She had sat down beside the empty cups and now began to nibble at a biscuit.

The Earl, perceiving that she had no intention of retiring to her chamber as she had been commanded, and fearing another confrontation between the two, shook his head, reiterated the need to return to his own house and made for the door.

"I'll see you out," Julia Thetford said, reaching it before him and opening it.

They passed through it together and she led him towards the front door, complaining as she walked about her stepmother's behaviour.

"She was trying to seduce you," she said.

"Oh, I'm sure she wasn't," he countered, although he thought Julia was right.

"I should think that's what she did with Papa – and he, being rather older and less accustomed to young women throwing themselves at him, was quite taken in."

"She is not happy," he said.

"Oh, don't be fooled by the tears – or the sobs. Why do you think she buried her face in your chest except because she could not make her eyes run in the way she wanted?"

"I cannot think of any reason why she might want to seduce me," he said *naïvely*.

"Can't you?"

"She is only recently married," he argued.

"Yes, but in my opinion she's insatiable. If I were you, I believe I'd make sure I never found myself alone in a room with her again. Suppose for a moment," she went on, putting her head on one side and gazing at him, "that it had been my father who walked into the room?"

"I would have given him the same explanation," he said. "I assure you I did not instigate the – the embrace."

"I didn't for a moment suppose that you had," she said, adding, "Do you believe me now?"

"About?"

"That she poisoned Mama?"

"I really don't know, Miss Thetford. If she did, I would suppose she had done so in order to cease to be a governess and become instead a Viscountess. Since that is what she now is, I cannot think it anything but foolish to try to seduce a neighbour. What could she hope to gain?"

"A lover, I suppose. My father isn't very young."

"Young enough to get her with child," he returned.

Chapter 20

Lady Amberstone, having eaten her breakfast tranquilly, waved off both her niece and nephew to their morning meetings with members of the Thetford family and prepared to spend a peaceful morning with the remainder of the household.

Jenny and her husband proposed taking a walk with their children but the Marchioness, seeing little opportunity of engaging in speculation – or discovery – about the recent goings-on in such a pastime, declined to accompany them. She was thus left with Aunt Saffy, Mr Bodley and her friend Helena.

Mr Bodley, having been more or less instructed by Miss Thetford to look into her sister's accident as well as her mother's death, decided to call upon the representative of the local constabulary in the area. The Earl and his sister having both gone out, he could not ask them where this person might be found – or indeed how he could get there. He had come to Rushlake in a hired carriage, which had now gone back whence it came so that, unless he were to request some sort of transport from his host, he must walk.

"Do you know where I might find the local policeman?" he asked Jenny, presuming her to have some knowledge of the local area.

She looked startled.

"A local policeman?" she asked. "I've no idea. I suppose he must be walking up and down the streets in Shrewsbury. Is that not what policemen in the country do?"

Mr Bodley had no more idea of the usual behaviour of country policemen than she. He enquired where – and what – this town was and, further, how far away it was.

"Oh, some way," she replied airily. "You can't walk if that's what you're thinking. At least it would take all day and then you wouldn't have time to do any detecting, would you? But I'm sure Horace will be perfectly willing to provide you with a carriage."

Mr Bodley looked anxious at this generous offer for, in truth, he did not know what to do or where to go. He looked interrogatively at Miss Patchett, who said, "We could go out together if you like and, while you walk about the streets looking for the local policeman, I could do some shopping."

Lady Amberstone's ears pricked up at this suggestion.

"Would you mind if I came with you?" she asked. "We could wander round the shops together and perhaps find someone to fill us in on the

162

local gossip, for it's all very well talking to each other and indulging in endless speculation, but, really, there must be people out there who've heard the tales and will be bound to have an opinion about them."

Both Adrian Bodley and Helena Patchett brightened at this suggestion. Somehow, having the Marchioness in tow immediately made the trip more commonplace. Two women going shopping, stopping for coffee somewhere and falling into conversation with other women doing the same thing made the whole enterprise seem more respectable and would, Helena was convinced, make Adrian more confident about searching for the local policeman.

Aunt Saffy, having lived at Rushlake for a few years, joined the conversation at this point, telling them about the shops she thought they would like and suggesting they stop at the tea room in the high street. They would, she assured them, be bound to find plenty of people who would have an opinion on the goings-on in Rushlake. Shrewsbury, she assured them, was not far, not much more than half an hour in the carriage, and everyone would be bound to know most of what there was to know about the Thetfords.

"Would they know whether poor Lady Thetford was poisoned and, if so, by whom?" Lady Amberstone asked, amused.

"I should think they would be bound to have heard the rumours and to have an opinion upon them," Aunt Saffy said, "because people like to gossip about the nobility."

"Yes, you're quite right," the Marchioness replied more soberly. "Although their views are often somewhat embellished."

"If you go to Martha's Tea Room," Saffy said, "you'll meet the local gentry as well as less elevated persons. You can engage in conversation with whomever you choose."

"I think it sounds like a delightful way to pass the morning," Lady Amberstone said. "Will you come with us, Saffy? You can tell us where to go, indeed lead us to the right places, for it's my experience that, when one goes to a completely strange town, one is only too likely to walk in the wrong direction in the first instance and find nothing at all of the least interest."

"I would be honoured," Saffy replied, blushing with pleasure, although she did not suppose that it was her company which the Marchioness sought.

Jenny, clearly wishing she had not chosen to take her children on a long, tedious walk around the estate instead of being one of what promised to be a fascinating shopping party, ordered the carriage for them before taking herself off with her family for the promised walk.

"I believe, while we're waiting for the carriage, that I'll go and speak to Nanny," Saffy said. "She may know the policeman's name and even whether there is a police station, which would surely make it much easier to find him."

"I should think," Lady Amberstone said, "that there must be more than one in Shropshire and, Shrewsbury being the largest town in the area, I should imagine there would be bound to be one there and indeed several policemen."

"Yes, indeed." Saffy, pleased that her suggestion seemed to have found approval, rose from the table.

"If Nanny is the sort of person who's inclined to talk a lot," Lady Amberstone said as she reached the door, "do try not to spend the entire morning with her. We'll be waiting in the hall for both you and the carriage."

Aunt Saffy, afraid of displeasing her ladyship, made an unprecedently brief visit to Nanny who, upon being given the reason for Saffy's refusal to sit down, agreed wholeheartedly that the Marchioness must be obeyed.

She furnished her friend with the name of the policeman, Constable Collins, although she was not certain he was still to be found in Shrewsbury, or indeed whether he had been promoted to Sergeant, in which case she guessed there must be a constable as well.

"And, really, Saffy, I do think they need more than one to keep an eye on such a large town. I hope you find everything you want. And, yes, the place to drink a cup of tea is still Martha's in the High Street. It's a charming place and I'm sure her ladyship will feel quite comfortable there."

"Thank you," Saffy said, preparing to leave. "I'll come and tell you all about our trip when I get back."

"I shall look forward to it," Nanny said cheerfully.

When Saffy had been to her room, put her hat upon her head and her coat upon her back, she picked up her handbag and gloves and scurried down the stairs to find Mr Bodley and Helena waiting, but no sign of her ladyship.

"I think she's still putting her hat on," Helena explained.

"Oh, well, I'm glad I haven't kept her waiting," Saffy said with a sigh of relief and sat down on one of the elegant but unforgiving chairs arranged in the hall.

Lady Amberstone sailed down the stairs a few minutes later. It seemed she had not been adjusting the angle of her hat all this time for she clutched in her gloved hand a much thumbed copy of a map of Shrewsbury.

"I'm sorry if I've kept you waiting," she said, "but I thought it might be worth trying to find a map of the town and turned this up in the library. I believe Horace's father must have used it because it's become a little faded around the creases. However, I daresay it may be of some use."

"I'm sure it'll prove invaluable," Mr Bodley said and the party made their way through the front door and into the waiting carriage.

The Marchioness begged Saffy to sit beside her, which the good lady did not for a moment suppose indicated that her ladyship particularly wished to share the seat with her, but rather that she wanted Mr Bodley and Helena to share the other.

The drive was uneventful; the sun was out, which, Lady Amberstone observed, probably meant that Titania's outing with Veronica Thetford would be quite pleasant.

During the journey, Mr Bodley studied the map, although it was not the sort of document which features useful addresses; it merely depicted the roads both into and within the town.

"The police station is bound to be in the centre," Lady Amberstone said.

Accordingly, the coachman was requested to take them straight to the middle of the town where they would alight and wander about, looking at the shops and so forth. Mr Bodley's mission to find the policeman was not shared with the coachman.

Reaching the main street and pulling up outside Martha's Tea Rooms, which the coachman seemed to know might feature on the ladies' itinerary, they all disembarked. The coachman was instructed to occupy himself for the next few hours and be at the same place to pick them up in the early afternoon.

"Well, I don't think we can have tea immediately," her ladyship said. "We must do a *soupçon* of detecting first – otherwise we won't have earned our refreshment."

They set off all together until they came to the kind of general emporium which visiting ladies often find fascinating. Inside a large building there were a number of small businesses selling trinkets and silk scarves as well as bolts of cloth and haberdashery.

Mr Bodley, feeling *de trop* in this sort of environment and aware that his presence hampered the ladies' innocent enjoyment of looking at largely unnecessary but fairly cheap objects, said he would leave them to their shopping. For his part, he believed he would wander off in search of the police station.

Lady Amberstone insisted upon his taking the map and the party split up.

The ladies wandered about in what seemed to both Aunt Saffy and Helena, neither of whom was much given to making frivolous purchases - the one because she did not have the money, the other because she saw no reason to acquire such things - to be something approaching paradise.

"Why," Helena wondered aloud, "have I never spent much time in such an Aladdin's Cave before?"

"Probably because you have never wanted the sort of thing they sell in such profusion in this sort of place," Lady Amberstone replied, amused.

Aunt Saffy was fingering some pretty pastel scarves with reverence. She was intent upon choosing the prettiest, but she was unable to decide between a pale blue with little white blossoms dotted about it or a green with no pattern but a subtle variation of colour running from one side to the other.

"Are you thinking of buying one of those?" Lady Amberstone asked.

"I don't know; no, I don't think I will, but they are very pretty, are they not?"

"Charming," the Marchioness agreed. "I think the blue would suit you."

"Do you?" Aunt Saffy, who rarely bought anything and had never, or at least not for at least twenty years, considered what might suit her, looked up at the Marchioness with a pair of wide blue eyes, which, the older lady noticed, almost exactly matched the silk.

"Let me get it for you," her ladyship said, "as a late Christmas present."

"Oh no, my lady, I cannot let you do that," Saffy exclaimed, embarrassed. She longed for the scarf but thought she could not afford it and knew that the Marchioness knew that. For her, as a rich woman, whatever the cost, it was almost certainly trivial.

Lady Amberstone, unable to think of a tactful way to persuade the other woman to accept something which, to her, was nothing upon which to refine, but to the other her heart's desire, snatched the scarf from Aunt Saffy's caressing hands and passed it to the shopkeeper.

"Let us for Heaven's sake not argue over a scarf," she admonished Saffy. "I *will* buy it because I think the colour is almost perfect for your eyes and because I haven't bought you anything for Christmas. I came bearing gifts for my nephew and nieces – and indeed gave Helena a small gift – but have given you nothing. Think of this as the guilty remedy for an oversight."

The old woman opened her purse, passed some money to the shopkeeper, watched as the scarf was carefully wrapped and then, taking it, handed it to Saffy.

"Thank you so much, my lady!" Saffy said on a breath.

Helena, while this was going on, had wandered off to another stall where there were myriad bars of soap of every hue and scent.

"Oh, I love this sort of thing!" she exclaimed, chose a couple and was paying for them when the other two joined her.

"Well, now," her ladyship said, "you've both found something you wanted. What shall I get for myself? I believe we should each go home with some proof of how we've spent our morning."

Saffy, searching frantically in her mind and around the emporium for something she could afford to buy for the Marchioness – and what in the world did one choose for such a person? - spied some handkerchiefs, prettily embroidered, no doubt by the person selling them. She hurried over and chose two which she presented to her ladyship with a shy explanation that this was her Christmas present.

"Oh, my dear, you didn't have to do that!" her ladyship exclaimed, touched. "Thank you. They are quite lovely."

In fact the purchase of the handkerchiefs was a fortunate one in other respects because, as Saffy was negotiating with the shopkeeper, a woman in a rather shabby hat touched her arm and, upon Saffy turning surprised eyes upon her, exclaimed at this unexpected meeting with a member of the Rushlake Women's Guild in Shrewsbury.

"I haven't spoken to you for ages," this woman exclaimed, "although of course I did see you in church on Christmas Day. Have you returned to Rushlake permanently or is this just a fleeting visit?"

"I'm not actually quite certain," Saffy replied. "I came with his lordship and Lady Titania, of course, for Christmas. I'm not quite sure how long we're staying. Let me introduce you to my companions."

The woman, Mrs Hurst, was just the kind of loquacious person whom the three Rushlake ladies had hoped to meet. She was what might be described as a 'villager', a woman who had no pretensions to rank but who admired the aristocratic families living nearby. She admired them and they provided her with a constant changing drama. Her life, she would have maintained, was dull. She rose in the morning, busied herself around her little house and then went out to help clean other people's houses, notably those of the aristocrats, who, frequently, did not employ quite enough servants to keep their houses in the pristine condition in which they wished them to remain – particularly when they were expecting guests. Just before Christmas was generally a busy time.

As a result of this, Mrs Hurst was inclined to grill the servants in whichever house she had recently been assisting. Such gossip as she obtained this way kept her going for some time in her own little abode. She was a widow and her grown children had children of their own, so that, although she did see them – and indeed often helped them too – she lived alone and was frequently in want of entertainment and social interaction.

She was not the sort of person with whom any of the three Rushlake ladies would have thought of sitting down in a *café* to drink tea so that the conversation which followed was conducted while they stood around, not far from the stall selling handkerchiefs.

Lady Amberstone and Miss Patchett smiled in a friendly fashion but, having bowed and received Mrs Hurst's compliments, did not take part in the exchange. It was left to Saffy to extract whatever Mrs Hurst might have to impart.

Chapter 21

She began by exclaiming about the awful injury poor Miss Veronica had received.

Saffy nodded and added her own comment on the extent of the damage the girl had sustained.

"I'd been working there over Christmas," Mrs Hurst continued. "They were all at sixes and sevens – had a whole lot of relatives coming to visit."

"Oh, there must have been a deal of hard work to be done," Saffy agreed sympathetically, although, in spite of her lowly status, she had never in her life been expected to clean anything – or prepare any food.

"There was, I can tell you. Lord Thetford – you know I don't think he's as well provided for as he likes to make out – he doesn't employ half enough servants and the house – well, a lot of the time it's not very clean. I shouldn't say that, I suppose, but I couldn't help noticing that the silver wasn't polished and some of the tables had *marks* on them, which it didn't seem to me anybody had made the least attempt to rub away! Of course," she went on, lowering her voice to impart this piece of criticism, "I don't think her new ladyship knows much about running such a large house! She's very keen on having new curtains made – and such like – but she doesn't take much care of what's there."

"Oh, dear," Saffy murmured. "I daresay she'll grow more accustomed to managing the place."

"Huh!" Mrs Hurst's face registered something approaching disgust. "I don't think she notices! She wants people to bring her cups of tea and coffee and so forth all day – which means they don't have so much time for doing what they ought to be doing."

"Oh, dear," Saffy repeated.

"It's my belief," Mrs Hurst went on, leaning towards Aunt Saffy and clutching her arm in case she was so horrified by what she was about to impart that she ran away before her informant reached her conclusion, "that he's regretting his hastiness! Serve him right, is what I say!"

"Is he not an agreeable gentleman?" Saffy asked.

"He's not so bad – but hasty! It's *her* that's put the cat among the pigeons. Miss Thetford – she can't stand the sight of her – do you know, she thinks she poisoned her mother?"

"*Did* she?" Saffy asked.

"I wouldn't put it past her – she's that ambitious and selfish – but I don't see how she did it – although I s'pose nobody would expect me to know. The thing is, you see, that she made *him* believe she was expecting before Lady Thetford passed away, but it wasn't true – you know if you do the cleaning – so she'd have been bound to want Lady Thetford out of the way in order to nab him before he found out the truth."

"Lord!" Saffy exclaimed, genuinely shocked at this underhand manner of getting one's own way. "But I imagine he did too – if he really believed she was expecting. After all, just imagine how afraid he must have been that the governess would give birth to a boy before they were married! Do you think he might have poisoned his wife himself – or the pair of them together?"

"Might've, I s'pose, but he liked his wife – seemed heartbroken when she died, but then he upped and married that no-good piece almost before she was cold in her grave."

"But she is expecting now, isn't she? I mean she looks as though she is!"

"Huh! She didn't wait, did she? Pretended to lose the first one – *after* they'd got married - kept the pretence up until then. Now it seems she's genuinely expecting – unless it's no more than a cushion!" Mrs Hurst said with a dark look.

"So he married her, believing she was expecting, she pretended to lose it – although in fact she'd never been expecting at that point – and now claims she has another on the way?"

"Yes!"

Aunt Saffy frowned.

"When did she declare she was expecting again? I mean, he has several children already – he must know how long they take to grow – and how long it takes after a disappointment to – well, to be able to announce another one's on the way!"

This remark, coming as it did from a maiden lady, caused Mrs Hurst to laugh in a vulgar way which made poor Saffy – who had never discussed this sort of thing before – flinch. She was conscious of her friends loitering behind, probably listening and judging her handling of this excessively shameful subject inadequate, and endeavoured to force Mrs Hurst to move so that her back was facing them.

"What do you think of Miss Thetford?" she asked, believing that discussion of the new Lady Thetford's condition had run its course.

"Oh, she's a little madam, she is! She's always sending for something or other too so that, between her and the new mistress, the servants are running about all over the place. That Miss Veronica, though, she's a sweet girl – doesn't deserve what's happened to her."

170

"No," Saffy said sadly, "sometimes it does seem the world is rather an unfair place. People don't get their just desserts, do they? Perhaps they do later – when they …" her voice died away but the way she cast her eyes upwards made it clear what she meant.

"Apparently they all thought she was dead when she was brought back," Mrs Hurst said. "His lordship's been beside himself ever since."

"Is there anyone who can comfort him?"

Mrs Hurst's laugh this time was derisive rather than vulgar. "Certainly not her new ladyship. Miss Thetford's doing her best but she's not been used to think of anyone but herself. I suppose you know she's setting her cap at Rushlake."

"I rather thought so, but I'm afraid she won't be successful. Do you know if anyone has any idea how Veronica came to take a tumble? I suppose it was an accident."

Aunt Saffy had no wish to discuss *her* lordship's marital plans, of which she guessed he had no more idea than she, and wanted to get back to discussing the Thetfords' misfortunes.

"Miss Thetford doesn't think so – she's convinced that someone wanted to kill *her* – she'd lent her old riding habit to Miss Veronica, you see."

"Do you think she might be right – that it wasn't an accident?" Saffy asked, trying to looked shocked in an innocent sort of way.

"I wouldn't put anything past that governess-as-was," Mrs Hurst said. "She was there – in spite of his lordship ordering her to stay at home. He didn't want her putting his son – if it is one – in jeopardy."

"No. Do you know that he told her to stay at home?"

"Everybody knows. He was shouting, she was screeching – of course she did what she wanted in the end – ignored him. I don't suppose she cares two hoots if she loses it – what she wanted was the title."

"Dear me," Saffy said, adding, "It sounds as if he's quite gentle."

"You mean she's not afraid of him? No, she's not. If you ask me, it'd be better for everyone if he was a bit firmer with her."

"Yes," Saffy said musingly, "particularly if he killed his first wife. He would have done all that, presumably at her bidding – or with her help – and then finds himself tied to a virago."

Mrs Hurst smiled in a rather malicious way.

"Precisely. But, if you've killed one wife, I suppose it's a small step to kill another. She should look out."

"Indeed," Saffy agreed, becoming quite carried away with this line of discussion, "but, if *she's* killed one person, she might kill another – him.

171

Then she'd still be Viscountess – a dowager of course – but she wouldn't have to put up with him – and presumably, from what you say, she doesn't care for him."

"Well, yes, but the thing is that Miss Thetford is suspicious, so the first one to be rid of is her. If I were Miss Thetford, I'd be worried."

"Yes, that's true. So you think someone – the Viscountess presumably because surely Lord Thetford wouldn't want to kill his own daughter – meant to kill Miss Thetford and mistook Veronica for her?"

"Yes. She must be kicking herself. She'll try again, mark my words!" Saffy shivered.

She said, "Did anyone notice who was close to Veronica at the time?"

Mrs Hurst shrugged and Saffy suffered a spasm of disappointment. Of course, none of the servants had been on the hunt so that speculation was idle.

"Has Miss Thetford accused Lady Thetford of causing the accident?" she asked.

"Oh, yes, I'm sure she has. Everyone's talking about it but her ladyship hasn't taken any notice."

"She probably wasn't nearby," Saffy said. "Has Lord Thetford heard the rumours?"

"I can't see how he can't have done, but he hasn't said anything either. I think they just hope Miss Veronica will get better and don't want to think about whether anyone wanted her – or Miss Thetford - dead."

Saffy, perceiving that Mrs Hurst was far more interested in the manipulations that the second Lady Thetford had employed to become Viscountess than whether poor Veronica's fall had been precipitated by a deliberate act, judged that she had got all she was likely to from this particular source. She made some excuse and, Mrs Hurst, taking the hint, promised she would let her know if anything new turned up.

Saffy, relieved to be able to stop talking about such exceedingly unpleasant subjects, switched her attention to the stall she was standing beside, which sold various highly coloured sweets. She bought some for Jenny's children and soon found herself back in the company of Lady Amberstone and Miss Patchett.

"Well, you're quite the interrogator, aren't you?" Miss Patchett observed.

"I didn't find much out though, did I, except that nobody likes the present Lady Thetford, possibly even including Lord Thetford? But then, I think we knew that anyway, didn't we? Do you think he might be the murderer – got rid of his first wife at the behest of the present one and was then forced to try to get rid of his eldest daughter on account of her suspicions?"

"Apart from his new wife, he does seem the most likely candidate," Lady Amberstone agreed, "but I find it hard to believe he meant to hurt his daughter, even if it wasn't the more agreeable one."

Aunt Saffy, who had led a sheltered, if unexciting, life and had no children of her own, did not altogether subscribe to the view that people would never harm their own children. She rather thought that, if a man was selfish enough and determined enough to get his own way, he would not let anything, even a daughter, prevent him. If he had killed his wife because she had only given him daughters, it followed that he did not value those girls very highly. They were expendable.

As for the former governess, she had not spoken to her, but she had seen her in church, both before the previous Viscountess had died and after, and she had not failed to note the difference in appearance. As a governess, Miss Morris had been proper, neatly turned out and clearly in control of her charges – not in fact a very frequent occurrence with governesses, who were mostly rather drab, weak-minded individuals who were bullied by both their charges and their employers. Now that she was the Viscountess, she was excessively well-dressed and adopted an air of haughty confidence. No one who had not known her former employment would have guessed from her demeanour that she had once been little more than a servant.

She would, in Saffy's opinion, have been perfectly capable of poisoning the former mistress and trying to murder one of the daughters. The only thing that did not quite ring true was that she had somehow managed to hurt the wrong girl.

The three ladies, having completed their purchases and grown tired of the emporium, left and set off down the street towards where they had been told they would find Martha's Tea Rooms. After such an energetic half-hour of investigation on Aunt Saffy's part and efforts to be discreet on the others', they all felt in need of sustenance. None of them had been there before, Lady Amberstone and Miss Patchett because they came from Yorkshire and Aunt Saffy because she had not sufficient funds either for shopping or buying tea in a tea room.

The Marchioness's appearance ensured that they were shown to the best table where they were able to order coffee and cakes almost before they had sat down.

"Well, this is very pleasant," Lady Amberstone said, looking round.

There were a great many people in the room, indeed most of the tables were taken, but the spacious one in the window, to which the three had been shown, had perhaps been kept in case the establishment might be honoured with the visit of such an august personage as her ladyship.

"Do you know any of these people?" she asked Saffy.

Aunt Saffy, so intimidated by the excitement of sitting in a sort of restaurant, at a table with a spotless white cloth and a pretty bunch of flowers in a vase, had not yet looked around at the other people, but when she did she saw at once that there was indeed a woman she recognised.

"Oh, yes," she replied in a whisper. "Over there is Lady Mottbane. She is a friend – indeed I think she might be a relative - of the Thetfords. She lives, I believe, on the other side of Shrewsbury – nearer to England than Wales, if you see what I mean – but I have seen her in Rushlake when she has stayed with the Thetfords."

"Ah!" Lady Amberstone said, looking towards the table which Aunt Saffy indicated as accommodating Lady Mottbane. The woman was sitting with another woman as well as a young girl probably not yet out. She was exceedingly well dressed and very good-looking. The other woman was some years older, possibly an aunt, and the girl looked to be of a similar age to Veronica Thetford.

"I remember the Mottbanes," Lady Amberstone said at once, also speaking in a low tone so that the lady in question would not be able to hear her. "He – the one I knew, who is most likely dead now – was a well-breeched fellow – an Earl, as I recall. That woman must be his daughter-in-law, I should imagine, and the girl his granddaughter. I don't know whether he – the old Earl and presumably the young one too – is related to the Thetfords, but if, as you say, they are sometimes their guests, the girl may be friendly with Veronica. Do you know the older woman?"

"No, I've not seen her before. Would you like me to greet them in some way? I'm a little afraid she may think it presumptuous of me to accost her."

"You can explain that your friend was acquainted with the old Earl and is fairly longing to hear how the family has prospered in the last twenty or thirty years."

Aunt Saffy looked anxious and Helena, seeking to help her, suggested that she, Helena, could walk past the table and drop her bag close to Lady Mottbane's foot. She could then pick it up, apologise, and Saffy, having seen her friend's embarrassment, could approach and exclaim at the chance of seeing a lady she recognised. It would be a matter of little difficulty to bring Lady Amberstone into the conversation at this point, and she, after having enquired as to the family, could move easily on to the present situation with the Thetfords.

None of them having a better idea and all rather over-excited after Saffy's success with Mrs Hurst, they decided to put this plan into action.

Miss Patchett rose and, picking up her handbag, was heard to say that she rather thought she wanted a closer look at a picture on the wall which reminded her of a place she had once visited. Making her way towards the picture, she stumbled a little and dropped her handbag almost into the lap of the older woman.

"Oh, lud! I'm so sorry! I'm afraid I wasn't looking where I was going – my eyes were fixed on my objective – that picture over there," she mumbled, bending down to pick up the bag and blushing quite naturally at her own extraordinary temerity in acting out this little charade.

"Oh, goodness, not at all! It's easily done!" the older lady said at once. "I've always thought the tables were far too close together."

"Oh, thank you; I'm afraid I'm …"

But she was interrupted here by Aunt Saffy wafting into view, putting a hand under her elbow as though to support a particularly feeble person and exclaiming with – almost – unfeigned surprise at seeing a person she knew.

"Why it's Lady Mottbane!" she cried. "Fancy seeing you here! Are you staying with the Thetfords?"

"Saffy! I thought it was you when you came in but, never having seen you in town before, I believed myself to be mistaken," the younger of the two women returned in a hearty tone.

One might have thought, Saffy reflected, that she was pleased to see her; Saffy was certain she was not, for she, Saffy, was a dull, despised companion to a young lady with whom a handsome, fashionable woman such as Lady Mottbane could not possibly be supposed to have anything in common.

"Oh, I came with my lord's aunt, Lady Amberstone," Saffy explained, turning and gesturing towards the Marchioness, who had remained at the table and was looking towards them.

"Lady Amberstone!" the older lady exclaimed, adding more quietly, "I've never met her, but I've heard a great deal about her."

"Would you like me to introduce you?" Saffy asked, not in fact knowing the older lady's connexion to the younger.

"Oh, I would, if that wouldn't be too presumptuous!" the older one replied at once.

"This is my Aunt Amelia," Lady Mottbane said, perhaps sensing Saffy's dilemma. "She is my mama's sister and we have all been staying at the Thetfords. We didn't come for Christmas as we were entertaining our own family, but the idea was that we would spend New Year with them. Unfortunately, when we arrived, we rather wished someone had told us what a state they were in – one of the girls badly hurt the day before. We wouldn't have come if we'd known – and we've tried to absent ourselves as much as possible so as not to be in the way."

"Oh, dear, yes," Saffy replied at once. "The poor things have had an awful time. Did they tell you," she went on, doing her best to spread a bit of gossip in a wholly unfamiliar manner, "that at first everyone thought she was no more."

"Yes, we were told that. It has really *not* been a happy visit. We'd never met the new Lady Thetford before either."

"She hasn't," Saffy said, still acting in a completely uncharacteristic manner, "been Lady Thetford for long."

"No, indeed," Lady Mottbane replied, now in a sort of amplified whisper. "The late Lady Thetford was my aunt," she explained, "a younger sister of Aunt Amelia. We came to her funeral, when she sadly died, but never expected him - Uncle Vernon – to marry again so soon. We didn't," she added in a disapproving tone, "attend the wedding. Was it a grand affair?"

"I don't believe so," Saffy admitted. "I wasn't here at the time – I'd gone to London with Titania. Ah, here is Lady Amberstone – allow me to introduce you."

While Saffy and Lady Mottbane had been exclaiming over the goings-on with the Thetfords, Miss Patchett had gone to fetch the Marchioness, returning with her in tow as though she wished to share a prize.

Chapter 22

Lady Mottbane was so overawed at meeting such an august lady that she stood up and, upon being introduced, bobbed a curtsey.

"I was used to know your father-in-law," the Marchioness said. "Not well, but we attended the same parties aeons ago."

"I'm sorry to have to tell you that he died a few years ago," Lady Mottbane said, although the fact that she was Lady Mottbane made it clear, without any explanation, that her husband was now Lord Mottbane.

"I'm sorry to hear that," Lady Amberstone said. "What I did not know then was that he was – your family is – connected with the Thetfords."

"Oh, yes, but then I don't think they were when you knew my father-in-law. The connection is through the first Lady Thetford – Margaret. She was my mama's sister – and this," she gestured towards the older woman, "is my Aunt Amelia, another sister of the first Viscountess."

Everyone greeted each other, more coffee was ordered and Lady Amberstone moved determinedly forward to her purpose.

"You must have been very upset when your Aunt Margaret died," she said.

"I was, although she had been ill for some time – off and on. What distressed me far more was the unseemly haste with which my uncle married again."

"Yes, I'm not surprised," Lady Amberstone agreed. "It does sound as if it was somewhat rushed. Was there some reason for that?"

"Of course there was. The governess – governess if you please! – was already expecting. He and that creature had not waited for a decent interval – any interval at all indeed – before embarking on some sort of *liaison*."

"It must have been awkward," Lady Amberstone murmured. "Did you attend the wedding?"

"No. We couldn't face it, I'm afraid, so soon after poor Margaret's funeral and now that we've met her – the new Viscountess - we're relieved we didn't. The creature is excessively vulgar. I know – or at least I must assume – that Vernon wants a son, which my poor aunt was unfortunately unable to provide – but I can't help hoping that it doesn't happen because the idea of a child of that harpy becoming Viscount one day is quite dreadful!"

Miss Patchett, sitting on the periphery of the group and exchanging small talk with the surviving aunt, heard this forcefully expressed view and hoped that it would not lead to another female death in the Thetford family.

"You say your Aunt Margaret had been ill for some time before she died," Lady Amberstone said. "Have you heard that Julia Thetford believes she was poisoned?"

"By the harpy? Oh, yes, she tells everyone and now seems to believe that poor Veronica was mistaken for her and injured in an attempt to remove her and her suspicions. I wouldn't be a bit surprised if it were to turn out to be true. Poisoning can be done, I understand, in a number of ways – some of them resulting in sudden and unexpected death, but not all. A clever poisoner, I believe, takes their time about it so that it looks, to everyone else, as if the poor departed had been ill for a long time."

"Oh dear! But that puts her – Julia – in a great deal of danger. Is she not afraid that next time whoever wants to be rid of her will be successful?"

"I warned her of that – and of course, since Veronica's accident, if it was an accident, she has conceded that she's in a dangerous position, but she seems to be engaged on a sort of crusade to right her mama's wrongs – and now Veronica's too."

"But do you not think she's refining upon her dislike of her stepmother and her grief at the loss of her mother and coming to an erroneous conclusion?" Lady Amberstone asked gently, determined to come to a definite conclusion about the accusations and counter-accusations in the Thetford household.

"No, as a matter of fact I don't. I believe her – and, on that account, am quite reluctant to leave. I feel someone should try to keep an eye on her – and the other girls."

"Good God!" Lady Amberstone exclaimed. "Do you think this murderous person might harm the younger girls too?"

"I don't know, but, if it's the governess-as-was, I shouldn't think she'd stop at anything."

"Is there anything we can do to help?" the Marchioness asked.

"I doubt it, but you could try telling Thetford what's going on."

"But surely he must have some inkling?"

"He shuts his eyes to anything which disturbs him – and anything which might make him realise what a dreadful mistake he's made."

"I suppose," Lady Amberstone said, "that he's in love with his new wife."

"I doubt it," Lady Mottbane snapped. "I should think it was a case of nothing more than the grossest lust - and now I think he almost detests her. He's beside himself with anxiety about Veronica, infuriated with Julia and …"

"Mama," the young girl interrupted. It was the first time she had spoken. "Pray, Mama, poor Lady Amberstone doesn't want to have to inspect *all* our dirty washing."

"I assure you I don't mind in the least," her ladyship returned at once, afraid that this interfering girl was about to prevent her unwise mother from spilling any more beans. "I'm an old woman and nothing can shock me."

"It might if it were your family everyone's talking about," Lady Mottbane retorted with some acidity.

But Lady Amberstone was perfectly equal to dealing with this sort of reaction. She assumed a sympathetic expression, nodded sagely and returned in a gentle voice, "You're perfectly right; I am fortunate, at least at present, to be unaware of anything disgraceful in my family – that doesn't mean it hasn't taken place – or that it won't – simply that at present I'm spared knowing about it."

Lady Mottbane smiled. "You're right. Dear, I find myself wishing I didn't know. The thing is," she confided, "you have sons, I have a son, there is therefore no particular need for our husbands to replace us with a version which they hope will be more successful at providing them with the one thing they all seem to want above everything else. You'd much better not listen to this, Selina, because it may come back to haunt you when you're married."

"I suppose," Lady Amberstone suggested, "that if one were to marry beneath one – choose anyone other than a nobleman with a line to maintain – one would not have to worry so much. The thing was, when I married, I was wildly in love with my husband and it never entered my head that he might want to replace me."

"No, mine neither," Lady Mottbane agreed, "but only think of Henry VIII."

The girl, Selina, who had been looking a trifle anxious, giggled at this. "Do you think," she asked, "that it would be preferable to be poisoned rather than beheaded?"

"I suppose it might take longer for poison to take effect – and it would almost certainly be painful, while, in Anne Boleyn's case, I believe her husband was thoughtful enough to engage a specially qualified French executioner to strike her head off with a sword rather than chop at it in

179

the usual way as though she were a joint of beef. Really, dear, I don't know, but I think you should heed Lady Amberstone's advice and look around for a nice gentleman without a title but plenty of money. The Thetfords haven't even got that," she finished with some disapproval.

During this curious conversation Aunt Saffy and Miss Patchett were having some difficulty in containing an embarrassing desire to laugh. It was too absurd, but it seemed that diverting the discussion about the Thetfords' problems on to Henry VIII and his wives had succeeded in distancing it from the present because Selina looked reassured.

"I don't think I'll marry at all," she declared with an emphatic nod.

"Oh, that's exactly what I've always thought!" Miss Patchett could not help exclaiming.

"And are you not married, ma'am?" the girl asked.

"No."

"Not yet," Aunt Saffy murmured, which made Helena blush.

"Have you got an admirer?" the girl asked, not too young to interpret the blush correctly.

"He's on the point of making an offer but is too shy to do so," Lady Amberstone said, "which is silly because neither of them is very young and really should be getting on with it, especially if they want any children – boys or girls."

"Isn't he a nobleman?" Selina asked.

"No," Miss Patchett replied, laughing. "Far from it."

"But does he have money?" the girl persisted.

"No," Helena said, "but I do."

This conclusion made everyone laugh so much that the other people in the *café* looked at them.

When they had all calmed down a little, Lady Amberstone repeated her offer to help in any way she could.

Lady Mottbane thanked the Marchioness for her excessively kind offer but repeated that she believed that the only way she might be able to assist was in trying to get through to Lord Thetford.

"I will do that willingly," the Marchioness said at once, "but fear he would think it odd if I were to seek an audience with him. It might be better if my nephew, Rushlake, were to approach him. What do you feel someone else can say more easily than you?"

"Ah," Lady Mottbane said with a sigh, acknowledging that Lady Amberstone had perfectly understood the dilemma.

"The thing is, you see," she went on, "that I am quite a deal younger than he so that I would imagine he'll think I'm interfering in his affairs with little justification – and there is little of which I could inform him that he does not know much better than I!"

"Well, yes," the Marchioness agreed, smiling, "but, apart from the difference in age, will he not think I'm even less well placed to comment upon his situation? So far as age is concerned, I daresay he might think I'm a silly old woman whose judgment is bound to be at fault."

"I don't think he could possibly think that – and as for your nephew approaching him – he's *very* young, is he not? The thing is, you see, that, from my observation, he wishes – strongly – that he had not married for a second time, at all, but certainly not *that* woman and not that hastily! That's why I think the *bons mots* of an older, wiser woman might be more acceptable than anything your nephew could say – or I. I'm a relative, which makes it particularly difficult for he is almost bound to take it badly."

Lady Amberstone laughed at this.

"So that it would be preferable if he were to take offence from an interfering old woman who will no doubt go back to immure herself safely in the north almost as soon as she has delivered herself of her opinion?"

Lady Mottbane had the grace to blush and the Marchioness nodded.

"Certainly I will do so. I should like to meet the rebarbative new wife too!"

"Yes, of course. I can't tell you how grateful I am! I've never even met you before but have admired you from a distance for years. I can't believe I've had the temerity to ask for your help almost as soon as I've set eyes upon you."

"Oh, pray don't refine upon that aspect!" Lady Amberstone exclaimed, amused. "I always think it's much easier to ask a favour of a person with whom one is not acquainted than one with whom one is."

After this, the three Rushlake ladies took their leave and set off down the road, their sole aim now being how to pass the time until they expected the coachman to return to their meeting place.

"Well, I think we've been quite successful," Miss Patchett observed as they paused to stare purposelessly into a shop window.

"I don't think we should pin too many hopes on my visit to Thetford," Lady Amberstone said. "I shall have to think of a suitable reason to call and, if he's there, she will no doubt stick to him like a burr and I won't be able to quiz him about her, although I own I'm curious as to the sort of female she is."

"Shall I come with you?" Aunt Saffy asked. "When you've had enough of her, I could take her aside and badger her about organising some sort of charity sale in the village. It's the sort of thing people will expect me to be thinking about," she added in a self-deprecatory manner.

"Would you, my dear? That would be very helpful – and then we could compare our impressions afterwards."

"Certainly," Aunt Saffy said, although her heart quailed within her at the degree of force that might be required to prise the Viscountess from her husband's side.

Passing a small restaurant a little later as they ambled down the road, Lady Amberstone, aware of Saffy's probable exhaustion after such an energetic morning, suggested they pause again for a 'spot' of luncheon. This was welcomed with relief by both the others, although it added a new worry for Saffy, who began immediately to be plagued with anxiety as to who would pay for it.

"It will be," her ladyship said, leading the way inside and once again divining the former companion's concern, "my pleasure to buy you both luncheon. It has been, I believe, a fruitful morning and we have definitely earned a small reward."

"Oh, my lady," Saffy said, "I can't let you do that – why, you paid for the coffee earlier."

"Pray don't let us argue about it," the Marchioness returned. "I would like you both to be my guests. I'm excessively fatigued after all that detecting and really feel I *must* sit down for a little while. Let us hope," she added uncharacteristically, "that there will be no one whom we recognise and therefore no necessity to grill anyone else about that exceedingly tiresome family."

"There's not the least likelihood of either you or I recognising anyone," Helena said, "and Saffy must sit with her back to the door so that she won't either."

Having thus disposed themselves around a small table, a light luncheon was ordered and the ladies settled down to eat it. Saffy looked neither to right nor left and basked in the approval of the other two, only expressing anxiety about whether Mr Bodley would have found something to eat.

"Oh, I don't think we need to be exercised about him," Lady Amberstone said. "Gentlemen never have the least difficulty in finding an inn to serve them a glass of ale and a pie of some sort."

After luncheon, they set off again and soon found a pleasant enough park where they sat down close to a small lake. Saffy, no longer ordered to turn her back on anyone passing whom she might recognise, soon did see someone familiar - a young man from Rushlake. He was walking with a young lady, the two of them deep in conversation as they circumnavigated the lake.

"Oh, there's a fellow from Rushlake!" she exclaimed, nodding towards him.

"Really?" Lady Amberstone asked. "He seems to have a great deal to say. Do you know who *she* is?"

"No; I've never seen her before, but he – I've seen him riding – when I've been out walking, you know."

"Was he on Rushlake land then?" the Marchioness asked, thinking it unlikely that Aunt Saffy's perambulations would have taken her very far.

"I suppose he must have been, but he is – at least he's dressed as – a gentleman."

"Yes," Miss Patchett said. "He was on the hunt – the one where poor Veronica was hurt."

"Was he?" Lady Amberstone asked, metaphorically pricking up her ears. "Was the young woman there too?"

"No, I don't think so. They seem very close, don't they?"

"Indeed; I should say he was courting her – and she's certainly not discouraging him."

"Do you think we should try to speak to him?" Aunt Saffy asked.

"Lord!" the Marchioness exclaimed. "I suppose we should, but how in the world are we to find an adequate reason to interrupt him while he's clearly laying out the advantages of an alliance to whomever the young woman is?"

It was, once again, Aunt Saffy who put herself forward in fear and trembling, but it seemed to her that, since she was the local resident – or had been – it must be up to her to take the lead in accosting someone she recognised.

"I could - if I went through the trees there, I could probably fetch up in front of them," she said, "for they're not moving fast. Then I could approach from the opposite direction, recognise him and exclaim at the extraordinary chance that we should be walking in the same park! I suppose he might feel he had to introduce me!"

"Do you know who he is though – his name and so on?" Miss Patchett asked.

"I can't just at present recall it," Aunt Saffy admitted, too nervous at the thought of the coming encounter to engage her mind in trying to remember the man's name, "but I don't suppose that matters. I'll say I recognise him but don't recall his name."

"If you're sure you don't mind," Lady Amberstone said gently. She could see that poor Saffy was, although professing eagerness to be helpful, extremely reluctant to do what she had herself suggested.

"I do mind," Saffy admitted, "but, if a greater good is to be achieved, I believe one must occasionally suppress one's reluctance to put oneself forward."

With which, without waiting for any further encouragement or advice, she rose from the bench and darted into the belt of trees, whch had been thoughtfully planted to add to the apparent naturalness of the pond.

In a few moments, she emerged beside the lake several yards in front of the young couple and, adopting a bright and interested expression, fixed her eyes upon the ducks which were waddling about near the water's edge.

"Don't you feel the cold?" she enquired of the ducks, bending down to address them and rising suddenly and without warning almost in front of the young couple.

"Oh, I'm so sorry – I didn't see you there – I'm afraid I was talking to the ducks! Oh, why, it's Mr Tipley, isn't it?"

Finding herself face-to-face with the young man, she recalled his name – or more or less – in the very nick of time.

"Topley, as a matter of fact! It's Miss Hemsted, isn't it – from Rushlake?"

"Yes, yes, indeed. Fancy seeing you here!" she exclaimed, all a-flutter.

"I thought you'd gone to London," he said, smiling at her rather stiffly so that she thought he was not at all pleased to see her.

"Oh, I did – we did – but we've come back for Christmas."

"Ah! Will you be staying long?"

Saffy, beginning to realise that he had no intention of introducing the young woman, smiled and said, "Well, I don't know, to be sure. I must do what his lordship wants – and Lady Titania of course. I don't believe I've met you," she added to the young woman.

"Oh, this is Miss Pritchard – and Miss Hemsted, who is Lady Titania's companion," the young man said hastily but with such a lack of enthusiasm that Aunt Saffy was again certain that he wished she would go away.

"Miss Pritchard," she said, smiling in what she hoped was a friendly fashion. "Are you a local as it were?"

"Oh no, Ma'am, I've come from some way away – Derbyshire. I too came for Christmas, to stay with my aunt, Mrs Miran. Mr Topley and I met on that most unfortunate day when poor Miss Thetford was thrown. Do you know how she is? At first, you know, we all thought she was dead – it was quite dreadful – but I've heard that she is well on the way to recovering."

"She's certainly alive," Aunt Saffy replied soberly, "but I would not say that she's precisely on the way to recovery. She's lost the use of her legs."

"Oh, how awful!" the young woman exclaimed with such genuine horror that Saffy warmed to her. "That poor person must feel quite dreadful!"

"Oh?" Saffy asked, wondering which person and why that one should feel so particularly bad.

"The horse nudged hers," Miss Pritchard explained. "I've been wondering why her companion was so clumsy ever since it happened because, you see, there was plenty of space."

Chapter 23

While Lord Vincent conversed amicably with the girl about whom her relatives were so exercised, she, relaxing and growing in confidence, whipped up the horses until they were trotting along briskly. Since they had been doing that under Titania's control, he said nothing but Titania, watching from the back, saw how alert he had grown and trusted that he would intervene if necessary. It was only when Veronica, glancing teasingly at Lord Vincent, applied the whip once more and the horses broke into a canter that he began to look seriously worried.

"That's too fast," he said. "This isn't a suitable road along which to be bucketing at such a rate."

"Nonsense!" she cried. "Don't you like to go fast? We can go faster still!"

"Don't you dare!" he said in an avuncular tone. "I'll stop you if you do anything so silly."

"How will you do that?"

"Quite easily – I'll take the reins."

"I think you should take them now," Marcus Stapleton, who had grown white with fear, begged from the back. "You're going too fast, Veronica."

"Oh!" she cried. "I thought *you* of all people liked to take risks!"

"Depends upon the risk," he returned. "You're putting us all in danger."

"I don't care!" she declared. "What can happen to me? I'm already crippled."

"Do you want us all to be killed?" he asked quite angrily and Lord Vincent, exchanging a glance with Titania, leaned across and snatched the reins from the girl at the very moment when she whipped the horses again.

Speeding up in response to the whip and confused by the tug on the reins, the horses reacted with the same fear as the people in the carriage. Schooled to do what they were bid, they interpreted the confusing signals as instructions to go faster and veer to the left, a result which propelled them off the road and into a field while at the same time trying to gallop.

Lord Vincent, who was no mean whip, struggled to control them, sliding along the seat until he had pushed Veronica out of the way. She, suddenly terrified by what she had done and her own helplessness, began to scream and Marcus, less accomplished as a whip but more frightened, scrambled across the seat, pushing Titania out of the way, and snatched the girl from behind, dragging her into the back.

Titania, displaced, tried to move to the other side as the carriage bucked and tottered across terrain over which it had not been designed to drive. However, it was not long before, fearing that she might be catapulted to the ground if she stood up, she was forced to abandon the attempt. She huddled in her corner, Mr Stapleton with Veronica upon his lap, pressed up against her until he had managed to slide along to the other end.

Lord Vincent eventually succeeded in slowing the horses, but the rolling and bumping carriage continued to disturb them so much that from time to time one or the other still tried to make a break for freedom.

Titania held on to the seat for dear life and Marcus continued to hold the sobbing Veronica in his arms as they swayed backwards and forwards, hitting his shoulder on the side as the carriage shuddered to a halt.

Titania jumped down immediately and went to the horses' heads, along with Jim, who had somehow managed to clamp himself so firmly to the back that he was still with them. Between them, they calmed the animals, Lord Vincent remaining where he was with the reins in his hand, ready to take control again if they bolted.

Nobody spoke apart from Titania and the boy, who both continued to murmur soothingly to the horses. She glanced up at Lord Vincent.

"Be careful!" he said in a low voice. "They're very disturbed and may try to run off at any minute. You'll be sent flying if that happens."

"I know, but, as we don't want them to do that, I think it's best if we try to calm them down."

"I don't want you to be hurt," he said.

"I don't want to be hurt, but I arranged this outing, I allowed Veronica to take the reins – Lord, I never thought she'd be so silly."

"She's not much more than a child," he pointed out, "and she's been incarcerated and incapacitated since the accident. I daresay it's that which caused her to act so foolishly."

"Why didn't you say something if that was what you thought?" she snapped, albeit in not much more than a whisper.

"If you want to argue with me, you'd better come away from the horses," Lord Vincent said quietly. "Jim can manage them. They look calmer now in any event, but your getting worked up won't help."

"I know. It's all my fault."

"Don't be silly and self-indulgent. Get back in the carriage."

Considerably to his surprise, Titania obeyed him, disdaining Jim's offer of a hand up and clambering into the seat beside Lord Vincent. She glanced behind her and observed Veronica still in the Reverend Marcus's arms, she sobbing, he stroking her hair from which her hat had long since fallen.

"What shall we do about them?" she asked Lord Vincent with a despairing look.

"Nothing. I don't see what we can do at present and they can't do much in a carriage with us sitting in front, but I do wonder how long they've been engaging in what strikes me as a romantic entanglement of longer standing than the last five minutes."

"I wonder too and believe we should try to stop it. She's only sixteen – far too young to be making love to anyone, let alone a penniless curate."

"Would he be such an unsuitable lover? He's your kinsman – don't you feel able to support his suit?"

"No; she's too young."

"Oh, how hard and unromantic you are!" Lord Vincent exclaimed, teasing.

"I'm a horrid old maid," she retorted, "and I realise that my age forces me into the role of chaperone. But, as I said, I organised this outing and am therefore responsible. If they're to spend the next half-hour, while we wait for the horses to calm down sufficiently to try to get them back on to the road, carrying on in that fashion, what will happen in the future?"

"I imagine he'll have to speak to her father."

"And I doubt that's what he wants. He doesn't strike me as in the least ready to settle down, even if he does seem to have formed a *tendre* for her. He's the same sort of age as Horace – barely out of Oxford and far too young to take on the burden of a wife, particularly one who's crippled."

"That's a very proper – and practical – attitude to take but if people fall in love, they fall in love and there's not much to be done about it, unless one is to forbid them to see or speak to each other again – a line which rarely leads to anything but heartache, very likely on both people's parts, and may lead to tragedy."

"They're not Romeo and Juliet," she snapped, irritated. It was bad enough to discover that the man she had thought admired her was already more than half in love with another without Lord Vincent adopting a perfectly infuriatingly pragmatic line.

"There's nothing wrong with Marcus's background; only with his lack of fortune and his youth. As for her, I suppose she must have a respectable portion, but she's too young and now she's crippled. She would be a burden on a young man; I can't see how he could provide for her even if she does bring some sort of a marriage settlement. You talk as though they're in love – I don't think he is, at least."

"Why not?"

"Because he's – I don't know; I just don't believe he's thinking sensibly about what he's letting himself in for."

Lord Vincent smiled. "A man in love doesn't think of that sort of thing; all he thinks about is his beloved's bright eyes and when he can arrange the next episode of love-making."

"Oh dear! You speak as though you know all about it. Are you in love?"

He smiled a trifle secretively but did not reply.

"What in the world do you mean?" Titania demanded. It seemed that she, now clearly in the role of disapproving spinster, had furnished her carriage with two men, both of whom were romantically entangled with someone or other – quite possibly, she thought bitterly, with the same woman – or girl.

"From what you've just said, a man in love can think of nothing but his beloved – if that were the case, I cannot see how you can be so uncertain of your feelings. Who is she?"

But Lord Vincent seemed reluctant to name the young lady, pleading the uncertainty of her reception to his suit.

"But," he added, "I am by no means uncertain of my own sentiments."

"I suppose," Titania said in a hard voice, for she was peculiarly annoyed to hear her old friend had succumbed to the sort of tender feelings which, so far as she could see, made a man melt in a thoroughly disagreeable fashion into something closely resembling a fool, "that she is not Miss Thetford?"

"Julia? Good God, no. She is not at all the type of female I admire."

"No, I daresay not," she snapped. "Most likely, like everyone else, you prefer someone like Veronica."

"She is certainly infinitely more appealing than her sister, a circumstance which is unfortunate for the elder girl, but, no, I'm not interested in schoolgirls."

"Is she still a schoolgirl? Marcus seems very taken with her."

"He's not much more than a schoolboy," Lord Vincent replied.

"No, but …"

189

Titania turned round again to cast another glance at the pair in the back seat. She did not think either was behaving much in the way that one expected from people still at school, although, not having left the schoolroom such a very long time ago herself, she knew that people of that age were not above dreaming – indeed fantasising – about romantic interludes. Nevertheless, there was something disagreeable about their apparent need to remain locked in each other's arms.

"You're not hurt, are you, Veronica?" she asked abruptly in the voice of a stern governess.

"Oh, oh, no, I don't think so – at least not *more* hurt!" the girl answered, struggling to evade Marcus's clasp. Her face was red and still streaked with tears but her eyes were bright.

"Good, because I don't think your mama would approve of your behaviour."

"Mama – Mama is dead!" the girl cried, shuddering.

The curate pulled her back into his arms, apparently believing that would comfort her.

"Stop that at once!" Titania exclaimed. "I didn't bring you out for you to carry on like a pair of hayseeds! I think we should take you home at once. Vincent – will you drive?"

"Yes, but first we must get the carriage back on to the road," he pointed out.

They were sitting, a little crookedly, in a field with Jim still standing by the horses' heads.

"How do you propose to do that?" she asked. She was so irritated by the lovers that her usual good sense seemed to have deserted her.

"We'll have to lead them," he said. "I suggest you take the reins and Marcus and I will get out and try to push, pull and encourage the horses to get back on the road. Will you be able to handle them if they take exception to what we're doing and hurtle off somewhere as soon as they reach the road?"

"I suppose so," she replied, less confident than usual.

He looked at her speculatively.

"You seem rather rattled," he said gently. "Shall we wait a little longer until you've calmed down?"

"No; the longer I wait with those two carrying on in that fashion in the back, the more irritated I will become."

She turned round once more.

"Get out!" she said to the curate, "and help Vincent get the carriage back on the road!"

Mr Stapleton, pausing only to wrap Veronica more securely in the rug and rearrange the rapidly cooling bricks around her, did as he was bid.

Together with Jim, the men managed to turn the horses and carriage in the rutted lane in which they had ended up, and lead them back to the main road. Jim, who seemed to have a deep understanding of horses, patted, stroked and encouraged them during this difficult manoeuvre, leaving the two noblemen to do the heavy work of supporting the carriage as it turned.

Once it was safely on the road, Titania ordered Lord Vincent to drive and Mr Stapleton to sit beside him while she took her place beside Veronica.

"How long have you been romantically involved with Marcus?" she asked.

"Oh, oh, I'm not! I hardly know him! He – I think he thought I was frightened!"

"No doubt! Were you?"

"Well, I own I was. The thing is, you see, that not being able to move properly, I felt – I did feel horridly helpless. Oh, Titania, do you think I'll ever get better?"

"I've no idea, but I shouldn't think engaging in hanky panky with my cousin will facilitate feeling returning to your legs. They're not," she added sharply and unkindly, "connected to your heart."

"No! Oh, I wish it hadn't happened!"

"What?"

"The accident."

"Do you remember it at all?" Titania asked, deciding belatedly that castigating the poor girl for taking the man she had herself wanted would not help anyone discover the truth about either the possible poisoning or the 'accident'.

"No. The last thing I remember was the first hedge I jumped. I don't remember the bank – Julia tells me Minna stumbled as she came down and I fell off into the ditch at the bottom."

"Yes, you were certainly in the ditch. Who were you riding with before – when we set out and went over the first hedge?"

"Papa and Julia. I think Mama was there too, although she was a bit behind. She doesn't," Veronica confided, "get along very well with Julia so I think she probably hung back for that reason."

"Was there anyone else close?"

191

"Mr Stapleton was there; he was talking to Julia, I think – although one can't really talk much when one's jumping a hedge. Where were you?" she added.

"In the front when we went over the hedge; I was with Horace, my brother. I didn't notice any of your family, I'm afraid, because you were all behind us. Vincent was with us too."

Titania frowned in an effort to remember the formation of the riders.

"I think the Master was with us too, but not any of the rest of my family. My sister, Jenny, was behind – she doesn't hunt very often so is a little nervous – and our other guests were definitely behind. Were you and your family – and Marcus – just behind us, do you think?"

"Yes."

This time it was Veronica who frowned as she tried to recall with whom she had been riding at the beginning.

"You said," Titania went on, "that Lady Thetford was just behind you at first. Did she catch up later – and did your father go on ahead a bit?"

Titania was recalling the people who were in the lower field when Veronica fell into the ditch. Lord Thetford had certainly been there, as had his wife and Julia. If they had already got down the bank when Veronica fell, they must have been ahead of her. Why, she wondered, had Veronica arrived there later? She was – had been – by all accounts a more bruising rider than Julia – and surely more than the former governess, who it seemed unlikely had spent her childhood on horseback.

"Mama," Veronica said slowly, her memory beginning to return, "was not in a good mood. She had had an argument with Papa, who didn't want her to ride at all that day – because, you see, she's expecting and he was afraid she might get hurt. She's not a particularly good rider – at least I don't think so and I don't think Papa does either. I think she didn't want to ride close to Papa in case he went on at her, but she didn't want to be left behind either. When we set off, Papa, Julia and I were together and she was behind. I think Mr Stapleton joined us a bit later – when we passed his house – he wasn't there when we set off. At first he was speaking to Mama and Julia dropped back to speak to him, I think. I'm sure she didn't want to speak to Mama – she hates her, you see – but I think she quite likes Mr Stapleton."

"Does he like her?" Titania asked abruptly.

Veronica smiled in a way which disturbed Titania. There was, she thought, something proprietorial about it. "Yes, I think so. He likes Mama too. He's your cousin, isn't he?"

"A very distant one," Titania admitted in a cold voice, adding with what she was afterwards afraid was intentional cruelty. "It sounds as though he likes women. Does each of them think he cares particularly for her?"

Veronica almost jumped and something wholly at variance with her reputation for sweetness of nature passed across her face.

"Very likely; isn't that the essence of charm?"

"Up to a point, yes, but not so much that each thinks he's in love with her. I would call that the mark of a seducer and *not* a desirable characteristic in a man of the church."

"Oh!" Veronica exclaimed. "But the old ladies love him; he charms them like birds in the trees and they all come to church to see him."

"Surely not the point of going to church?"

"No; but does it matter *why* they go so long as they do?"

"Yes, I should say so. I mean, if you were to go to church to steal the collection, I don't think God would consider that a valid reason for attending."

"You don't seem to like him," Veronica said. "Why? Do you know something to his detriment?"

"Enough," Titania said in a surly tone. "Seducing old ladies – and young ones – is an unpleasant habit."

"Papa likes him," Veronica said.

"Does he? Does he approve of him making love to you?"

Chapter 24

"I'm sure he would," Veronica murmured.

"If he knew? I'm fairly certain he would not; you're sixteen. That's far too young to be looking at suitors and hoping your father will like them."

"People can be married at sixteen," Veronica pointed out sulkily.

"Has he asked you?"

"No – not yet."

"But you believe he will now that he's kissed you?"

Veronica blushed deeply.

"I – I didn't …," she muttered.

"Did he though? And you may not have actually kissed just now in the back of the carriage, but you might as well have done – and a lot more besides. Have you met him secretly?"

"Not – not precisely."

Titania nodded. She could see that Mr Stapleton had behaved much as he had done with her: lain in wait when he suspected she might be going riding and fallen into step with her. No doubt, when they'd been going for a bit, he would suggest they pause, dismount and let the horses graze a little while he and she whispered together and locked eyes.

As she thought of it, Titania felt her anger rising: she had been hoping for just such an encounter with her distant cousin, had indeed dreamed of it, thought it would be bound to happen sooner or later for, her own blood pulsing in her veins under his warm gaze, she had been certain his was too. She had even thought that, with her – with her fortune as additional sweetener, for she had not much confidence in her ability to prompt real love in a gentleman – he would make an offer before Horace took her back to London.

Now, in her company, indeed in her own family carriage, the wretched curate had made love to Veronica; she supposed she would have to take it that he preferred the younger girl, or did he think that his charms were so irresistible that she would forgive him and allow him to whisper into her ear in a similar manner?

While Titania had been grilling Veronica in the back, the two men remained silent in the front, presumably listening to every word behind them. Lord Vincent drove the carriage at a walking pace and Titania, behind him, saw how square and straight his shoulders were, how stern and unapproachable that portion of his neck between his collar and the brim of his hat appeared, and wished that it was he who was raking the wretched girl over the coals instead of she. He looked neither to right nor to left, except as his driving required, and did not glance at the curate beside him. Titania felt his disapproval and feared that it would fall upon her shoulders for suggesting such an unwise outing.

Mr Stapleton did not glance behind him either, but he did not sit up particularly straight, preferring to lounge in his seat with the sort of easy grace that Titania, until she had seen his manner with Veronica, had found so appealing. His gaze was not upon Lord Vincent, although his face was turned slightly in that direction, probably, Titania hazarded a guess, because he wished the two women in the back to have the benefit of his profile rather than the back of his head. He was several years younger than Lord Vincent and the back of his neck was still slender, a little too much so to support his handsome head, in Titania's opinion, and his shoulders in the well-fitting coat were narrower than Lord Vincent's.

For the first time in her life, she looked at Lord Vincent as a man, not simply as her old playmate and she found, to her surprise, that he bore comparison with the handsome curate. She had never considered him to be good-looking, but she realised now that he was in a well-bred sort of way. She could not see his face at the moment but she did not need to, for she knew him well. He had neat dark brown hair, the bottom tendrils of which she could see curling beneath his hat, fine hazel eyes under straight black brows, an aquiline nose and a mouth whose smile prompted a quivering of her own lips as she recalled it. He was, she was certain, a good, reliable man who was wholly trustworthy.

Clearly, Mr Stapleton, in spite of being a man of God, was none of those things, although, being young, it was possible that he would become them later – if he could control his urge to seduce any half-decent looking female.

Veronica, beside her, had fallen silent. She was looking straight ahead but, as that was at Mr Stapleton's profile, Titania did not think it showed any degree of regret for her behaviour – or any less interest in the man.

Irritated, and longing to be rid of all these people, Titania leaned forward and touched Lord Vincent on the shoulder.

"Do we have to proceed so slowly?" she asked.

"I thought it might be as well after our recent accident. We want to get back safely, don't we?"

"Yes, but we do want to *get* back – preferably before it gets dark."

"Would you like me to go a little faster, Madam?" he asked, turning his head slightly to acknowledge her presence and speaking in a humorous tone.

"Yes, please – if you think you can control the vehicle sufficiently."

"Very well."

A moment later they were proceeding at a trot, the horses moving efficiently and with their accustomed style. Lord Vincent was a good driver.

"What time were they expecting you home, Veronica?" Mr Stapleton asked, turning his head to look at the girl.

"Papa didn't say, but it won't be dark for hours yet. Couldn't we – I know we had a little picnic in that field – but couldn't we find somewhere to have luncheon? I don't want to go home yet."

"We could go to the inn," the curate suggested. "Would you like that?"

"Oh, yes, I would. Could we do that, Titania?"

She turned her eager face towards Titania and she, who had been indulging in uncharitable thoughts about the girl, found herself once more charmed by the pretty face, the engaging manner and – she could not deny – the way the girl clearly acknowledged her as being in charge, as having the ability to make this – still, in spite of the accident – into the sort of outing she had originally intended.

"Have you time to stop at the inn, Vincent?" she asked.

"If that's what my lady wants," he replied, still teasing.

"Yes, if *you*'ve got time," she retorted, transferring some of her irritation to him.

"My time is entirely at your disposal," he returned, leaving off the bantering tone.

"Thank you. Can you – between you gentlemen – take Veronica inside?"

"Of course," they replied together and she wondered whether there would be a stand-off as to which would be honoured to carry the girl inside.

The party continued towards the inn in a more amicable frame of mind after this, although neither the men nor the women spoke until Veronica turned to Titania and spoke in a low voice.

"I'm sorry. I was behaving foolishly earlier. Will you forgive me?"

"I don't think I'm in a position to forgive or not," Titania said stiffly.

"You won't tell Papa, will you?"

"Ah, is that what's worrying you?" Titania asked rather unkindly.

"He would be angry with me, but he would be very angry with Marcus," Veronica confided. "He would probably forbid him to visit us again and – and not many people do visit us. I would miss him."

"I don't doubt it, but you should have thought of that before you allowed him to make love to you. You're far too young for that sort of thing."

"I know. I won't do it again – I promise."

Titania did not think that a promise given under such circumstances or concerning such a matter would be likely to be kept, but she believed that her cousin's behaviour could more easily be brought under control if she told her brother about the matter. He could take Marcus's job away from him and send him back to his family with little prospect of finding another in the same line. He would have to make his way in the world in a different manner. She did not think he would mind giving up the church since she was by no means certain that he took his career seriously. He would infinitely prefer to join a regiment, she suspected, but wondered whether even that would be possible if Horace were to make his recent behaviour known – and of course someone would have to buy him a commission.

When they arrived, the carriage was handed to the ostlers, Jim was sent to find some luncheon in the servants' quarters and the four young people went inside.

Titania had never been inside The White Hart, although she had met the hunt in the forecourt on numerous occasions. She was recognised, as was Lord Vincent and Mr Stapleton. Veronica had certainly never patronised the establishment but, the village being well aware of her injuries, was identified as soon as she was carried inside in Lord Vincent's arms.

He, having taken charge of the party, had told the curate, as he drove into the forecourt, that he would carry the girl inside and, such was his tone and air of authority, that no argument ensued. Indeed, Titania, watching and waiting for one, noticed that Mr Stapleton barely glanced at the girl as Lord Vincent lifted her. It seemed that, without saying a word, his lordship had managed to convey his disapproval.

"I'm sorry if I displeased you," Mr Stapleton said, falling into step beside Titania.

"You did," she replied coldly. "I was shocked at the overt partiality which you displayed towards a very young girl. I hope you have not raised hopes which you will inevitably disappoint."

"I did not mean to do so," he replied. "I believe that the initial joy of the occasion – the poor girl being outside after such a long spell indoors and after such a horrible accident with its terrible consequences, followed by the frightening accident she herself caused - affected me to

197

an extent that I'm much afraid did lead me to behave in an irresponsible fashion. She was terrified and I believed she needed comforting. Will you forgive me?"

She did not look at him but knew that his eyes were pleading and that, if she had glanced in his direction, she would immediately have been swayed.

"It's not up to me to forgive," she snapped. "I believe you should apologise to Veronica – and may have to, with much more serious consequences, to her father too."

"Thetford? Are you intending to tell him? Pray do not! It will make him angry, yes, but also anxious, and he is already quite worried enough as it is. I won't repeat my offence, I promise."

"Will you not? When Veronica pleads with you, weeps, forgives you, for God's sake, throws herself into your arms, will you not weaken and reassure her?"

"No, never, if *you* will forgive me! And, yes, you do have something to forgive, for I do not think you can have misinterpreted my manner towards you. *That* was genuine, not inspired by any transitory situation, and, if I have hurt you, I beseech you to put it down to my inexperience and youthful wish to make an injured girl happy."

She stopped, letting Lord Vincent go ahead towards the private room to which they were being shown.

"Really? I think I must have misinterpreted it if there was anything out of the ordinary in your manner towards me. You and I are cousins. I assumed any warmth you showed towards me was the familial one of relatives who, due no doubt to geographical distance, have never met before."

He stopped beside her and took her hand, although she tried to evade his fingers.

"Don't deny it, Titania! You know there was – is – something between us. You felt it as much as I."

"I felt nothing!" she returned mendaciously. "You seem to have refined needlessly upon what was nothing more than the condescension due to an indigent relative on whom my brother had taken pity. I meant only to show consideration."

Titania had never in her life shown condescension to anybody; she had in fact little sense of her own position as the sister of an Earl and, uncertain of her own charms, had no belief in her ability to throw her weight around and get her own way, but she saw at once that she had hit him where it hurt. His face, at which she tried but failed not to look, revealed a level of pain and humiliation which surprised her – and gave her hope that he was telling the truth.

Tossing her head as though she had been an acclaimed beauty, she withdrew her hand and followed Lord Vincent and Veronica into a comfortable private room where a log fire burned brightly.

Lord Vincent laid Veronica upon a settle which the innkeeper drew closer to the fire before leaving the room, promising to bring a blanket for the invalid.

"Oh, isn't this lovely?" Veronica exclaimed with her usual optimism. "I'm so glad we came here! Do you think they'll be able to provide a good luncheon as well?"

"I don't see why not," his lordship replied, smiling indulgently upon the girl. "Are you hungry?"

"I own I am – although I've not done much to work up an appetite."

"I think you did a good deal," Titania told her, amused. "You drove the carriage with such gusto that we nearly overturned. If that's not doing enough to work up an appetite, I'd like to know what is!"

"Oh, pray – I'm sorry. I've not been an ideal guest."

"This whole outing was got up to please you," Titania told her, "so, if springing the horses and driving into a field pleased you, I for one will not complain."

The landlord returned with a blanket which Lord Vincent took from him and tucked tenderly around Veronica's legs.

A menu having been decided, the landlord withdrew and everyone sat down, Titania opposite Veronica and Marcus and Lord Vincent a little way away.

"He's not speaking to me," Veronica complained in a low voice to Titania, glancing at the curate's sullen face.

"I think he's embarrassed because I castigated him," Titania explained lightly.

"It was my fault as well," Veronica said.

"Nonsense! He should have known better – and *you* will now. Look, here comes the first part of our luncheon."

A pair of waiters came in carrying dishes and, pulling up a table close to the settle on which Veronica lay, set out plates, knives and forks. The other three moved to the table and everyone was soon eating enthusiastically. Perhaps the earlier drama and anxiety had sharpened their appetites, or perhaps it was the cold weather outside and the delightful warmth inside, or perhaps it was simply that they were all young, but the food disappeared from the dishes on to their plates and from thence into their bodies in no time. The gentlemen drank ale and the ladies lemonade.

Chapter 25

As luck would have it, Lord Rushlake, escaping from the embarrassment of his interview with Lady Thetford, ran into Lord Thetford returning from his trip round his estates.

They met upon the doorstep. Lord Thetford looked delighted to see his neighbour and exclaimed upon the mischance that had taken him from home at precisely the moment when the other had chosen to call upon him.

"I don't suppose you have time to come into the library for a few moments," the Viscount said, "but it would surely be a pity if we missed this opportunity of speaking."

"Indeed," the Earl agreed readily. "Lady Thetford has very kindly been entertaining me in your absence," he added obliquely.

"Has she?" the Viscount asked, a slight spasm passing across his features.

The two men went into the library where the Earl was offered more coffee, declined it, and was offered a glass of whiskey instead. Feeling rather in need of a fillip to his spirits, he accepted this. The Viscount summoned the butler and requested he bring two glasses and a jug of water. The whiskey was kept in the library.

Putting a log upon the fire and inviting his guest to sit down, Lord Thetford poured the whiskey, offered water, which was declined, handed his guest his glass, picked up his own and sat down opposite the Earl.

"To your very good health, sir!" the Viscount said, raising his glass in the direction of his guest.

"And to yours!" Rushlake replied, echoing the gesture.

"Health," the Viscount said in heavy tones, "is something which seems to be at something of a premium in this household."

"I'm sorry! How is your daughter?"

"Which one? I have, I believe at the last count, four of 'em, although I nearly lost one – sadly, the best!"

"Is she improving?"

"Not really. At least, she looks well – she is blessed with a sunny disposition – can't think where she gets that from – and that is reflected upon her face, whose smiles raise one's spirits briefly – until one remembers all there is to repine over in her case."

"I'm sorry," Rushlake repeated.

"You knew she was alive when I'd given her up! Have you anything else to tell me?"

"I haven't seen her since that day, but my sister has taken her out today – as you know."

"Yes. That was a kind thought. She was so looking forward to it. God, when I think of what that girl had – should have had – and what she has lost, I – I wonder how I can go on."

"It's a blessing that she has a sunny disposition," Rushlake said helplessly.

"I suppose it is – for her. But, for me, to see her so blighted breaks my heart."

Rushlake nodded. It occurred to him that, if he wished to persist in this new hobby of his – investigating crime amongst the nobility – he had willingly – although he had not thought of it at first – put himself in a position where people were bound to be going to confide their deepest despair to him. Not himself being particularly blessed with a sunny disposition, but rather with one which found itself restlessly seeking explanation, he began to think he had chosen a singularly unsuitable hobby.

"Does the doctor hold out hope that she will walk again one day?" he asked.

"No; he seems to think she has severed something essential in her spine. I don't know how he knows – and pray that he is wrong – but his prognosis is not encouraging."

Rushlake took a sip of his whiskey and felt the warmth slide down his throat. Lord Thetford was miserable, understandably, but it did not seem to Rushlake that he was in the grip of any sort of fantastical notions. On the contrary, his outlook was drearily realistic. His favourite daughter had been cut down before she was fully grown, his other daughters seemed to be categorised only by their number and perhaps position *vis-à-vis* each other – and his new wife, what of her? He had not been married for long, a matter of months; was he still in the grip of romantic love or passionate lust – whatever had prompted him to marry such a frightful woman?

"How has your wife taken it?" he asked.

"Vera? I've no idea! Veronica is not, of course, her daughter, but she was her pupil at one time and I would have expected her to be upset, worried about her. She doesn't appear to be except in so far as she's afraid she'll not marry now and we'll be left with her for ever."

"Is that what she's said?" Rushlake asked, struck by the fact that the woman, who had presumably expressed some degree of affection for the

Viscount's children while she was still hoping to persuade him to marry her, no longer bothered to conceal her real sentiments.

"Yes – and I suppose she may be right. The thing is," the Viscount said, trying to pull himself together and adopt a more positive tone, "that I wouldn't mind Veronica staying with me for ever, but that doesn't seem to be the case for Vera."

"Perhaps she's thinking about her own child – am I right that she's expecting one?"

"Who knows?" the Viscount asked, his brief moment of positivity vanishing abruptly. "She was apparently expecting one before – before we married – but it didn't materialise. I wouldn't be surprised if the same thing happened this time."

"I don't know much about it," Rushlake admitted, "but I understand there are often false starts and abrupt endings to such things. I hope she will retain her health this time."

"Very kind, but she didn't lose it last time. I'm beginning to think she wasn't telling me the truth when she said she was expecting the first time. That was before Margaret died."

"I see. From what did she die?"

A spasm passed across the Viscount's features.

"Julia's convinced she was poisoned."

"Yes, but – what do you think?"

"I don't know. I'm beginning to wonder if Julia's right. At first, I thought she was simply overcome with grief at her mother's death, but now – now I wonder if there's anything in what she says."

"If someone did poison her, do you have any idea who it might have been?" Rushlake asked.

Lord Thetford's face darkened. For a moment, the Earl feared that he had gone too far but, when the Viscount spoke, he realised the anger was not directed at him.

"Vera, of course! And then she pretended to be expecting to force my hand!"

"Is that what Julia says?"

"Yes, but I think she may be right because, you see, it turned out there was no child."

He finished his whiskey in a gulp, slammed the glass down so hard upon the table that Rushlake feared it would break.

"I've been a fool!" he said.

The Earl, unable to deny this, murmured something about everyone making mistakes from time to time.

"You don't seem to!" the Viscount snapped.

"Oh, I do - it's only that I haven't had so much time yet. And then," he added more sympathetically, "we all hide our mistakes, don't we – if we can!"

"I should have dismissed her long ago when …" The Viscount came to an embarrassed stop, before plunging on, "Did she … just now?"

The Earl nodded.

Thetford said, "Do you think I could divorce her?"

"I suppose so."

"But it would be difficult – and expensive."

"Yes."

"And, would she kill us all before she went?"

"I shouldn't think so. I mean, if she tried to do that, she'd be arrested, tried for murder, hanged."

"Cheaper than divorce," Thetford said with a fleeting, cynical little smile.

"Yes, but even more painful, I should imagine – and just suppose if she managed to kill one or two of you first."

"Julia's convinced she meant to kill her when she caused the accident – because she'd given her old habit to Veronica."

"But did she? How could she have done so?" Rushlake asked, pulling himself together and trying to concentrate. He had been wondering how much longer he would be obliged to listen to Thetford's litany of regrets and reflecting that doing so required a degree of tact he did not think he possessed. The man was miserable, he wanted a confessor as well as an adviser, but it did not seem to Rushlake that he was quite the right man. He was, to begin with, too young. He had never been married – and was rapidly going off the idea of ever doing so – so that he had no idea, from the inside, how people could change their minds so radically – or perhaps how, once married, people made so little effort to try to maintain the agreeable *persona* they had put forward before.

"Prodded the horse, tripped it – I don't know. I say," the Viscount's face brightened as an idea came into his head, "do you think that detective fellow you've got staying with you could help?"

"I believe Julia's already asked him."

"And has he agreed – or did he think she was exaggerating or – or had convinced herself there was something amiss when there isn't?"

"I think you'd have to discuss that with him. What was your initial belief about the cause of Veronica's accident – before Julia told you her theory?"

"I don't think I thought anything particular. I mean, it's a steep bank and much obstructed by greenery; anyone could slip there, although Veronica's a good rider."

"If someone did give the horse a push, or tripped it up, have you any idea who was near her at the time? Was she riding beside you or Lady Thetford, or indeed Julia?"

The Viscount frowned while he thought about this.

"We all set off together, but then, when we met the villagers – and the various other people who joined the hunt – at the inn, our formation, if you like to call it that, changed a bit. As I recall, I was with you, in the front. I think the girls, and indeed Vera too, fell back a bit."

"You and I – and the Master – led the party down the bank so that we were already in the lower field when she fell. Did you see it – the fall? I own I didn't. I was already going hell for leather, together with the Master, across the lower field."

"I was behind you," the Viscount said, now staring into the middle distance, clearly trying to picture what had happened. "Titania was with you, wasn't she? She's a tearaway rider, by the way, isn't she?"

"Yes. I think I left her at Rushlake too long; she had nothing else to do but ride. What about Lord Vincent? He's her usual companion; did you notice him?"

"No, I didn't. Vera was behind me; I think she meant to be because we'd had a disagreement about whether she should come or not. I said I thought hunting was too dangerous for a woman in her condition but now I wonder if she *is* in point of fact in a delicate condition. Julia isn't such a keen rider as Veronica and she was definitely further back – but so, oddly, was Veronica. I would have expected her to be in the front, although I don't think she rides to hounds so much as your sister."

"Were they riding together, Julia and Veronica?"

"I think so, yes, but I shouldn't think Vera was with them – on account of Julia's dislike of her, you know."

"Yes. Did they have any men with them?"

"Potential suitors, do you mean? I don't think the curate was far away. It's my belief he was riding with Vera, and Julia and Veronica were together."

"Ahead of Lady Thetford or behind?" Rushlake was still wondering whether it was the Viscountess who had caused the accident, although there was no doubt that she was already in the lower field when the crisis unfolded. Had she tripped Veronica's horse and then rushed down the bank herself to arrive before Veronica?

"I can't say, I'm afraid. Mr Stapleton might be able to confirm where he was – and whether he was riding with Vera at the time."

"I'll ask him," Rushlake said. He was about to take his leave when he recalled the sort of thing that he believed detectives asked.

"Was Veronica's mood just as usual that morning?"

"I didn't see her until we set off. I'd had breakfast earlier – young people don't seem to get up very early, do they? But, when we set off, she was in good spirits. Julia was a trifle crotchetty and Vera and I had had a disagreement, as I told you."

"Did Julia confide what was upsetting her?"

"Not in so many words, but I'm certain it was her usual disgruntlement with Vera. She was wearing a new riding habit so that I had expected her to be more cheerful, but she wasn't. I live with too many women, Rushlake, and yet have learned very little about their moods or what discomposes them. All I do know is that Julia resents Vera and picks a fight with her whenever she sees the smallest opportunity. She hadn't been able to that morning because I had been quarrelling with Vera."

The Earl smiled in what he hoped was a sympathetic manner and made his *adieux*, begging Lord Thetford to send for him at once if he thought of anything else germane to the enquiry.

"I will, I will; thank you, Rushlake, for listening to me. If you want to send round your detective fellow, I'll be as co-operative as I can."

"I'll tell him," Rushlake promised and left the room, not waiting for the butler to escort him to the door, but finding his own way.

He went home by way of the curate's small residence, dismounting and hooking his horse's bridle over the gatepost before walking up the path and knocking upon the door. It was opened by a young maid who seemed surprised to see him.

"Mr Stapleton isn't expecting me," Rushlake admitted, "but, as I was passing, I thought I would call in."

"He's not at home, my lord. He went out quite early this morning on horseback. Would you like to come in, my lord, while I try to find out if anyone knows what time he's expected to return?"

"Yes, thank you."

The maid showed him into a small sitting room and went off to enquire if any of the other small band of staff who served the curate knew either where he had gone or when he planned to return. It was not long before she returned to tell him that she believed he had gone out in a carriage with Lady Titania and Miss Veronica Thetford.

"Oh!" Rushlake exclaimed. "I wonder if I was supposed to know that. I did of course know that my sister had gone for a drive with Miss Veronica but did not realise that Mr Stapleton was to be of the party."

"I think, my lord, that he'd heard there was to be such an outing and went along to Thetford Hall in the hope that he might be asked to accompany them."

"Oh, well, I'd better be on my way then!"

His lordship, who had not sat down and was standing by the window when the girl entered, smiled and made his way towards the door, brushing awkwardly against a small desk as he went. It was not like the Earl to be clumsy and he knocked a large pile of papers on to the floor as he passed.

"Oh dear!" he exclaimed, quite in the manner of his aunt. "I'd better pick them up."

"Oh, don't trouble yourself, my lord! I can do it!" the maid exclaimed, coming back to help.

His lordship had already bent down and was picking up the papers, forming them into a neat bundle as he did so. Unless one were to hold papers upside down – and most people don't when attempting to form them into a pile – one is almost bound to see what some of them concern.

In this case, there proved to be several written on fine linen paper and smelling of roses. He was unable to read more than the first line or two of these missives, but they all began with, '*My dearest Marcus*' and were written in the sort of flowing hand which generally indicated the sex of the correspondent to be female. One of these fell again as he shuffled them clumsily and, bending to pick it up, he found himself reading the end. This time, the writer signed off as '*Your devoted sweetheart*'.

Afraid that the maid might begin to suspect he was looking at the papers, Rushlake placed them on the desk and joined her in the doorway. She ushered him out, but, at the front door, his lordship enquired whether she was Mr Stapleton's only servant.

"Oh no, my lord; there's a cook and a man who sees to the rough work."

"I see. Well, I'm sure you work very hard and I'm sorry to have taken up so much of your time."

"Not at all, my lord." She smiled again and blushed and his lordship reflected that a combination of his rank and looks had most likely filled her mind to such an extent that she would be unlikely to think he had spent too long picking up the scattered papers.

As he went home, he pondered on what he had discovered that morning and began, for the first time, to wonder whether he had made a mistake in appointing his distant kinsman to his position without so much as meeting him first. He reflected that nepotism was probably a bad thing although almost everybody he knew practised it.

The thing was that a letter which began in such an intimate fashion and ended in an equally emotional style was something which ill became a new curate, a man who should have been above behaving in such a morally questionable manner.

He guessed there had been a good deal of flirting for the Earl had seen the young man with his sister and knew that he was an accomplished flirt. It might be that the rose-scented correspondent had jumped to an erroneous conclusion, but there was a proprietorial flavour to both the opening and closing of the letter which indicated that she had not done so entirely without reason. Indeed, unaware at the time of the curate's skill in capturing the affections of the opposite sex, he had wondered if he would make his sister a good husband. He was certain now that he would not – indeed wondered whether he made a good curate. He might be able to compose and declaim a moving sermon – he was, after all, well-educated and clearly possessed a certain gift for using words in a persuasive manner – but he doubted that he was altogether to be trusted. Engaging a young woman's affections to such a degree as that indicated in the letter amounted to seduction and, while to be deplored in a well-behaved gentleman, might be considered positively wrong in a man of God.

Chapter 26

He was joined for luncheon by his sister Jenny and her husband, the other women being out. His nieces and nephew were taking their luncheon in the schoolroom, so that the three grown-ups sat down together.

"Did you enjoy your walk?" he asked his sister.

"It was very pleasant," she replied, "although at first I felt a trifle discontented as I wished I had gone to Shrewsbury with the others. Do you think they will have found out anything new?"

"I've no idea. Do you mean the women or Bodley?"

"Well, I didn't want to go with Bodley to talk to policemen," Jenny replied in her forthright manner. "I can't conceive what I would have said to them. No, I wished I had gone to look at the shops in Shrewsbury. I'm sure they must be cheaper than London."

"No doubt, but I daresay their goods are inferior," her brother reassured her, amused.

"I daresay you're right, but it would have been amusing to see what a provincial town has to offer. Do you suppose Aunt Mildred will have found anything to buy?"

He laughed. "Well, I suppose she sometimes buys things in Yorkshire and I don't see why Shrewsbury should be so vastly inferior to the North."

"I think," Sir James interjected, "that it's a very good thing you didn't go, Jenny, because you would have been thoroughly scornful of whatever they had to offer but would have felt bound to look for the same thing later in London, hoping it would be better. It would certainly have been more expensive."

"I hope," she said, arching her brows at her husband, "that you're not implying I'm extravagant."

"Of course not, dearest," he replied with a tender look which, as usual, reconciled his wife to his criticism.

"What have you been doing, little brother?" Jenny asked.

He grinned.

"I went to visit Thetford and was entertained – and subjected to an energetic attempt at seduction – by his wife. When he came in, he confided that he regretted his o'er hasty marriage. I wasn't surprised and, although I didn't tell him how she had thrown herself at me, he presumed she had. I parted from him even more convinced that marriage presented all sorts of problems – although you two have done your best to negate that depressing opinion – and, passing Marcus's humble abode, rang the bell. He wasn't there either – apparently he'd managed to inveigle his way into the carriage in which Titania was driving Veronica Thetford. I'm beginning to wonder," he went on, deciding not to mention the letter he had seen, "if our kinsman is a little over-keen on the ladies."

"He's young," Jenny said, "and most young men, if they haven't grown as cynical as you, little brother, are never free from dwelling upon the female of the species for long. He's also excessively handsome – as indeed are you."

"I see. Do you suppose he will have received the same attentions from Lady Thetford as I?"

"Certain to have done, I should think."

"What worries me," he said, "is that he may have succumbed to them. I'm not convinced he's a committed man of God."

"Probably not – not many of them are," his cynical sister said. "He's the third or fourth son and wasn't, so far as I can gather, offered much choice in the matter of a career."

"Has he made a play for you?" he asked.

"No; probably I'm too old – or perhaps he's worried about what you and James might say. He's definitely made an approach to Titania. Perhaps he doesn't like to try two sisters in the same family – he might be afraid they'd discuss their conquests and then he'd be exposed for the seducer he is."

"I'm afraid Titania may have lost her heart to him," Rushlake said more soberly.

"Do you think so?" Jenny seemed determined to maintain a light note. "I've never seen any evidence that she has a heart before so I suppose we should be glad she's fashioned like other females. I'm beginning to worry about you, though, Horace. Miss Thetford is in hot pursuit – what do you think of her?"

"Very little, although I'm beginning to think she may have a point when it comes to her stepmother – the woman's a horror. What sort of portion do you think she has?"

"Not as generous as Titania's, which is why Marcus *has* been pursuing *her* in a more serious fashion. I wouldn't be surprised if he put in an offer for her and I fear, if you're right about her heart having been engaged, she might be eager to accept. All the same, she has to marry someone and, as we said before, it doesn't particularly matter if he's poor since she has more than enough for two."

"I don't want her to marry a loose screw," Rushlake said stubbornly. "What do you think, James?"

"I? I own I don't care for the fellow – wouldn't like him in the family."

"He's already in the family," his wife reminded him.

"Only vaguely. I agree with you, Horace, I don't think his choice of career is one made from belief and, if he were to marry Titania, I suspect he would either leave it – and live off her – or not bother to try to move up the hierarchy. I don't see him as a bishop, do you?"

"Oh, I don't know; I've never been particularly convinced by either the faith or the morals of many of our bishops," Horace replied. "I've seen too many of them in inappropriate places in London. Many of them, particularly as they rise up the hierarchy, spend more time in London than in their parishes. Having a rich wife might help him to acquire promotion, but I don't trust him around women and, as time passes, Titania will cease to be young while he'll continue to be idolised by young women. I don't want her heart broken."

"Are you regretting appointing him?" Jenny asked curiously, seeing with a degree of tenderness how strongly he wanted to defend his unmarried sister against life's vicissitudes.

"Do you know, I think I am. I should have interviewed him, not relied upon his connexions."

"Probably you should have, but I doubt many people in your position do – and would you have known, interviewing him by yourself with no women present – that he was a seducer?"

"Probably not."

"I suppose you could sack him," she said, "if you don't think he'll be good for the parish."

"I don't think I can do that simply because he makes eyes at women. I suppose I'll have to speak to the vicar, see what he thinks of his junior."

"Good idea!" James said.

"What about Lord Vincent?" Jenny asked.

"What about him? I think he's gone for the carriage ride as well."

"Would he make Titania a good husband?" she asked.

"I'm sure he would, but I don't think either he or she has any idea of embarking upon that kind of thing."

"Do you think I should try to put the idea into her head?" Jenny asked.

"No," both the men replied as one.

"Put her off if you make that sort of suggestion," Horace said, "and, in any event, no use persuading her if he isn't interested. Leave well alone, Jenny, is my advice."

"And mine," put in her husband.

211

Jenny looked a little crestfallen but soon rallied, suggesting that Nanny might be able to drop a hint in the tiresome young woman's ear.

"She won't take any notice of her," Horace replied. "Tania's quite independent-minded and very likely takes Helena as a role model."

"Oh, but she, if only she can persuade that wretched detective to declare himself, is about to come off the shelf," Jenny pointed out. "That might persuade Tania to follow suit."

"I doubt it, and, if she's fallen in love with Marcus, we'll have to wait until she gets over him before we can present anyone else. I'm afraid disappointment may have a negative impact on her sensibilities."

"Everyone has to fall in love eventually," Jenny said unsympathetically, "and most people lose the first one and have to make do with the second – or even third."

"Is that what I am?" her husband asked.

Jenny flushed uncomfortably but denied that she had ever felt affection for another.

Sir James, who was too pragmatic to make a fuss about something in the distant past, glanced at his brother-in-law with some amusement.

"Fortunately, your little brother was far too young to notice where your affections fell when you were a girl," he observed.

There was not much any of them could do in their quest to discover whether the first Lady Thetford had met her end by foul means or whether Veronica's injury had been caused deliberately until the others returned, so they went their separate ways after luncheon.

His lordship took the opportunity to go round his estate, speak to his bailiff and generally check on how his inheritance was being maintained.

Meanwhile in Shrewsbury, Mr Bodley, having parted from the women, set off to find the police station. This did not prove to be as difficult as he had feared for he soon met a member of the constabulary pacing along the street with, so far as Adrian could see, little to do.

"Excuse me," Mr Bodley said, approaching this man, "I'm a detective with the Metropolitan Police and am visiting this area for a few days. I wonder if you could direct me to the police station."

The constable was delighted to meet him and offered to accompany him to Swan Hill, where it was situated.

"Are you just touring, sir, or do you have an enquiry you wish to make?" the constable enquired as they walked.

"Well, in point of fact, I do have something I wish to bring to the attention of the Chief Constable. At any rate, I would like to ask his advice on a somewhat tricky matter."

"I'm afraid I don't think Captain Mayne will be there today," the constable admitted. "He doesn't usually come in to the station except when there's something to which he must attend. This area is quiet, sir – not a great deal of crime – I expect there's far more in London."

"I don't doubt it," Mr Bodley agreed cheerfully. "It's rather a delicate matter, the one on which I wished to consult Captain Mayne. Would it, do you think, be possible to call upon him at home? I'm staying with the Earl of Rushlake," he added by way of establishing his credentials as the kind of person the Chief Constable might be ready to meet.

"Lord Rushlake?" The constable seemed surprised, but impressed, which reinforced Mr Bodley's self-evaluation as a man so far beneath his host that other people would struggle to believe they were friends.

"Yes. He spends most of his time in London," Mr Bodley offered by way of explanation for the oddity of their being acquainted.

"Yes, yes, of course," the constable agreed.

They had by this time arrived in front of a large brick building which proclaimed itself to be the headquarters of the Shropshire Constabulary. The constable went up the steps, accompanied by Mr Bodley. Inside, there was a clerk sitting at a desk to whom the constable spoke, explaining Mr Bodley's wish to speak to Captain Mayne.

"He's not here, as you well know," returned the clerk with a lugubrious air.

"Yes. Mr Bodley is a guest of Lord Rushlake and desires an audience with Captain Mayne."

"Ah! If you like to write a note, sir, I'll see that it's delivered to his house," the clerk told Mr Bodley and, when that gentleman admitted he had no paper or writing implement about him, produced both.

The constable waited patiently while Mr Bodley, directed to another desk in the corner of the room, wrote his message. This was not easy as he did not feel he had the right to request an audience with such an august personage as the Chief Constable. He was certain that Lord Rushlake could have managed it without the least difficulty and would, moreover, have immediately been granted whatever he desired.

When he had written something bland - for he was unwilling to state the reason for his wish to speak to Captain Mayne and could do no more than once again use the Earl's name as a sort of 'open sesame' to the Chief Constable's ear - he approached the clerk again and asked the direction of

Captain Mayne, hoping thereby to learn his address so that he could pass it on to Lord Rushlake, who would no doubt contact the man directly.

"I'll see it gets to him, sir," the clerk informed him unhelpfully.

There was nothing that Mr Bodley could do to force this person to divulge the Chief Constable's address, so he folded his missive, wrote "Captain Mayne' upon the outside and handed it to the clerk.

"Thank you for your help," he said as courteously as he could, although he did not consider that he had been afforded much assistance and did not at all take to the clerk's ill-natured manner.

After that he found himself at something of a loose end. He had arranged to meet the rest of the Rushlake Team at three o'clock at the spot where the carriage had dropped them that morning. It was now approaching midday and he had achieved almost nothing except that he now knew there was a police presence in Shrewsbury and that the Chief Constable was called Captain Mayne. Guessing the man must now be retired, he wondered in what service he had been a captain.

Judgng that he had not done enough to warrant stopping at an inn for luncheon, he wandered aimlessly about the streets, keeping to the less populated ones for fear of running into the female contingent and having to report on how little he had done. While thus occupied, he passed a jeweller's and paused to gaze at the glittering objects in the window. His eye was inevitably caught by what he guessed were the sort of rings gentlemen gave ladies to whom they were affianced. What, he wondered, would Helena like? He did not think she was the sort of person who would want a huge ruby or even an emerald and decided that she would probably prefer something quiet and unassuming such as a pearl. Having come to this conclusion, he moved to the part of the window behind which there were a number of pearl rings. The next stage of his speculation involved what sort of an arrangement she would favour. Would she prefer a large single gem or a band of smaller ones? Personally, he preferred the bands and he could not help thinking that wearing a gem the size of a pea on one's hand would be exceedingly inconvenient. Would it not keep catching on her clothes?

He spent so long gazing at – and mentally comparing – the rings that eventually one of the shopkeepers came out and accosted him.

"Pardon me, sir," this gentleman said, "you seem to be taking a long time assessing those rings. Is there any way in which I may be able to assist you?"

Mr Bodley blushed and made a furtive movement to run away as fast as he could before remembering that he was a man and, if he really wanted to acquire a wife – and a particular one at that – he must pull himself together and make a decision.

"I doubt it," he said in a low, uncertain voice. "The thing is, you see, that there is a lady – a lady whom I admire – and I was wondering what sort of ring she would like."

"Yes, of course, sir. Is the lady to become your wife?"

"Oh," Mr Bodley exclaimed, suddenly overcome with the need to confide in someone – and someone, moreover, who knew neither him nor the lady in question, nor any of the circumstances surrounding his uncertainty. "I wish it might be so!" he finished on the sort of longing note that a child might use when contemplating an ice.

"Would you like to come in and discuss your situation? I, we, might be able to be of assistance."

"I wish," Mr Bodley said, so low that the shopkeeper could barely distinguish the words, "that I had the courage to ask her."

"It's a difficult thing to do," the man said sympathetically. "But perhaps if you were to buy her a small present – not something so very overt as a ring – it might facilitate a discussion of the subject which could lead to you being able to put the matter before her."

"Oh!" Mr Bodley exclaimed again, this time in the tone of one experiencing a revelation. "What an excellent idea!"

The shopkeeper bowed and, concealing his smile of satisfaction at enticing a customer into his shop, ushered the hesitant lover inside.

He was seated in a comfortable chair, a cup of coffee was procured, along with a plate of small biscuits, and the shopkeeper set himself to discover not only the nature of his customer – which he had in truth already discerned – but also that of the recipient of the lover's token.

The shopkeeper did not produce any rings for his customer's approval, sticking instead to bracelets, necklaces, lockets and brooches. He brought these items out, displayed discreetly upon dark velvet and soon began to get a picture of the admired lady.

She was neither extravagant nor vain; nor was she of the type who flaunted herself – or her jewellery. Indeed, it seemed that she was discreet, tactful, a trifle retiring but not lacking in confidence and that – and this last lightened the heart of the jeweller – she had excellent taste. Good taste is always expensive and the shopkeeper wished to make a substantial sale, although years of experience had also equipped him to size up fairly accurately his customer's means. These were not great, but the strength, although unstated, of the gentleman's sentiments was substantial.

Chapter 27

It soon became clear that the customer would prefer the first piece of jewellery he bought for his lady to be a brooch rather than something more intimate – and more expensive – such as a necklace or pendant. A pendant, which generally seemed to consist of a gold or silver case, sometimes embellished with pearls or brilliants of some kind, hinted at the hope that she would keep a lock of the gentleman's hair therein. Mr Bodley shied away from expressing such a definite sentiment.

The shopkeeper, well aware that this particular customer might back away at any moment, immediately agreed that a brooch was just the thing. Having come to this conclusion, the two men were able to focus upon the different sorts of brooch available.

Brooches were much worn by ladies although Mr Bodley admitted that he had failed to notice the style – or indeed the presence – of any that the lady already owned.

"Does she wear a necklace sometimes?" the shopkeeper enquired.

"She has a little gold pendant," Mr Bodley admitted. He had noticed this because he had not been able to tear his eyes away from the manner in which this modest little ornament nestled just below his beloved's collar bone and the way it moved with her breath. "I don't know if there is a picture or a lock of hair therein."

"She may have a picture of one or both of her parents inside," the shopkeeper suggested. "Perhaps you could ask her."

He thought, no doubt, that enquiring as to the contents of the pendant would likely lead his customer to lean closer to his beloved, might encourage her to remove it – an action which might require the help of her admirer – and should, if these two clearly shy people could be sufficiently impassioned, lead to their lips meeting. That, the shopkeeper reasoned, might result in a further visit to his shop to purchase a ring.

At first, once they had decided on a brooch, Mr Bodley felt relieved that he had made a decision and began to experience a sense of achievement. This did not unfortunately last long for there seemed to be an almost infinite choice that would have to be made between the innumerable brooches which the shopkeeper laid out for him.

Here, more exact questioning was required in order to ascertain whether the lady would prefer one depicting a flower – or bunch thereof – or whether she would prefer a straight bar of jewels – or pearls if the customer thought she would favour these – or whether she would appreciate an unusual shape or the representation of a particular object.

Mr Bodley did his best to answer these questions but found, after a depressingly short time, that his head began to ache for he really could not come to a conclusion. In the end, he was unable to decide between a bar with five beautiful but modestly sized pearls arranged in a row or a spray of flowers, this time composed of sapphires, which winked and shone.

"I'm afraid the sapphires might offend her," he said at last. "I've only ever seen her wear pearls; she might think that one too 'flashy', if you understand what I mean."

The shopkeeper, thinking that he had at the back a particularly delightful sapphire ring that would match the brooch wonderfully and would make an excellent engagement ring, suggested that perhaps the lady wore pearls because she felt unchallenged by their gentle glow, but that she might, if presented with sapphires, find herself entranced.

"Oh, but she might consider them vulgar!" Mr Bodley protested.

"Sapphires can never be vulgar," the shopkeeper opined. "And that piece is modest but beautiful. I would advise you to take a chance and present her with that. It might," he added slyly, "open her eyes to all sorts of things of which she has never thought."

"I doubt that," Mr Bodley returned. "She is a highly intelligent lady."

"In that case, the brightness of the sapphires will stimulate her imagination," the shopkeeper said, seeming to have a ready answer for any of the detective's quibbles.

Mr Bodley, who, if the truth be told, was extremely taken with the sapphires himself, was at last persuaded, although he had one last anxiety.

"But how can I present her with a gift just after Christmas? I already gave her one at the festival. She will – well, what will she think?"

"I would suggest she will realise how much you admire her, sir, something of which perhaps she has not until that moment been entirely certain. Just give it to her, sir – and I guarantee she will fall into your arms!"

Mr Bodley could not quite visualise Miss Patchett doing anything so silly, but he did realise that, if he wanted to make her his wife, he would have to ask her and presenting her with a gift, valuable and carefully chosen, but not *too* valuable, might be a useful way of approaching this hitherto frightening step.

He bought the sapphire brooch, saw it placed in a blue leather box, wrapped in tissue paper and finally inserted into a small bag. Now all he had to do – apart of course from the terrifying moment when he must offer it – was pay for it. Modest though it was, it was a large sum to pay for a man who had no inheritance and lived entirely by the – cerebral – sweat of his brow.

He wrote a cheque and, pursued by good wishes, bade farewell to the shopkeeper and went back into the street.

He paused for a moment just outside the shop, so disoriented by his experience, as well as his knowledge of what a huge step he had taken in his relations with Miss Patchett, that he could not remember which way he had come and could not decide which way he should go.

The door opened behind him and the shopkeeper emerged to ask if sir was lost.

Mr Bodley laughed awkwardly and admitted that he could not remember whether he had come from the right or the left, he not being a native of Shrewsbury.

"Oh, where have you come from, sir?" the jeweller asked.

"London, but I'm staying with Lord Rushlake."

"His lordship?" the shopkeeper exclaimed, clearly even more taken with his customer than he had been at first and perhaps wishing that he had ascertained this fact earlier in their acquaintance.

"Yes. I came into Shrewsbury with some ladies, who have left me to my own devices while they have gone shopping."

"Ah!" the shopkeeper said. "Do you know where you're meeting them?"

"Oh yes, but I'm not doing so for some time so must find something else – rather less expensive – to occupy my time until then."

The shopkeeper laughed and said, "Well, since you've already spent a good deal in my shop, why don't you come into a place where you'll be safe from temptation and I'll tell you something of Shrewsbury so that you can visit the most interesting spots?"

Mr Bodley, who now had a strong desire to leave the shop – and his new, rather overpowering, friend - muttered something about going to look at the church.

"Ah! The most interesting ecclesiastical building is probably the Abbey. Come in for a moment, sir, and I'll give you directions."

Mr Bodley, forced by the exigencies of courtesy to return to the shop, did as he was bid, sat down once more in the chair in which he had been sitting before and waited while the man, who had seemingly become his host, fetched a map.

But it soon transpired that the jeweller's motive for persuading the detective to re-enter his premises was not so much his desire to assist the gentleman in his wish to visit an interesting church as to enquire closely into the almost tragic events which had taken place on Boxing Day.

More coffee and biscuits were brought, along with the map, and, spreading out the plan of the town, the jeweller immediately enquired, under the guise of solicitude, into the health of the injured young lady.

"I'm afraid she has not yet regained the use of her legs," Mr Bodley said, "but we have not given up hope that she will recover completely – in time."

"Yes, indeed," the shopkeeper replied at once. "She is a Miss Thetford, is she not?"

"Yes; they're neighbours of Lord Rushlake," Mr Bodley admitted, wondering what was coming next.

"Oh, from all I hear – the town, you see, is positively buzzing with gossip about that family – there've been some distressing goings-on recently," the shopkeeper said with an enthusiasm which made Mr Bodley shrink before a sudden memory of what his job was and the purpose of the visit to Shrewsbury made him realise that perhaps, just possibly, he had not in fact wasted some considerable time and a great deal of money in this establishment; perhaps he might, even now, be able to extract some useful information from the man who was trying to extract it from him and return to the Hall with something useful to add to the investigation.

"There's talk," the jeweller confided, "of the first Viscountess having been poisoned by the second!"

"Good God! Do you think there's anything in it?"

"Most people seem to think there is," the shopkeeper said.

"Has anyone reported it to the local constabulary?"

"Well," the shopkeeper almost whispered, "in the strictest confidence, one of the maids did and the police are investigating."

"Did she have any evidence? Did she find poison or something of that sort?"

"I gather she did find something of that nature – or evidence – amongst the poor lady's linen – of her last illness, which I understand was quite sudden, having been brought on by the administration of a deadly poison."

"Good God!" Mr Bodley exclaimed, thoroughly taken aback. "Do you know what poison is suspected?"

"I've heard a rumour that it was strychnine," the jeweller said in a low and doom-laden voice. "Apparently her ladyship had been prescribed it – in small doses – to alleviate tension and agitation brought on, it was believed, by giving birth to another girl when everyone knew his lordship wanted a boy – and when she must have known that his lordship was paying an unnecessary – and quite unwarranted – amount of attention to the governess. In my humble opinion, that was what had upset her ladyship so greatly."

"Yes, indeed, I daresay it did," Mr Bodley agreed. "Have the police interviewed the maid?"

"Oh, yes, I think so. She came all the way into town to report what she had noticed."

"How very loyal of her! Was she her ladyship's personal maid?"

"No, I don't think so; I believe she was a laundrymaid."

"Do you know the name of the policeman to whom she spoke?"

This question produced an almost lighthearted titter from the jeweller who said, "We only have two constables in Shrewsbury, so it must have been one of them. I believe it was Tom Darke, but I wouldn't swear to it. The other one is Joe Collins, but I don't think it was him. And then, that poor girl – it makes you wonder if what happened to her was an accident."

"Yes, it does," Mr Bodley agreed soberly, adding, "Does the town have an opinion of why the person who might have murdered Lady Thetford wanted to kill her daughter too?"

"Oh, I suppose she was afraid she suspected her!"

"Her?"

"Well, the governess of course. She was soon Lady Thetford – he waited less than six months to marry her. People say she was expecting and he wanted to legitimise the child in case it was a boy, but what I've heard is that there never was a baby!"

"From the same source, I suppose – the laundrymaid?"

"Yes. They know a lot about their employers, you see. You can't hide much from a laundrymaid."

"No," Mr Bodley agreed. "Well, I believe I might visit the police station," he went on, "to see if I can find anything out."

"I shouldn't think they'd tell you though, would they? I mean all that sort of thing must be confidential, especially when it involves an aristocratic family."

"Yes, but, you see I'm a detective so they might want me to help them in their investigation – since I'm a near neighbour at present."

"Good God! You're a detective?"

Mr Bodley nodded humbly.

"Why didn't you say so before?" the jeweller asked, clearly a little hurt at his customer's retention of such an exceedingly important piece of information.

"I didn't know there was anything to detect," Mr Bodley said untruthfully. "I came in to buy a present for the lady I admire," he added with rather more veracity, "and was unaware that my profession would be of any interest in such a venture."

The jeweller, understandably looking a little hurt at this rebuff, denied that the customer's profession was of any material value, pointing out instead that he was of the belief that they had become friends and that this was the reason they had strayed on to the subject of recent events in the neighbourhood.

Mr Bodley endeavoured to soothe his new friend's hurt feelings, knowing that, although he had been inveigled into the shop to buy a piece of jewellery for his beloved, he had originally come to Shrewbury with the intention of discovering all he could about the Thetford case and had indeed leapt at the opportunity to pump the jeweller for any information he might have on the putative crime.

"I own I did not know that the unfortunate events in Rushlake would be of any interest to anyone in Shrewsbury," he said pacifically.

"Do you tell me you do not rely on gossip in the metropolis?" the jeweller asked.

"No! It would be very wrong to rely on gossip about such an extremely serious matter. One must have evidence."

"Of course, of course," the other replied, adopting a soothing tone in his turn, "but, having been alerted to the possibility of a crime having taken place by gossip, it is surely the police's job to search for evidence."

Mr Bodley, beginning to realise that he and the shopkeeper could engage in this fairly tedious game of alternately soothing and ruffling the other's feelings for an inordinate length of time without coming to any conclusion, said, "Is it the town's firm belief that a crime has taken place?"

He wondered as he asked the question whether the crime was that of murdering the first Lady Thetford or trying to murder her second daughter.

"I think," the jeweller responded, "that there was a strong suspicion that the first Lady Thetford had been poisoned, but no one was sure, so that when we heard about Miss Veronica's accident everyone thought that provided evidence that the Viscountess's death was arranged."

"I see – by the governess?"

"Yes, although there is some doubt about whether his lordship was directly involved or simply the reason for it."

Mr Bodley nodded. This was very much what he had thought and, in truth, he did not feel much vindicated to learn that the local gossip agreed with him.

"But, if he was involved in his first wife's demise, did people really think he might have planned his daughter's accident?"

The jeweller shook his head.

"His lordship is not popular in the town," he admitted, "but I don't think anyone seriously believes he would try to kill his own daughter. That must have been the hand of the governess."

"Do you," Adrian Bodley asked, "happen to know the name of the laundrymaid who reported her suspicions to the police?"

"I believe her to be called Betsy or Bessie, or some such."

"Thank you. Do you know anything else which might help in my investigations?"

"Are you intending to take it on?"

"I'll call upon the police first; it would be improper for me to interfere without their knowledge and permission."

"Of course."

Judging that he had probably received all the information – and it was, after all, nothing but gossip – that the jeweller had to impart, Mr Bodley made his way back to the police station.

The constable who had taken him there earlier and with whom he believed he had managed to forge some sort of a connexion, had, to his great delight, swapped places with the unhelpful one. This impression was confirmed when the man smiled in recognition.

"You're back!" he exclaimed unnecessarily but with what appeared to be pleasure.

"Yes! May I speak with you about a matter which I understand has been reported to you recently?"

"Of course. What is it?"

Mr Bodley repeated the gist of what the jeweller had told him.

"Ah!" the constable said. "Was that what you wanted to speak to Captain Mayne about?"

"Yes. I didn't know, earlier, that information had been lodged and that you were already investigating the matter."

The constable nodded warily.

"I'm staying, as I told you, with Lord Rushlake, who is a near neighbour of Viscount Thetford. I have heard the rumours but believed them to be just that – rumours – so that, while I wanted to discuss the matter with Captain Mayne, I did not consider that I had anything specific to report."

"No," the constable agreed.

Mr Bodley, not surprised at the other man's reluctance to engage in further gossip and rather pleased than irritated by his restraint, mentioned the laundrymaid.

The constable nodded, but said, "I'm afraid I'm not at liberty to discuss the case since you're not a member of this constabulary until and unless Captain Mayne gives me permission to share our knowledge with you. I'm sure you understand that, as it involves a local aristocrat, there is even more reason to tread carefully."

Mr Bodley agreed with this and reassured his new friend that he perfectly understood. He would, he said, tell Lord Rushlake about their conversation and leave it to him to speak to Captain Mayne if he thought he should.

"Good idea!" the constable responded, relieved. "He doesn't live far from Rushlake."

"Oh, good. I suppose we may pass his house on our journey home later this afternoon."

"Almost certainly, I should think. It's not far off the road – indeed you will pass the gates, probably about halfway between the town and Rushlake Hall."

Mr Bodley, recognising that the constable was giving him enough information to call in on his way back – when he would be accompanied by the eminently respectable and aristocratic Lady Amberstone – nodded and prepared to leave.

"Thank you; you've been extremely helpful," he said, turning back to hazard a guess as to the nature and recognisability of Captain Mayne's abode.

"I suppose it's a manor house."

"Oh, yes – stone. Very fine gates and a lodge in the same style."

Chapter 28

Titania, rendered complaisant by the serenity of the atmosphere during the early part of the luncheon in the inn and, in spite of herself, warming once more to Mr Stapleton, ceased to pay so much attention to Veronica even when she and the curate began once more to talk animatedly between themselves. She was therefore taken by surprise when the girl dropped her knife and fork with a clatter, cracking her plate and scattering pieces of food over the table.

"What, whatever is the matter?" she asked, irritated.

"I don't know; I didn't mean to cause so much trouble. I – my fingers have gone stiff – that's why I dropped the cutlery." The girl was white and trembling but her hands, which lay upon the table did look stiff, the fingers oddly rigid

"What? Is it …? How do your legs feel?"

"I can't feel them, you know I can't, although I had thought, earlier, that some sensitivity was returning. Oh, don't tell me it's spreading, this paralysis, that I won't be able to move my hands or arms soon! I believe I truly would rather be dead than become as stiff as a board!"

"No, I'm sure it's not," Titania murmured, herself beginning to tremble. She leaned across from her chair and made to take Veronica's hand, but the girl, her couch between the two men and opposite Titania, flinched and cried out. Her arms began to jerk.

"I can't … help me!"

Titania, appalled, turned not to Marcus, at whom she did not even glance in her panic, but at the older man, Lord Vincent.

"What shall we do?" she asked.

Lord Vincent addressed the suffering girl, "Do you think it may have been something you've ingested – something in the luncheon which doesn't agree with you?"

"How can I have? None of you is ill!"

She was shaking, jerking and now began to gasp, her chest heaving.

"We must go – get her to a doctor at once!" Lord Vincent decided.

"Why don't we send for him to come here?" Marcus asked, rising and going to the door.

"Will that be quicker, do you think?" Titania asked.

"Probably." The curate left the room as he spoke, the door swinging behind him.

"I think you must have eaten something which disagreed with you," Lord Vincent said, "and the sooner it leaves your body the better, I should imagine."

He rose, picked up the girl in spite of her protests and followed Mr Stapleton out of the door, Titania trailing behind them.

Lord Vincent carried the girl outside into the courtyard, she still jerking and now gurgling as though she could not even scream or cry out. As soon as he reached the outdoors, he ceased to cradle her but instead held her, as though standing, against his own body, bending her forward. Then, locking his hands together around her middle, he began, quite violently, to squeeze, all the time exhorting her to cast up her accounts, for whatever she had ingested must be regurgitated as quickly as possible. At last she was sick, throwing up everything she had just eaten. But, in spite of this, she remained alarmingly stiff and seemed to find it difficult to breathe, dragging air into her lungs with a frightening wheeze.

"She's been poisoned!" Titania concluded. "What can we do?"

"Wait for the doctor," he returned. "He may have an antidote."

"But will he know what she's taken?" she asked.

"I suppose Stapleton will tell him the symptoms."

Lord Vincent, the girl now hanging, bent almost double over his locked hands, laid her upon the ground, face down, and began to thump her upon the back.

"I've no idea whether I'm helping or hindering," he commented, glancing up briefly at Titania.

The innkeeper, having heard the commotion, came out.

"What's happened?" he asked.

Furnished with a brief description, he suggested Lord Vincent bring the patient inside again and take her up to a bedroom.

Laid out upon the bed, Veronica continued to jerk and shake, her body now arching upwards in a horrifying arc; her teeth chattered, her eyes rolled up inside her head. The only sounds she made were the desperate gasps for air for it seemed she no longer had strength or leisure to scream.

The innkeeper fetched extra blankets which Titania and Lord Vincent endeavoured to wrap around her, but her convulsive movements threw them off as fast as they put them on.

"Should I try to make her sick again?" Lord Vincent asked the innkeeper.

"I don't think it'll help," the innkeeper admitted. "She's clearly been poisoned."

"You don't think it could have been something she ate?" Titania asked.

The landlord, looking displeased by this suggestion, which he no doubt took as an aspersion upon the luncheon, shook his head.

"Looks like strychnine to me," he said, "and the reaction is so strong that I doubt she'll survive more than an hour or so."

"Strychnine! But how would she have got it?"

"Probably took an overdose somehow. She may have been prescribed it for her illness and inadvertently took too much."

"But is there nothing we can do?" Titania, increasingly panic-stricken, repeated.

"I doubt it. I'll get the doctor."

"Our other companion went for him," Titania said.

"Probably not found him. I think I might know where he is – woman down the road is about to give birth – probably started. I'll send someone – no, I'll go myself and see if he's there."

Upon which the innkeeper left the room and Titania, standing on the opposite side of the bed from Lord Vincent, met his eyes.

"I wish I hadn't arranged this outing," she said.

"Not your fault – and she was enjoying it until just now."

"Is she going to …?" Titania stared at him imploringly.

"I'm afraid so, yes."

"Oh, my God!"

Whether Titania was merely exclaiming in horror or actively beseeching God to intervene, neither knew, but, with a sigh, Titania sat down upon the bed beside Veronica, took her hand in hers and held it fast.

"Dearest," she said, "try not to worry!"

It seemed an idiotic thing to say when the girl was obviously in extreme pain as well as frightened of what was about to happen. Her eyes, in the brief pauses between convulsions, clung to Titania's with an expression of terror.

The doctor arrived a few minutes later, took one look at the patient and confirmed Lord Vincent's diagnosis.

"She's obviously ingested a good deal," he said, "so much that I don't think there's anything to be done. I'll give her some of this, but I don't hold out much hope that it'll do the trick. My lady," he added to Titania, "best not to touch her – there may be traces of poison on her person or her clothes."

"Oh, no – I cannot – she must not be left alone and friendless," Titania exclaimed, her eyes filling with tears of sympathy.

"Best do as he advises," Lord Vincent said, coming round to the same side of the bed as Titania and drawing her away.

"Have you touched her?" the doctor asked sharply.

"Yes."

"Well, I suppose you're both as contaminated as each other," the medical man concluded with a shrug and Lord Vincent took Titania in his arms, where she leaned against him with her eyes closed.

The doctor opened his bag and brought out a small brown bottle and a spoon. He poured some of its contents into the spoon and, waiting for a moment when Veronica had subsided momentarily on to the bed, tipped it down her throat. He followed this first dose with several more, although they were interrupted by the patient's continued convulsions until she fell into what appeared to be an uneasy sleep, her body at last relaxing and ceasing to jerk.

Titania, knowing from the absence of sound that Veronica was either dead or at least no longer moving, raised her head from Lord Vincent's chest and turned to look at the patient.

"She's still breathing," she said.

"Yes," the doctor agreed. "But I'm not hopeful that she will survive. What I've given her won't do her any good in the long run. She'll probably start vomiting soon," he added, looking round for a suitable receptacle.

"She did earlier – in the courtyard," Lord Vincent said.

"Ah! No doubt that brought out some of what I suspect to be strychnine, but the tannic acid I've given her will make her sick too."

"How would she have come by strychnine?" Titania asked.

"I prescribed a small dose to help with her injuries from the riding accident. She must have taken too much."

"How – was it in the form of pills?" Titania asked.

"Yes. It seemed to be helping – until now."

The doctor sighed. "The trouble is patients often think that when a medicine makes them a little better, taking more of it will make them a lot better. That's rarely true, certainly not with something as dangerous as strychnine."

As he was speaking, the patient stirred, her complexion grew even whiter if that were possible and her features began to twist.

"Give me the receptacle!" he ordered. Clearly, he had seen this before because he raised the girl into something approaching a sitting position and held the chamber pot in front of her. It was not long before she began to vomit repeatedly. There was nothing left in her stomach but tannic acid and this she hurled into the pot with violent contortions of her upper body.

Nobody spoke, but Titania shuddered and clung to Lord Vincent, whose face remained stony.

"There, there!" the doctor said. "Bring it all up – there's a good girl! You don't want any of that stuff in your stomach."

Veronica needed no second bidding for she heaved and spat for some considerable time, less and less liquid joining that already collected in the chamber pot. At last, she ceased these paroxysms and, without apparently having been conscious at any time during the frenzy, fell into what looked, at first glance, to be death.

Titania, raising her face from Lord Vincent's chest, detected the girl's chest moving faintly.

"She's still alive!" she exclaimed as though neither of the others might have noticed this fact.

"Yes," the doctor said, "but now she will lie still for some time, after which she may come round or she may slip into death. It's impossible to predict."

"Should she remain here?" Lord Vincent asked, "or should we take her home?"

"I don't think taking her home will affect the outcome," the doctor said.

"No!" Titania exclaimed. "She mustn't go home – someone's poisoned her – I'm certain she didn't take any extra pills herself. Someone wanted her dead – wanted her dead before – that's why her horse fell – someone did something – prodded, tripped it. She'll never get better if she goes home because someone will suffocate her or something!"

Neither the doctor nor Lord Vincent looked surprised by this conclusion.

"Can we take her back to Rushlake, do you think, or should she stay here? If she remains here, someone trustworthy must be with her at all times or the murderer will manage to get at her again."

The doctor nodded.

"Is that your carriage outside, my lady?"

"Yes; I took her for a drive, which I thought she'd enjoy. Instead, she's almost dead – and it's my fault."

"I'm sure it isn't," Lord Vincent said.

He turned to the doctor.

"Where do you think she would be best off?"

"I shouldn't think it would make any difference," the doctor said gloomily. "Her chances of survival are extremely poor, my lord."

"We can look after her, keep her safe at Rushlake," Titania said.

The doctor nodded, perhaps more to placate Titania than because he thought anything anyone could do would be of the least benefit to Veronica.

"Take her back in your carriage and I will drive to Thetford House and tell his lordship that she was taken ill close to Rushlake so that it seemed best to take her there. I will further add that I don't think she should be moved."

"Oh, thank you!" Titania exclaimed in heartfelt tones. "I know you think she's not going to get better but, if she is to do so, she will undoubtedly have a better chance with us. Someone can sit with her at all times and we won't allow anyone to visit – not anyone," she added with emphasis.

"I don't think you'll be able to refuse her father entry," Lord Vincent pointed out.

"No," Titania agreed, "but, useless though he's been – and worse than useless to marry that harpy – I can't believe he would want to kill his own daughter. But even he, even he, won't be permitted to visit her by himself – one of us must be there all the time."

The doctor shrugged and, no doubt impressed – or intimidated – by Titania's forcefulness, gave his permission for the patient to be carried to Rushlake forthwith.

"I'll visit again this evening," he promised and left, not waiting while the girl was picked up again, carried downstairs and laid once more in the carriage in which, earlier, she had been so happy and animated.

"You drive," Titania told Lord Vincent, "I'll sit with her."

Lord Vincent took the reins, Jim, who had been waiting with the horses since consuming his own sustenance in the kitchen, took up his position at the back and they prepared to depart. Lord Vincent paused as the landlord stood waving them off to ask whether there had been any sign of Mr Stapleton since he had dashed off to fetch the doctor.

"No, my lord," the innkeeper replied. "He may still be looking for him; I found him where I'd expected."

"If he does return, pray tell him we have gone to Rushlake," Lord Vincent said and directed the horses out of the inn's yard.

Veronica lay as inanimate and pale as a doll during the journey. Titania stroked her hands, her cheek and her hair and bade her rest peacefully and wake refreshed.

"There's no hurry," she said, "although I own I'm impatient to speak to you again, but you must take your time. You've been horridly ill and will need to recover. I'm certain you will," she added on a falsely positive note.

Lord Vincent said nothing but took the carriage expertly along the roads and in at the gates of Rushlake, pulling up in front of the main door.

The butler, no doubt informed by an alert footman of their arrival, opened the door to be greeted by a somewhat dishevelled and distraught young mistress, who informed him that Miss Veronica had been taken ill over luncheon and that she had decided she would receive the best nursing at Rushlake.

"Yes, my lady. I'll send someone to bring her in and order a room to be prepared."

"Lord Vincent can bring her in," Titania replied, "but, yes, pray arrange for the room next to mine to be prepared at once."

Lord Vincent, taking his order in good part, handed the reins to Jim with instructions to take the carriage back to the stables, climbed into the carriage and once more picked up the girl. She was still breathing, still warm, but might as well have been a corpse apart from those hopeful signs.

Titania led him up the stairs to the room she had designated. As they walked along the corridor, a couple of maids appeared carrying bed linen and a warming pan.

They all entered the room together and Lord Vincent stood, with his burden in his arms, while the bed was made and the warming pan passed across the sheets. At last, the maids indicating it was ready for its occupant, his lordship laid the girl upon the sheets and he and Titania drew up the blankets around her.

"Is anyone in the family at home?" he asked. "His lordship?"

"I don't think so; I imagine the party that went to Shrewsbury is not yet returned and Horace – well, I don't know where he is, but I'm certain Perkins will inform him of the presence of a new guest. I daresay my sister's here," she added. "She and her family were simply going for a walk today so I should think they'd be back by now."

"Perhaps you should inform her of the guest," Lord Vincent suggested tentatively.

Titania frowned. "You mean that, being the youngest, I've taken too much upon myself to bring her here without their permission?" she asked, beginning to simmer with resentment.

"Yes," he answered, smiling at her boldly. "I think you should tell them what you've done before they find out through the servants and take exception to your not having informed them yourself."

"Oh! But what else was I to do? Someone wants her dead and it's most likely to be someone in her own household. She's not safe there, especially in this state where she hasn't the least idea what's going on."

"I think you did the right thing," he said more seriously, "although I don't know that she will survive. The doctor seemed very pessimistic."

"Oh, he's always like that! He probably doesn't want to be accused of having given us hope that was dashed – we might blame him. If she does survive, he'll no doubt claim it was the second poison he poured down her throat in the inn. Do you think I should go and look for Jenny – or Horace?"

"No; you promised you wouldn't leave her alone and I don't think you should. Get a servant to fetch one of them."

"You could stay with her, couldn't you?"

"Yes, but I might be the murderer. Dear Titania, you were quite right when you said no one could be trusted – and you shouldn't trust me either. Ring the bell."

"Why in the world would you want to kill her?"

"Who knows? There are any number of reasons: perhaps she knows who killed her mother and perhaps that was I – or perhaps I'd been courting her until you turned up when I transferred my attention to you."

"But why would that prompt you to try to kill her?"

"I might have seduced her and she was preparing to tell you how badly I had behaved and thus ruin all my plans."

"It sounds a bit far-fetched. You've never shown the least interest in me."

232

Chapter 29

When Aunt Saffy parted from the young couple and rejoined the other two ladies, they greeted her with scarcely controlled curiosity.

"You were speaking to that young woman for a long time," Helena said.

"So far as I could see, she did most of the talking," Lady Amberstone said. "Did she tell you anything of interest?"

"Well, yes, she did, but I think she must be mistaken. She told me someone was coming down the bank at the same time as Veronica and that this person's horse nudged hers – and, in short, that was how it stumbled and she fell off! She didn't," Saffy continued, "say she thought it was deliberate but she did say there was plenty of room so that she didn't understand why this other rider was so close."

"Good God!" Helena exclaimed. "So someone did try to kill her?"

"It looks that way, yes."

"Who was it?" Lady Amberstone asked.

"She wasn't sure," Aunt Saffy admitted.

"Is she certain this person nudged her horse on purpose in order to send it flying or was it perhaps merely an unfortunate result of the horses getting too close in spite of there being space around them?" Lady Amberstone persisted, by no means certain that the young woman had not refined upon what she had seen and, after the event, come up with a dramatic conclusion.

"Why in the world didn't she say anything at the time?" Lady Amberstone enquired.

"Well, I didn't quite like to ask that – at least not so bluntly. I asked if she was certain or whether she had come to this conclusion afterwards. She was adamant that the fall had been caused by the horses touching. She said she hadn't mentioned it before because she didn't like to make trouble or question the nobility."

"Oh, my goodness!" Lady Amberstone exclaimed impatiently. "Even the nobility aren't permitted to kill people on purpose! Was it your impression that she believed the person – was it a man or a woman? – she must have noticed that - was an aristocrat?"

"I don't know, but I think she was anxious about interfering in the Thetford household, there being already such a deal of gossip about them."

"So far as I'm aware, there aren't any men in the Thetford household," Helena said, "so that, if it was a member of the household it must have been a woman - unless if was Thetford himself. Did she notice what the person was wearing? Not pink, I presume?"

"No, not pink. At least, I didn't ask her that, but I'm sure she would have mentioned it if it had been. I asked her what he or she looked like."

"Yes?" Lady Amberstone asked.

"She said she wasn't sure because she was behind, you see, and, really, everyone looks alike from the back."

"Men don't look like women, and women don't look like men," Lady Amberstone said, "unless it was a woman riding astride – or a man on a side saddle – and everyone else would have noticed that. Surely she could tell whether the person was male or female! She's a very poor witness. You were the only one of us who was on the hunt," she added to Helena, curbing her impatience with difficulty. "Did you happen to notice who was talking to Veronica?"

"No. I was even further behind. But I don't think is is easy to identify a man on a hunt, particularly if he isn't in pink. They all dress in a similar fashion and all wear almost identical hats, beneath which it's not easy to be certain of hair colour – or features. Even a woman, from a distance, might be mistaken for a man because I don't suppose your witness was paying much attention to how the person was sitting on the horse. She noticed two horses close together and then saw them collide. Both the riders were presumably in dark clothes – almost everybody was - and would have been wearing hats – why, some women these days wear hats very similar to men's!"

"Perhaps," Lady Amberstone conceded. "Did she have anything to say about the size of the horse?"

"I'm afraid I didn't think to ask that," Aunt Saffy said apologetically.

"Well, never mind. It would be helpful if we knew whether it was a man or a woman though, although I suppose both might have had a reason other than murder to get so dangerously close - a woman might have wanted to confide something and a man - I haven't met Veronica Thetford – is she a taking little thing?"

"Oh, yes, I should say so," Helena replied. "She's not tall, very slender and graceful – or she was when she could walk – and has a lovely little face – just the sort that men particularly warm to, I should think – you know, large eyes, a good complexion and abundant hair. And then, she's very young – sixteen. Most girls are taking at that age."

"No," Lady Amberstone corrected, "beautiful ones are often not so very taking – they grow into their beauty a little later, but quite ordinary looking females – the kind that 'go off' quite early – are often charming at that age. I always think mothers who want their girls married should make a pragmatic judgment of their daughters' looks and act accordingly."

"Oh, I don't think she'll 'go off,'" Helena returned, laughing. "She's undoubtedly pretty. I wonder," she added thoughtfully, "if I was one of those that 'went off'. My mother should have presented me earlier."

"I should think she would have been well advised to do so in any event," Lady Amberstone said, "for she must have known your character and it would be bound to become more determined later. So, we've established that the poor girl is pretty, sixteen – is she a good rider?"

"Yes, very."

"So that, in that setting, hunting, she would have stood out and attracted the attentions of most of the men. I think we'd better try to ascertain just who was on the hunt, men and women, and what they were wearing – style of hat and so on - and eliminate some of them from our enquiries," Lady Amberstone concluded.

When they got back to the square where they had agreed to meet Mr Bodley and the carriage, they found the carriage but not Mr Bodley.

The coachman opened the door and the ladies climbed in, sitting down with a sigh of relief upon the squabs. They were all three tired and had had quite enough of Shrewsbury for the time being, although, as soon as they were seated, Aunt Saffy unwrapped her new scarf and fell to contemplating it with pleasure. Lady Amberstone, watching her, smiled. She was glad she had bought it.

"I suppose Adrian's still following up clues," Helena observed.

"I'm sure he must be," Lady Amberstone agreed, "which, irritating as it is to be obliged to wait, is surely a good sign."

The coachman enquired whether they wanted to wait for the gentleman, to which Lady Amberstone replied briskly, "Well, of course we don't *want* to wait, but we must. I daresay he's busy."

"Yes, my lady."

It was at least a quarter of an hour later that Helena saw Adrian Bodley striding across the square towards them.

"Here he is!" she said with sigh.

"He looks big with news!" Lady Amberstone observed.

They all three watched as he saw the carriage and made his way towards it.

"I'm sorry I'm late!" he exclaimed, arriving at the door, which the coachman opened.

"Not at all!" Lady Amberstone replied politely. "Have you had a successful day?"

"Well, I have and I haven't, so to speak," he said, subsiding on to the seat beside Helena as the coachman shut the door and prepared to depart.

"Could we," he asked, "that is, do you know where Captain Mayne, who is the Chief Constable here, lives?"

Lady Amberstone, who knew this part of England not at all, shook her head, as did Helena, but Aunt Saffy said she thought she knew which was his house and that they would more or less pass it on their way home.

"Oh, splendid!" he cried. "I thought that might be the case. Do you think we could stop there?"

"I don't see why not," Lady Amberstone said, trying to adopt an enthusiastic note which she did not feel. She was tired and wanted nothing more than to sit beside the fire at Rushlake and drink a cup of tea.

"There is something which I would very much like to ask him," Mr Bodley went on, becoming a trifle wistful, "although I don't suppose he'll want to speak to me. I wondered, dear Lady Amberstone, if you could be the spokesperson – I'm certain he would be delighted to welcome you into his house."

"He may not be there," she said, "and, in truth, I think it would be better to ask Horace to approach him. He must, after all, have met him once or twice, whereas I, although I acknowledge that I have the reputation of a grand lady who gets what she wants, am a perfect stranger to him."

Mr Bodley was forced to concede the truth of this and, after he had told his companions what he had discovered, they agreed that, although things were becoming urgent and it was fairly clear that at least one crime had been committed, they were not so urgent that it behoved them to act impulsively.

Back at Rushlake, Titania had overseen the arrival of their latest guest, made sure she was comfortable – as comfortable as anyone could be who was as close to death as Veronica was – and, having sent the maid who had lit the fire to fetch her sister, awaited her with some trepidation.

Jenny entered the room very soon after she had been called. Titania rose from her chair beside the bed and joined her sister just inside the door. It did not take long to retail a short version of the drive which had been intended as a treat for the girl.

"My God!" Jenny said on a breath, approaching the bed and staring down at the waxen figure upon it.

"She is at least quiet now," Titania said. "It was simply awful when she was writhing and vomiting – terrible. What she must have suffered!"

"It doesn't bear thinking about," Jenny agreed. "What do you intend to do now – and where is Vincent?"

"I think he's downstairs; he didn't want to come up, thought it improper, I believe. He's very correct, Jenny."

"I should hope so; I own I've been horrified since I've been here by the gross impropriety of so many people whom one would have expected to know better.

"What," she continued on a different note, "did you think Marcus's sentiments were – are?"

"He's in love with her, but I can't think where he's got to since he rushed off to find the doctor, which he didn't succeed in doing in any event. The innkeeper found him – he was attending a confinement a few doors down from the inn."

"Perhaps he went to her house, thinking she might have been taken there. I think we should send for Thetford, let him know we have her as safe as she can be – which is not very safe at all – and wait for him to turn up in a panic. Marcus, if he's gone there, will no doubt come with him."

"Where's Horace?"

"He went out again after luncheon, saying something about checking on the estate. I daresay he'll be back soon; in fact, I suppose he might be hiding in the library. Why don't you go and look for him – and see what Vincent's doing – while I sit with Veronica?"

"Perhaps I will. Thank you."

Titania went straight to the library where, to her surprise, she found Lord Vincent being entertained by her brother.

"I didn't know you were here!" she exclaimed accusingly.

"I've just come in and found Vincent sitting in the hall. I assumed he'd come to see me, but he's told me something of what took place on your drive and I now realise he's been waiting for you. You look frazzled, dear sister – tell me what's troubling you."

"If Vincent's told you what happened I can't imagine why you don't already know what's disturbing me. Lord, but it was an awful day – lurching from one disaster to another. I let her drive and she – well, I assume it was a mistake – lost control and we ended up in a field and then, over luncheon, which I was beginning to enjoy – and so was she – she suddenly became violently ill."

"Vincent's been telling me that the doctor thinks it's strychnine poisoning, brought on by her taking too many of the pills she'd been prescribed."

"That's what he said – and it's my opinion that telling her to take something which could prove fatal if she took too many was an irresponsible thing to do. What were those wretched pills supposed to do if she'd taken the right amount?"

It was Vincent who answered. "Calm her down and alleviate some of the stiffness she was suffering."

"Make her able to walk again?"

"I suppose he might have hoped so."

"Well, it didn't and now she's probably going to die! She's suffered appallingly. Also," she added, working herself up into a passion, "she wasn't agitated – she never is – she's a calm girl."

"Perhaps it was the pills which stopped her being agitated," Vincent suggested tentatively.

"I don't believe it! I think he just wanted to be seen to be doing something – and no doubt charged a vast amount for his attendance as well as for the pills."

"But do you think her seizure was caused by an overdose?" Rushlake asked quietly.

"I'm fairly sure it was strychnine," Lord Vincent said, "but whether the overdose was caused by her taking too many pills of her own accord, or someone else giving her too many – or indeed by someone else administering the drug in a different form – I'm not certain."

"Do you think her mother died of the same thing?" Titania asked.

"I don't know precisely what her symptoms were, but I think this second attempt to remove Veronica makes it more likely that she too was poisoned," Horace said.

"But I still don't see why anyone would want to kill *Veronica*," Titania said. "I can perfectly understand that the wicked governess had to get rid of the mother before she could become the stepmother, and I can understand that someone – the same person – might want to kill Julia – and mistook Veronica for her because she was wearing her habit – but what's Veronica done to annoy this person?"

"I wonder if you need to look for a different motive," Horace murmured. "You're convinced the murderer is the wicked stepmother – and I agree she would make an excellent murderess as she has motive

238

as well as the sort of character that stops at nothing to get what she wants – at least so far as the first Viscountess was concerned – but perhaps the person who wants to remove Veronica has a different reason for his or her actions."

"Why would anyone want to kill her? She's sixteen and completely harmless!"

"But, is she?"

"Yes!"

"Think, Tania! What are the usual motives for killing someone?"

"Greed, anger, ambition, resentment, hatred – I don't know – I suppose it's usually about wanting something they've got, isn't it? Or not wanting them to spill the beans. Did she know who'd killed her mother while Julia was only guessing? That was why I thought the riding 'accident' happened – because she'd been mistaken for Julia and Julia knew too much about her mother's death and kept talking about it. She'd even told Adrian about it – wanted him to investigate."

"Yes – and all that points to Vera Thetford, if that is the reason for the attempted second murder. But what if this was a wholly different matter which people have naturally tried to link to the first suspicious death? What if the first attempt at removing Veronica – pushing her down the bank – was nothing to do with her mother's suspicious death and that, that having gone awry, the person had to try again and this time was determined there wouldn't be another mistake?"

Chapter 30

The party which had gone to Shrewsbury arrived back at Rushlake in time for tea.

"His lordship is in the library with Lady Titania and Lord Vincent," Perkins announced as they entered the house.

"Ah! Perhaps you would be so good as to tell him we've returned," Lady Amberstone said. "I'm going upstairs for a little while; it's been a tiring day. What about you, Saffy?"

"Yes, I believe I'll go up too – just for a few minutes, you know."

"Quite."

The two older ladies allowed themselves to be divested of their hats and coats and then made their way up the stairs together, leaving Helena and Adrian Bodley in the hall.

"I suppose you'll want to join Horace in the library," Helena said.

"I will, but, unless you also want to rush upstairs immediately, I'd very much like to have a few words with you first," the detective said, the presence of the brooch positively weighing down his pocket.

"Will you ask him to seek out Captain Mayne?" she enquired, leading the way into the morning room, although it was by no means morning.

"Yes, but that can wait for a few moments. It's you I particularly wish to speak to," he insisted, following her.

"Do you think we can send for tea?" she enquired, "or should we be waiting until everyone's gathered in the drawing room?"

"I'm sure we can," he said at once, although he had never been less interested in tea.

She rang the bell before sitting down beside a fire which was languishing in the grate.

Mr Bodley, impatient to say his piece and present his gift before someone else came into the room, poked the fire and threw on a couple of logs with the result that it looked almost insulted by this attempt to revive it, adopting a grey and exhausted look which struck him as a depressing omen for the reception of his gift.

The butler, appearing in answer to the bell, promised that tea would immediately be forthcoming and left the room. Mr Bodley, once again forced to delay his speech, went to look out of the window at the garden.

"You don't have to wait for the tea before you speak," Helena said, aware of his impatience and wondering what he wanted to say so urgently.

"Yes, I do, because I'd rather not be interrupted once I've launched into it," he returned a trifle testily.

"What does it concern?" she asked, her usual *sangfroid* deserting her in the face of his agitation.

"You and me," he replied in a disagreeable voice.

"Oh! Have I done something wrong?"

"No; how could you?"

"Easily, I should think. You seem annoyed."

"Not with you – never with you. It's just that I'm anxious about who will be the next person to burst into the room and disturb us."

"I shouldn't think anyone would; that's why I came in here, because I don't believe it's usual to go into the morning room in the afternoon."

He blinked.

"You mean you didn't want to be disturbed either?"

"No; if you have something to say to me particularly, which is what you said, I would infinitely rather you had the opportunity to do so. I'm sorry I requested tea, but it's been a very long day and I felt in need of refreshment."

"Of course."

Fortunately, at this moment the door opened and the butler appeared with the tea, which he placed upon a table near Miss Patchett.

"Would you like me to mend the fire, sir?" he enquired of Mr Bodley.

"Yes, yes, please do," the detective replied, although in truth he simply wished the man out of the room.

The butler poked the fire a little more but with rather more science that Mr Bodley had employed, inserted a couple of small logs, built up the whole with some coal and, pausing for a few moments to make sure that it was responding, bowed his way out.

The two were now alone, the fire had begun to look more lively and Helena, without either enquiring whether her companion wanted tea or how he wished to take it, poured out a couple of cups and handed one to him.

"Thank you."

She sipped her own and waited for him to speak. As so often, he reflected that she had a delightfully calm way about her. She neither made a joke nor begged him to open his budget but simply waited with the air of one who had all the time in the world.

"Helena," he said at last, and then, having no idea how to begin, thrust his hand into his pocket and brought out the little package, holding it out to her with a blush.

"I bought you a little present in Shrewsbury," he said. "I hope you'll like it."

"Why, thank you!"

She took the little box, judged that it did not contain a ring, for it was the wrong shape, and enquired whether she might open it.

"Pray do!"

She undid the ribbon which bound it, lifted the lid and saw the pretty brooch, whose sapphires winked at her as the new flame in the grate reached upwards.

"Oh!" she exclaimed. "It's beautiful! Thank you! But why did you buy me another present? You gave me one scarce a week ago for Christmas."

"Yes, but that was a dull thing. I wanted – I saw this – and I wanted to give you something more exciting."

She lifted the brooch out of its box, opened the pin and attached it to her dress, where it sat so comfortably that it might have been made for that very dress worn by that very woman.

"Doesn't it look pretty?" she asked, her head bent and slightly twisted to look at it.

"Very. It becomes you."

"Does it? I've never had anything half so lovely."

"Oh, I'm sure you must have – after all – after all, you – you are ..." His voice faded away.

"So rich." She completed the sentence and, after a pause, said, "Yes, I've inherited a great deal of money but not much jewellery and no one has ever bought me anything like this. It's – it's of enormous value to me."

She looked up at him and the blue eyes, whose colour he had noted only recently and which had prompted his choice of sapphires, were swimming in tears.

"I wanted ...," he began, and his own eyes had grown unusually bright. "I wanted to give you something as a token of my affection."

"Is your affection so strong?" she asked on a breath.

"Yes - and deep," he said, surprising himself by how he seemed to have lost his uncertainty. Afterwards, he supposed that, having as it were thrown himself off the cliff, he had found courage and determination waiting for him.

"Oh!" was all she could manage, his previous uncertainty having transferred to her and rendered her almost dumb. Was this, at the age of thirty-five, her first proposal?

"I didn't dare," he went on, "believe that you would consider my suit anything but an insult and so – well, I thought that if I gave you a brooch, you would – it was possible – you would not mind so terribly."

"Bribe me, you mean?" she asked, finding a little humour to carry her forward as she glanced at the jewellery sitting confidently beneath her shoulder.

"I didn't see it that way," he admitted. "I just wanted to give you something but, more than that, I wanted – have wanted almost since the moment we met in Yorkshire some time ago now – to confess my sentiments. But I was too much of a coward."

"I think it's because we're so old – I mean, not precisely old, but past the usual age for declaring sentiments and giving meaningful gifts," she explained, also gaining in confidence.

"I've never felt this way before," he continued, "so that I have no experience of how to approach a lady – or how to put my foot in it, so to speak – and I was so afraid that I would mess it up and lose you completely that I'm afraid I bottled it back in London."

She, aware that he had still not said the words, or asked the question which she felt, hoped, was on the tip of his tongue, smiled encouragingly and agreed that she'd never felt quite this way before.

"*Quite?*"

"Never!"

Both fell silent as the words, and the future, hung between them.

"I've fallen in love with you," he said at last.

"And I with you," she returned.

"Truly?"

"Truly."

He rose, and for an awful moment, she thought he was going to mend the fire again, but he did not; he moved a few feet towards where she was sitting and, with a surprising degree of grace, got down upon one knee and, reaching for her hand, managed, albeit in a rather strangled voice, to say the words.

"Will you become my wife, dearest Helena?"

"Yes, of course I will – with the greatest pleasure!" she exclaimed, clutching his hand in her turn.

"I didn't get you a ring," he confessed.

"Who cares about a ring?" she asked, throwing caution to the winds and tugging at his hand to make him rise and take her in his arms. "It's how we feel that matters."

"Yes," he breathed and kissed her.

Meanwhile, in the library, Lord Rushlake, who had been informed that the town party had returned, wondered aloud when someone was going to tell him about the outing.

Lord Vincent, feeling that his presence was superfluous now that the family had been reunited, took his leave.

Titania, disdaining her brother's offer to request Perkins to show him out, offered to perform this duty herself and led her friend to the door.

"Thank you again," she said fervently as they stood in the hall, the footman waiting to open the door while they made their *adieux*.

"Not at all; thank you for inviting me to come on the trip."

She gave a hollow laugh, saying, "I should think you wish I had not – or you had had the forethought to provide yourself with an excuse."

"It was an unfortunate set of events," he agreed, drawing her further from the door and speaking in a low voice, "but I'm glad I was there to help. I hope the poor girl rallies."

"Do you think she will?"

"I've no idea; I'm not a doctor and have no experience of people being poisoned so severely. May I call later this evening to enquire after both her and you?"

"Of course. Would you like to join us for dinner?"

"I would be delighted."

This having been settled to their mutual satisfaction, he turned his steps towards the door again, which the footman opened, revealing that there was neither carriage nor horse to convey his lordship back to his home.

"How are you going to travel?" she asked, as he prepared to step outside.

"I'll walk."

"It's a few miles. Let me call a carriage or you'll only just have got home when it'll be time to set off again to join us for dinner."

He smiled.

"I'll go across the fields and, to tell you the truth, will quite enjoy the walk. It'll help to clear my head and perhaps lead to unexpected insights into the situation."

"Very well."

She gave him her hand, which he pressed briefly before turning and striding off down the drive.

Titania went inside and up the stairs to relieve her sister of her bedside duties and to see how the patient was progressing. She found Jenny sitting beside Veronica, who did not appear to have moved or changed in any way.

"She is still breathing?" she asked as she came in.

"Yes; she hasn't groaned or sighed or indeed stirred since you left."

"I believe the drug stiffens the limbs – and eventually the lungs – so that, if she's still breathing, I think that must be a good sign."

"Yes," Jenny said with a marked lack of optimism. As the mother of three children, she was perfectly accustomed to nursing ill persons but was not used to sitting beside someone who did nothing; her usual patients groaned and cried and either coughed or vomited at frequent intervals. Generally, too, they had a high temperature and flushed cheeks. This patient was pale as milk and did not move – possibly could not move.

"Would you like me to relieve you?" Titania asked, to whom the quietness of the girl was a relief after the awful twistings and turnings which had characterised her illness at the beginning.

"Yes, for a little. I believe I should see what my children are doing."

Titania nodded and took her sister's place beside Veronica. There did not seem to be much that she could tell her but she reiterated, with no little exaggeration, the doctor's opinion that she would soon be well, her own hopes that this would not be long delayed, and her apologies for taking her on an outing which had proved to be not so much enjoyable as nearly fatal.

"I wonder," she said after a long pause while she wracked her brain for another topic, "how soon it will be before Marcus comes to enquire after you."

As she spoke, she scanned the girl's face for any change and thought – believed or imagined – that there was the slightest, faintest suspicion of a tremor on the beautiful lips.

"I couldn't help noticing," she went on, encouraged, "that you and he seemed to – to like each other and, I'm not sure whether you can hear me, although I think you can, but I'm going to admit to you – never to anyone else so pray don't mention it when you're able to speak again – but I had, there was a moment when I had hoped that he might be interested in me. While we were out, or at least in your presence, I realised that I was deluded, that he cared nothing for me, probably only for my fortune, for that's what everyone finds most attractive in me; indeed it's the only thing that's ever attracted anyone and that not for long; when they find out more about my character, they generally abandon hope of it; you see, I'm obviously too awful a prospect even when sweetened by my money. It's a lowering thought that no one will have me, but I shouldn't complain as at least, so far in any event, no one has tried to kill me; they probably would if they married me. I daresay the disagreeable nature of my character would soon drive them to such lengths. But who could possibly want to kill you? You're one of the most agreeable people I know, although of course I don't know you very well, and perhaps, beneath that soft and compliant exterior, you're a selfish, demanding person.

"Is it – was it – that you know something about your mama's death that has rattled her murderer? Can it possibly be that? Because, you see, we thought that perhaps you'd been mistaken for Julia, as you were wearing her old riding habit, but now that someone has taken such a very drastic step to remove you, I wonder if it's not Julia who knows something, but you. And, now I come to think of it, if Julia did, does, know anything, I'm certain she would have said so, whereas you may not have known that what you knew was so dangerous.

"I don't suppose I'm making much sense, but, if you do know something about someone which nobody else has noticed, it would be advisable, in my opinion, to tell someone – although for Heaven's sake not the wrong person – to tell someone who means you no harm, like me.

"For, the thing is, whether Marcus likes you better than me, and clearly he does, I don't mean you any harm and – dearest Veronica – pray wake up soon, for it is quite awful to be on such tenterhooks lest you never do."

During some of this monologue, Titania had been watching the other girl's face, had been holding her hand, hoping to see either a flicker of movement upon the still features or feel a slight pressure upon her fingers, but during some of it, as she reflected bitterly and a trifle self-pityingly upon her own misfortunes, she had stared off into the distance. Since she was sitting with her back to the window, she had had nothing upon which to focus but the door and that had not been inspiring.

"I believe I'll pick some flowers for you when Jenny comes back. I'll put them on the table beside you because I always think scent can be quite stimulating, although of course there's not much in the garden at this time of year. What there is, though, is generally scented – perhaps some winter honeysuckle or wintersweet, which is not pretty but smells lovely. The honeysuckle is quite pretty and its rather ramshackle appearance might be interesting to study."

She fell silent, aware that she was rambling and beginning to wish that someone would come to relieve her for, although she wished poor Veronica all the best, sitting beside her was tedious. Looking round the room for something to remark upon, her eye fell on a bookshelf and she jumped up and chose a book almost at random.

Sitting down again, she began to read.

Chapter 31

Lady Amberstone and Aunt Saffy stayed in their rooms for some time, unaware that Adrian and Helena were far too taken up with themselves to discuss their discoveries of the morning with their host, and also unaware of the result of Titania's well-meant drive.

Lord Rushlake, having bidden *adieu* to Lord Vincent, went in search of Adrian and Helena. Finding them sitting very close upon the sofa in the morning room, he retreated without them having noticed his presence and went upstairs to find Titania and his unconscious new guest.

He knocked upon the door as Titania was finishing the first chapter of what was turning out to be an unutterably dreary book.

She looked up, relief upon her face.

"Are you very bored?" he asked sympathetically.

"I own I am a little, although it is not at all Veronica's fault. You see how still she lies – but I suppose it's better than writhing around as she was when she first swallowed the poison. Oh, Horace, what do you think will happen? Have the others got back from Shrewsbury?"

"Yes, but Helena and Adrian are sharing their deepest thoughts with each other in the morning room and Aunt Mildred and Saffy have taken to their beds, so I've no idea whether they discovered anything of importance. I've sent word to Thetford that his daughter's here, so I daresay he will arrive soon."

"I don't want her to be left alone for a moment," Titania said.

"No, but I suppose we can leave her with her father."

"I don't think we should; if it was he who poisoned her mother, I wouldn't trust him with his daughter."

"He's devoted to her; you didn't see his manner when he carried her home after the accident. Whoever is harming people in that household, I'm certain it isn't he."

"I don't care," Titania said stubbornly. "I won't leave her – and you musn't either."

"I don't think we both have to sit here until eternity," he said. "Who do you think is responsible? When you were out with her this morning, did you see anyone interfere with her food in the inn?"

"What in the world do you mean?"

"Did anyone pour her a drink or put some vegetables on her plate or anything?"

"No, of course not. There were only four of us."

"Yes, but one of those four might have introduced a stronger dose of the poison. She was taken ill very suddenly and dramatically."

"Well, it wasn't I!" she exclaimed. "Are you accusing Vincent or Marcus?"

"I'm wondering, that's all. Who poured her drink – and what did she drink?"

"Lemonade, as did I. It came in a jug and Vincent poured it – at least he did after the waiter had initially filled our glasses."

"And what did she eat?"

"We had a sort of nuncheon – nothing very exciting. There was ham, beef and some chicken. It was all sliced up and laid out on large dishes, which were put on the table. Then there was bread and butter and cheese – again laid out on the table. The bread was cut up in the kitchen; it came in large chunks. And there was a big dish of fruit with oranges, apples and pears. There were peaches too – she had a peach."

"And did anyone peel it for her?"

"Yes, Marcus did."

"And what sort of fruit did you have?"

"An apple – and he peeled that for me. He was quite adept with the fruit knife. Vincent peeled his own orange."

"And had she finished eating when she was taken ill?"

"Yes. She didn't have anything I didn't have, except the peach, and I think she ate chicken although the rest of us stuck to the beef and ham. Perhaps that was poisoned, but why should anyone in the kitchen do something like that?"

"I don't suppose they did."

"Then how did she get it?"

"Did she take any pills while you were in the inn?"

"No, I don't think so."

He sighed. He looked very grave; indeed she had never seen him look so solemn, not even at their father's funeral. His face was almost grey.

"It's a terrible thing," he said. "Go and find Jenny and ask her to take your place; you've sat here for long enough. If Thetford arrives, send for me and I'll come down, leaving Jenny here. Are we expecting the doctor again?"

"Yes; he said he'd come later."

She found Jenny in the nursery playing a game with her husband and children. Explaining that Horace wanted her to join him in the sick chamber, Titania bore her off to the lower floor where Veronica was lying.

As they came down the stairs she heard a knock upon the front door and, rounding the corner, they both saw Lord Thetford being admitted.

"I suppose he's come to see her," Jenny said.

"I should think so; Horace is with her now. Do you think we should go down and speak to him?"

"I'd much prefer it if Horace did," Jenny said, pulling a face.

The sisters backed up the stairs and went to find Horace, who was still sitting beside the patient.

"Thetford has just been admitted," Jenny told him.

"Why don't you speak to him?" the Earl asked Titania. "You know exactly what happened."

She sighed, but, reminding Jenny to stay in the room all the time the Viscount was there, complied.

Downstairs, the footman informed her that his lordship had been admitted and shown into the small sitting room. Apparently, Perkins was already on his way to inform the Earl.

"He knows," Titania told him, "and he's asked me to speak to Lord Thetford."

She found the Viscount pacing restlessly up and down and begged him to be seated.

"*You've* come to speak to me!" he exclaimed furiously. "Haven't you done enough? My daughter hadn't recovered from her accident when you took her out this morning and now I understand she's close to death!"

"I'm so sorry," she said. "Pray sit down and let me tell you exactly what happened while I was with her."

"And why the devil have you brought her here instead of taking her home?"

"She was excessively unwell, sir," Titania replied, sitting down herself and gesturing for her visitor to do so as well. Too well brought up to refuse, the Viscount perched uncomfortably and anxiously upon the edge of a chair facing Titania.

"She was taken by such a violent fit of ... she was writhing, gasping – we thought she would die there before our eyes," she said, gazing at him so earnestly that some of his anger drained away. Titania was a tall and handsome young woman – not the sort that generally prompted a male desire to protect - but she was still young enough to make an anxious father feel paternal towards her.

"We brought her here because it was closer and we wanted to get her somewhere comfortable as soon as possible. The innkeeper did make a chamber available and we took her up there to begin with, but, after the doctor had seen her, we decided – with his agreement – to bring her here rather than take her all the way to Thetford. I'm sorry if that wasn't what you wanted – well, of course it wasn't – but there was also the fact that the doctor thought she had been poisoned – that – in short, that someone wanted her dead and – forgive me, sir – but we, I, was afraid that that someone was a member of your household."

"*What?*"

Titania almost jumped, his voice was so loud, but she rallied and said apologetically, "There've been too many accidents – and death – in your house recently for one to be able to discount the possibility."

"There has been one accident – to Veronica!" he shouted.

"Yes; but your wife died under suspicious circumstances not very long ago; it's hard to escape the notion that something monstrous may be going on. I wanted to save Veronica."

"Thank you," he said stiffly. "Would it be in order for me to see her?"

"Yes, of course. I'll take you up."

Once they had climbed the stairs and were no longer within earshot of the footmen in the hall, he said, "I suppose you're reacting to Julia's outrageous accusations against my wife."

"Yes."

"Julia's deluded," he said. "She hates her new mother and will do anything to discountenance her."

Titania did not reply, but she thought that calling the former governess Julia's 'new mother' would be bound to exacerbate her dislike and resentment.

She knocked briefly upon the door of Veronica's chamber before opening it and leading the Viscount inside. Jenny was still sitting beside the bed, as was Horace.

"My daughter seems to be a favourite with your family," the Viscount said, still firmly seated upon his high horse.

"Indeed, she is," the Earl said gently, standing up to greet his guest. "There hasn't been much improvement, in truth not any that is noticeable, but at least she hasn't deteriorated since she was brought here. The doctor has promised to return later."

The Viscount approached the bed and Titania, receiving an almost imperceptible nod from her brother, withdrew.

When she went into the drawing room she found Lady Amberstone and Aunt Saffy sitting alone.

"Where are Helena and Adrian?" she asked.

"Plighting their troths, I presume," Lady Amberstone replied.

"We haven't seen either of them since we got back," Aunt Saffy explained, "but, judging by his nervous agitation on the drive home, we suspect he's plucked up courage to make a declaration."

"Oh, good," Titania said. "It was about time he did – or she might have had to wait for the next leap year. I daresay you've heard with what disastrous results my outing with Veronica Thetford ended," she went on.

"No!" they both exclaimed.

"Oh!"

Titania spent some time explaining what had happened and was gratified to observe that her tale caused both their faces to become more and more grave as she continued.

"What do you think?" she asked at last.

"I think someone wants her dead and I suspect that it's not because she knows something this person is afraid she might reveal," Lady Amberstone said, "but because of something between herself and the person."

"Good God!" Titania exclaimed. She had not thought of this, although Lord Vincent had suggested the same thing. She had discounted it on the grounds that Veronica was too young to have acquired such a deadly enemy.

She asked them about their experiences and received a minute description of the various people to whom they had spoken, culminating in what Aunt Saffy had been told by the lake.

There was no time to discuss the importance of this piece of evidence because a moment later Perkins announced that Mr Stapleton had arrived.

"Oh, pray show him in," Titania said at once.

Perkins, who had not left the room immediately, coughed and explained that Mr Stapleton had asked to speak to Lady Titania alone.

"Good lord!" Titania exclaimed, blushing. "I'll come down. Where have you put him, Perkins?"

As she accompanied the butler downstairs, Aunt Saffy expressed the hope that there might be a positive outcome to this interview too.

Titania, going into the small blue sitting room into which the curate had been shown, greeted him cautiously. She was still wondering why he had taken so long to come to enquire after a young woman for whom he had rushed off in search of the doctor.

"Thank you for seeing me," he said, looking, as well he might, a little embarrassed.

"Not at all," she returned, gesturing for him to sit down.

He did and she took a chair opposite him.

"I've searched high and low for the doctor," he began. "He wasn't at home and his housekeeper told me he was attending a confinement. She didn't seem to know where precisely so I went back to the inn and found you'd all left. There, I learned that the innkeeper had found the doctor, who had seen Veronica and given permission for her to be brought here. Is she still alive?" he finished with an anxious look.

"In a manner of speaking," Titania told him. "She breathes but has not moved since – since what you saw in the inn."

"It's terrible!" he said with a stricken look.

"Yes."

"Is someone with her?"

"Yes – at all times, but at present her father is there."

"Thetford? Are you certain it's safe to leave them together?"

"What do you mean?"

"There have been so many 'accidents' in that household; I hope they will not now transfer to yours," he said darkly.

"We will do our best to look after her," she reassured him.

"Good. But what of you? Your kind gesture in arranging the outing led to a scene which must have distressed you unutterably."

He leaned forward as he spoke and reached for her hand. She looked into his dark eyes and drowned therein. His evident concern for her had a dramatic effect upon her.

"Yes, it did. I feel dreadfully guilty."

"There is nothing with which you need to reproach yourself; what you did, you did with the best intentions – and her father was perfectly willing for you to take her out."

"Yes, but how did she come by the poison?"

"I should think she took too many pills by mistake – if it was not that someone made sure she did. Ever since her mother died, there has been danger in that household."

"But it was not she who was accusing her stepmother of hastening their mama's death – it was Julia. How could anyone want to kill Veronica?

She is all sweetness – you've felt that yourself. You were – I could see you were taken with her when we were out. You two were whispering together like lovers."

"Not like lovers!" he exclaimed, looking almost insulted. "She's not much more than a child. I was trying to animate her, make her day out a pleasure – I'm sure she couldn't have mistaken my intentions. May I ask," he added with a different look, "whether you interpreted my kindness as flirting because it mattered to you?"

She flushed.

"I was worried about her – flirting with a grown man at her age – I didn't think her father would approve."

"I'm sure he wouldn't – and of course I have very little to offer – only my heart and my pedigree."

"I'm sure your heart would be enough for a lady who – whose own heart recognised yours," she returned, not sure whether he was offering these trifles to her.

"Would it? Would it be enough for you, Titania?"

"If …" Her voice died away.

"If?" he prompted.

"If my heart was engaged, I don't think I'd care about the pedigree, although I daresay Lord Thetford might."

"I'm not interested in what he might like; I'm asking you, Titania. Would you consider me? We're very distantly related, but not anything like enough to present problems of the kind that concern people; you know I have nothing material to offer, nothing at all; I have only myself and my love."

He paused and she could only say, "Oh!"

"We haven't known each other long," he went on, "but I knew as soon as I saw you that you were what my heart has dreamed of ever since I grew to man's estate."

There seemed to be such a large lump in her throat that she could not speak at all, could not even manage another 'oh' and, gazing into her eyes, he rose from his own chair and pulled her up from hers into his arms where his lips found hers.

Titania, in spite of having reached the advanced age of five-and-twenty and having been pursued by a number of gentlemen in London, had never kissed or been kissed by a grown man. It was the most exciting thing that had ever happened to her; it was sweetness itself, the gentle pressure growing stronger, the firm embrace promising safety and hope. She leaned against him as he kissed and kissed her until, at last, so affected that she could not help returning something of his passion, she threw her arms around him and held him as close as he held her.

"You do feel it!" he exclaimed at last. "Will you have me, dearest Titania? Will you wed me? I promise I'll do my best to rise up the church hierarchy. It wouldn't be so very bad to be a bishop's wife, would it?"

She laughed. "It would be very heaven to be a curate's wife," she said and they fell to kissing again.

Chapter 32

Miss Patchett and Mr Bodley, eventually returning to their senses, went to their rooms to repair whatever dishevelment had resulted from their exchange of mutual affection and, having done this, made their way to the drawing room where Lady Amberstone and Aunt Saffy were waiting, a trifle impatiently to order tea.

Neither of these ladies, having spent a day in the company of the lovers, needed to enquire what had delayed their arrival but Lady Amberstone, being of a more impatient disposition than Aunt Saffy, heaved a sigh of relief and directed the gentleman to pull the bell so that they might have their tea.

"You shouldn't have waited for us," Helena said, but, although there was a genuine wish that the older pair had not sat thirstily awaiting them, there was also such a glow of happiness surrounding her that she could hardly keep her mouth in a straight line.

"Oh, we wanted to," her ladyship assured her.

"Where's his lordship?" Mr Bodley asked. "I made sure you would have told him everything that we learned today."

"We were about to, but he went off for some reason and hasn't returned. I believe Lord Thetford arrived; he may be with him," she said.

"Oh! Was there a particular reason for him to call?"

"Oh, yes, indeed!" This time it was Aunt Saffy who answered and, between them, the two ladies retailed something of Titania's day, which perfectly explained the presence of the Viscount in the house.

Tea at this point arriving, there was a pause while it was poured, cups were passed around, cake cut and distributed and so on.

Sir James joined them as they were discussing whether it would be an unnecessary indulgence to have a second slice of cake. More tea was sent for and enquiries made as to how his day had turned out. Where, indeed, was Jenny, Lady Amberstone wondered.

"Oh, I daresay you've heard about our new guest," Sir James said. "I believe she's sitting with her."

"There seem to be a great many people up there," Lady Amberstone observed, "for Horace is there with Thetford, I understand."

"Oh! Well, I should think Jenny will be down soon then. One shouldn't, in my opinion, conduct a party around a person who's unconscious."

"Oh, I don't know," Lady Amberstone said. "It might wake her up – all that chattering. Do you know, I believe I'll forgo a second slice of cake and go up myself. If Jenny's there, I'll send her down."

"I very much want to speak to Horace," Mr Bodley said.

"Oh! In that case, I'll send him down too. What about Thetford? Does anyone particularly wish to talk to him?"

"Not just at present," Mr Bodley said obscurely.

"Well, if it's just he and I up there, I'll see if I can get him to open up a little," Lady Amberstone said with a conspiratorial smile and left the room.

Her ladyship had not in fact met, or seen, Veronica before and thought, as she entered the bedchamber hard upon her knock, that she looked like a portrait of Ophelia after she had been extracted from the river and laid out as though she were only asleep. Ophelia, seen on the stage in this sort of pose, was of course always pretending to be dead and therefore looked as though she was asleep. Veronica was, to the Marchioness's eye, not asleep. She was as close to death as a person may be while yet still breathing. She had never seen a living person quite so still or pale. She did not think there was much cause for optimism on anyone but the murderer's part.

Both men, who were sitting one on either side of the bed, looked up in relief, for finding a topic of conversation was proving difficult once the usual expressions of sympathy and hope had been exchanged.

"I hope I'm not disturbing you," she said in her most gracious manner. "I'm Mildred Amberstone. You must be Lord Thetford?"

The older gentleman rose to his feet and took the hand held out to him.

"Yes. I've heard a lot about you, my lady."

"Really? I hope it was flattering. I was so sorry to hear about your daughter's illness and hope you will feel able to trust us to look after her to the best of our ability."

"Rushlake has already pointed out that no household can be so dangerous to her as my own," the Viscount said heavily. "It seems to be a haven for criminals."

"I don't doubt that's an exaggeration," she returned pleasantly, "although I believe you may harbour one."

"One is enough," he said.

"Indeed; one is too many. I came to tell my nephew that he is required downstairs. May I take his place for a little while?"

The Viscount, bowing to the inevitable – that he was not to be left alone with his daughter – expressed gratitude for her kindness and held out his hand to the Earl, who had risen.

"She has not changed one iota since I came in," he told his aunt, "but so long as she breathes – and you see, she does, quite evenly – I believe there to be hope."

"Indeed."

The two men retreated together to the doorway where they exchanged a few words in low voices, before Rushlake left the room and Thetford returned to the bedside.

Lady Amberstone had already sat down in the Earl's vacated chair and the Viscount now resumed his own seat.

"What do you think?" he asked, clearly hoping for a more positive view from this new person.

"I do not know," she admitted. "I've seen a number of unwell persons, some of whom have recovered and some of whom have not, but this, this particular form of illness is something of which I have no experience."

"My wife," he began, "my first wife – you know that people are saying she was poisoned too, but her illness was not like this."

"What was it like?"

"She was sick a great deal, lost weight and was in a great deal of pain. This: your niece described what happened in the inn and it doesn't sound in the least similar."

"It may have been a different poison – they don't all have the same effect," Lady Amberstone said. "But – was your wife ill over a long period, getting worse?"

"Yes. She had begun to be ill before she knew she was expecting again, and then it got gradually worse. Once the baby was born, we could all see how thin she had grown and then, you see, she didn't recover very well after the birth. She was in increasing pain, which at first we thought might be related to the birth, but – well, the doctor thought it was something else."

"He didn't think she was being poisoned? You see, a subtle murderer can administer poison over a long period so that it can look like an illness."

"No. He thought she had contracted an illness which gradually destroyed her from inside. It sounds horrible – and it was."

"It does indeed," Lady Amberstone agreed sympathetically, "but I don't suppose we'll ever know now unless, when we find the person who wanted to kill your daughter, we realise he or she might also have had reason to kill her mother.

"I believe," she went on, now in a very grave tone, "that we must put all our effort into trying to discover who wanted your daughter dead and apprehend that person before he or she does any more harm."

"Yes."

The two fell silent for a little while until the Viscount, after glancing, as he thought surreptitiously at the Marchioness, said, "Do you think it might be my present wife? Could Veronica know something about her – or about what she did to my first wife – which would make Vera want to silence her?"

The Marchioness looked up and met his eyes.

"Is that what you think – that your present wife may have killed your first one and that she is trying to kill Veronica?"

"I don't want to think it, but I can't escape the fear that it's possible. My eldest daughter, Julia, believes it. She's convinced Vera killed my first wife and indeed thought that the riding accident was meant to kill *her*. Veronica was wearing her cast-off riding habit, you see."

"Yes, but was she anywhere near Veronica when the horse lost its footing?"

"No, she was with me. Veronica was behind."

"Do you know who she was with?"

"No. When we set off, she was riding with us, and then, when we met up with the rest of the hunt outside the inn, she was with Mr Stapleton, the curate, as well as Julia, but I don't know if he was still close to her when she fell. My wife and I had gone on some way ahead and indeed were already halfway across the lower field when the accident happened."

"So it doesn't look as though it can have been your wife who pushed her – or prodded the horse – or whatever it was that caused the incident. Of course, it could have been a genuine accident, I suppose?"

"Yes."

He did not sound convinced and Lady Amberstone reflected how exceedingly unpleasant it must be to think that one of the people of whom one was fond had tried to kill another. On the other hand, looking at his anguished face, she suspected that he had become a trifle unhinged by both the events as well as the attendant gossip.

After this, the pair fell silent and Lady Amberstone, who had promised she would not leave any member of the Thetford family alone with the patient, began to wonder how long she could reasonably remain as chaperone when the other person was the girl's father.

While the minutes passed and turned into quarter hours, Lord Rushlake, having gone first to the drawing room where he found his family drinking tea, apart from Titania and his aunt, requested Mr Bodley's attendance in the library.

"Aren't you going to have tea?" Jenny asked.

"Not just at present. Adrian and I have something to discuss which really can't wait while I drink tea. Where's Titania?"

"Oh, I imagine she's still with Marcus," Jenny replied.

"What?"

"He requested an audience with her," Jenny explained, looking a little startled by her brother's question.

"Where are they? Did you know this, Adrian?"

"No; she wasn't in here when Helena and I came in. We'd – we've only just arrived ourselves."

The Earl, looking suddenly years older than the four-and-twenty summers to which he laid claim, rang the bell.

"Where is Lady Titania?" he asked the butler when he appeared.

"I believe she and Mr Stapleton are in the blue sitting room, my lord," the butler returned.

"Thank you."

His lordship nodded at Mr Bodley and he and the detective followed his butler out of the room with swift strides, only pausing when Jenny demanded what he thought he was doing interrupting what she was convinced was a romantic interlude.

"Romantic interlude, my foot!" his lordship exclaimed inelegantly and disappeared.

Those left in the drawing room looked at each other with some confusion.

"What's the matter with him?" Jenny asked rhetorically, not really supposing that any of the others would know.

"I think he's afraid something unpleasant may take place if he doesn't avert it," Aunt Saffy explained diffidently.

"I didn't think he objected to Marcus as a suitor," Jenny argued. "Of course he hasn't a bean to his name, but Tania has plenty for them both."

"Well, I'm sure I don't know, but he did seem to be in rather a hurry to intervene," Saffy said.

"Do you know anything about this?" Jenny asked Helena, clearly assuming that Saffy did not.

"I'm afraid not; I've been rather taken up with my own affairs since we got back," Helena admitted with a blush.

"Are you going to marry Adrian?" Jenny asked bluntly.

"I hope so; certainly, we have agreed to tie the knot," Helena admitted, "unless of course Horace has taken Adrian away to forbid such a thing."

"He can't do that!" Jenny exclaimed. "You aren't his sister!"

"No – and I'm a long way past the age where anyone else needs to give their consent."

"So is Titania," Jenny said, "although I daresay he could refuse to release her portion if he doesn't care for her choice."

Helena, who had been much involved with Lord Rushlake's previous case, did not think that either the gravity of his expression or the speed with which he had dashed out of the room could be entirely connected to whether he approved of the curate as a future brother-in-law, did not comment. It was her opinion that the Earl had something else on his mind when he ran off with her betrothed.

She rose and went to the window which would have had an excellent view of the garden if it had not already got dark. She stared out, wondering if Titania was still in the house and certain that, if she was, Rushlake would find her. If, on the other hand, she had gone outside into the cold darkness with the man on whom she was fairly certain her guarded emotions had settled, she was almost certainly in extreme danger and her brother chasing after her would assuredly alert the curate to his own imminent danger.

"Can you see anything?" Saffy asked, appearing on soft feet beside her.

"No, not a thing except light spilling from some of the windows downstairs. Do you think one of those is where Titania is?"

She spoke quietly because she did not particularly want to include Lady Wendell in the conversation, knowing that she had no inkling of the suspicion which had clearly assailed the Earl and which had, she knew, been troubling both her and Saffy ever since the older woman had spoken to the couple in the park.

"Yes, I think one is the library," Saffy said, peering down. "Horace is bound to go there."

"What about that one to the left?" Helena asked. "Is that the library too?"

261

"No; I think it's a small room where there's an old harpsichord. Nobody goes in there much, which," the older woman said on a breath, "makes there being a light coming from it so very peculiar."

"I believe I'll go down and have a look," Helena said. "Can you see any other glimmers of light from up here?"

Aunt Saffy pressed her face against the window and looked right and left as well as up and down.

"There's the one from the bedroom where that poor girl is," she said. "Perhaps Titania's gone back up there."

"I don't think so. If she had, Lady Amberstone would have come down."

"So she would. You go down, Helena, and investigate the little harpsichord room and I'll stay up here and keep checking on the lights. When you get downstairs, make your way towards the library and, just before you get there, there is a slight turn in the corridor, which you may not have noticed. If you turn to the left rather than going on to the library, you'll see the door to the harpsichord room ahead of you.

"Be careful," she added. "You know what happened to you before. In fact, would it not be better if I went down and you kept watch up here? After all, my wandering about in a doddery sort of way is unlikely to alert anybody to my spying upon them – or, if it does, they will simply think I'm a prurient old lady."

"I don't want you put in danger," Helena returned.

"I don't think I will be – and in any event it's my turn. You had the nasty experience last time."

With which, the older lady moved away from the window, mumbled something to Jenny about the weakness of old age – although she was not in point of fact much above forty – and hurried out of the room.

"What were you looking at out of the window?" Jenny asked, becoming suspicious.

"Oh, nothing in particular, but I find the shadows at this time of the evening fascinating," Helena said vaguely, stepping aside slightly to allow the other woman to join her.

Jenny, knowing the house well, immediately noticed the light in the harpsichord room.

"Whoever do you think is in there?" she asked. "Nobody goes in there."

"What not even to play the instrument?"

"No; there's a better one in the pink sitting room. That one's really very poor – it's not been properly looked after. Do you think Titania and her swain might be in there? I suppose, if they wanted privacy, she might have taken him in there because, if she'd gone to the library, she might expect to be interrupted by Horace at some point.

"Tell me," she went on, moving away and no doubt hoping Helena would follow, "have you fixed a day for the wedding yet?"

Chapter 33

Titania and Mr Stapleton were so lost to the world and everyone around them that they did not notice someone opening the door, although they did hear the click as it shut again.

The curate looked up, still holding his new *fiancée* within the circle of his arms, and perceived that there was no one in the room.

"Your house is as bad as mine at home," he observed, "always someone coming in."

"No one has," she pointed out.

"No, but they tried to, presumably saw what we were doing and went out immediately."

She laughed.

"It doesn't matter. It was probably Aunt Saffy – my erstwhile companion; she's always coming and going, but is much too tactful to stay if she considers herself *de trop*."

"Well, she was quite right; we don't want her in here just at present. Is there anywhere we can go where we aren't so likely to be disturbed? Oh ...," he added, seeing anxiety cloud her face. "I don't mean to do anything more improper than kiss my betrothed, but all the same I'd prefer it if we could be undisturbed for just a little longer."

"We could go next door," she said. "It's a very small room, almost entirely filled with an ancient harpsichord. We'd be most unlikely to be disturbed in there – nobody ever goes in."

"Then let us repair to that haven without delay," he said at once.

She smiled, took his hand and led the way out of the blue sitting room, back into the corridor and, turning the opposite way from that which would have taken them to the library, led him into the harpsichord room.

It was exceedingly small. Besides the harpsichord there was a somewhat bedraggled sofa, a small table and an armchair. The curate, his eye alighting upon the sofa with eager anticipation, led his betrothed to it and drew her down into its sagging depths where he resumed kissing her.

Titania, nothing loth to engage in such a delightful pastime, allowed herself to be almost swallowed by the sofa and more or less submerged into it by the weight of her lover pressing upon her. It did not, at least at first, occur to her that his onslaught was perhaps a little too enthusiastic but, as his hands began to move from hers to her arms and, by gradual degrees, to other parts of her anatomy about which there was little doubt that he knew considerably more than she, she did at last begin to worry that perhaps he meant to go a little further in his seduction than she had expected.

Unnerved by this too swift progression and suddenly acutely aware that their acquaintance had been short and their betrothal even shorter, she struggled to free herself. Whether he had expected this she could not tell, but it was clear that he had no intention of heeding her exertions for, murmuring something or other which she could not discern, he drew her firmly back into his arms.

"No!" she exclaimed, suddenly affronted.

"What, what's the matter?" he asked, his voice, while still tender, nevertheless acquiring a slight edge which made her withdraw further.

"You're … I'm not used to this," she explained, trying to push him away.

He was still more or less on top of her and, in spite of being a tall, athletic woman, she was a great deal weaker than he – and smaller. He did not move except to caress her.

"Stop it!" she cried, straining to prevent what was rapidly becoming an assault and endeavouring to extract herself from beneath him.

"There's no need to be rough!" he exclaimed, clearly taken aback by what he recognised belatedly as a reaction to his having moved too fast. If he had been a little older, he would surely have known that Titania, while inexperienced in the matter of lovemaking, was not the sort of person who would respond well to coercion. "I'm not trying to rape you!"

"Aren't you?" she countered.

"No! You like it – you know you do!" he said, trying for a wheedling tone but failing to achieve it.

"Yes, I do," she acknowledged, ever honest and fair, "or rather I did, but what you're doing now isn't proper and – really, Marcus, I do love you, but we're not alley cats!"

He reared up, away from her, clearly insulted to have his lovemaking described in such an unromantic fashion, and she took the opportunity to pull herself out of the treacherous dip in the sofa and get to her feet.

"We're to be husband and wife," he reminded her.

"Yes, but aren't that yet," she retorted, "and I will not engage in what should wait until we're properly wed in this shabby little room. I must say," she added, becoming heated, "I do not think your behaviour fitting for a minister of the church."

"Oh, don't be silly," he chided, again trying to draw her back.

Giving him the benefit of the doubt, she allowed herself to be brought back to the sofa but the first heady pangs of passion had fled; she was no longer deceived either by his blandishments or her own response to them. She thought, although not so coherently as to form the opinion in words, that he was either trying to please himself at her expense – although she was no longer sure that his whole manner was not an act – or that he was trying to coerce her.

She, by no means confident with regard to the opposite sex and her own appeal, began to experience the usual recurring self-judgment about her fortune and its greater allure.

"I thought," she said, avoiding the treacherous hollow in the sofa by perching stiffly upon the edge, "that you were in love with Veronica."

"Veronica!" he exclaimed and there was no doubt that his tone held contempt.

"Yes. You were whispering into each other's ears this morning; it was positively embarrassing."

"Only because you were jealous," he said with distressing accuracy. "I was talking to her, trying to make sure she enjoyed the outing; I thought you would approve."

"I don't," she returned haughtily, "approve of young men making love to girls of sixteen in an open carriage."

"No?" he asked, laughing. "Would you prefer it if I'd made love to her in private?"

"Of course not. You shouldn't be making love to her at all, particularly when, a few hours later, you make love to me. For whom do you care? Or do you feel nothing for either of us?"

"I care for you," he said at once. "I've just asked you to marry me; I haven't asked her."

"No," she agreed, with sudden devastating acuity, "you didn't have to, did you, because she succumbed immediately. What have you done with her? Have you – have you done what you were trying to do with me?"

"Of course not."

But she did not believe him. She had intercepted Veronica's glances towards him – and his to her. She knew he found the girl attractive – or had done so once when she was able-bodied and before he became convinced that her, Titania's, fortune was within reach.

"Have you seduced her? Did you tell her you loved her? Did you, indeed, make a declaration? Probably you did because that would have convinced her - as it did me for a little while - that you were serious, that eventually she would be honestly married to you?"

As she spoke, she began again to try to remove herself from his grasp but now he had clamped his fingers around her wrist and held on to her.

"I want you," he said, holding her eyes with his.

"You want my fortune and she is too young to marry in any event. Her father would never consent at this juncture."

"She's crippled," he murmured, "and will probably be dead by tonight."

She felt a cold wave of dread pass through her body as the truth forced itself upon her.

"Was it you," she asked, holding his eyes and feeling her heart break, but not, in spite of this, sensing her danger, "that tripped her horse?"

"Are you mad?" he asked, attempting to laugh.

"Did you get her with child?" she demanded, still trying to pull away from the iron grip upon her wrist. "Is that why you wanted to kill her – still want to kill her?"

"You're mad, deluded with jealousy," he said with that infuriating certainty that, in the face of her own recent almost overpowering desire for him, made her for a moment doubt her own conclusions.

"Let me go!" she demanded.

When he did not, but on the contrary tried once more to pull her into his arms, she raised her free hand and slapped him as hard as she could across his handsome face.

She saw his expression change immediately, the way, apart from the red mark left by her hand, his face turned white with anger.

"You she-devil!" he exclaimed and twisted the wrist he held with such violence that she heard it crack.

She did not scream, she barely winced, but she began to fight for her life, hitting him as hard and as frequently as she could make contact with him, while he, dropping the broken wrist, took hold of both her arms and threw her upon the floor.

"You'll pay a heavy price for that!" he muttered in a threatening manner, now breathing heavily in a way which she was convinced owed more to his rage and determination to dominate her than to his passion.

"You'll pay with your neck!" she returned gamely. She knew she did not stand a chance against his strength, but she would not yield.

Aunt Saffy, hurrying down the stairs as fast as she could, tripped over her own skirt, stumbled to her feet and went on running, making her way towards the harpsichord room.

She heard the heavy breathing, the gasping, the bangs and something of the furious interchange between the people inside the small chamber before she reached the door.

She opened it, saw her erstwhile charge upon the floor with a man on top of her and noted the desperate struggle in which the young woman was engaged, not only to retain her honour but, to Saffy's horror, her life too. As she burst through the door, she saw him abandon whatever attempt he had until now been making to make love to the young woman in favour of trying to strangle her. She could not help noticing that he had very large hands with long, strong fingers and that he had no difficulty in encircling Titania's slender neck with one hand while the other grasped her hair.

"Stop that at once!" she cried in the sort of outraged tone she might have used to a big child trying to impose his will upon a smaller one. Lacking a weapon, she took off one of her shoes and began to hit him over the head with it. It was not, unfortunately, a very substantial shoe since she had changed the walking boots in which she had tramped around Shrewsbury for a pair of indoor slippers and she was horridly aware that it was quite inadequate for the purpose.

"What the devil?" he exclaimed, looking up to see the older woman and batting away her feeble attack as though she had been no more than a fly. "You silly old fool! Don't you think it'll be the matter of a moment to choke you?"

"I don't care what you do to me!" she almost snarled, lit up by a passion she had never before experienced, "but you'll leave her alone!"

He paused, one hand still around Titania's throat and the other, having dropped the hair, raised to repel the older woman's pitiful defence of her charge.

"Very well. I'll deal with you first and then go back to her," he said smoothly with something of his old charm.

He leaned towards Saffy, pulling Titania with him by the neck, snatched the shoe from her hand, threw it across the room and administered a sharp blow to her face, which sent the older woman flying. She fell backwards, hitting her head upon the corner of the harpsichord as she went.

He sighed and turned back to Titania.

"Do you really want to save this until our wedding day?" he enquired.

"There won't be a wedding day," she managed to gurgle through the grip around her neck.

"Oh, yes there will, if you want to live. I can throttle you now or we can get married in a week or two. I must admit I'm rather taken with your spirit. I warn you, though, if you tell your brother anything about this, it will go ill for you. Tell him, an you love me – which I know you do – how happy you are to become my wife. You will be – you were very eager a few minutes ago; I can't think what came over you to become so proper suddenly."

"You frightened me," she whispered as his hold upon her throat eased momentarily.

"I'm sorry; I didn't mean to; I got carried away," he told her and now the hand which had been choking her caressed her neck.

"What have you done to Aunt Saffy?" she asked, allowing him – although now it made her shudder – to kiss her again.

"I've no idea but I think she may be dead, killed by the harpsichord. She tripped, didn't she, as she came to protect your honour?"

"I must see to her," she insisted, pushing him away again with an assumed lingering reluctance. She wanted to avoid angering him again.

He smiled indulgently, apparently deceived, and did up the buttons on the front of her dress with something approaching tenderness.

"Go on, then," he said.

She got up with difficulty for she was bruised and frightened and found she could hardly move her limbs for the trembling which had overtaken her.

She staggered towards where Aunt Saffy lay. She had despised, disliked and been almost murderously irritated by her companion for years but, recalling how she had run to her aid without thought for herself and how cruelly she had been felled, she found her heart beating painfully as she kneeled beside her.

The older woman lay in an awkward position with one leg bent and trapped beneath her body. There was a large bruise already forming on her jaw where the curate had hit her and her eyes were closed. She had, Titania noticed with surprise, exceedingly long eyelashes, which lay like spiders on her cheeks. Her skin was very pale, as though it had been painted with chalk.

"Aunt Saffy," Titania said, laying a hand across the other woman's forehead and finding that the skin was clammy.

"Can you hear me?"

There was no answer until Mr Stapleton said, "Of course she can't. Leave her alone: she'll either come round on her own or she won't.

There's not much you can do except pretend to be sad. This room's too small for that harpsichord – it was a death trap."

"She's not dead," Titania said. "Pray, Saffy, open your eyes – or press my fingers."

She took the limp fingers in hers, once again noticing something she never had before: that they were long and slender with neatly pared nails. This woman, whom she had derided, seemed to possess many features that, if she had made more of them, might have been prized.

There was no response from the woman on the floor, but the little pulse at the base of her neck continued to flutter.

In the silence, Titania – and no doubt Marcus – heard footsteps outside. In a moment, he was beside Titania, pulling her up and clamping one arm across her breast to pin her against him as the door opened to reveal the Earl and the detective.

"My God!" the Earl exclaimed. "Let her go!" he added in a menacing tone, taking a step towards the curate.

"I didn't think you'd approve but I must admit I didn't expect quite such a hostile reaction," Mr Stapleton said, striving for a gently chiding note. "Your sister has agreed to become my wife," he added, putting the other arm around Titania and holding her close, although she was facing the same way as he.

"Really? And what's the matter with Saffy? Was she so shocked to hear the news that she fainted?" the Earl asked.

While he was speaking, Mr Bodley was moving away from him, around the back of the sofa.

"She tripped and hit her head on the corner of the harpsichord," Mr Stapleton explained. "She seems to have lost her senses."

"He hit her," Titania said bluntly.

"Nonsense, darling! That was the joke we were going to tell people, remember."

"Let me go!" Titania said quietly. "If Horace is to give his consent, we must attend to poor Saffy. My brother will never agree to our marriage if you go on holding me like that. It looks as though I'm unwilling, which I've already proved I'm not."

She turned her head and kissed the curate upon the only part of his face she could reach: his jaw. Out of the corner of her eye, she could see Adrian Bodley moving around the sofa so slowly he appeared to be stationary. The Earl still stood in front of the door through which he had entered and Mr Stapleton faced him. She was not sure whether he was aware that the detective was in the room at all. She suspected that his opinion of the man was so low, for he was nothing but a common fellow, that he discounted his presence.

Lord Rushlake moved towards Saffy, not apparently looking at his distant cousin, although he said curtly, "Please do as my sister requests."

"You've already checked that she's still breathing," Marcus said to Titania. "I don't think you took her pulse though. Do you want to do that?"

"I'm not sure I know how to," she murmured. "Should we not send for the doctor?"

"Definitely we should," the Earl agreed. He had reached Saffy and dropped on one knee beside her. "You do that, Tania, and I'll carry the poor injured lady up to her room – or at least to that conveniently placed sofa."

"I'll ring the bell for Perkins," she said as the curate removed his arms. The bell, hanging beside the mantelpiece, was in front of her. She wanted the young man to watch her so that Adrian could make his move quietly from behind.

She was not, however, permitted to reach the bell, the curate following her with one stride and taking hold of her again.

The Earl, his fingers on Aunt Saffy's wrist, said, "By the way, I'm sure you'll be surprised – and of course delighted – to hear that Veronica has recovered her senses. She's been asking for you, Tania."

"Oh, I must go to her!" she exclaimed. "Do you think, Horace, that Aunt Saffy will be better soon?"

"I'm sure she will."

Titania tried to move towards the door but was detained once more by Mr Stapleton. However, no longer so afraid of him killing her now that both her brother and the detective were in the room, she struggled and he, trying to deceive the Earl into thinking he meant no harm, allowed her to pull him forwards a little way, far enough for the Earl, glancing up quickly to check where Mr Bodley was, to remove his hand from Saffy's wrist and grasp the young man's ankle.

At the same moment, Mr Bodley, having reached his objective of being one stride behind the curate, stepped forward and hit him upon the head with a large pot plant which he had been able to pick up as he passed the window.

Chapter 34

As the curate fell, Lord Rushlake lifted the insensible Aunt Saffy out of the way moments before the second body landed where she had been. He laid her upon the sofa, pillowing her head on a cushion and covering her with a rather moth-eaten rug which lay upon the arm. Having done this as tenderly and rapidly as he could, he went to the assistance of the detective to secure the curate's wrists with one of his own stockings, Mr Bodley not having considered it necessary to equip himself with a pair of handcuffs on a Christmas visit.

"Call the doctor!" the Earl shot at Titania, who ran out of the room to find Perkins, judging it inadvisable to ring the bell and bring the butler in on such a scene.

She went to the hall and despatched one of the footmen to fetch the doctor as quickly as possible before returning to find her brother and the detective barefoot, having trussed up her erstwhile lover in a business-like way with the aid of both pairs of stockings. He was already beginning to come to himself whereas poor Aunt Saffy still lay motionless.

"I'll take her upstairs," the Earl told his sister. "Will you send the doctor up as soon as he arrives?"

"Yes, of course. What are you going to do with him?" she asked Mr Bodley, nodding at the man on the floor.

"Send word to the local constabulary to come and fetch him to jail," he said.

"But – you can't leave him – suppose he were to get away!"

"He won't, but I won't leave him. You're quite safe now, my lady. Are you hurt?"

"No – or at least not seriously. I'll probably have a few bruises and my pride is sadly wounded, but I daresay I shall come about."

Titania spoke bravely but her whole world had collapsed. She had been a fool, taken in by glowing dark eyes and a pair of knowing hands. She supposed Veronica had suffered in a similar manner, but feared that the seduction had gone further in her case. There must be a strong reason why he had wanted to kill the girl so much that he had tried a second time when the first attempt had failed.

"Would you like me to send word to the constabulary so that you can continue to guard him?" she asked. She had a strong desire to leave the room before Marcus fully regained his senses.

"Yes; thank you."

"I'll write a note and get someone to take it directly," she said, "or perhaps Horace can go himself. I believe I'll go up to Aunt Saffy now."

"Of course," he said. "Never fear, he's safe here and the plant pot is to hand if I should need it again."

She smiled tremulously and left the room.

As she passed the hall, she spoke to the remaining footman, telling him to send the doctor up to Miss Hemsted's room as soon as he arrived.

The Earl, with Aunt Saffy in his arms, made his way up the stairs to her chamber where he laid her gently upon the bed and drew the covers over her. He put a match to the fire and, finding a carafe of water on the bedside table, sprinkled a few drops on the former companion's face. This seemed to be a successful manoeuvre for she began to stir at once, her eyelids fluttering up and a soft moan issuing from her lips.

"Dear Saffy," he said tenderly, taking her hand and pressing it. "You hit your head on the harpsichord, I'm told, although I suspect it was that accursed curate's hand which did the damage, either propelling you into the corner of the instrument or simply knocking you down. I see you've lost one of your shoes. Did you take it off? And did you hit the wretched man with it in defence of Titania? You see how essential you are. Heaven knows what he would have done to Titania if you hadn't gone to her defence. Adrian and I were rather tardy, having gone first to the wrong room."

"Is she hurt?" Saffy asked weakly, coming to herself.

"Not much. She was able to go out of the room on her own legs to send for the doctor. Don't talk if it tires you, but I can't help wondering what made you go to the harpsichord room."

"I saw the light was on when I looked out of the drawing room window. I knew you'd probably go to the blue sitting room so I thought I'd look in the little room."

"Did you know Marcus was a bad man?"

"No, but you and Adrian seemed so anxious to find Titania that it made me suspicious. Poor girl! She was in love with him, wasn't she?"

"Yes, I think so, but I daresay she'll get over it."

"No," Saffy said with sudden firmness. "She may not. One's first love – and it is hers, isn't it? – can linger in the memory and the heart for ever. Don't, I beseech you, make light of it."

"Has yours?" he asked after a moment.

"I suppose so, but mine – he never looked at me, never noticed me at all so that really there was nothing to be making a fuss about. He,

Stapleton, he was kissing her and – well, I don't know what besides, but, when I went in, he was all over her."

"Was she all over him?" the Earl asked, pouring more water from the carafe into a glass and holding it for Saffy to drink.

She struggled to sit up and, putting the glass down, he helped her and placed several pillows behind her before proffering the glass again.

"Not by the time I went in," Saffy said. "She was trying to get away. That was why I hit him. I wouldn't have done if she'd been enjoying it; I would have gone out again tactfully. I mean, it may not be right to carry on like that before she's married, but, if that was what she wanted, I don't think it would have become me to intervene."

"Would you have done when you were her companion? Wouldn't that have been your duty?"

"Yes, I suppose it would, but I don't think I am her companion now, am I? In any event, I did try to get him to stop."

"How?"

"Well, I told him at first, but he didn't take any notice of that – was quite rude to me as a matter of fact, which I suppose isn't surprising. Then, when he went back to her, I took off my shoe and hit him with it. That didn't achieve much either, except that he became quite angry and let go of her in order to hit me. Is there a bruise forming?"

The Earl peered at her and agreed that one was.

"I don't suppose you remember whether you hit the harpsichord."

"No; I remember him hitting me, that's all. It was a punch! Has he gone?"

"Not yet. We'll have to wait for the constabulary to take him away. Adrian and I tied him up and Adrian's guarding him.

He stayed with her until the doctor arrived.

The medical man examined the back of her head where there was a nasty cut which was bleeding sluggishly, but, after carefully wiping it with boiled water, he assured his patient that it had fortunately not damaged any material part of her head and that, although she would no doubt have a headache for some time, he believed she would make a full recovery.

"You mean I won't be any more stupid than I was before?" she asked humorously.

The doctor smiled.

"You will be no less intelligent than you were before. I would like you to remain in bed for the next twenty-four hours and, indeed, not leave it until I've seen you again."

He prescribed some laudanum and, a maid having been sent for to sit with Saffy – for one must always keep a close eye on anyone who has injured their head – accompanied the Earl to Veronica's room.

Lady Amberstone was still there but Lord Thetford had left and, in his place, sat a distressed-looking Titania.

"You said she had come to her senses!" she accused her brother as he came in.

"Yes, I did, and I'm sorry to have deceived you," he said, "but I wanted to unnerve your attacker. I would have confessed before you came up but was busy with Saffy."

"How is she?"

"She'll be right as rain in no time," the medical man said, "but I've ordered her to remain in bed until tomorrow. It looks," he went on, staring at the young woman, "as though you've acquired some injuries too. Would you like me to examine them?"

"No; I don't think they're anything of importance."

"Your wrist looks a bit odd - broken, I suspect. Do you mind if I have a look?"

She shrugged but held out her arm. The doctor took it and gently moved her hand, a movement which caused her to gasp with pain.

"Yes, it's definitely broken. I'll strap it up in a moment." He was still peering at her and, after a noticeable pause while he fixed his eyes upon her neck where there was a deep red mark, asked "Did somebody try to strangle you?"

"I don't think he meant to kill me," she said mildly, "only constrain me."

The doctor nodded and, seeing the despair in her eyes, tactfully turned his attention to the other young woman, the one lying motionless in the bed.

"Has she shown any sign of returning consciousness?" he asked.

"No – at least not while I've been here," Lady Amberstone replied.

"All the same," the doctor said with an attempt at the sort of optimism that patients and their relatives generally seek, "she is still alive and that, after ingesting such a large quantity of strychnine as I believe she did, is remarkable in itself. I have high hopes of her recovering – in time."

"How do you think it was administered?" Lord Rushlake asked.

"I'm afraid that may be partly my fault," the doctor admitted. "I had prescribed a small amount in order to help her with her movement – or lack thereof – and the agitation from which she was understandably suffering. She may have taken too many pills herself."

"How soon would they have an effect?" Titania asked.

"Within about a quarter of an hour – less than half an hour in any event."

"So that, if she'd taken too many pills by mistake – or even on purpose – she would have been taken ill before she left her house, or certainly before we had gone far," Titania concluded.

The doctor nodded and neither the Earl nor the Marchioness spoke.

"We'd been out for some two or three hours when we went to the inn for luncheon," Titania said in an expressionless voice. "We ordered drinks and luncheon. She became unwell – extremely, excessively, frighteningly unwell – when we had eaten luncheon. Do you think someone could have inserted the poison into her food at the beginning of the meal?"

"Yes, although he – or she – would have run the risk of someone else in the party noticing. If it was a deliberate act," the doctor said in a grave tone, "it's most likely he or she delivered it by means of a liquid rather than a large number of small-dose pills. That is how vermin is killed."

Titania shuddered. Somehow the word 'vermin' made her so angry and shocked that for a moment she could not speak. It seemed to her the height of infamy that the man to whom she had been so appallingly attracted could have wanted so desperately to be rid of a previous conquest that he would be prepared to try to eradicate her as though she had been no more than a rat. And all, she reflected with disgust, because he wanted her, Titania's, money.

"Have you," she said when she had mastered herself a little, "examined her for any other conditions?"

"I did when I was first called, after she had fallen from her horse," the doctor said.

"Did she – was she with child?" Titania asked.

Her words fell into a silence, the Earl and Lady Amberstone registering shock.

"I cannot tell you that," the doctor said apologetically. "My dealings with the patient must remain between her and me."

"Yes," the Earl said, speaking for the first time. "But a felony has been committed, indeed more than one, and the girl has almost been killed. The perpetrator, who has also attacked my sister and Miss Hemsted, is detained downstairs until the police get here. It will add immeasurably to the evidence that Miss Veronica was the victim of attempted murder if you can answer my sister's question."

The doctor nodded but he did not speak.

"Has she lost it?" Titania pursued, undaunted.

The doctor said, "Miss Veronica was exceedingly ill when I attended her after her riding accident. You know that, I know that, and her family knows that, as well, of course, as she herself. If I am asked the question you have just asked in a court of law, I may be required to answer it, but I cannot divulge the extent of her injuries otherwise. You will have to wait," he added with a small smile, "until she is able to tell you herself."

"Or until she's dead, I suppose," Titania said, "when no doubt the coroner will ask the question and you will no longer be under an obligation to refuse to speak."

"Just so, my lady," the doctor said.

"Have you divulged the full extent of her injuries to her father?" the Earl asked. "She is a minor so that I suppose you were compelled to tell him everything."

The doctor did not answer this; he was busy examining the patient: listening to her chest, taking her pulse and at one point lifting one of her eyelids to peer at her eye.

"I think she's improving," he said at last. "Her pulse is steady, as is her heartbeat, and there is more reaction in her pupils. I believe she may come to her senses within the next few days."

With this the others had to be content and Lord Rushlake accompanied the doctor downstairs when he had splinted and bound Titania's wrist, afterwards arranging a sling to hold her arm in the correct position.

Lady Amberstone and Titania finding themselves alone with Veronica, Titania enquired, after a small silence, whether her aunt knew where Helena Patchett was.

"I think she's somewhere downstairs, tactfully keeping out of the way. Did you want her?"

"I thought she might like to sit with Aunt Saffy. At the moment there is a maid there and I will return soon, but I wanted to see Veronica, having been erroneously informed by Horace that she had not only regained her senses but was asking for me."

"I'll go and find her and, if she isn't able to sit with Saffy, I'll do so myself," the Marchioness replied at once, thinking that the two women who had been mistreated by the curate might, if only the unconscious one would regain her senses, have a good deal to say to one another.

When she had gone, Titania began to tell Veronica what she believed she had discovered as well as how the wretched man had tried to seduce her – only, she stressed, because she had so much money. It was that, she insisted, which had attracted him, although she, Titania, had been foolish enough to fall for his blandishments.

"We have both been horridly misused," she said sadly.

She had never considered whether an unconscious person might be able to hear what someone was saying but, as she fell silent, she heard a little sigh and saw, upon fixing her eyes upon the girl's pale face, that something had changed. The pretty mouth twitched, the long eyelashes fluttered and, after several minutes, rose to reveal a pair of blue eyes, which, as they found Titania's, filled with tears.

"I was with child," the young woman said, confirming Titania's suspicions, "but, perhaps fortunately, the riding accident dislodged it. How did you know? Did the maids talk?"

"No, I guessed because there had to be some strong reason why he wanted you dead. Dear, dear Veronica – you have been appallingly treated and have suffered most dreadfully."

"You have too," the girl said softly.

"Oh, no; the greatest wound I've received is to my pride. Pray don't give it another thought. How long have you been able to hear what people say?"

"Always, I think, but I couldn't reply. People have spoken of my slipping into death, of my being permanently damaged, paralysed and perhaps rendered idiotic. It's been horrible. It was only when you said what you did, about what Marcus did, that I wanted to speak so much that somehow or another I did!"

"Perhaps you'll find you can move your legs too," Titania suggested.

"I can feel them," Veronica said. "I couldn't before, but now I can feel pins and needles in my toes, so perhaps I will recover. Do you truly think I can?"

"Yes! Did you love him very much?"

"I thought I did."

"So did I, but now I realise that he - we were cruelly deceived. I don't think I love him any more. I realised suddenly when he was making love to me – somehow it didn't seem real, at least it didn't seem to come from the heart – and – well, of course I always knew he was after my money, for he could not have loved me more than you."

"Of course he could. Yes, I did think I loved him too, but, when I told him about the child, he was horrified. I can understand that he might have been afraid of Papa, and that he might have been afraid for his career in the church too, but I thought, if he loved me, he would have been concerned for me. He wasn't – not at all. He started talking about ways – oh, shocking, horrible ways – to get rid of it."

"But that must have been before the riding accident."

"Yes – and I don't think it was an accident. He was riding very close to me; I'm sure he tripped Minna on purpose – she's normally so sure-footed."

"But you were still keen on him when we set out on the drive the other day," Titania reminded her.

"I couldn't help it. I thought perhaps he'd arranged the accident so that I lost the baby, which I did. I convinced myself he didn't mean for me to be so badly hurt."

"I don't suppose he did, but you might have been killed."

"And you'd seen how he made love to me and yet you still let him do the same to you," Veronica pointed out.

"Yes – and it was utterly shocking. I'll never forget how stupid I've been, but there was something horridly attractive about him. We both felt it, didn't we?"

"Yes. I'll never marry now – or have babies," Veronica said.

"You will if you want to," Titania said.

"I think I should go into a nunnery," Veronica said in a despairing tone, "but they probably wouldn't have me if I can't walk. I wouldn't be able to kneel, would I?"

"I'm sure they wouldn't mind that. They're supposed to be sisters of mercy, aren't they? But don't be silly, Veronica, you don't have to do that; you can recover and one day you'll be able to dance at your own ball."

Chapter 35

It was not until the following day when the party met in the drawing room for tea that they were able to discuss the recent events.

Aunt Saffy had been discharged by the doctor and, although she was nursing an enormous bruise upon her chin and wore a bandage around her head, she was in good spirits.

Mr Bodley and Helena had formally announced their forthcoming nuptials, which were, they decided to take place in Yorkshire. Lady Amberstone had offered to put them all up as well as organise the wedding breakfast.

Veronica Thetford's feeling in her legs was gradually returning and the doctor was now firmly of the opinion that she would recover completely and be perfectly able, as Titania had suggested, to dance at her own ball in a couple of years' time.

Since the culprit behind Veronica's woes had been uncovered, Julia Thetford had dropped her accusations against her stepmother. She would never like her, she insisted, but, after a long talk with the doctor, she no longer thought her mother had been poisoned and accepted that her demise had been caused by some malignancy in her body which had very likely been exacerbated by her condition.

For her part, Lady Thetford offered to present her stepdaughter in the spring with the promise to do the same for Veronica in a couple of years' time.

Lord Rushlake, putting down his teacup, said sadly, "I should never have appointed that wretched man as curate. It is I who am mainly at fault for I allowed the distant connexion between us to persuade me to give him the position even though I had never met him – indeed never met any of his immediate family. I shall not do anything so careless and lazy again, I promise."

"I don't think you should castigate yourself too severely, Horace," his aunt said. "We were all completely taken in. It is fortunate that no lasting damage has been done, except of course to the two young women."

"Oh, I daresay we'll recover. *I* shall at least; like Horace, I have had my pride dented and will, I promise be more humble in future," Titania said.

It was not until nearly dinner time that Lord Vincent, who had been invited to join the family again, arrived. Titania went down to greet him alone.

"I heard something of what happened," he said. "You have all my sympathy."

"I don't think I deserve it," she said. "I was foolish and hope I've learned my lesson. The person most damaged is poor Veronica, although she is getting better. What did you think of him?"

"I didn't like him, but I put that down to having my nose put out of joint by his attention to you. I didn't suspect him of hurting Veronica, and I didn't think for a moment that he was after your money, as you insist. I thought he was in love with you – and I didn't find that at all difficult to believe."

"That's very kind of you," she said, blushing.

"No, it's the truth. I've always admired you, Titania, and will continue to do so."

"And I've always liked you," she said shyly.

"*Liked*," he agreed, "but not found attractive."

"I never thought of you that way," she explained. "We've known each other since we were children so that I didn't, haven't – you're my best friend."

He smiled and said, "I would like to be more than that one day, but perfectly understand that declaring myself at this juncture would be unfeeling and insensitive."

Titania refrained from pointing out that, although he had not made her a formal offer, he had in fact declared his sentiments – as well as his intentions. She was grateful for his restraint and comforted by his belief in her. That, for the moment, was enough.

Printed in Great Britain
by Amazon

42961858R00155